The chopper rose before the sliding door was fully closed

Bolan stood and charged the aircraft as it banked and turned, emptying the AKSU's magazine in a futile attempt to breach the armored undercarriage.

In his fury, he wasn't surprised or startled by the sound of a familiar voice behind him. "So, they have the nuke, then?" Jacob Gellar asked.

"There it goes," Mack Bolan replied.

"Pashenka should have taken out the bird first thing."

"Too late for that. We need to know their destination. The target. And we're running out of time."

Behind him, in the forest clearing, all was silent death. How long, Bolan asked himself, before some major city looked that way? How long, and where?

DON PENDLETON's
MACK BOLAN®

A DYING Evil

THE TYRANNY FILES

BOOK III

A GOLD EAGLE BOOK FROM
WORLDWIDE®

TORONTO • NEW YORK • LONDON
AMSTERDAM • PARIS • SYDNEY • HAMBURG
STOCKHOLM • ATHENS • TOKYO • MILAN
MADRID • WARSAW • BUDAPEST • AUCKLAND

First edition September 2001

ISBN 0-373-61480-2

Special thanks and acknowledgment to
Mike Newton for his contribution to this work.

A DYING EVIL

Fanaticism consists of redoubling your effort when you have forgotten your aim.
—George Santayana,
The Life of Reason, 1905

I remember my aim, and it's time to redouble my effort. If my enemies really believe they're on a Divine mission, they shouldn't mind meeting their maker.

—Mack Bolan

For the 130 American law enforcement officers
who died on duty in the final year
of the twentieth century. God keep.

CHAPTER ONE

Odessa, Ukraine

The house was unremarkable, resembling any other in the run-down neighborhood. A casual observer wouldn't have surmised that anything significant had ever taken place within its dirty, off-white stucco walls. It wouldn't be presumed that this drab house held anything worth murdering or dying for.

The casual observer would be wrong.

The neighborhood might be run-down, but it couldn't be called low-rent. Nothing was cheap these days in Odessa, third-largest city in Ukraine. A decade of freedom from the former Soviet Union had failed to shake off the deadweight of crushing economic problems, with Ukraine still dependent on failing Russia for forty percent of its foreign trade. Inflation was rampant, and even seedy neighborhoods such as this one, well removed from the Black Sea waterfronts and beaches, still commanded relatively exorbitant prices.

In Odessa, nothing came cheap—except, perhaps, human life.

Mack Bolan, aka the Executioner, crouched in darkness, waiting for the others to reach their positions before he made his move against the house. If his allies weren't in place in another fifty-seven seconds, he would have to rock and roll without them.

Either way, the hit was going down at 4:00 a.m.

It was the time of night—or morning—when most people were fast asleep, while those required to stay awake by duty to a job or something else almost inevitably felt their spirits and their eyelids start to sag. It was the hour when guards were lowered, when watchmen went for badly needed coffee, when some sentries dozed off for the last time in their lives.

Bolan had taken out one guard already, as a prelude to the main event. It had been wise of his enemies to plant a man across the street, but they hadn't been wise or generous enough to spring for two. If they had doubled up the guard, it would have been more difficult for him to approach. If nothing else, those dwelling in the target house might have been warned that death was on its way.

Too late.

He hoped the other guards would be as easy to dispose of as the young man stretched out in the darkness, three long paces to his rear. He had no great concern for Jacob Gellar at the moment, confident that the Israeli agent could hold his own, would do whatever was required to see the mission through. As for the young Ukrainian—Grisha something or other—Bolan knew nothing more than that he was a sometime contract agent for Mossad, supposedly an expert on the movements and motives of neofascist groups within his native land.

Crouched in the darkness, running down the doomsday numbers in his head, Bolan hoped Grisha Something lived up to his reputation. If he didn't, all of them could easily be dead within the next few moments.

They had found their first target on schedule, posted sentries telling Bolan that his enemies believed someone or something inside the house was worth guarding. He didn't care particularly who or what it was, since he already knew who it *wasn't*. Closure would have to wait a while. This strike was Bolan's first stop in a brand-new hunting ground. He thought it only proper to check in and introduce himself.

The weapons the soldier and his comrades carried were of Russian manufacture, for the most part. AKSU assault rifles—the stubby "bullet hose" model that was basically a shrunken version of the standard-issue AK-74, chambered in 5.45 mm—with apple-green RGD-5 antipersonnel grenades for backup, just in case. Their side arms, while not of Russian manufacture, were still SovBloc classics: the AT-2000 version of the Czech-manufactured CZ-75 autoloader, exceptionally accurate, with ambidextrous controls and a finish superior to that of the parent weapon, sporting a 15-round box magazine in 9 mm Parabellum.

Bolan checked his watch again: twelve seconds.

Rising from his crouch, he slipped the AKSU off its shoulder sling and double-checked the safety. There was no need to confirm the live round in the weapon's chamber, or to check the pistol slung beneath his left arm in a horizontal fast-draw harness. The grenades, spare magazines and the stiletto he had used to kill the sentry were distributed about his person with an eye toward balance, comfort and convenience.

The last thing any soldier needed in the middle of

a firefight was to wind up sitting on his frag grenades or groping for a spare clip that he couldn't find.

Nine seconds.

Bolan left the comfort of the shadows, moving toward his final jumping-off point. If the target house had other guards out front, he couldn't spot them. He would have to deal with them when *they* saw him and opened fire.

Assuming he was still alive and able to respond.

He pictured Gellar and the young Ukrainian in motion, hoped that they were on their marks and hadn't stumbled into danger prematurely. There had been no sounds of gunfire, no alarms, but Bolan knew his enemies wouldn't be anxious to rouse the neighborhood. The sentry he had killed was carrying a Chinese Type 64 submachine gun, muzzle-heavy with its eighteen-inch combination sound suppressor and flash-hider shrouding the weapon's 9.5-inch barrel. It was an assassin's weapon, accurate only at close range, quiet enough to kill without drawing attention.

Bolan had considered taking the SMG with him, but settled for pulling the curved 30-round magazine, tossing it into some nearby bushes. He wasn't concerned about noise from this point forward.

In fact, a bit of racket might be beneficial to the cause.

He crossed the street, thankful that streetlights in this quarter of Odessa were few and far between. He watched the windows, ready with his AKSU as he closed the gap with his target, moving boldly toward the front door of the house. No lights were showing through the drapes in front. With any luck—

A burst of automatic gunfire resounded from the

middle distance, somewhere at the rear of the house. Bolan steeled himself, prepared to rush the door.

So much for luck.

ZIVEN ZHENECHKA WAS a disappointment to his parents. They had both been raised on stories of the brutal Nazi occupation of Ukraine during the Great Patriotic War of 1941–1945, and they would never understand his allegiance to a cause they deemed traitorous and depraved. He believed that they would never forgive him for joining the Temple of the Black Hundred, Ukrainian youth wing of the Temple of the Nordic Covenant, and he didn't expect them to.

Still, things could have been worse.

At least they weren't Jews.

The news that Gerhard Steuben, founder of the Temple, would be visiting Ukraine this week had spread like wildfire through the ranks, although it wasn't public knowledge. So far, Ziven Zhenechka hadn't seen his leader, couldn't even swear that Steuben was in town, but all troops had been placed on full alert for the duration of his stay, wherever he might be.

There had been trouble, Zhenechka understood, although if asked, he couldn't have provided any details. Killing, certainly—that much was known among his fellow skinheads. As to where the killing had occurred, reports were vague and contradictory. Some said in Germany, while others named Croatia, Bosnia—one rumor even mentioned Moscow. More important than location was the identity of those who had been targeted for death.

The Temple of the Nordic Covenant was under siege.

The image of his comrades dying for their cause aroused conflicting emotions in the man. While he was furious, outraged at the arrogance of their enemies, another part of him felt pride at the bold sacrifice of his Aryan kinsmen. And yet another part of him felt pure, visceral excitement at the prospect of battle.

Zhenechka had seen his share of action in street fights and skirmishes with left-wing radicals around Odessa, plus a few exhilarating raids into the country-side, striking at Jews and immigrants farther afield, but he was still untested in the face of serious opposition. The last days were coming, he knew, with Armageddon looming on the horizon, and he would feel better able to confront those challenges once he was blooded in serious combat.

Besides, the young women who found themselves drawn to the Black Hundred always preferred real fighters, the rugged types with battle scars to go with their tattoos.

Instead of being sent to battle, though, Zhenechka had been detailed to guard the house in Old Odessa where his unit of the Black Hundred—styled as Strike Force 17—stored various supplies, including weapons. The duty was far from glamorous, but a good soldier did as he was told.

Zhenechka knew his time would come, but he had no good reason to believe that it would come this night.

Something had roused him from his restless sleep. What was it? He couldn't recall the interrupted dream in any detail, but it hadn't been disturbing, nothing that would jar him back to full and sudden wakefulness.

Two other skinheads, Moriz and Fedor, shared the

small bedroom, both still fast asleep and snoring like a pair of swine in muck. He didn't wake them as he rose, still vague on what had roused him, dreading how foolish he would look if it was nothing but a dream.

Zhenechka scrabbled for his pants, wadded up on the floor beside his cot. Just blue jeans, nothing to take care of, since they weren't allowed to wear their khaki uniforms around the neighborhood. A fat SIG-Sauer pistol lay across the polished toes of his combat boots. He scooped it up and placed it on the cot beside him as he pulled on the boots.

He was sweating now, unable to say why.

There was a sound, but Zhenechka couldn't place it. Chair legs scraping on the kitchen floor perhaps? A stubborn window opening? The muffled and distorted sound of snoring from another bedroom?

There were fifteen skinheads assigned to security in the house, with five of them on watch at any given time. The rest, when not on duty, were at liberty to sleep, watch television, read, do laundry, feed their faces, polish boots or weapons—anything, in short, that didn't jeopardize the house, its occupants or any merchandise contained therein.

Another sound. Zhenechka thought that this one sounded more like someone shuffling cards, except that he had to have the largest deck and strongest hands that anyone on earth had every seen or heard of. It was more like canvas ripping and—

The first faint smell of cordite reached his nostrils, and he didn't need to stop to think about what that meant, in conjunction with the riffling noise. An automatic weapon with a sound suppressor. There could be no mistake.

Zhenechka drew his pistol from the waistband of his trousers and rushed back to the bedroom, slapping Fedor and Moriz across their shaved scalps to wake them, hissing at them in his fear of making any undue noise.

"Wake up, for God's sake! Hurry!"

"Who's that?" Fedor challenged.

Moriz muttered, "I don't like this fucking game."

"No games," Zhenechka told them, speaking through clenched teeth. "There's shooting."

"What? What shooting?"

"I don't hear—"

The sudden, unmistakable report of a Kalashnikov assault rifle drowned out whatever else Fedor had meant to say.

"Do you hear *that?*" Zhenechka growled.

"What is it?"

"Trouble!" he replied. "Now, grab your guns and follow me!"

EACH TIME HE FOUND himself confronting death in some strange country, Jacob Gellar wondered whether he would ever see Israel again. He had no conscious fear of death, though he preferred that it be swift and painless. Still, there was something, more akin to bittersweet nostalgia, that recalled the memories of Israel each time he suspected he might die.

Like now, for instance.

Coming up behind the house with the Ukrainian, Grisha Pashenka, he was on alert, prepared to cut loose with his AKSU if they met the slightest opposition. They had taken down one guard—a teenager, he seemed to be, though he had struggled manfully as

Pashenka cut his throat—and so far they were in the clear.

So far.

The final part of the approach was where the danger lay, of course. Gellar had taken up the dead youth's SMG, grateful to find it suppressor equipped. They were on schedule, and this way they could blow the lock on the back door without alerting every sleeping neo-Nazi in the house.

Gellar had grown up hating Nazis, schooled by the survivors of a family that had been whittled down in Hitler's death camps, understanding early on that brownshirts and turbans were often motivated by the same irrational, deep-seated hatred of Jews. It was a sin, the Torah said, to return hatred for hatred.

But he would take his chances on that score.

God needed warriors at the moment, as much as he needed rabbis, teachers and optometrists.

Ten paces from the house, Gellar froze in his tracks as the back door swung open. Another young skinhead emerged backward, turning on his heel to face the darkened yard, a steaming mug of coffee in each hand. He blinked at Gellar and Pashenka, dropped the mugs to spill and shatter at his feet, trying to reach the weapon that was slung across his shoulder.

He never made it.

Gellar fired a short burst from the liberated SMG, stitching a line of holes across the startled skinhead's chest. His target staggered backward, sat down hard, the clatter of his weapon on the pavement louder than the gunshots that had killed him.

And the door was open, waiting for them, pale light spilling out across the stoop, the corpse, the lawn.

Gellar didn't consult his watch. Whether the time

was right or not, they had to move, and rapidly, before they were discovered by another enemy and somehow blocked from entering the house. The first rule of a fighting man was to seize opportunities as they arose.

"Come on!" he whispered in Russian, Grisha close behind him as they rushed the house. Already there was movement in what had to be the kitchen, someone stepping closer to the open door.

Gellar was tempted to explode with cursing as a round face peered around the doorjamb, swiftly drawing back again, but he restrained himself and instead fired another silenced burst of Parabellum rounds. They gnawed the door frame, but he knew that he had missed his mark.

The Israeli knew they were in trouble then, at least as far as a surprise attack on the house was concerned. He heard a sharp, metallic click-clack sound from somewhere in the kitchen, knew a weapon had been armed and was already dodging when an unaimed burst of AK-47 fire erupted from the open doorway.

Speed was all that mattered now—to hell with stealth. He sprayed the doorway with his captured SMG, emptied the magazine in seconds flat and dropped the useless weapon on the lawn. Pashenka was milking short bursts from his AKSU, circling closer to the kitchen door, when Gellar called a warning out.

"Stay back!" he snapped. "Grenade!"

The RGD was in his hand, the pin already tossed away. He didn't care about the skinhead in the kitchen, if the Nazi bastard heard his warning cry or not. If he retreated, they would still have access to the kitchen. All that mattered now was gaining entry to the house. Whether they killed the guards in one room or another was irrelevant.

He thought about the neighbors, wondered which of them had working telephones and were already dialing the police hot line. Gellar pitched the grenade and watched it sail in through the doorway, bouncing once on old linoleum before it wobbled out of sight, off to his left.

Three seconds...two...one...

Hand grenades weren't generally as powerful as Hollywood portrayed them. Antipersonnel grenades weren't designed to level houses or sink battleships. The RPG-5 contained 110 grams of TNT—a hair under four ounces—and the average kill radius of its serrated shrapnel was sixty feet. In short, while it was deadly in close quarters and would definitely trash a room, it shouldn't under any circumstances be mistaken for a blockbuster.

Gellar was crouching when the RGD went off, leery of shrapnel coming through the stucco walls, and Pashenka beat him to the smoky doorway, moving with the reckless zeal of youth. A short burst from Pashenka's AKSU told Gellar the skinhead hadn't managed to escape. He didn't bother checking out the corpse as he went in, scanning instead for any adversaries who were still alive and fit for battle.

Gunfire from another quarter of the house told Gellar that his traveling companion and partner in crime, Mike Belasko, was fighting his way inside. The Israeli swallowed an impulse to help him, concentrating instead on the primary mission: annihilate defenders in the house and destroy whatever they had been assigned to protect.

One small step for Gellar and Belasko.

With any luck, one giant loss for Nazi-kind.

There was a single exit from the kitchen to the interior rooms of the house. No door, per se, but simply an open arch, with darkness lurking where the kitchen lights couldn't reach. Gellar sensed danger there, but they had no alternative approach.

"Come on!" he said. It was superfluous, since Pashenka was ahead of him, already moving closer to the shadowed doorway. Gellar stopped short when the young Ukrainian froze in his tracks, staring down at the floor, between his feet.

And this time it was Pashenka who cried out, "Grenade!"

Gellar recoiled, already diving toward the nearest cover when a heavy-metal thunderclap enveloped him.

ZIVEN ZHENECHKA HUGGED the floor as bullets punched holes in the wall a foot or less above his head. He couldn't tell if it was friendly fire or hostile rounds, but the result would be the same if any of the bullets met his flesh.

Behind him, stretched out in the hallway, Fedor was cursing a blue streak, his shrill voice grating on Zhenechka's nerves. There was no sound from Moriz, and Zhenechka wasn't sure what he should make of that. The silence was welcome at this point, but he wondered whether Moriz had been hit.

Zhenechka couldn't turn and look without pushing up on his elbows and edging away from the wall, two moves that would only serve to make him more vulnerable, a better target for his unseen enemies. Clutching his pistol, still unfired in this engagement, he wasn't prepared to take that risk.

How many shooters were there in the raiding party? And what did they want?

The second question was no great riddle. This attack had to be part of the general persecution targeting the Nordic Temple and its affiliates. It had taken some time for the shock waves to reach Ukraine, but now Gerhard Steuben was here, and so were his enemies.

If only Zhenechka could get a clear shot at one of the bastards! Just one glimpse, long enough to aim and fire...and preferably without getting himself killed in the process.

Another burst of AK fire tore through the wall and showered him with plaster dust. Fedor gave out a squeal that could have indicated fright or pain. Zhenechka didn't try to ask him which it was, for fear his own voice might betray him to the enemy. Instead, he pressed his face against the worn-out carpet.

One chance. Just one clear shot.

At least they were no longer using hand grenades. Zhenechka had been worried that the house might catch on fire, that he would fry before he could escape. This way, his only risk was being shot by friends and enemies alike, as he lay trembling on the floor.

It shamed him, lying there, his jaws clenched to keep his teeth from chattering like castanets. If Kiryl, the commander of their team, could see him now, he would be furious. What kind of soldier would Zhenechka make if he was terrified the first time guns went off?

He had to do something, and soon, before it was too late!

When in doubt, attack!

It was a slogan popular among his fellow fighters of the Black Hundred, and while it was more commonly heard in bars, over drinks, than in actual combat, it still seemed to capture the essence of the moment.

But whom should he attack, and how? Where were his enemies? Were they inside the house, or—?

Suddenly, as if in answer to his question, one of his comrades staggered backward through a door that served what some would call the family room, some fifteen feet ahead of where Zhenechka hugged the floor. He recognized Edik, another of his comrades and a sometime drinking friend, although his face was torn and smeared with blood. Zhenechka watched as Edik took another burst of automatic fire dead-center in the chest. The impact slammed him against the nearest wall, pinning him there for a moment, until gravity took over and dragged him slithering downward.

That tore it! One of his enemies was just beyond that threshold, murdering his friends and comrades. All Zhenechka had to do was walk or crawl another fifteen feet, and he would have his clear shot at his foe.

Why was it, then, that when he urged his arms and legs to move, they stubbornly defied him?

Cursing, feeling hot tears in his eyes, Zhenechka struggled to his hands and knees, bruising the knuckles of his right hand as he kept a firm grip on the automatic, lurching toward the open doorway like some oversize child in a playpen. He was tempted to look back and see if either Fedor or Moriz would follow him, but then he pictured both men dead, lying in blood, and knew that if he saw it in the flesh his will would break.

He paused outside the doorway, awkwardly working himself into a crouch, his legs folded under him, his back against the wall. At any moment, the Ukrainian feared, another burst of automatic fire would rip the plaster, dump him sprawling, lifeless on his face.

If he was going to attack, he had to do it now.

Zhenechka checked the safety on his pistol one last time, thumbed back the hammer, wincing at the loud metallic sound it made, and bolted to his feet. The sudden move made him feel giddy, like a vodka buzz, with bright spots swarming for a moment in his field of vision.

He lunged around the corner, the SIG-Sauer braced in both hands, sighting instinctively on a tall, dark man who occupied the center of the room, surrounded by chaos and carnage. The stranger seemed to be expecting him, made no real effort to raise the weapon he held at waist level, its stubby muzzle angled toward the door.

Zhenechka squeezed off two quick shots and saw a window shatter, well behind the stranger. Then he saw brass spewing from his adversary's weapon, felt the impact of a giant fist beneath his sternum and was conscious of a weightless moment as he vaulted backward, tumbling through the air.

And by the time he landed, he knew nothing anymore.

IF BOLAN HAD BEEN called upon to grade the skinheads, he would probably have ranked their overall preparedness around C− or D+ while giving them a B for effort once the hit went down. They were determined but disorganized, gung-ho but poorly trained—or maybe they had simply never faced a challenge where the lives at stake turned out to be their own.

The young neo-Nazis scattered around him, sprawled in awkward attitudes of death, had failed the only test that mattered for a fighting man. There was no makeup test, no second chance, no extra-credit work that they could do at home, in their spare time.

This night their time had all run out.

In combat, barring miracles or flukes, a soldier got one chance to prove himself, and only one. Confronted with the enemy, he either lived or died—and living meant that he had spilled the blood of others, stolen lives from others like himself, who followed orders, did as they were told and paid the price for failure in an unforgiving world.

Six dead so far, and Bolan heard more firing from the back part of the house, where Gellar and his local contact had engaged the enemy. How many more skinheads were left inside the house? How long before police arrived with flashing lights and whooping sirens? Where was the material—arms cache, supplies, whatever—they had come here to destroy?

He pulled the AKSU's nearly empty magazine, replaced it with a fresh one, moving cautiously but swiftly toward the door. Along the way, he chose the youngest, thinnest of his recent kills and dragged the skinhead after him, propelled him through the open doorway with a straight-arm shove that sent him tumbling right across the hall, to slump atop a fallen friend.

The corpse had drawn no fire, and while that didn't prove the corridor was safe, at least it indicated he would have a fighting chance. Bolan went through the doorway in a shoulder roll and came up on one knee, his AKSU tracking, seeking targets.

There were two more skinheads in the corridor, both lying prone and making no attempt to bring him under fire. One of them twitched and moaned, the other lying deathly still, and both of them were leaking blood into the mouse-gray carpet. Rising, moving closer, Bolan gave each one of them a head shot to make sure, then moved on toward the sound of firing from the back part of the house.

He estimated he was halfway there, when suddenly a door flew open, two nude figures spilling out into the corridor. One of them was a girl, not bad, a little thin for Bolan's taste; her sidekick was a skinhead with a pimply face and various tattoos, the body art and blemishes ignored as Bolan focused on the shotgun in his hands.

He shot the naked skinhead, three or four rounds in the chest from something close to point-blank range. The kid went down without a whimper. Bolan, covering the girl, was surprised when she bent down to take the shotgun from her lover's grasp.

''*Nyet!*'' he warned her.

She snarled and babbled something at him—curses, he assumed—and then she had the shotgun, swinging it around to aim the sawed-off muzzle at his chest.

No time. No choice.

The AKSU stuttered and the girl slumped over backward, into a pose that could have been alluring if you took away the gun, the background and the blood. It was Bolan's turn to curse now as he stepped around her, scooped up the shotgun and pitched it left-handed down to the end of the hallway.

''Anybody else?'' he challenged silent doors on

both sides of the corridor. "Who wants to die for the half-assed master race?"

He started kicking doors and checking rooms. Inside the third one he found guns, lots of them racked and stacked, some of them crated, all with extra magazines and ammunition, hand grenades and high explosives.

Neo-Nazi toys.

A scuffling footstep brought his AKSU back around to pin two figures in the hallway. Gellar and his contact, Grisha Something, waited for his eyes and brain to catch up with the combat reflex, making the ID.

"All done?" he asked Gellar.

The Mossad agent nodded. "Have you found something?"

"The candy store," Bolan replied, and stepped back, let the other men examine the Black Hundred's arsenal.

"It is convenient that they have plastique," Gellar remarked. "Before we blow it, we should maybe take some ammunition for ourselves."

"Sounds fair," Bolan replied. "We earned it."

Four metal boxes filled with loaded AK magazines were set aside before Bolan and Gellar began distributing the plastic explosive, seating detonators found in a separate box, on a high shelf away from the plastique. The timers were simple but effective.

"How much time?" Gellar asked.

"Make it five," Bolan suggested. "It should blow before the cops pile in."

Three minutes later, they were in the car and rolling, no one looking back. They slowed at the sight of squad cars rushing toward the recent firefight scene, letting the lights and sirens pass them by. The plastique blew while officers were scrambling from their cars and double-checking weapons, talking over entry routes and plans.

All gone.

"That wasn't bad, all things considered," Gellar said.

"What now?" their driver asked.

Bolan felt weary as he said, "We keep on going."

CHAPTER TWO

The long chase had begun in the United States, where one-eyed Gary Stevens—better known to his neo-Nazi disciples in the Temple of the Nordic Covenant as Gerhard Steuben, reincarnation of an SS captain killed on the Eastern Front in World War II—had been linked to an escalating series of terrorist incidents. The Temple was considered more extreme than its various fascist competitors, based on Steuben's apocalyptic vision of a war to end all wars that would enthrone the proud blond remnant of the master race to rule humankind. It was considered more dangerous than other neo-Nazi cliques because of its size and scope, with active tentacles or hard-core allies in countries ranging from Europe to the Mideast and South Africa.

Bolan's first pass at the Nordic Temple, stateside, was an inconclusive sparring match, but he had come away from the clash with an ally of sorts. Marilyn Crouder was a deep-cover agent for the ATF—Alcohol, Tobacco and Firearms—who had spent the better part of eighteen months inside the Nordic Temple, absorbing the cult's secrets and memorizing faces, names, relationships. Somehow her cover had been blown, and she was marked for execution on the very night Mack Bolan struck the Temple's main U.S. bivouac and training facility. They got away with their lives that time, but it wasn't the end of the story.

Despite her sudden lack of cover, Crouder's people at ATF were strangely reluctant to bring her in from the cold. First they placed her on loan to Bolan, via Hal Brognola's Stony Man connection, to assist in rolling up the Temple of the Nordic Covenant. Then, when the action in Chicago and Los Angeles turned bloody, no arrests but lots of bodies, Washington got hinky in a hurry. Overnight, it seemed, Marilyn Crouder was cut adrift from the agency she had served, working without a net.

Bolan supposed that moment of abandonment, as much as anything, was the factor that persuaded him to let her tag along when the hunt went international.

From the States, they tracked Gary Stevens and his little clique of bodyguards to Germany, where Bolan hooked up with Mossad agent Jacob Gellar for the first time—another match arranged by Hal Brognola's Stony Man connections. Together, they took down some Nazi players, frustrating the would-be führer's plan to launch another Kristallnacht attack on German Jews and to retrieve an alleged holy relic, the so-called Spear of Destiny, that was supposed to render its owner invincible in combat.

When it turned out that his German troops were anything but bulletproof, Stevens fled again, this time to troubled Croatia, where a history of collaboration with Nazi killers during World War II had provided a leg up on latter-day ethnic cleansing. Still playing connect-the-dots on his lonely road to Armageddon, Stevens psyched up his Croatian cronies for a murder attempt against the nation's chief of state. Exactly what the Nordic Temple hoped to gain from that was anybody's guess, but Bolan believed rationality had little to do with the thought processes of a neo-Nazi fanatic who worshiped the old Nordic gods of war.

Personally, Bolan couldn't have cared less if Stevens and company wanted to dance naked in Times Square on Christmas Eve, sacrificing chickens to Thor and Odin while singing "Hello, Dolly." Religious peculiarities concerned him only when they involved violence and coercive behavior, trampling on the rights and lives of others. For Gary Stevens and his self-styled Aryan warriors, adherence to their one true faith meant setting off a string of international explosions that would rock the world and, at least in theory, change the course of history.

Bolan had no reason to think that Stevens could ever accomplish his goal of setting the world on fire, much less emerging from the ashes intact himself to rule the planet, but he was already responsible for dozens of deaths, and his flight from Croatia to Ukraine had placed him within arm's reach of weapons built for the last days.

The breakup of the Soviet Union, while hailed as a miracle by anti-Communists worldwide, had created a whole new list of problems for diplomats and soldiers in what was once known as the "First" or "Free World." Spies, assassins and scientists thrown out of work by the fall of the old Red regime were suddenly free agents, hawking their knowledge and skills to the highest bidder, without regard to nationality or ideology. More frightening yet, vast arsenals of weapons— including tactical nukes—survived in the new, chaotic and impoverished nations that had recently been strictly managed Soviet republics. Much of that hardware had gone up for grabs, and was for sale. Ukrainian dealers ranked among the most active, well-stocked arms merchants in post-Soviet Europe.

All of which meant trouble if a group of die-hard fanatics like the Temple of the Nordic Covenant should come into possession of a nuclear device. It was Bolan's great fear, Israel's waking nightmare, but even without a nuke in the equation, fascist violence in Ukraine could still unleash a grisly tide of blood and suffering.

It was their job to dam that bloody tide by any means available, and hopefully stop Gary Stevens in his tracks before he could move on to other battlefields, send other brownshirts marching off to racial holy war. And failing that, it was their task to minimize the damage, see to it that the majority of casualties were suffered by the Temple of the Nordic Covenant.

By such means was a grim war of attrition won.

"All right, we've scored first blood. What's next?"

The question hung between them, Bolan watching Jacob Gellar and their local contact—who spoke passable, if somewhat awkward English—waiting for an answer.

"Obviously," Gellar ventured, "what we need most is a line on Steuben's whereabouts."

"Agreed," Bolan replied. "That's obvious. It's also obvious that we don't have a single lead so far on where he's hiding out."

Gellar was too experienced—or maybe just too tired—to take offense at Bolan's tone. "We simply haven't asked the proper person yet," he said.

"That may be it," Bolan replied. "Or then again, there may not be a proper person in Ukraine for us to ask."

"Meaning?"

A shrug from Bolan. "I was thinking, what if this was never meant to be his final destination in the first place? What if he was running from Croatia and he just passed through Ukraine, headed to somewhere else? We know he's got connections in the Middle East, an outfit in South Africa, some people in New Zealand and Australia."

"No," Gellar said, frowning as he shook his head. "Grisha's connections are convinced that he is still here, somewhere in Ukraine."

"All due respect," Bolan replied, "but those connections haven't seen him, right? They're passing on what they've been told, and some of them are tight with members of the Nordic Temple, maybe Nazis themselves. I don't care if the herring's red or Aryan. It smells the same."

"No," Gellar said again, still frowning. "I believe that he is here. It makes sense for a man attempting to initiate a series of events around the globe. Where better for one of his patented massacres than in a former province of the USSR?"

"In that case, why not Moscow?" Bolan challenged. "He's got people there, from what I understand."

"A handful only," Gellar said. "His troops are stronger here, the raw materials of death more readily available."

"All right. Let's say we trust your instincts this time," Bolan said. "We can't afford to thrash around the fringes of his operation while he puts the ball in play. We need better connections, better information, and we need it now."

"You're right, of course."

Gellar turned to Grisha Pashenka and said, "We need to keep the pressure on, you understand? But not just anywhere. We must find out where Steuben is and what he's up to."

"Yes, of course," the young Ukrainian replied. "His chief lieutenant in my country is Hedeon Onoprienko, a notorious fascist with a long criminal record."

"You can find this man?" Gellar asked.

"Possibly. Though finding him and reaching him may be two very different things. He travels all the time with bodyguards and lets his guard down never. It is said he keeps a man outside the bathroom door each time he takes a shower or relieves himself. Same thing when he has sex, at least one man outside the door to listen in and make sure there are no surprises."

"We can deal with bodyguards," Bolan remarked.

"Onoprienko also has no regular—what do you say in English?—fixed address," Pashenka said. "To often move, he thinks, is making him secure. It may be true, since he is still alive and free."

"He'd be the one to know where Stevens is, if anybody does," Bolan said.

"But if we go for him directly," Gellar said, "the odds are good that someone else will tip off our rabbit and give him time to run before we find his lair."

"Somebody else, then. Stevens would have guards, support troops, maybe somebody to feed him, maybe a chauffeur. It's hard to keep that kind of duty quiet when the big boss comes to town."

"We need an intermediary," Gellar stated.

"A quartermaster," Bolan said. "Find someone midway up the ladder of command who handles the logistics details. Maybe someone from the Nordic Temple, or an officer from the Black Hundred, if they spread the work around.''

''We could try both,'' Gellar suggested.

''What we can't do,'' Bolan countered, ''is waste any time. The sooner we run Stevens down, the better chance we have of ending this before he can arrange another fireworks show.''

''Agreed.'' Gellar turned back to their Ukrainian associate. ''You understand what we require, Grisha?'' he asked.

Pashenka nodded. ''Someone who may know where Steuben hides, and who may disappear without the big alarms.''

''Exactly,'' Gellar said. ''Can you locate someone like that?''

''I have my sources.''

''Right. There's no time like the present, then.''

''I use the public telephone outside,'' Grisha informed them as he rose to leave.

''That's my cue,'' Bolan said. ''I need to check on Marilyn and maybe touch base with the States.''

''I'll be here,'' Gellar told him, and prepared to clean his weapons one more time.

MARILYN CROUDER TOOK the semiauto pistol with her when she went to answer the door. Because it was a double-action weapon with a live round in the chamber, she didn't thumb back the hammer. It would be no problem firing through the hotel's wooden door, if she should find a hostile-looking stranger in the corridor outside.

The peephole was old-fashioned, like a tiny trapdoor that you had to open from the inside, peering

through a metal minigrate. There was a certain risk
involved, since any shooter on the far side of the door
could have his weapon pressed against the grate and
ready when you offered him your eyeball as a target,
so she took a chance, stepped off to one side of the
door and called, "Who is it?"

"Mike Belasko."

She could feel herself relaxing at the sound of his
familiar voice—and tingling, too, dammit—but she
still checked the peephole, leaning into it, the muzzle
of her side arm held a slim inch from the door so any
recoil would not sprain or snap her wrist.

It was Belasko, and seemingly alone.

"Nice you could make it, guy," she told him as
she stood aside to let him enter. Even as she spoke
the words, Crouder wondered if they sounded as ridiculous to him as they did to her.

"We had some business," he replied, waiting while
she checked out the corridor from force of habit,
closed and double-locked the door behind him.

"Right," she said. "No problems, then?"

"No problems with the hit," he said, and she could
smell the cordite on him, maybe in his hair or on his
clothes. The smell was too familiar to arouse her, but
it got her ticking, all the same. "We're still no closer
to the target, though."

"You're sure he's in the country?"

"We're pretty sure," Bolan replied, sitting in one
of the room's two available chairs. The bed looked
big and empty, up against the wall behind him.
"We're pursuing angles, trying to find out."

She didn't ask if there was anything that she could
do to help. It would have been an idiotic question.
What could she do in a country where she didn't speak

the language, didn't know a living soul, most likely couldn't find her way across town if her life depended on it?

Nada. Zip. The old goose egg.

Instead, she asked, "What angles would those be...if you don't mind my asking?"

"I suppose Grisha will find some locals he can bribe or squeeze. There's not much I can do from here on out, until we find a target."

"It's rough, the waiting. I know all about that end of things."

Bolan shrugged. "We have to wait, we wait." He didn't seem upset or agitated; neither was he bored, as far as Crouder could tell. She had the sense that he was used to waiting, in between the bouts of bloody action where he so excelled. It was a hunter's trait, she realized. The best cops had it down—stone killers, too, apparently.

"One thing," she said, "in case it helps. Stevens or Steuben, call him what you want, is every bit as strange to this part of the world as we are. What I mean to say, he may have been here, but he doesn't speak the language. If he wants a cup of coffee or a roll of toilet paper, he's relying on interpreters, the same as we are. Just in case you start to think he's got an edge."

"He does have one," Bolan told her solemnly. "He's got disciples on the ground here, natives who can walk him through whatever steps he has to take along the way. He's got support, hardware, maybe political connections we don't know about. Between the Nordic Temple and its youth auxiliary, the Black Hundred, he's got at least 450 people in the country, ready to salute when he walks in the room."

She couldn't think of anything to say that would reduce those killer odds, and so instead she asked him, "Does it ever bother you?"

"What's that?" Belasko asked, pretending not to understand.

"The killing," she replied.

"It's what I do," he said, no need to pause to think about his answer. "When I catch a target, he's already skated through the system, proved himself to be above—or maybe just beyond—the law. I don't preempt the courts and lawyers. I get called when there's a job nobody else can handle—or nobody wants to touch."

"So you're the court of last resort," she said.

"Not even close. I don't judge anyone. They judge themselves. They've been convicted and condemned by their own actions. I'm just taking out the trash."

"A sanitary engineer," she said, frowning.

"Just a soldier, once removed," he said. "I know you understand the check-and-balance thing. The military doesn't formulate policy, it executes policy."

"But you're not military," she replied, the urge to prod him proving irresistible. "I mean, you can't be, right? The military has no law-enforcement function, short of martial law, and there's no jurisdiction in the States."

His narrow smile had frost around the edges. "Are we working up to something here? A question?"

She considered it, then shook her head, her shoulders slumping. "Never mind," she said. "You wouldn't answer it, and something tells me that I'm better off not knowing anyway."

"I'll second that," Bolan said, and seemed to visibly relax. "The less you know when you go home, the happier you'll be."

"Go home to what?"

"There must be someone, something waiting for you," he replied.

"Big no to someone," she informed him. "There's been no one...I mean, other than..." Dammit! She tried again. "I'm flying solo. Have been since before I took the mole spot in the Nordic Temple."

"Family and friends," he said, no comment on the fact that she had almost said, "Other than you."

"My parents aren't around," she said. "No siblings. The rest of the family, who needs them? You watch Jerry Springer?"

That earned her a smile as she continued. "As for friends, I have—or had—two kinds. There was the college crowd, of course. You know how that goes. Everybody swears they'll stay in touch, but once the summer after graduation's over, ninety-nine percent of them are history. I couldn't find three of them on a map of the United States to save my life. The other bunch was friends from work, at ATF. Of course, it seems that I'm no longer part of ATF. In fact, smart money says I'd be about as welcome as flesh-eating virus if I tried to get in touch with them. Know what I mean?"

"Their loss," Bolan said.

"Why does it feel like mine?"

"You'll make new friends. You're a survivor."

"Gets lonely, though," she said.

"I've been there."

"Have you?" Startled by the flicker in his eyes, she said, "I'm sorry. What I meant was, well, I get the sense that it was your choice, how you live and all.''

"My choice," he said, "but not my plan. Nobody plans a life alone. Well, maybe old man Hoover at the FBI."

"He had Clyde Tolson," she reminded him.

"That's right." A smile this time.

"I'm curious...."

"That killed the cat."

"But satisfaction brought her back."

"That's something I can't promise, satisfaction."

Crouder was on the verge of telling him that he did all right last time, but caught herself. Instead, she said, "Why don't you humor me?"

"For what?"

"You said yourself, I need to make new friends."

"So, put me on the list," he said. "I'm sold."

"I need to know you first."

"You have a question."

"Yes."

"I may not have an answer," he replied.

"That would be your decision."

"Go ahead, then."

"I'm just wondering how you got into this...this line of work," she said. "You're obviously not a psychopath—or what's the PC term these days—antisocial personality disorder? It amazes me, the things you do and how you came to this."

Bolan thought about it for a moment, then replied, "No details. They'd be useless to you, anyway. Long story short, I was a soldier, like I said. I went to war and did my job. Somewhere along the way, an obstacle was placed in front of me that couldn't be removed by any ordinary means. There's no more uniform, but I can't seem to shake the war.''

"You ever think of going AWOL?'' Crouder inquired.

"Just once," he said. "It didn't help.''

"I'm sorry."

"Don't be. Like I said, we all make choices.'' Glancing at his watch, he said, "And now I need to make a call."

She rose and intercepted him before he reached the door.

"Right now?" she asked. "It couldn't wait five minutes? Maybe ten?"

He stared into her eyes and said, "Maybe fifteen. Who knows?"

Washington, D.C.

THE TEN-HOUR TIME difference meant Hal Brognola was starting on his second cup of morning coffee when the black telephone rang. It was his private line, a bypass that circumvented the building switchboard and his secretary's desk, thus theoretically avoiding taps. He swept the line each morning, just in case, and used the built-in scrambling device religiously. It angered his secretary to hear the black phone ringing, when she couldn't screen the calls—and that was something of a bonus, in Brognola's view.

This day he picked up on the second ring and said, "Hello." No name or other greeting was offered as he waited for the caller to identify himself. Despite the line's unlisted number, Brognola got nuisance calls—wrong numbers, telemarketers and sundry shills for Jesus—on an average of two, three times per month. Sometimes he traced the calls and had a little fun himself. Two sleazy telemarketers had suffered audits by the IRS this year alone, for interrupting Brognola at lunch, and one prank caller dialing random numbers from his house while playing hooky from a D.C. junior high school was surprised to find a pair of burly G-men on his doorstep.

This time, the caller was legit.

"It's me," he said. Just that, and the big Fed immediately recognized the deep voice of a man who ranked among his best and oldest living friends. Not that the guy was old, per se; Brognola's friends involved in heavy field work simply had a tendency to die before their time.

But not this guy.

Thank God.

"Striker," he said by way of greeting. "I'm scrambling now."

"Right with you."

The big Fed reached out and tapped a button, watched a little red light blink three times, then wink out as the green light to its left came on.

"Okay," he said when they were set. "What's cooking where you are?"

"We're holding at the moment," Bolan said, "hoping for confirmation on a target. In the meantime, I was hoping that you might have turned up something on the reason why we're here."

"No luck," Brognola said. "You know, I used to sit around and think that life would all be so much simpler if the Evil Empire fell apart. Turns out, it's just the opposite. Instead of one united enemy, with orders coming down from Moscow, now it's like somebody opened all the cages in the zoo at feeding time. I tapped the Company and NSA, but they've got nothing—or, at least, they're not inclined to share. Strike three with Interpol. They're nowhere close to getting any kind of decent hookup with the former SovBloc countries. Bottom line—I wouldn't know where *you* were if you didn't tell me. As for Adolf Jr., hell, it's anybody's guess.''

''I was afraid of that,'' the Executioner replied. ''Did you come up with anything at all about that other thing?''

The nukes, he meant. Brognola felt a tight knot forming in his stomach, tried to wash it clear with coffee, but it didn't help.

''Officially,'' he said, ''they're clean. Have been for years. You know the party line, no pun intended. Still, we keep on hearing stories about dealers from Ukraine, Georgia, Azerbaijan. I wouldn't want to say it's smoke without a spark or two behind it.''

''But we can't confirm delivery of a package from your end,'' Bolan said.

''Nothing solid, sorry,'' Brognola replied. ''We've picked up rumors that some of your basic Nazi types are shopping for the ultimate in fireworks, but you hear that about every crackpot east of Belfast. Last July, one of the local spotters swore he'd seen a clone of Tim McVeigh shopping for warheads at an arms bazaar in Kazakhstan. The guy he picked out of the photo lineup was a fifty-year-old G-man from Des Moines—who had a fairly decent alibi, in case you're wondering.''

''I hear you,'' Bolan said. ''We'll have to work it from this end and see what floats when we turn up the heat.''

''For what it's worth,'' Brognola said, ''remember

that the players where you are have been a little schizo since the Kremlin cut them loose. Besides the economic problems and the old boys' club that wants to resurrect Joe Stalin, you've got zealots, kooks and crazies everywhere you turn. It's like a bughouse with the inmates in control.''

''I think we've got an extra straitjacket,'' Bolan replied.

''One other thing,'' the big Fed said. ''About your friend…''

''What's that?''

''With the Mossad…well, you know what I'm getting at. They have their own agenda, and it doesn't always matter what they're saying to your face, okay? It's understood that if they have a choice of helping Tel Aviv or playing by the rules agreed on in advance, the rules go out the window faster than a cut-rate gigolo. Okay?''

''I'll make a note.''

''Nothing against the guy they sent you,'' Brognola went on. ''Sounds like he's done all right so far. But keep an eye out if there's any way his team could benefit by hosing you.''

''Affirmative.''

''I mean to say it hasn't been that long since we caught one of their guys…well, let's put it this way— the Mossad would just as soon spy on their friends as on their enemies.''

''As for the home team,'' Bolan said, ''I'm proud that we would never do a thing like that.''

''Except with the most honorable motives,'' Brognola replied. ''Just watch your back, okay? No matter who's standing behind you.''

''Roger that.''

"And speaking of the lady…"

"Anything on that from ATF?"

"My last call never got returned," Brognola said. "They've hurt my feelings, if you want to know the truth."

"Bureaucracy is cruel."

"I'll live," Brognola said. "The risk is all at your end of the line, as usual. I'm thinking that you may be wise to send her back, ASAP."

"It's not a problem at the moment," Bolan said. "She's cool."

"She's one more target for the heavies," the big Fed reminded him. "Even if she's not playing in the street, there's still a risk."

"I'll handle it," the Executioner replied. His tone didn't suggest that he was open to protracted argument.

"Okay. Your call. For what it's worth, I don't think anyone at ATF intends to push for prosecution on the shootings in Chicago or L.A. Not on your friend, I mean."

"I didn't know they were considering it," Bolan said.

"Between the press and oversight from Congress," Brognola replied, "you'd be surprised what they'll consider when it's time to duck and cover. Anyway, the twist they're going for right now is blaming everything on Stevens and the Nordic Temple, which is only fair. They've got some shills from ATF on hand to take the bows for dropping Fletcher and his people."

Sean Fletcher, former chief of security for the Temple of the Nordic Covenant, had died along with his strike force when Bolan and Marilyn Crouder interrupted Fletcher's strike on an old civil-rights group's anniversary convention. Brognola was hazy on specific details as to who shot whom, and he was perfectly content to let it stay that way.

"I'm glad they saw the light," Bolan remarked. "I've got enough to do without a visit to the ATF."

Brognola forced a smile at that, reminding himself of Bolan's pledge that he would never drop the hammer on a lawman under any circumstances. Still, he didn't like to think about the kind of havoc Bolan could inflict while stopping short of homicide, if he was properly inspired. It was enough to make him pity those on the receiving end, whether they were deserving of concern or not.

"That wouldn't be the best idea you've had all day," he said, squeezing a chuckle out to make it seem as if he thought the Executioner was joking. "Anyway, as screwed up as they are at ATF, they might not even notice—"

"Hal? Relax."

"You bet. Bygones. About this other deal, where you are... I'll keep looking into it, but realistically, it's doubtful I can help you much. Since '91, it's like the fascist fringe has staged the mother of all comebacks in what used to be the Eastern Bloc. Check out Poland, you'd think they never heard of Auschwitz or Treblinka. Hitler and his goons have got a whole new lease on life. To hear the new breed tell it, they were just misunderstood, precocious anti-Communists."

"I'd better let you go," the soldier said. "We're on a whole new schedule over here."

"And miles to go," Brognola said.

"At least."

"Okay. Stay frosty, guy."

''No choice,'' Bolan replied, and broke the link.

Brognola thought of several things he wished that he had said, too late for any of it now, the dial tone humming in his ear. He hated being half a world away from where the action was, but part of him acknowledged it was better this way than to have the battle waged in his backyard. Whatever happened next, whichever way it went, deniability would be preserved.

His hands would still seem clean.

CHAPTER THREE

Gerhard Steuben held his left eye underneath the tap and rinsed it, warm water dribbling through his fingers as he turned and rubbed the orb to make sure it was clean.

The eye wasn't one of his specials, marked with an iron cross or swastika. It was simple and unremarkable, enabling him to pass inspection points without a second glance from the authorities.

The daily cleaning ritual was a damned nuisance, but he still preferred the glass eye to a simple patch that made him look like someone's idea of a pirate, waiting for his ship to sail. Despite the fact that he had lost his left eye honorably, battling African savages in a jailhouse assault, it still felt demeaning for the would-be führer of the planet to appear imperfect, incomplete, when he addressed his followers. He preferred to put his best face forward when the good name of the Nordic Temple was concerned.

Good name?

He almost had to laugh at that, his bitter smile reflected in the fractured bathroom mirror. After years of persecution by authorities and slander by the Jew-owned media, Steuben and his Temple had been "libel-proof" by the courts of the United States and Germany. He could recall the wording of the judgment handed down in Alexandria, Virginia, two years earlier:

> With views so odious, outlandish and inflammatory, plaintiff's claims of malice on the part of those who criticize said published views must be dismissed as frivolous and insupportable.

Not that it mattered.

Gerhard Steuben and his Temple thrived on calumny and condemnation from the Jew-run government and Jew-deluded sheep who were facetiously described as journalists. Had Hitler been deterred by criticism or imprisonment? Far from it. Had his shock troops been afraid of scathing editorials when they were fighting Jews and Bolsheviks in the streets of Berlin? Ridiculous!

Heroes were made of sterner stuff than that.

When he was satisfied with the condition of his glassy orb, Steuben replaced it, still damp, in his empty left eye socket. Another moment to adjust it, seating it just so, and he washed his hands again, the water nearly scalding now. His hands felt almost feverish as Steuben dried them on a threadbare towel and went to greet his waiting guest.

Hedeon Onoprienko was tall for a Ukrainian peasant, fully six feet, tipping the scales at 210 pounds. Most of that was muscle, from the look of him, and none of it was hair, his buzz cut a concession to the onset of male-pattern baldness. The zigzag scar that ran between his right ear and the corner of his thin-lipped mouth resembled a pale lightning bolt, as if he had branded himself with the dreaded emblem of Hitler's SS.

Hedeon Onoprienko was Steuben's chief lieutenant in Ukraine, commander of the Nordic Temple's forces there, liaison with the Black Hundred's youthful skinhead auxiliary. Like Steuben, he had earned his disfigurement in combat, though the details were vague and had a tendency to change somewhat between one telling of the legend and another.

No matter, Steuben thought. If the man could rally troops and lead them on to victory, so be it. If he could deliver on his promise of a weapon that would make the enemy take notice, he was worth his weight in platinum.

"You have the merchandise?" Steuben inquired, coming directly to the point.

"Not yet, sir," the Ukrainian replied. "I'm meeting the supplier in—" he paused to check his watch "—two hours and fifteen minutes."

"Are you confident that he has what I want?" Steuben asked. "What we need?"

"If not, he can procure it," Onoprienko said.

"And the expense?"

"Will be considerable, sir." The visitor didn't flinch from delivering bad news. "Such articles are rare and in great demand. It is what the American's would call a seller's market, yes?"

"Our resources are not unlimited, as you know well enough."

"Of course. We have, however, made certain preparations. Extra cash has been obtained...and there is still the possibility we may not be required to pay in full."

Steuben could only frown at that, uncertain of Onoprienko's meaning. A display of ignorance wouldn't be helpful at this juncture.

"Oh?" he said, waiting.

"The dealer I've contacted is a former Communist," Onoprienko said. "He's an outlaw, also Jewish. It's unlikely anyone will miss him if he disappears. As far as the authorities can say, in fact, he vanished years ago. His people aren't the sort to file complaints or protests."

"But they may retaliate in kind," Steuben suggested.

"Let them try." There was ironclad confidence in the Ukrainian's tone. "We've dealt through cutouts until now. I'm meeting the supplier for the first time this morning. I shall use a cover name, of course, but if he finds out who I am—" a finger brushed across the lightning bolt that marked his cheek "—what can he do?"

"Increase the price, perhaps?" Steuben suggested.

His lieutenant shrugged. "What of it, sir? I simply promise anything he wants upon delivery. It doesn't matter if he wants the moon and stars. He'll get a bullet for his trouble. In the meantime, if he tries to squeeze me for a larger cash deposit than we've already agreed upon, I simply threaten to go elsewhere."

"Is there somewhere else to go?" the would-be führer asked.

"Undoubtedly," Onoprienko said, "but it won't come to that. This pig would rather get his money now, perhaps inflate the final payment on delivery, than see the whole thing slip away."

"I hope you are correct in your assessment of this

Jew. The schedule won't allow us to go searching for a second source.''

"I can assure you," his lieutenant said, "there's nothing to concern yourself about."

"You're right, of course," Steuben replied. "If anything goes wrong, it is not I who will be held accountable. If you are fully satisfied with the arrangements as they stand…"

He let the silent threat hang there between them, like a dangling blade, enjoying the expression on his subordinate's face. Racial solidarity aside, it was always wise to reinforce the bonds of fear from time to time. He saw the glint of fear in Onoprienko's dark eyes—swiftly covered, but there all the same—and he could guess what Onoprienko was thinking. He would be calculating odds and numbers, gauging the reaction of his men should anything occur to spoil the blueprint of their master plan. He would know those men, how swiftly they could turn upon a comrade who was branded as a traitor to the Temple and the master race.

"I pledge my life," the scar-faced soldier said at last, "that nothing will go wrong."

"We understand each other, then," Steuben replied.

"Yes, sir."

"How much are we required to give this Jew as a down payment on the merchandise?"

"One million *hryvnias,* sir. That equals roughly two hundred thousand U.S. dollars at the current rate of exchange."

"And you obtained this money from the membership?"

Onoprienko seemed as if he were about to laugh before he realized that it would be a terrible idea. He closed his mouth instead, wiped the expression from his face and tried again.

"No, sir," he said. "We were required to raise the money elsewhere, on short notice."

"And this was accomplished...how?"

"A tax on certain Jewish shops raised some of it. We offered them security. The bastards always think they can buy friends, no matter where they are. Throw money at a problem, and it goes away."

"And for the rest?" Steuben already knew the money had been raised by some illegal means. He didn't care what methods had been used, particularly; he was simply curious.

"There was a bank in Dubno, führer. It is owned by Jews, I'm fairly certain...or at least by those who gladly deal with Jews. I thought—"

"It makes no difference," Steuben told him, waving it away as if the robbery were nothing. "I commend you for displaying such initiative. You have done well—"

Onoprienko smiled, his eyes glittering.

"—so far."

The smile lost something on one side, began to sag. Onoprienko felt it going and retrieved it, saved the moment.

"Yes, sir. Thank you, sir."

"You should be going now, I think. We mustn't keep the Jew boy waiting, eh?"

"No, sir. All will be well. You'll see."

"Of course," Steuben replied, deliberately reserved. "You have my utmost confidence. I'll just stay here and have a brief word with your second in command while you arrange for the delivery."

GRISHA PASHENKA DIDN'T relish undercover work, where religious or political fanatics were concerned. He much preferred to deal with honest criminals whose motives could be ascertained and understood by anyone with basic common sense. Greed, sex, revenge—these were the motives that provoked most criminal activity, with greed by far the favorite of hoodlums everywhere. It was a universal constant, common to all thieves and racketeers, whether in Odessa, London or Las Vegas. Thieves stole because they wanted things that they couldn't afford and suffered from an allergy to honest toil. So had it been since time began; so would it always be.

Fanatics were another breed entirely. They were irrational by definition, fixated on strange creeds and theories, marching to a tune that only true believers ever heard. Grisha Pashenka wasn't sure if he feared the religious zealots or political fanatics more, but he was certain of one thing: the very worst of all were those who mixed religion with their crazy politics and managed to convince themselves that God or some bizarre equivalent had given them their marching orders.

All things considered, Ukraine wasn't a likely haven for religious fanatics. Controlled by Russia from 1654 until August 1991, Ukrainians had been ordered to worship the god of their czar for 263 years, and were then officially barred from worshiping any god at all for the next three-quarters of a century. Faith didn't flourish in such an atmosphere, but where it put down roots, those roots were often gnarled and twisted, drawing meager sustenance from bitter soil.

The same was true of politics, where absolute loyalty to a "divine" autocrat had been replaced overnight, and at gunpoint, by the rule of an all-powerful party. There was bitter irony, for those with eyes to see it, in the fact that methods of suppressing individual dissent changed little, if at all, as one regime replaced another. The czar's Cheka was replaced by the Party's MVD, OGPU and finally the KGB—but there would always be Siberia, the firing squads, the midnight knocking on selected doors.

As with religion, where political dissent survived in such an atmosphere, it tended to be radical, extreme, potentially explosive. It also tended to be anti-Communist, since there was nothing else for dissidents to rail against, and rabid anti-Communists learned swiftly from the German Nazis during World War II. As far as anti-Semitism went, the peasants of Ukraine could teach the Einsatzgrüppen how to deal with Jews. Who had invented pogroms, after all, more than a century before the Wehrmacht turned its guns and armor to the east, in June of 1941?

Pashenka himself had grown up being taught that Jews were different, which meant undesirable, perhaps less human than their Gentile neighbors, to some small degree. Those childhood lessons were a part of him, even today, but they had little impact in his daily life. He dealt with Jewish merchants and informants—even secret agents—when the need arose, and sometimes laughed at racist jokes behind their backs. Who suffered from a joke? Who cared if he laughed about some made-up tale about the meeting of a priest, a rabbi and a prostitute?

The die-hard Nazis and their ilk, though, were a breed apart from other human beings. Whisper "Jew" to one of them, and you could see his eyes glaze over, angry color rising in his cheeks. Shout it where brownshirts had assembled, and the odds were fair that they would take off shrieking after anyone you pointed at. The Temple of the Nordic Covenant had lately moved beyond mere anti-Semitism, elevating hatred of the Jew and nonwhite races to the pitch of a divine crusade—which made the new crop of fanatics doubly dangerous.

Pashenka knew that he was gambling with his life each time he made a move against the Nordic Temple or its teenage goons in the Black Hundred, but he had faith in his own ability to walk that tightrope like a skilled professional. He also understood the sort of difficulties that he might encounter if he tried to back out of a deal with the Mossad. It was one thing to take their money and renege; for that, they might chastise him with a beating that would send him into hospital. If he attempted to play fast and loose when they were chasing neo-Nazis or the like, though, Pashenka knew he was as good as dead.

Besides, if what he heard from his two recent visitors, the Mossad agent and the tall man whom he took for an American, the Nordic Temple's latest plans involved much more than simply brutalizing Jews. It seemed as if they had a master plan this time, a plan that might spell grim disaster for Ukraine, and for the world at large.

So, he would do his best to try to stay alive, while digging up the information that his paying customers required. If he couldn't find Gerhard Steuben, there was still a somewhat better chance that he could locate Hedeon Onoprienko—or, at the very least, find out what the Ukrainian chief of the Nordic Temple was up to these days.

Pashenka's contact was an informer named Borya

Bolodenka, a scrawny ferret of a man who somehow managed to ingratiate himself with nearly everyone he met. He had contacts on the police force, in the ranks of those who worked and schemed for a return to hardline communism, and among the neo-Nazi putschists who stood at the other extreme. Borya rubbed shoulders with them all—and made a living selling off their secrets to the highest bidder any time he could.

Informing was a dangerous profession at the best of times, more so when one was dealing with fanatics who were both well armed and unafraid to kill—or die, for that matter. Borya Bolodenka had survived this long, to the ripe old age of twenty-eight, because he watched his back and made a point of knowing who his buyers were. If push came down to shove, and he was caught red-handed dealing information, he wasn't above betraying his initial customer—but only for a price, of course.

Pashenka had arranged to meet his stool pigeon at a public park near the heart of Odessa. It was 10:05 a.m. as he approached the meeting place in a "borrowed" Citroën sedan. Aside from the AT-2000 automatic pistol that he carried in a shoulder holster, he also wore a smaller handgun, the venerable Walther PPK, in an elastic ankle rig. Beneath the driver's seat, inside a greasy paper bag, he had a Skorpion machine pistol.

All unnecessary, Pashenka told himself as he found a parking place and killed the engine. Borya was no fighter, despite his given name.

Still…

It was better safe than sorry in such matters. Most particularly where the Nordic Temple was involved.

Pashenka reached beneath the driver's seat and took

the wrinkled, greasy bag of death along with him as he locked up the car and moved into the park.

KOLYA ARKADY WAS a businessman, no different from any other trying to survive and make ends meet in tough times. Some businessmen owned factories, while others sold the merchandise those factories produced; still others serviced said merchandise when it broke down or failed to function as prescribed. Because he had no skill at building or repairing anything more complex than a sandwich, it had come to Arkady early in his working life that he had to find his niche in sales.

The only question still remaining to be answered was what should he sell?

And the compelling answer to that question was anything that others longed to buy.

Egalitarian by nature, Arkady never knowingly discriminated against any paying customer, regardless of the buyer's personal desires. Beginning at the tender age of fourteen years, Kolya had dealt, at one time or another, in narcotics and prescription drugs, pornography and prostitution, untaxed alcohol and cigarettes and a phenomenal array of stolen goods. Kolya Arkady handled items large and small. His stock included cameras and electronic gear, objets d'art, jewelry, clothing, fresh veal and caviar, two- and four-wheeled vehicles of every size, aircraft, the occasional luxury yacht.

And weapons.

There seemed to be no end of human desire for lethal hardware in the post-Soviet era. Rebellion and oppression, competition between criminal cliques, assassination for hire or simple personal defense—there was a tool for every need, and each came with a price tag attached. The larger, more complex and more devastating the weapon, the more it cost.

Naturally.

Kolya Arkady had made so much money from weapons in the past ten years that he had little time for handling anything else. It had never been his intent to specialize in death, but a wise businessman followed the money wherever it led, without pronouncing judgment on his customers.

All things considered, a conscience was one luxury he couldn't afford, at any price.

He had been discreet, therefore, when a friend of a friend had inquired about the availability of limited-yield nuclear warheads. Certain inquiries were unavoidable—not only to locate the merchandise, but to assure that Arkady wasn't himself the target of some devious entrapment by authorities. Once satisfied that he wasn't the victim of a sting, he had reported back that such devices could indeed be found—although, of course, their scarcity and all the risks involved would obviously be reflected in the retail price.

The prompt response—that money was no object—had been music to his ears. The rather stiff down payment was a test of sorts, establishing the buyer's bona fides. In the United States, they would have called it "earnest money"—to be forfeited, of course, in the event that Arkady's customer should have a change of heart.

The nuclear device wouldn't go begging, either way.

Not in these interesting times.

That morning's meeting was a simple matter of collection. Arkady would collect his money and arrange for the delivery, at which time he would take receipt of the outstanding balance.

Low yield for them, Arkady thought. High yield for him.

He saw the black Mercedes-Benz approaching, nearly glanced around to make sure that his shooters were in place, then stopped himself. The gunmen wouldn't get their pay until the meet was over, and they would earn nothing whatsoever if he died—or suffered so much as a flesh wound, for that matter. There was no percentage in their skipping out on him. Arkady trusted them to serve their own best interest and remain on duty, watching over him through telescopic sights attached to SVD Dragunov sniper rifles.

He didn't recognize the man who stepped out of the black Mercedes on the passenger side, but that wasn't important. As the snipers covered him, so a third employee would be snapping photos with a telephoto lens, recording the buyer's face for posterity and future research. They hadn't met so far because no money had changed hands. Indeed, this scar-faced man might not be—probably wasn't—the principal buyer. But he was further up the food chain than the small-time go-between who had been carrying his messages so far.

The scar-faced man was carrying a small suitcase. He approached the bench where Kolya Arkady sat, standing before the dealer with his shadow blotting out the morning sun.

"Luka Kropotkin?"

"In the flesh," Arkady replied. He never gave his real name to a client, understanding that illegal business—whether of the most benign variety or something worse—required certain precautions if he wanted to retain his loot and liberty.

"The bag, perhaps, is meant for me?" Arkady teased.

"Perhaps." The scar-faced man sat down beside him, with the suitcase to his right, where Arkady would be forced to reach across the other's body if he tried to grab it. Not that snatch-and-grab theatrics were his style. Kolya Arkady was a businessman, and he wasn't afraid of Scarface, while his snipers had the stranger and his comrades covered.

"To receive the bag," Scarface said, "you must tell me what I want to hear."

"A challenge," Arkady said, playing along. It crossed his mind that this could be a sting, the scar-faced buyer a policeman tricked out in more stylish clothes than most Ukrainian detectives could afford, but he dismissed the notion for two reasons. First, he knew the go-between who had arranged this meeting, had done business with him in the past, and there had never been a problem with the law, no hint that his connection was a turncoat or informer. Second, Kolya Arkady had chosen the meeting place himself, in Kiev's largest public park, for its view of surrounding streets, and he could see no vehicles resembling police cars within two long blocks. If Scarface and the others *were* policemen, they would all be dead before they snapped the handcuffs on his wrists, and Arkady would be gone before the echo of the gunshots died away.

"A challenge, if you like," Scarface replied.

"Very well." Arkady forced a smile at the ritual's absurdity. "You have an interest in pyrotechnics, yes? Please stop me if I'm wrong. You want fireworks, but not just any fireworks. You require the best, the biggest, for the celebration you have planned. Am I correct so far?''

"Go on."

"You want to throw a party that will make your friends and enemies alike take notice and remember you for always, yes? You want, I think, to fire a shot heard around the world."

"You can supply the merchandise I need?" Scarface asked.

"I've already told your boy Nikita that it will not be a problem. I require one million *hryvnias* in advance, for my contacts. You pay the rest upon delivery. No credit, no discounts and no delays."

Scarface reached down, picked up the bag and handed it to Arkady. It was heavy, in a pleasant way. He placed the suitcase on his lap and cracked the lid, enough to see the stacks of notes inside. He riffled one stack with his thumb, then closed the bag again.

"I take for granted that the full amount is here," he said.

"It is."

"Because, if it is not, well…"

"You would threaten me?" Scarface seemed more surprised than angered by the thought.

"I threaten no one," Arkady replied. "I'm not a man of violence. It is simply that my contacts will demand to count the money in my presence. If it should be short by even one or two *hryvnias*, there will be no further meetings, certainly no merchandise."

"I've counted it myself," Scarface informed him. "One million, as required. If your contacts have any problem with arithmetic, perhaps they cannot count so high, I will be happy to assist them.''

''That won't be necessary,'' Arkady said. ''I'll call Nikita with a time and place for the delivery.''

''I need the merchandise no later than tomorrow night,'' Scarface informed him, leaning closer, so that Arkady caught a whiff of garlic on his breath. Garlic and something even more unpleasant. ''Will that be a problem?''

Arkady shrugged, a heartbeat away from raising his hand to scratch his scalp, the signal that would drop this pig and his companions on the spot. If Scarface touched him—

''No problem. But for a rush delivery like that, expenses may be somewhat higher.''

''How much higher.''

''It is difficult to say.''

''Make the attempt.''

''Another million, on delivery.''

''Agreed.''

Scarface got up and left Kolya Arkady with his suitcase, sitting on the bench, a fortune resting in his lap and visions of an even greater payoff playing silently behind his eyes.

Low yield, high yield.

It all depended on your point of view.

HEDEON ONOPRIENKO WAS pleased with himself. He had maintained his temper when the rat began to squeeze him for more money—and why not, since he didn't intend to pay another penny for the merchandise? The million he had just delivered might be lost, no realistic hope of ever seeing it again, but it was mostly stolen money anyway. There was a saying in

America that he had heard of: easy came and easy went, or words to that effect.

He had good news to help his führer's mood now, and he only hoped that it would be enough. The difficulties Steuben had endured for the past few weeks, the losses suffered by the Nordic Temple, had put him on edge. Anyone could see that, and who would deny him the right to be upset?

Still, a leader of such stature—one who hoped to rule the world within a year or less—should probably be made of sterner stuff. It wouldn't do to let the Jews or any of their other enemies detect a sign of weakness in the führer. Something had to be done to demonstrate his courage and resolve.

Something spectacular.

Onoprienko was doing his best to bring that about.

Steuben was waiting for him when Onoprienko returned to the safehouse outside Kiev. With Steuben in the den was the American whom he had introduced on arrival as his new chief of security, a hulk of a man named Eric Glass. The two of them stood with their backs to the cold fireplace, an arm's length apart, both watching Onoprienko as he let himself into the room.

"It's all arranged, sir," he told Steuben, ignoring the hulk.

"You have a time and place for delivery?"

"Well, um, no, sir. They will call and make arrangements later in the day."

"You left the money, and you didn't even set another meet?"

The question came from Glass. He looked amused, although his tone was cold.

Onoprienko ignored him, addressing his answer to

Steuben. "We know where to find the man, führer. Should he attempt to cheat us—"

"Then the money will be lost," Glass said, "and you'll have shit to show for it."

Reluctantly, stiffly, Onoprienko turned to face the stranger. "This is my country," he said. "These are my people. I know how they think and how to deal with them. We gain nothing by imagining betrayals that do not exist in fact."

"We gain preparedness, mister." The American's smile was fading by degrees. "We gain a chance to salvage something if it starts to fall apart."

"I have anticipated any difficulties," Onoprienko replied, addressing himself to Steuben once again. "If I don't hear from the supplier by one o'clock this afternoon, he will have visitors and much to answer for."

"Will that get us the bomb?" Herr Steuben asked.

"I think it will. Yes, sir."

"You think?"

Glass mocked him. Onoprienko did his best to ignore it.

"We should think about transporting the device," Onoprienko said. "It may not be entirely safe—"

Entirely *sane* was what he meant to say, but Steuben cut him off, and he could feel Glass glaring daggers at him from across the room, though he refused to meet the stranger's eyes.

"My mind is quite made up on this point," Steuben said. "There can be no room for argument. I have debated the potential uses for this mechanism and am confident that I have made the proper choice."

"Yes, sir. Of course. I was considering the transport problem only," Onoprienko lied. "It's such a long

way to the target destination, after all. There are so
many closer targets, all along the way, where this device could deal our enemies a grievous wound. I simply thought—''

''The führer said no arguments!'' Glass bellowed
at him, taking one step closer before Steuben reached
out and caught him by the arm, drawing him back to
the hearth.

''Eric,'' he said, ''we're all comrades and brothers
here. Hedeon has served us well, brought us this far.
He has some understandable concerns and wishes
nothing but complete success. Is that not true, Hedeon?''

''Yes, sir! Exactly, sir!''

Onoprienko despised the tremor in his voice, hated
the hulk named Glass for putting it there. If it were
just the two of them, and Glass without the führer's
shadow to protect him...

''What you fail to understand,'' Steuben pressed on,
''is the condition of our combat forces. There's no
reason you should know the details, since they don't
concern you in your local work. For now it is enough
to say that all of our recruiting has not managed to
inflate our fighting ranks enough for us to face even
the smallest army on the planet. Think of it, Hedeon!
For the legions of the master race to be defeated by
some inferior rabble. It's intolerable. You agree?''

''Yes, sir. But I thought...I was told...I mean, the
Spear of Destiny—''

''Is lost to us,'' the führer interrupted him. ''At least
for now. Our enemies were too resourceful and more
daring than I gave them credit for. The blame, of
course, must be entirely mine.''

''No, führer! With the Jews—''

"Thank you, I'm sure. My point, Hedeon, is that we shall be needing reinforcements. It is not enough to simply smite our enemies, unless we have the strength to knock them down and keep them down. You would agree?"

"Yes, sir."

"Of course. That's why I've made my choice and shall remain unshakable in my resolve. We need those reinforcements. We must go directly to the source."

CHAPTER FOUR

"Why are the Carpathians familiar to me?" Jacob Gellar asked when they were more than halfway to the mountains, visible ahead of them as hulking shadows on the skyline.

"It's Bram Stoker," Bolan said. "Count Dracula. The children of the night. Dark mojo working."

"How can that be?" Gellar wondered. "Dracula was found in Transylvania, yes? And Transylvania is a district of Romania, if I am not mistaken."

"That's today," Bolan reminded him. "The Carpathian Mountains cross the border up ahead. The northern half of them has been Ukrainian for going on a hundred years."

"What happens to tradition, eh?"

"The big battalions draw new maps," Bolan replied. "I'm more concerned with Nazis than I am with zombies at the moment."

"Silver bullets!" Pashenka offered, grinning back at Bolan from the rearview mirror. "Stops the werewolf, yes?"

"If anyone gets close enough to bite you, you're in trouble," Bolan told him, but their driver merely laughed and bobbed his head.

Grisha Pashenka's contact had produced coordinates for the meeting point—an alleged meeting point, anyway—where a certain "neutral" dealer was supposed to be delivering a low-yield nuclear device to members of the Nordic Temple around sundown that day. Preparations for their trip had consumed the best part of two hours, and they had been driving for five, forced to skirt the Ukrainian border with Moldova, in lieu of following the straight-line path between Odessa and Chernovtsy.

They would still be well ahead of schedule for the meet, Bolan thought. And he could only hope that one or both sides of the deal were not so paranoid that they turned out long hours ahead of schedule, staking out the high ground for themselves.

It wouldn't suit his purposes if he was forced to kill the dealers—or the buyers, for that matter—before all the parties were present and accounted for. Above all else, he needed to dispose of the device itself, trusting Jacob Gellar's assurance that he was adequately schooled in such matters to defuse the warhead without any problem.

Beyond Chernovtsy, where they stopped for fuel, the road began to climb and wind through foothills that grew taller and more rugged by the mile, sprouting forests that would certainly have seemed less sinister without the baggage of pulp fiction and horror films spanning more than a century. At one time or another, Hollywood had used the Carpathian Mountains—or their cardboard-cutout equivalent—as the root of almost every lurking evil but Godzilla and the IRS. Vampires and werewolves, ghosts and witches, curses and the evil eye.

Ironically, none of it could measure up to the apocalyptic evil Bolan and his tiny crew were hoping to avert this day. No demon from the wild imagination of a fiction scribe had ever posed the threat to humankind that a person could fit inside a backpack, suitcase or valise if he or she possessed the right technology.

Doomsday, he thought. And if they let the instrument slip through their fingers, they were absolutely clueless on the nature and location of the target.

"How much longer?" Bolan asked Pashenka.

"Half an hour, maybe. Possibly three-quarters. We must leave the car and walk at least the final mile to keep from being recognized."

Bolan knew that already, and he understood that it was unavoidable, although he didn't relish being so far separated from their wheels. Escape didn't concern him so much as the matter of a possible pursuit. The best intentions in the world wouldn't permit them to run down a fleeing motor vehicle on foot.

He had already double-checked his weapons and resisted the impulse to triple-check. It was a sign of nerves and weakness, like a poker player sorting through his cards incessantly. Once guns were locked and loaded, live rounds didn't disappear from firing chambers; magazines didn't unseat themselves and drop away; safeties didn't switch off and on without a human touch.

He focused on the hike, across a mile or more of rugged, unfamiliar ground, and what would follow afterward. If they weren't too late, there would be time for them to pick out fields of fire, conceal themselves and settle in to wait. Conversely, if the soldiers of one side arrived ahead of them, they would be forced to fight at once, without adequate preparation or cover.

And they would probably die.

It came down almost to a coin toss, one time when the paranoia of his adversaries might work out to Bolan's mortal disadvantage.

Let it go.

He had already taken every possible precaution. There was no way he could alter time, turn back the clock and buy himself more breathing room. The Executioner would have to work with what he had.

And it would either be enough, or it wouldn't.

"We should stop here," Pashenka said, braking before his passengers could speak, nosing the dark sedan into cover behind a copse of trees, concealed—they hoped—from any traffic passing on the mountain road behind them.

Piling out and changing into forest camouflage, strapping on their guns and gear, the three hunters used up more precious minutes, the doomsday clock ticking loud and clear in Bolan's head. Their armament was much the same as on their last strike: AKSU rifles, side arms, antipersonnel grenades, a choice of strangling wires and fighting knives for silent work if there were sentries to be taken out up close. The sole addition to their arsenal was an RPG-7 grenade launcher, slung across Pashenka's back with its muzzle pointed toward the earth, two of the nose-heavy rocket-grenades riding his left hip in a canvas sling, wrapped in burlap to prevent them from clanking together as he walked.

A mile, Bolan thought as they started out, wasn't that far.

And there were only ten or fifteen different ways the mission could go wrong, blow up in their faces, leaving them dead or stranded in the middle of nowhere, cut off from anything resembling aid.

Not bad.

He had faced worse odds in his time, and he was still alive.

The adversaries he had faced on those occasions couldn't say the same.

KOLYA ARKADY WISHED he could have skipped the actual exchange, but Scarface would expect to see him there, and Arkady wouldn't trust five million *hryvnias* to any middleman. He had brought six gunners along with him on the delivery, all armed with automatic weapons, and he had broken tradition by arming himself with a Beretta RS 202 M-3 military shotgun, a concession to his own poor marksmanship, with twelve buckshot rounds in its detachable box magazine.

Of course, he hoped that there would be no shooting. An ideal exchange was quick and easy, merchandise and money changing hands, perhaps a few bland pleasantries, well-wishes to the customer whom he would never see again. Arkady had insisted on the men and guns because his cargo, this time, was so very special, and because the retail price was nearly triple any he had ever pocketed before. Even deducting his expenses, paying off the troops, Arkady would emerge from this day's work a wealthy man.

He checked his Rolex Oyster wristwatch and saw that it was still a good half hour before Scarface and his companions were supposed to show themselves. Arkady had no doubt the buyer would be bringing reinforcements with him; he could only hope that they wouldn't be stupid and try to take the merchandise by force in lieu of paying what they owed.

If they tried anything like that, someone was bound to die.

Arkady chain-smoked while he waited, lighting one butt from another, staring at the point in front of him where the narrow mountain road emerged from brooding forest into a clearing of sorts. He had begun to picture snipers creeping through the undergrowth, surrounding his own party, when a new, distant, vaguely familiar sound intruded on his senses.

Where and when had he heard such a sound before. Was it...?

"A helicopter!"

Startled by the sound of his own voice, Arkady repeated the warning, louder this time. "A helicopter's coming! Everyone on guard, now!"

Stepping from the car, he left his shotgun on the seat. Standing behind the open door, which Arkady hoped might shield him if Scarface and his companions started shooting, he could reach the weapon swiftly, easily. It was already primed and cocked, the safety off. All he would have to do was aim it, more or less, and squeeze off rounds in rapid fire until the magazine ran dry.

Of course, if Scarface chose to strafe them from the air, then they were all in deep, deep shit.

"Stand ready, now!"

His final warning was unnecessary, as the helicopter suddenly came into view above the treetops, drawing closer, hovering before it settled down to earth. It seemed to be a modified civilian version of the Russian Mil Mi-4 "Hound," a twelve-seater normally used for transport and for antisubmarine warfare. This Hound was painted navy blue, instead of military camouflage, and seemed to be unarmed.

The same couldn't be said for Scarface or the men who disembarked behind him, once the helicopter's rotor blades began to slow. Arkady noted that the helicopter pilot didn't turn off his engines, remaining at the stick, prepared to lift off on a moment's notice from the man in charge.

Scarface and his companions were advancing, three men bearing heavy suitcases in either hand—the cash—while their companions sported automatic weapons, slung and gripped in able-looking hands.

Kolya Arkady plastered on a smile and told his soldiers, "Watch them!" as the pickup team advanced. He had already calculated that his people were outnumbered two to one.

"My friend!" he called to Scarface, when the teams were still some fifty yards apart. "It seems you plan on celebrating your new acquisition with a hunting party!"

Scarface shrugged and spread his hands, two automatic pistols showing underneath his jacket, tucked inside the waistband of his slacks. "Such merchandise demands a fair degree of caution," he replied. "But we are all friends here, of course."

His left hand kept on rising, well above his head now. Arkady wondered if the bastard could be fool enough to try to take the merchandise by force.

The raised hand was dropping—as a signal?—when a spout of crimson suddenly erupted from the pointman's chest, his dark eyes glazing over as he toppled over backward in a boneless sprawl.

The echo of the gunshot reached Arkady's ears a fraction of a heartbeat later, stunning him as much as what he had just seen.

"Who fired that shot!" he shouted at his men, already reaching for the shotgun on the seat. "Who fired that goddamned shot!"

But none of them could hear him, as all hell broke loose.

FOR JUST A MOMENT, watching the tableau in front of him, Bolan had pondered letting the assembled gunners kill one another, leaving him, Gellar and Pashenka to mop up the various survivors and retrieve the nuke with minimal exposure to themselves. It was a tempting notion, but he finally decided to continue with the plan they had worked out while waiting for their targets to arrive.

The first shot had been his, nailing the scar-faced neo-Nazi whom he recognized from mug shots as one Hedeon Onoprienko, an ex-convict with a long record of violent felonies, lately converted to the master-race mumbo jumbo of Gary Stevens and the Temple of the Nordic Covenant.

The echo of his AKSU round had barely reached the hostile troops in front of Bolan, when they opened fire. Some members of the helicopter party obviously thought their leader had been shot by one of those on the delivery team, and in another heartbeat the two sides were trading bursts of automatic fire and curses, as they scattered in a search for cover. Others of the new arrivals, though, weren't immediately duped. They seemed to be Americans—or English-speakers, at the very least. One stocky member of the expedition called out to them, "We've got a sniper in the trees! Lay down some cover fire!"

The shooters he was talking to, approximately half the pickup party, instantly began unloading on the tree line, throwing everything they had at targets that were still invisible. It was impressive, even so, with bullets from the first wild fusillade passing within a foot of Bolan's head.

He couldn't tell if Gellar and Pashenka were returning fire, enveloped as he was by sounds of combat, but he took for granted that the two would hold their own. The milling chaos of the firefight would help cover them, to some extent, but he didn't delude himself about the skill of those escorts who had determined his position, at least vaguely, on the basis of a single shot.

Their leader was a pro; that much was obvious. The question was could he manage to control Onoprienko's troops, or even speak their language in a pinch? The answer seemed to be a major negative, the burly soldier concentrating on his own men, barking orders at them, more or less ignoring the Ukrainians who were still dueling with their fellow countrymen.

The cars were taking hits downrange, a pair of four-by-fours that had been stylish and expensive-looking moments earlier, before the shooting started. Both of them were pocked with shiny bullet scars by now, one with a pumpkin-sized hole in the middle of its tinted windshield. Bolan wondered which, if either of them, carried the tactical nuke, wondering what would happen, how bad the contamination would be, if a wild shot cracked the radiation shield.

The voice in Bolan's head reminded him that it might not even be there. Which would mean, of course, that they had gained precisely nothing by this risk of life and limb. If they had stepped into the middle of a double or a triple cross, then they were simply wasting precious time, potentially throwing away their lives.

For nothing, right.

He focused on the up side, sighting on the leader of the English-speakers from a range of forty yards or so. It was a bit far for the AKSU's stubby barrel, but his only other option at the moment was the pistol that he wore beneath his arm.

No good.

Bolan was taking up the trigger slack, squeezing the way he had been taught in boot camp, so that he couldn't anticipate the moment of the "break" and thereby flinch involuntarily to spoil the shot. He felt it when the trigger went, and could have shouted curses at the heavens when another member of the pickup team, one of the wild-eyed locals, ran across his field of fire.

The 5.45 mm bullet struck his unintended target in the upper chest, perhaps three-quarters of an inch below the clavicle. Its impact jolted the Ukrainian off stride, put rubber in his legs. He wobbled, staggered, dropped to one knee like a drunkard who had missed his footing, stepping off an unseen curb into the gutter. Shock was written on his face. His lips moved silently—or maybe he was praying to forgotten gods, his breathless supplication lost amid the sounds of combat.

Bolan left him to it, trying to correct his aim, but he had lost his mark. The stocky soldier was already moving, waving to the troops who understood his orders, leading them through streams of interlocking fire in the direction of the bullet-riddled vehicles.

IT HAD BEEN SAID of Eric Glass that he preferred combat to sex, the act of killing to the act of love. Those who had made that observation—in Grenada, Panama,

Somalia, half a dozen mercenary brushfire wars before he found the Temple of the Nordic Covenant and called it home—were only partially correct.

Glass did prefer combat to sex, but he could only draw a blank when love was mentioned, since he hadn't even the most hazy, ill-defined concept of what love was. For Glass, sex was the simple scratching of an itch that he experienced from time to time, at intervals that were increasingly prolonged. As for combat—well, that was something else.

That was the only time he truly felt alive.

The pickup was supposed to be a milk run. They would verify the merchandise, then waste the dealer and his bodyguards, retrieve the nuke and fly it to an airstrip on the outskirts of Kiev. If there was no resistance from the dealer, it would simply make his execution that much easier. Upon arrival in Kiev, Glass would receive new orders and would take the merchandise wherever he was ordered by his führer.

Simple.

But the plan had blown up in their face, as "simple" schemes so often did when greedy men with weapons were involved. Someone had smoked Hedeon Onoprienko with the first shot fired, and while Glass couldn't identify the shooter, he *could* swear the shot hadn't come from the clutch of nervous-looking gunmen grouped around the four-by-fours. He had been watching them when it went down, and from the angle of the hit, the general direction of the sound, he knew the shot had come from somewhere in the trees beyond, behind the dealer's party.

Eric Glass had one job now, and only one. He had to grab the merchandise they had been sent for, shift it to the waiting helicopter and get out of there before he and his men were KIA. Failure was more intimidating than the thought of death, which Glass had long regarded as the act of simply nodding off and never waking up again. It made no lasting difference if death was painful or serene, although a wise man would avoid whatever pain he could. In either case, the end was all the same.

But Glass had no desire to meet his end that afternoon.

Not with his mission incomplete.

He milked a short burst from his Uzi, firing toward the dark wall of the forest, then swung toward the vehicles and shot a young man with an automatic rifle who was taking much too long on target acquisition for his own sake.

Live and learn, Glass thought. Or not.

The rub, aside from having bullets buzz around him like a swarm of killer bees, was that he didn't know which car the nuke was in. The truth was he couldn't swear it was in either car, but he would have to check them both. What else was he to do, under the circumstances?

"Keep your heads down!" he commanded gruffly. "Check both cars! Without that package, it's a one-way trip."

That wasn't strictly true, of course. His führer would be disappointed—make that raving mad—if they came back without the merchandise, but Glass couldn't produce the nuke if it didn't exist, and he didn't intend to sacrifice himself in penance for somebody else's double cross. Still, it was always good to motivate the troops, give them a sense of purpose, keep them on their toes.

He saw the rocket coming, from the tree line. First

it was a puff of smoke in his peripheral vision, then a streak that trailed more smoke and noise behind it, rattling across the open ground in the direction of the vehicles.

"Incoming!" Glass shouted, hitting the turf. He tried to pinpoint the location of the rocketeer and knew that it was hopeless. If the guy had any brains at all, he would have been in motion even as he squeezed the trigger, dodging the return fire.

Glass was startled when the rocket missed both cars, passing a yard or so above the nearest one and maybe six feet to its left. It slithered through the trembling air above him and exploded somewhere to his rear, its shrapnel sprinkling the battlefield.

A sudden chill of panic seized Glass as he thought about the helicopter. He pushed up on one elbow, cranked his head around and felt near orgasmic relief as he saw the whirlybird intact, still sitting there. Granted, its pilot wore a nervous face, but Glass believed that he wouldn't desert his comrades unless it was clear that none of them were coming back.

Still watching out for any further rockets, Glass was scrambling to his feet, almost erect, when one of his commandos shouted, "Over here! I've got it, sir!"

JACOB GELLAR COULDN'T believe his eyes when the RPG round exploded harmlessly, two hundred yards downrange. He was relieved, of course, that Pashenka hadn't detonated either of the cars—their goal was to retrieve the nuclear device, not rupture it and scatter its contaminants across the countryside—but it amazed and mortified him that the helicopter still survived.

What was the damned boy playing at?

Gellar would cheerfully have snatched the RPG from Pashenka, taken out the helicopter on his own, except that they had separated to avoid giving the enemy an easy target. He couldn't see the Ukrainian now, had no clear fix on his location and couldn't afford the time to go and search for him while Belasko fought their adversaries all alone.

Dammit!

He understood the young Ukrainian's confusion to a point, since they hadn't discussed the possibility of taking out a helicopter. Who could know the Nordic Temple would dispatch its pickup team by air? Still, from a combat veteran's point of view, it should have been a simple choice, what the Americans liked to call a no-brainer: when in doubt, disable any means of transportation that might let your enemy escape with what you hoped to steal.

Simple.

He lined up on a moving target, one of those employed to guard the shipment prior to its delivery, and dropped the gunner with a short burst from behind. It would have looked bad in the movies, but in real-life combat situations there was no such thing as chivalry. You didn't warn an enemy that he was in your sights, and you most certainly didn't allow him the first shot—unless, of course, you had a death wish and were anxious to explore the next plane of existence.

Not this day, Gellar thought, lining up another shot.

Playing no favorites, he chose as his next mark a member of the pickup team. A patriarch of Gellar's family once had told him he should never miss an opportunity to kill a Nazi, and he heeded that advice, firing a 3- or 4-round burst of 5.45 mm rounds into the skinhead's chest, snuffing his life as one might pinch a candle's wick to kill the flame.

He felt nothing.

That was the worst of it, in fact—that he had learned to kill without compunction on the orders of his government, or even on a private whim. Sometimes, in brooding private moments, Gellar wondered how he differed from his enemies, a question always answered when he told himself that *he* was in the right, while *they* were in the wrong.

Of course, these neo-Nazi bastards would have said the same.

It was a matter of perspective, when he thought about it at his desk in Tel Aviv or in some foreign hotel room.

Here, on the firing line, it was a simple matter of necessity.

Gellar avoided firing at the cars directly, though he seemed to be the only one who gave the nuclear device and its lead shields even a passing thought. The four-by-fours kept taking hits, tires flattened, windows shattered, paint jobs decorated by bright, shiny holes, as if some madman with a railroad spike had run amok and stabbed them both repeatedly.

Still, if they had a bit of luck—

He saw the raiders separate, three men rushing one car, four sprinting toward the other, cutting down the scattered opposition they encountered on their way. Before he had a chance to open fire on them, they had doors open, leaning in and pawing through the vehicles, two men to a car, while their comrades stood watch and kept off the jackals. A moment later, one of them called out in English, words lost in the swirl of battle, but the others cheered him, two of them wrestling a shiny metal suitcase from the back seat of the four-by-four farther from Gellar's position.

They had it!

He would have to stop them now, if possible, before they reached the helicopter. That meant firing at the men who carried the device, but it couldn't be helped. They were obscured from his view for a moment, moving between the two cars, shielded, but Gellar was waiting for them when their leader emerged, his eyes everywhere at once as he scanned the killing field, intent on reaching their destination with the cargo intact.

The second RPG round seemed to come from nowhere, and it didn't miss its mark this time. The closer four-by-four stood on its nose, riding a spout of smoke and flame that instantly obscured Jacob Gellar's field of fire. He squeezed the AKSU's trigger anyway— better to fire blindly, sometimes, than not at all—but even as the weapon bucked and rattled in his grip, he had a sinking sense that he was already too late.

BOLAN CURSED as the rocket found its mark and the four-by-four exploded, riding a fireball aloft as its fuel tank exploded. Roiling smoke obscured his view of the retrieval team, made it impossible for him to tell if they were down and out or beating a swift retreat to the waiting helicopter. Was the metal suitcase with the nuclear device inside it breached by shrapnel? Was it leaking radiation, even now? Were the runners as good as dead from fallout, sprinting for the whirlybird?

He almost fired into the smoke screen, then restrained himself at the last moment, with his AKSU's trigger more than halfway to the break. This wasn't the same thing as dealing with some kind of wild-ass charge when the enemy came storming at you through the choking mist of battle and you had to cut them down at any cost, to save yourself. Bolan had been there, done that, and he recognized the crucial difference.

This called for more precise and cautious work—at least until he found out whether it was already too late for caution to do any good.

His mind made up, he broke from cover, moving from the shadowed tree line toward the smoky, corpse-littered battlefield. At least half the original gunners were already down, and Bolan cut another's legs from under him as he advanced, the squealing target silenced in another instant as he fell across the AKSU's line of fire.

It was so easy when you had the proper tools. A finger twitched, and someone died. The trick was making sure you had the *right* someone, and that you didn't trespass into wasteful, potentially disastrous overkill.

That wasn't always quite as easy as it sounded...even for the Executioner.

A wounded gunman staggered toward him, cursing in a language Bolan didn't understand—presumably Ukrainian. He spotted Bolan, did a groggy double take and raised an automatic weapon with his one good arm.

Too late.

A burst from Bolan's own Kalashnikov produced tidy crimson holes across the shooter's chest and slapped him over backward, tangled legs assisting with the drop. Bolan couldn't be sure that he was dead, nor did he care. Disabled was as good as dead right now, his focus on the package and its where-abouts.

Heat from the burning four-by-four baked into the soldier's face and body as he circled toward the shattered vehicle. If anyone had been inside the car, they had to be toast. His interest lay beyond the wreckage, on the killing field still blocked from view by twisted metal, leaping flames and drifting smoke.

He found one member of the armed retrieval team curled on his side, still breathing, though it didn't look as if he would last much longer. The close-range explosion had scorched one whole side of his body, and he was bleeding from several ragged shrapnel wounds that the fire hadn't managed to cauterize. Alive or dead, he was out of the action, no visible weapon within reach of his blackened hand.

The rest of the team, however, had nearly reached the helicopter, making good time across the field of battle. Bolan mouthed another curse, moving in that direction as he saw one of them scramble aboard the chopper, quickly reaching back to snare the shiny metal suitcase from the grasp of a companion.

He squeezed off a burst toward the chopper without really aiming and tagged the last shooter in line, waiting to climb aboard. The guy went down without a whimper, as far as Bolan could tell, although the combination of gunfire and revving helicopter engines made such things impossible to tell.

Two other members of the boarding party saw him fall and turned on Bolan at once, laying down cover fire from their own automatic weapons. One of them was the team's apparent leader, the American, firing what could have been a Spectre SMG, or possibly a Heckler & Koch MP-5 K. In any case, the bullets came too close for comfort, making Bolan hit the deck, spoiling his aim while the last two shooters leaped aboard the Hound.

It rose before the sliding door on its port side was fully closed, some kind of giant, prehistoric dragonfly retreating from a lily pad where predators lurked in the shadows. Bolan rose and charged the aircraft as it banked and turned, firing off the rest of his AKSU's magazine in a futile attempt to breach the armored undercarriage.

In his fury, he wasn't surprised or startled by the sound of a familiar voice behind him. "So, they have it, then?" Jacob Gellar asked.

"There it goes," Bolan replied.

"Pashenka should have taken out the bird, first thing."

"Too late for that. We need to know their destination now. The target. And we're running out of time."

Behind him, in the forest clearing, all was silent death, except for the rustling sound of hungry flames devouring the blasted four-by-four.

How long, he asked himself, before some major city looked that way? How long, and where?

CHAPTER FIVE

"I don't know how they tracked us, but the shooters were in place when we arrived," Eric Glass reported. "Their first shot nailed Onoprienko, and it pretty much went to hell after that. I lost two of my people before we pulled out."

"But you *did* get the device?" Steuben demanded, keeping his priorities in proper order.

"Yes, sir. It's secure downstairs. About the ambush—"

"I'll miss Hedeon, of course," Steuben remarked. "He could be headstrong, almost insubordinate at times, but he knew the people here—how to control them, get things done. He won't be easy to replace."

"Is that something you need to think about right now?" his new chief of security inquired.

"There's no time like the present."

"With all respect, sir, we need to consider what just happened at the pickup. We were ambushed, we lost personnel and someone very nearly intercepted the delivery."

"Could it have been an effort by the dealer to collect his money without giving up the merchandise? What addicts call a rip-off, I believe?"

Glass thought about it for a moment, frowning, then

replied, "I doubt it, sir. Truth is, the dealer's body-guards all looked surprised when the first shot went off. They weren't ready, you know? Then, of course, Onoprienko's people started shooting at them, and the whole set went to hell."

"You're blaming a third party for the interference, then." It didn't come out sounding like a question.

"Coupled with the hit on the Black Hundred earlier, and the attacks we've suffered in the past two weeks, I'd say the odds were ninety-ten against the dealer pulling this himself. On top of which, he could have minimized his risk and left the merchandise at home if he was out to bag the cash without delivering."

It all made sense, of course. Steuben was still pursued by demons he couldn't identify, couldn't escape, couldn't destroy. The ferocious, relentless pursuit almost made him suspect it was the hand of destiny at work.

Almost.

Fortunately, the would-be führer had already glimpsed his destiny and knew that it wasn't a lonely death, shot down by faceless men who sought to stop him short of greatness that was preordained. The bastards were an obstacle, a challenge to be overcome, but he could still emerge victorious and save the dying world for members of the blessed master race. In order to achieve that goal, he simply had to persevere, stay strong and use his wits to keep the hunters guessing, scrambling, as they tried to run him down.

"It's clear what we must do, Eric," he said, breaking the silence that had stretched between them for the better part of two full minutes.

"Sir? I'm not sure I—"

"You must deliver the device as planned, on schedule. Nothing must be allowed to interfere with the timetable."

"Sir—"

"While I," the führer said, as if Glass hadn't tried to interrupt him, "must proceed to the next destination on my list. Also as planned."

"But, sir—"

"Eric." It was enough to still the soldier's voice. "Our enemies defeat us only if they frustrate our design and thereby block fulfillment of the final prophecy. They may disrupt our progress, even keep us from the Spear of Destiny for now, but if we persevere until the end, we shall emerge victorious. You understand?"

"With all respect, sir, it appears to me that if these bastards get a halfway decent shot at you, there'll be no prophecy and no fulfillment. They're efficient, ruthless and professional—in other words, just like Mossad or the Israeli paras. They won't stop until you're dead, or they are. And I can't protect you properly if we split up this way. My men—"

"Are trained and blooded, yes? Surely you aren't about to tell me that you chose less than the very best we have for this most critical assignment?"

"No, sir." Eric's face had reddened. "What I'm saying is that in the present circumstances, sir, our best may not be good enough."

"Be cautious, Eric," Steuben chided him. "If someone other than myself should hear you voice such sentiments, denigrating your own elite troops, it could be catastrophic for morale. If we don't trust ourselves to win the fight, for Wotan's sake, how can we ever get new converts to the cause?"

"I didn't mean—"

"I know exactly what you meant," Steuben replied, cutting him off again. "And your concern for my welfare is commendable, Eric. You must remember, though, that nothing takes priority over our duty to the planet and the master race. The only way in which we can fulfill that duty is to forge ahead, without regard to fears or personal concerns."

"Yes, sir."

"The stratagem I've planned will put us in the lead, Eric. Our enemies will not expect it, much less the result. In the vernacular, they'll never know what hit them."

"No, sir."

"Your role is critical, however. You're aware of that, Eric?"

"Yes, sir."

"You must not hesitate or question orders. You must do as you are told and see your mission through."

"I will. Yes, sir."

"Good man. I knew that we could count on you. As for the other matter, if I leave today, I'll buy some time. I may evade them altogether, but it seems unlikely, given their persistence. Still, as long as they are tracking me, they won't be after you. Once they lose track of the device..."

He left the sentence dangling, spread his hands in a gesture that left Glass to draw his own conclusions. And his chief of security was nodding, still grim faced but going along.

It was enough. Steuben needed compliance at the moment, not good cheer.

"The charter flight has been arranged?" he asked.

Shipping the warhead via a commercial flight would be a risk that he wasn't prepared to take.

"All done, sir," Glass replied. "The pilot should be ready by the time we reach the field."

"No questions asked?"

"Not at the price we're paying, sir."

"And he will take you all the way?"

"To meet our connection in western Australia, yes, sir. With mandatory rest stops and refueling, we should be there day after tomorrow. Our own pilot will be standing by at Wagin, for the last leg of the journey."

"It appears you've thought of everything," Steuben said.

"It *is* my job, sir," Glass replied. "We could have changed the route, of course. If I accompanied you as far as Durban—"

"No," Steuben interrupted him. "We'll have no deviations from the plan agreed upon."

"But your security—"

"Is not enhanced by flying with the cargo you will be transporting. We mustn't put all of our eggs in one basket, Eric. Yes?"

"You're right, of course, sir."

"Yes." Steuben was always pleased when his subordinates agreed with him. "Besides," he added, "if the enemy persists in tracking me, they will defeat their own purpose and lose the device. It works to our advantage, as you see."

"I understand, sir, but your personal security—"

"Shall be entrusted to our friends of the Iron Guard. You've spoken to them, I assume?"

"Yes, sir."

"And you've impressed them with the crucial nature of my mission?"

"They seemed anxious to cooperate," Glass said.

"It is enough, then. Even with the changes in their government, the Iron Guard still knows how to deal with mud people and Jews."

"Yes, sir. Of course."

"And I will have the bodyguards you have handpicked for me."

"The best, sir."

"I expect no less." Steuben recalled something that he had meant to say before, deciding it might be his last, best chance. "You know what happened to Sean Fletcher, don't you, Eric?"

"He was killed, sir."

"I mean why."

"Um, well…"

"Because he overestimated his ability to deal with unknown enemies and underestimated their ability to deal with him. You take my meaning, Eric?"

Glass was frowning at him. "There will be no carelessness on my part, sir."

"I don't mean carelessness," Steuben replied. "It's one thing to believe in prophecy, but it is quite another thing—a fatal error, in fact—to think that our success in this particular attempt is preordained. The prophecy will ultimately be fulfilled, of course. The Jews cannot prevent it, not with all their gold. But they may still stop us, postpone the day of glory for another generation, if we fail in any way."

"I understand, sir."

"As I knew you would." That settled, Steuben rose to shake his chief enforcer's hand. "You will be anxious to depart, I know. Good luck! I'll see you soon."

"Sieg heil!" Glass barked, with the straight-arm salute, when they had shaken hands.

"Sieg heil, my friend."

The crisp sound of the closing door reminded Steuben of an ax blade biting into wood—or bone.

Whose neck? he wondered. And how soon?

"WE NEED TO KNOW if Steuben's running," Jacob Gellar said, "and if so, where he's going. Can you find that out or not?"

His question was directed to Grisha Pashenka, the only member of their trio who had any hope at all of uncovering the required information. Gellar's tone was stern, as he meant it to be, but without being overly harsh or accusatory.

"I believe so, yes," the young Ukrainian replied.

They hadn't spoken of Pashenka's failure to destroy the Nordic Temple's helicopter when he had the chance, and thus prevent their enemies from fleeing with what all of them assumed had to be a nuclear device. Two rockets blasted from the RPG, one shot a total miss, the other wasted on a Land Rover already riddled with small-arms fire, flat tires and all.

Grisha Pashenka recognized his error, had approached them with profuse apologies in the immediate aftermath of the firefight, slamming the heel of one palm into his forehead repeatedly, with such force that Gellar finally grabbed his arm to stop him before their guide concussed himself. Gellar believed that there was nothing he could say to make the lad feel worse, certainly nothing that would let them turn the clock back and correct the fatal error.

Belasko felt the same, apparently, since he said nothing of the matter to their young interpreter. It wouldn't be his way, Gellar decided, to waste time brooding about mistakes already in the past. He would focus on what could be done to remedy the problem, rather than bog down in pointless recriminations.

But next time, Gellar knew with equal certainty, the tall American wouldn't want the Ukrainian handling the RPG.

"Who will you ask?" Gellar pressed him.

"I'm not sure yet," Pashenka answered. "There are two or three who might know something. Please, about the helicopter—"

"Let it go," Bolan said. "They took us by surprise, that's all."

His words were true enough, but only to a point. The helicopter *had* been a surprise, but once it had arrived and was identified so obviously as the pickup vehicle, it should have been destroyed without a second thought, before the nuclear device could go aboard. Instead, Pashenka had fired his two rockets at the Land Rovers, and had missed with one of those. It was a mark of inexperience, and there was nothing they could do about it now.

"I can go back to the Black Hundred," Pashenka said after a moment's contemplation. "It is risky now, of course. They will be on their guard, but—"

He hesitated, waiting, but if he was expecting anyone to talk him out of it, he was doomed to disappointment. Having missed the one best chance to place the warhead in their hands, he now remained their only hope of retrieving it before the damned thing was detonated or transported out of the country for parts unknown.

"And is there someone else," Gellar asked him, "in case the Black Hundred aren't talking?"

"I know someone in the Temple of the Nordic Covenant," Pashenka replied. "It will be even more risky than talking to the skinheads. Still, there must be some confusion in the Temple now, with Onoprienko dead. They'll have to pick another leader in a hurry. Maybe I can find out who he is and locate someone close to him. It could cost money."

Gellar dug a roll of notes out of his pocket, dropped it on the bed between them. "Spend whatever's necessary," he instructed the Ukrainian. "Just make sure you get our money's worth."

"I'll do my best," he said. "If no one's talking, though…"

"Then we'll just have to try another way," Bolan said, grim faced.

And Gellar knew what that meant. He had witnessed the American engaged in what Belasko called "rattling" their enemies, had even joined him in the rapid-fire attacks that were designed to terrify, disorient and shake loose information from otherwise tight-lipped fanatics. It was a deadly pastime, but it might turn out to be what some Americans were wont to call the only game in town.

"And when we find out where the warhead is…"

"We go and get it back," Bolan stated. "We do it right this time."

"And Steuben?"

"If he's sitting on the bomb, so much the better. If he's not, we need to focus on the nuke, first thing. That has to be job one. It won't matter what happens to a one-eyed Nazi if his goons turn Tel Aviv or Washington into another Nagasaki."

"We should think about potential targets in that case," Gellar remarked. As if the subject hadn't occupied their minds these past few hours, since they missed their chance in the Carpathians.

"They'll want something symbolic," the American replied, "but opportunity will be important, too. You've notified your people, I assume?"

"Of course."

"Okay. Same here. Even if they've got skinheads lining up to volunteer as kamikazes, they're no good without at least a fifty-fifty chance of scoring on a decent target. Otherwise, the whole thing is a waste of personnel and hardware."

"Steuben is obsessed with Armageddon," Gellar said, thinking aloud. "He does not have to strike at Washington or Tel Aviv to start a chain reaction, yes? Given the proper circumstances, he could do as well by setting off the bomb in London, Paris, Moscow— any number of cities where the governments have power to retaliate in kind."

"Against an enemy who may not even be responsible," Bolan said, picking up on his train of thought.

"Precisely," Gellar said.

"A bomb goes off in Moscow, for example, and the Russians blame the British or Americans?"

"There would be efforts to communicate after the blast, of course," Gellar replied.

"Which could be useless, if the cooler heads have gone up in the mushroom cloud," Bolan said.

"And once retaliation has been ordered..."

"Treaties kick in. The fallout starts to drift, and self-defense takes on a whole new meaning. There's your chain reaction. Bam-bam-bam."

"Would he be mad enough?" Gellar asked.

"Who, our boy? The one who thinks that he's possessed by some dead German officer from World War

II? The one who picks up private messages from ancient Viking gods?"

"My God!"

"It's not God we have to think about right now," Bolan replied. He turned to Pashenka, speaking with a voice as cold and sharp as stainless steel. "You need to make those contacts," he instructed. "Do it now."

THE CHARTER FLIGHT had been no problem to arrange, though it was costly hopping from one continent to another with a pilot who was absolutely barred from asking any questions about his passengers or cargo. Eric Glass had deliberately avoided using anyone associated with the Nordic Temple or the neo-Nazi movement generally, a stratagem he hoped would make it that much more difficult for the Temple's unknown enemies to track him while he carried out his orders from the führer.

Glass still resented being exiled, as it were, at the moment when his leader and the cause appeared to need him most, but he also knew how critical his mission was, how great the rewards would be if he succeeded.

No problem, he told himself, standing on the tarmac while the aircraft was loaded and fueled, but he kept one hand in his pocket, fingers crossed, just in case.

The easy part, if such a term could even be employed under the present circumstances, would be transporting the nuclear device and setting it in place. As long as they weren't pursued immediately, Glass was confident that they could throw off any tail and reach their destination without major difficulty. Certain bribes might be required along the way, if they encountered a pushy customs inspector or a curious airport employee, but Glass might just as easily decide to solve the problem some other way, trusting concealment of the corpse to give them a fair head start.

It would all depend on his mood at the time.

His real misgivings—and he hated to admit it, since it was tantamount to confessing lack of faith—revolved around the issue of whether the bizarre scheme would actually work. Placing the warhead was one thing; detonating it would be a snap for the technicians Gerhard Steuben had retained.

No sweat.

But if it didn't work, if they didn't achieve the planned, desired result, what would be left for them to do, except die fighting, hopelessly outnumbered by their enemies?

It was the trusting part, the faith, where Eric Glass habitually came up short. He was a stone-cold pro at hating, judging others on the basis of their pigment, politics, religion or what have you. The explosive violence had been second nature to him for so long that he couldn't have said with any certainty when it began.

Faith, though…that called for inner qualities that Eric Glass wasn't sure he possessed.

Oh, he could fake it well enough. Glass was adept at covering his private feelings, such as they were, and presenting a face that would please his superiors, employers, whatever. Adaptation—or, more precisely, the appearance of adaptation—was critical for a mercenary living on the razor's edge.

It was a somewhat different matter with the Temple of the Nordic Covenant, however. Glass believed most of the cult's teachings: Aryan superiority; the need for global-cleansing racial war; even the fact that certain

Nordic deities predated those dreamed up by rabbis to intimidate their flocks of sheep in human form. He could accept the notion of prophetic visions, destiny and such, although the führer's credibility had taken a beating in that area, of late, with repeated ass-kickings by foes who remained unidentified.

Specifically, it was the goal and outcome of his present mission that was giving Eric Glass some troubling second thoughts. He didn't mind planting the bomb as ordered, and he had no compunction whatsoever about setting it off, casualties and the environment be damned.

He simply didn't know if it would work.

Okay, the whole thing made a certain kind of sense when Steuben ran it down, spelled out the details one-on-one, his slick voice urging and cajoling, filling in the blanks with personal beliefs and prophecy. The breakdown in credibility began when he was separated from his führer, when he started to examine the plan in the harsh, uncompromising light of day.

Could it succeed? Was any of it even true?

And always, when he started to dissect the scheme, Glass ultimately came back to a final question: did it matter?

The important thing, as far as Glass could tell with anything approaching clarity of thought, was to uproot and finally eradicate the Jew-Communist clique that dominated world finance, government and media. If that could be achieved, regardless of the cost in human life, it scarcely mattered whether some specific point of prophecy was realized in his lifetime. Even if the führer's present strategy turned out to be predicated on error, it made little difference, so long as the end result was satisfactory.

Which meant that Eric Glass had to concentrate, first and foremost, on delivering the warhead to its destination. To that end, he had selected half a dozen of his best men to accompany him, leaving the führer himself with only two English-speaking bodyguards for his own journey southward. The split had been Steuben's idea, and he had insisted that the escort team for the device be armed and ready to deal with any opposition they might meet along the way.

That much, at least, was guaranteed.

Their mobile arsenal included four Beretta AR-70 assault rifles and three Kalashnikov AK-74s as primary weapons. Should those somehow fail, there were five Uzi submachine guns and two of their Spanish clones, the Star Model Z-84s. Each member of the escort team also carried at least one side arm, several of them packing two, and the private plane was well stocked with surplus ammunition, plus a case of antipersonnel grenades. His troopers each wore Kevlar body armor underneath their street clothes, and the team had walkie-talkies, some of them with hands-off headsets, to permit communication at a distance.

All things considered, the small group was better equipped than most military units Eric Glass had served with in his time, before or after his unfortunate dishonorable discharge from the United States Marine Corps. They were trained, committed and professional, armed to the teeth—in short, well able to defend themselves against any hostile force of roughly equivalent size and strength.

Which wouldn't help them in the least, of course, if they were blasted from the sky, cut down by long-range snipers or splattered across the tarmac by rocket-propelled grenades.

Suddenly nervous, Glass turned to scan the perimeter of the airstrip, searching for any out-of-place person or object, anything at all that might suggest a threat before or during takeoff. He didn't believe his unknown adversaries had air power at their disposal, or the helicopter carrying the nuke would almost certainly have been shot down somewhere between Chernovtsy and Kiev. They *did* have rocket launchers, though, and one of those could send a plane cartwheeling all the way to hell if it scored a hit on takeoff.

The short hair on his nape was bristling, giving Glass the creeps as he boarded the aircraft. He was the last to go aboard, refusing to bolt in the face of his fear, stretching his final moments on the deck until the anxious pilot came back to the open door and, scowling, beckoned him inside.

Only when they were airborne, climbing well beyond the range of any simple RPG, did Glass allow himself a measure of peace. They should be safe for the time being, at least while they were airborne. The next dicey moment would be in Istanbul, when they touched down for refueling and filed the next leg of their flight plan, to Qatar.

So far to go. So many opportunities for failure and disaster, all along the way.

But Glass wouldn't allow it.

He would see his mission through, regardless of the risk.

That much, at least, he could believe in...even if it cost the life of every man on board.

"SOUTH AFRICA?" There was a steely edge of disbelief in Jacob Gellar's voice that made Grisha

Pashenka scuff his feet across the hotel's nappy carpet.

"It's what they're saying," the Ukrainian replied, defensive now. "I can't swear that they speak the truth."

"And who is they?" Bolan inquired.

Pashenka seemed happy for the chance to name his sources, thereby shifting the responsibility for any error or displeasure that his words evoked.

"A sergeant in the Temple of the Nordic Covenant who likes his vodka very much," the young man said. "Also two members of the Black Hundred. They've all heard the same thing. Steuben is leaving for South Africa today. Perhaps he is already gone."

"I don't think much of their security," Gellar remarked, "if every skinhead in the gang knows all their secrets and feels free to share them on the street."

"They think I am a comrade," Pashenka said. "We talk about the Jews and Africans, the holy day of reckoning. They want me to enlist, I think."

"Still." Gellar didn't sound convinced.

"Three possibilities," Bolan said, thinking aloud. "They may have poor security, or they may have been misinformed specifically to throw us off the trail."

"That's only two," Gellar reminded him.

"Or, third, it may be true our target's heading south, leaving a trail and hoping that we'll follow him."

"But, why—?" Pashenka began to ask, before the Mossad agent interrupted him.

"While the device goes somewhere else?"

"I wouldn't rule it out," Bolan said. "He may think he can outrun us, maybe ditch us once he clears the border...or he could be desperate enough to sacrifice himself to let the bomb get through.''

"A martyr complex," Gellar said.

"That wouldn't be my reading, at the moment," Bolan said, "but it's at least a possibility. If I were betting, I'd say Stevens thinks he's smart enough to lose us on the runaround, then maybe double back somewhere to catch the fireworks.''

"Have you considered that he may be traveling with the device?" Gellar inquired.

"I thought about it," Bolan answered him, "and ruled it out. Too risky, is the feel I get. Of course, I could be wrong."

"I don't think so," the man from Tel Aviv replied. "If we could only learn what has become of the device..."

"One chance for that, as far as I can see," Bolan remarked.

"Go after Steuben," Gellar said, not asking him.

The plan of action had inherent risks, of course. First, they couldn't predict what sort of timetable the leader of the Nordic Temple had in mind. The bomb might be intended to destroy its chosen target on that very day, or any day thereafter. It could detonate in France, in Britain—anywhere on earth, in fact—while they were chasing the man to the southern tip of Africa. Assuming it did *not* explode before they found him, there was no good reason to suppose that they would capture him alive, or that a spaced-out zealot, certifiably insane, could be induced to tell them where the nuclear device had gone.

"I don't see another way," Bolan replied to Gellar, utterly disgusted with his lack of options.

"No." The Mossad agent's tone was grim, resigned.

"I should go with you?" Grisha Pashenka asked, addressing his hopeless query to no one in particular.

His woeful tone and the expression on his face made Bolan smile despite himself. "I don't think we'll have any need for a Ukrainian interpreter in Jo'burg," he replied.

"No, Grisha." Gellar, as the young man's contact, made the word official. "You stay here. We go alone."

They had a brief glimpse of a thousand-candlepower smile, before Pashenka caught himself and tucked it out of sight, straining to make himself look disappointed at the news.

"I could go with you," Pashenka said, pressing, but not too urgently. "There may be something I can do, although I do not speak the language of South Africa and have no contacts there. And do not know the customs. And—"

"You've done enough," Gellar assured him, cutting off the litany.

To Bolan, then, "We should be on our way as soon as possible. If we could find out where Steuben is going, in South Africa…"

"I'll make a call," Bolan replied. "It may not help, but it's a shot, at least." He thought of Hal Brognola and the long, long reach of Stony Man.

"The woman, Marilyn, will wish to go?" Gellar asked.

"She may," Bolan said. "It was no problem this time."

Gellar responded with a shrug and let it go. He didn't have to say that she could be a problem next time, if she took it in her head to try another fling at front-line combat, mixing with the hostiles and ignoring Bolan's orders to lie low. Bolan, for his part, was already working on a way to make the next leg of the trip sound too damned boring, dangerous, whatever, for Marilyn Crouder to tag along.

The final choice, he knew, would be hers. Short of locking her up, there was no way to prevent her from following them, and even that option was lost to him in Ukraine, where he had no contact, no ''in'' with the authorities.

''Whatever is decided,'' Gellar said, ''if we are able to confirm Steuben's departure for South Africa, we should be after him without delay. I can't believe he went to all this risk and trouble for a nuclear device if he does not intend to use it soon.''

''Agreed. I'll make the call right now,'' Bolan said, ''then touch base with Marilyn. You and Grisha can get some kind of charter flight lined up, I hope. If we confirm a destination for our target, that way we can fly ASAP.''

And maybe die ASAP, he thought, but pushed the grim thought out of mind. The road ahead would certainly be rough and dangerous enough without the nagging adversary of defeatism working on Bolan from within.

They still had time, he told himself, and prayed that it was true.

CHAPTER SIX

They were airborne over water—the Atlantic, she suspected—when Marilyn Crouder felt the craving for a cigarette. She had quit smoking seven years before, sheer willpower, without the patch or any other scientific crutch to help her, but the yearning still came back full force from time to time.

Mostly when she was nervous, as it happened…and this qualified as one such time.

The former ATF agent didn't mind flying, even with a planeload of illegal arms and ammunition, zigzagging through airspace over countries where they could be locked up for a long, long time if they were tagged as gunrunners. There would have been a certain irony in that, after the years she had invested chasing weapons smugglers for Uncle Sam, but it wasn't her first concern.

At the moment, she was worrying that some of them might not survive their unexpected visit to South Africa.

They had avoided Libya and Algeria, Saharan Africa's worst trouble spots of the moment, by flying almost due west from Odessa, refueling in Budapest, again in Milan and once more in Barcelona before they made the hop to Africa. A mandatory rest stop in Morocco, then a new day dawning, with a hop to Dakar, then Accra and on toward Luanda, with the ocean gray and forbidding beneath them, their shadow skimming across the surface like a tiny flying fish.

Angola was potential trouble, Crouder knew. The country had been torn by nearly nonstop civil war for more than a quarter century, since Portuguese colonial forces withdrew in 1975 and left the natives to grapple for control of their homeland. At one time or another, military forces from Cuba, Russia, the United States and South Africa had been embroiled in the marathon bloodletting, interrupted by a brief UN-supervised cease-fire of sorts in the mid-1990s. Full-scale combat had resumed in early 1999, United Nations troops withdrawing en masse as the National Union for the Total Independence of Angola—UNITA—launched a new offensive against its chief rival, the Marxist Popular Movement for the Liberation of Angola—FNLA. Tourism had basically ceased, and it wasn't unknown for white visitors to run afoul of various unpublished rules, regulations and decrees.

Bribery was one apparent solution, and Jacob Gellar had assured them that he knew people in Luanda, that there should be no problem as long as they stayed with the plane, kept Crouder out of sight, refueled and departed from the airport with minimal delays.

It should be fine, he said.

And still, she found herself craving a hit of nicotine.

It was difficult for Crouder to pin down her apprehension, to give the fear a name. She wasn't terribly concerned that they would all be yanked out of the plane upon arrival in Luanda—though it was at least an outside possibility. She didn't think they would wind up in some Angolan dungeon, with their plane and weapons confiscated, charged with some bizarre conspiracy against the government.

Besides, she thought, and nearly smiled, what could they claim that was more outrageous than the truth?

She felt as safe with Mike Belasko—and with Gellar, too, of course—as she had felt at any time within her recent memory. Their present circumstance was grim, but not life-threatening in any sense that she could grasp.

At least, it wouldn't be that way for her.

And that, Crouder suspected, was part of the problem.

In her years with ATF, she had grown accustomed to living on the edge, surviving by her wits and skill when orders from the brass were garbled in transmission or were simply, obviously wrong. She had survived armed raids and undercover work—although, granted, the latter run had nearly finished her, before Belasko came along to pull her fat out of the fire.

Which, looking back, had been the obvious beginning of the change.

It was the trusting part that ran against the grain for Crouder. From childhood, growing up in a dysfunctional family, she had developed what the shrinks called "issues" around trust, responsibility, the whole nine yards. In recent days, dealing with Belasko, there were times when she believed that she was dealing with a whole new breed of human being, one who meant exactly what he said and always, always followed through—and that was frightening, all by itself.

Promise keepers got killed in Crouder's world, and she wasn't talking about the praise-Jesus, boys-only club that held periodic meetings in sports arenas. She had spent so much time in the world of compromise and sacrifice, delay, disappointment and double cross, where the only visible colors were all shades of gray, that she had trouble recognizing any other life.

It was ridiculous, of course. She saw where her own thoughts were going and headed them off at the pass. No way. No sale.

She hardly knew the man who called himself Mike Belasko, although they had been to bed several times, and she could vouch for his extreme proficiency in that department. Yes, indeed. Outside the sack, he was apparently some kind of soldier-civil servant with topflight connections in D.C., though she could never pin him down to a specific branch of government, much less to any given agency. He did the dirty work; that much was obvious. He killed without remorse or apparent enjoyment, almost mechanical about it—at least, it seemed that way, until you saw him in action, so ferociously alive.

It was enough to make a lady cringe and tingle all at once.

Her concern wasn't with Belasko per se, but with the current status of his mission. It wasn't *her* mission anymore, since her superiors at ATF had taken umbrage at her handling of events in Chicago and Los Angeles, suggesting—politely, of course, but with no room for argument—that she might consider an extended leave of absence, with an eye toward early retirement. They had washed their hands of her, the Temple of the Nordic Covenant, the whole damned thing. It had been dumped into Belasko's lap, or the collective lap of whomever he represented, and Crouder was simply along for the ride, a rootless wanderer with nowhere else to go, no real contribution to make.

She'd turned into a damned camp follower, Crouder thought, and almost smiled at that. It was not strictly true, of course—but close enough to sting and tickle all at once.

There was ambivalence in her concern about the latest convolution in their long pursuit of Gary Stevens and his Temple of the Nordic Covenant. The nuke, of course, made everything a thousand times more critical, regardless of the target Stevens had in mind. If it went off, wherever it went off, they could expect a catastrophic loss of life and property. So far, she didn't have the faintest clue as to how Belasko and Gellar hoped to find the warhead and retrieve it from their enemies.

But there was something else, as well. It was a trivial concern, admittedly, when she compared it to the possibility of nuclear annihilation, but it stuck with Crouder regardless, haunting her.

Quite simply, she had no idea what she would do, where she would go, if they survived the mission and emerged successful on the other side of it.

Her job was gone, and you could bet the farm that ATF wouldn't be writing any glowing references when she went hunting for a new position. She could pretty well kiss off any job in the law-enforcement field or any other branch of government, unless she found herself some rural backwater where Feds were hated like the plague. She had some savings, possibly enough to live on for a year or two if she was frugal to the max. If she took off for someplace cheap and sunny—down in Mexico, perhaps, or even farther south…

But what about Belasko?

What about him? sneered the mocking voice inside

her head. Did she think he was shopping for a soul mate? Maybe looking for that white house with the picket fence?

Ridiculous.

Forget about it. Just concentrate on getting through the next few hours or days alive, and let the future take care of itself.

Assuming that there *was* a future for the three of them, for anyone at all.

"Luanda coming up," their pilot's disembodied voice announced. "We're thirty minutes out and cleared to land."

THEY LANDED at an airstrip outside Upington, thereby avoiding customs at the major urban airports of South Africa. There was an agent in the tiny terminal, of course, but he was easily persuaded that they weren't importing drugs and pocketed his bribe as if he had been doing it for years.

Which, Bolan realized, was very probably the case.

A handsome black man decked out in a khaki uniform of sorts was waiting for them when they left the terminal, a dusty white Range Rover standing by. He introduced himself as Mitane Selepa and loaded their bags on a cart, which he then wheeled to the car for a swift, efficient transfer. They were on the road to Cape Town, Upington a smudge on the horizon far behind them, when their guide and driver opened up.

"You hunting Nazis, then," he said, all smiles. "That's sounding good to me, I tell you."

"You have your share of Nazis in South Africa, I take it?" Gellar said.

"Oh, sure," Selepa said, beaming. "Nazis are old news in my country. Long time before my father and his father born, the Germans plant their notions in South Africa. The Boers were German to begin with, yes. Come two world wars, they friendly-like with Germany, against the Brits they hate from 1890-something. Comes the day of victory in Europe, 1945, and all new German faces suddenly are seen around Pretoria, Johannesburg, Durban, Cape Town. Some have a strong resemblance to old faces from the camps where Jews and other folk be killed. They help the masters in Pretoria stand up to communism and make sure apartheid rules don't be forgot. Come our time, with the changes in South Africa, the sons and grandsons still be hoping that the old days come around again. They like their guns and uniforms even today."

"The more things change," Crouder said, "the more they stay the same."

"Tha's true, ma'am. Tha's for certain sure."

"You are familiar with the Temple of the Nordic Covenant, I think," Gellar remarked.

"Tha's right," Selepa said. "They one of six or seven groups would like to turn the clock around and see the old ways back, with pass books and the rest of it. They call it a religion, but they work right close with the Iron Guard, and everybody know what *they* about."

"Which is...?" Bolan inquired.

"Main thing, they kill black folk," Selepa said. "They don't care whether it be man or woman, big or small. Kill black, kill brown, make Jews unhappy so they run go someplace else beside South Africa."

"What of the law?" Gellar inquired.

"Police do what they can, most times," Selepa said. "Not all, you understand. You know about the Truth and Reconciliation hearings, yes? Much was recorded there about South African police and what they long time do to black folk. You heard maybe about the police commander called Prime Evil for the way he love to kill and torture, or the minister of justice they call Dr. Death? Some of those same police still on the force today, but mostly not. Is hard to catch the Nazis, anyway, when white folk and their money help the bastards hide.''

Selepa was still smiling as he finished, making Bolan wonder what it took to make him frown. ''We won't be working with the law,'' he said. ''That's understood?''

''Oh, sure,'' Selepa said. ''That's fine to me. They don't complain so much, maybe, if we all play the same rules, yes?''

''It's worth a shot,'' the Executioner replied.

''Has there been any word on Gerhard Steuben entering the country?'' Gellar asked.

''Nothing so far,'' Selepa answered. ''Good friends I have in immigration keep a watch for him, but there is difficulty. No flights from Ukraine, as you may know, but he would surely come from someplace else, as you have done. He does not use the passport in his given name, of course. We check for German tourists first, then other Europeans, Scandinavian, lastly Americans. Our tourist industry is still not large, but we have some three thousand names to study for the past two days. A few of them are women—maybe two, three hundred. Take them out, unless they travel with a man who could be Steuben in disguise, using a woman as his...how do you say—whiskers?''

''Beard,'' Bolan corrected him.

''Okay!'' Selepa seemed delighted with the English lesson. ''Most of the three thousand will be businessmen, some diplomats, reporters from America and Europe. We have to check them all, of course. The process of elimination is our only tool.''

''Who do you mean when you say 'we'?'' Bolan inquired.

''My friends,'' Selepa said. ''Have no fear, sir. They hate the Nazis very much.''

''The group you're checking won't have come by private charter flights, will they?'' Gellar asked.

''Some,'' the driver said, ''but not too many. If the man we seek has come into South Africa illegally, the search will be a waste of time.''

But one they couldn't afford to skip, as Bolan realized. He took a shot and asked, ''Bearing in mind that Stevens—Steuben, as he calls himself—would probably be traveling with bodyguards, have there been *any* likely prospects? Groups of three or four men coming out of Europe, anywhere at all?''

''In that regard,'' Selepa said, ''we have three prospects, as you say. Four men from Austria arrived this morning and identified themselves as string musicians, yes? There is a concert booked in Durban for tomorrow night, though it could be a ruse, perhaps.''

''Unlikely,'' Gellar said, frowning. ''They would draw too damned much attention to themselves by canceling. What else?''

''Three diamond buyers from the Czech Republic, traveling together. One of them is an older man. His passport claims that he is sixty-seven years of age. They landed in Johannesburg three days ago.''

''Too old,'' said Bolan, ''and the target hadn't left Ukraine when they arrived.''

''They are removed from the list.'' Selepa grinned.

"You said three prospects," Gellar pressed, reminding him.

"Indeed. A group of four men disembarked yesterday evening, in Pretoria. Their papers are in order, naming them as sportsmen. In South Africa, we still accommodate the great white hunters on occasion, if the price is right and they do not seek to destroy endangered species."

"Sportsmen?" Bolan said. "That means they brought in weapons?"

"I believe that they declared four rifles and four handguns, plus a quantity of ammunition, sir."

"That sounds more like it," Gellar said.

Their driver's smile appeared to falter for the first time since they had begun their journey. He wasn't quite frowning, but the sunny grin was definitely slipping into shade.

"We have considered them, of course," Selepa said, "but they appeared to be unlikely candidates for Nazis."

"Oh?" Bolan was curious. "Why's that?"

"Because they travel on Israeli passports, sir."

FALSE MODESTY aside, Gerhard Steuben allowed, using Israeli documents had been a stroke of genius. It could have proved inconvenient, granted, if some Palestinian freedom fighter had chosen to hijack their particular flight, but such incidents were rare in modern times, with all the various security devices and precautions that were spawned by the golden years of skyjacking in the early 1970s.

Flying commercial had its drawbacks, of course. Steuben and his three companions were limited in the type and number of weapons they could check through as cargo, but an inspector in Pretoria had mistaken the Heckler & Koch G-3 battle rifles for big-game hunting weapons, a simple error that had left him slightly more affluent than he was before he came to work that morning. Steuben had abandoned the alternative—taking a charter all the way and carrying a heavy-duty arsenal—when he had dozed off briefly in the air, somewhere over the eastern Mediterranean, and dreamed that they were captured with their weapons, jailed with filthy savages who raped them and infected them with AIDS before they could make bail.

The would-be führer had awakened from his nightmare bathed in clammy sweat and absolutely certain that he had to change his travel plans if he and his escorts were going to survive. The passports were a relatively simple thing—so many strokes of genius were, in fact—obtained from an Egyptian dealer who had asked no questions and was thus allowed to live. Their South African visas and hunting permits were completely genuine, albeit issued in the names of persons who did not exist.

"Feels weird to be a Jew," one of his escorts said as they were settling into their hotel suite, waiting for a call back from their contact in Pretoria.

"Good thing they didn't check my prick," another said with a grin. "The rabbi's clippers must have missed."

"The proper term is *mohel*," Steuben interrupted them, watching the childish grins drop from their faces.

"Sir?"

"The person who performs circumcisions on Jewish boys is called a *mohel*. He may or may not be a rabbi.

Know your adversary, gentlemen, if you expect to be victorious.''

"Yes, sir!" All three of them together, red faced with embarrassment at being chastised by the führer.

Steuben took a moment to reflect upon the wonders of the human psyche. These three were younger, stronger, trained in martial arts and skilled with weapons. Any one of them could knock him on his ass without breaking a sweat. Together, they could tear him limb from limb and fling the bloody pieces from the window of their ninth-floor suite to splash down in the swimming pool below—and yet, they would accept verbal correction, insults, even screaming tirades verging on complete hysteria, without lifting a finger against him.

It was simply marvelous.

Before he was transmuted into Gerhard Steuben, he had devoted tireless hours to studying the art of command, crowd control, demagoguery. He had watched old newsreels of Hitler, Huey Long and others, studying their movements, vocal intonations. After weeks of study, he had concluded that whatever he lacked in personal charisma and animal magnetism, he could make up with rehearsal and careful selection of initial converts. Part of a crowd pleaser's art was selecting the right crowd to please.

His followers, for the most part, were sheep. Despite their violent bigotry and the criminal records that were common to many, they were for the most part followers. Recruited from the military or from street gangs, they had always looked for someone else to make decisions, give the orders, spare them from the burden of responsibility. A few, like Eric Glass and the late Sean Fletcher, were qualified leadership material, but they still lacked vision, still fell short when it came to taking the long view.

They would always need a führer, and having selected one, would follow him to hell.

So had it always been, from the Crusades to the invasion of Kuwait and ethnic cleansing in the Balkans. There would always be strong men, militant shepherds to direct the herd—and to profit from its sacrifice.

"They should have called by now, sir," one of his young escorts said.

"They should have met us at the airport," yet another groused, judging the locals who had failed to put in an appearance as of yet.

"They'll be in touch," Steuben replied. "We're in a different world now, gentlemen. The mud people have seized control of the South African regime. They're working overtime to dismantle a civilization built up over 350 years. White patriots face opposition here that makes the FBI look like a high-school debating society. Some patience, gentlemen. Give them time."

"Yes, sir."

In truth, though, Steuben was struggling with furious impatience himself. Uncertain whether he had been pursued from the Ukraine by unknown enemies, without a means of checking Eric Glass's progress with the nuclear device, he felt cut off from the very movement he was meant to lead. It troubled him, but there was nothing he could do until—

The telephone made a disturbing honking sound. Steuben nearly jumped, but caught himself in time to save his dignity. The bodyguards stood waiting, watching him, until he nodded at the nearest of them to pick up the phone.

"Hello?" The soldier listened briefly, then said, "Sir, they're here."

Steuben allowed himself a stingy smile and said, "Have them come up."

Five minutes later, cautious rapping sounded on their door. One of the escorts went to answer it, the other two standing well back, their pistols drawn. There was no reason to expect a double cross, but so much that had happened in the past few weeks was unexpected, Steuben was in no mood to take anything for granted. He edged back toward the open doorway to his bedroom, where the H&K assault rifles were laid out on the queen-size bed.

The door was opened, and he recognized the first man through. Gert van Koch was a ranking minister in the Temple of the Nordic Covenant, handpicked by Steuben to supervise the cult's operations in South Africa. He was also the founder and leader of the Iron Guard, a quasilegal paramilitary unit pledged to restore apartheid in the face of opposition from native blacks, mixed races and world public opinion.

Whether that goal could be reached was open to debate, but it would scarcely matter in the scheme of things, if Steuben managed to fulfill his destiny. Apartheid would become superfluous when Aryans ruled the planet at large, with inferior races either reduced to the status of slave labor or eradicated from the face of the earth.

It was all a matter of perspective.

"Gert, it's good to see you." Steuben moved forward, with his arms outstretched for the embrace.

"My führer, welcome." As they stepped apart, the

large man said, "There were concerns that you might have been intercepted."

"I'm alive and well, as you can see, though not from lack of trying by our enemies."

"You have in mind a plan to make them pay for their impertinence, I hope." Koch was frowning, his expression mirrored on the faces of the soldiers who accompanied him.

"Indeed I do," the führer said. "But I require your help."

THE FOUR "Israeli sportsmen" had checked out of their hotel before Mitane Selepa arrived to get a look at them or snap their photo from a distance. He was disappointed by the news, but not especially surprised. His visitors—the *real* Israeli and the tall American with graveyard eyes—had already persuaded him that these were probably the neo-Nazi fugitives they sought.

The question now was, where could they have gone?

The gloomy answer, almost anywhere.

That wasn't literally true, of course. He thought it most unlikely, for example, that the men had left South Africa. Why come at all, unless they planned to stay at least a little while? Selepa's homeland wasn't geographically convenient, in the sense that it wasn't a midway point *from* anywhere *to* anywhere. The four "Israelis"—or, as he was now almost entirely convinced, American neo-Nazis—hadn't flown all the way from Eastern Europe to South Africa for the pleasure of saying they had been there, just to turn around and leave again.

A meeting? That was almost guaranteed, Selepa

thought, and he had put out feelers with his contacts, seeking the whereabouts of Gert van Koch and other Iron Guard leaders, from Pretoria and Jo'burg to Durban, Port Elizabeth and Cape Town. Koch had already turned up missing from his normal haunts around the capital, which also came as no surprise. Within a few more hours, Selepa should be aware of any major movements by members of the country's fascist fringe.

Which, he reflected sourly, wasn't at all the same thing as knowing what was on their minds, what they intended to do with themselves.

There was no easy route to discovery for one such as he, who was born with the wrong shade of skin. South Africa's fascists had a clear advantage there, over their comrades in Europe and North America. Here most of their adversaries were black or otherwise "colored"—a tag used in the old apartheid days to label Asians, Indians and anyone of mixed parentage. The sole exception, Jews, were also fairly obvious and generally known in their communities. As far as Mitane Selepa could recall, the government's admittedly halfhearted efforts to infiltrate white paramilitary groups had failed across the board. A handful of convicted terrorists had broken silence from their prison cells, but they had mostly spilled old news, filling in some historical blanks without endangering their comrades still at large. At present, if his information was correct and up-to-date, there didn't exist a single working spy within the country's fascist fringe.

The reasons for that ongoing failure weren't difficult to grasp. Some white police still sympathized with the terrorists, although they were less likely to boast about it over mugs of ale than in a bygone era. Likewise, many white South Africans, despite the smiles they wore these days in public, still lamented their loss of privilege, secretly—perhaps even unconsciously—gloating when the "kaffir" cause and government were threatened.

The real secret, though, lay with the homegrown fascists themselves. Unlike the neo-Nazis in America, who had never tasted victory, or the skinheads in Germany, living on the memories of what their grandfathers had done in the 1940s, South Africa's neo-Nazis had controlled the government and ruled a captive black population within living memory. They had seen that Aryan paradise slip through their bloody fingers, lost to them with stunning swiftness after generations of control, and their collective bitterness tainted every waking moment, colored every dream and nightmare they experienced. "Enemy" and "race traitor" weren't hollow propaganda slogans to the lily-white commandos of the Iron Guard and similar cadres. They would kill—or die—before they breathed a word to jeopardize their holy cause.

And of the several groups at large in modern-day South Africa, the Iron Guard and the Temple of the Nordic Covenant were more fanatical than most.

None of which meant that Mitane Selepa was defeated, however. Far from it. He would simply have to use his wits to outthink the neo-Nazi fugitives.

Where would they go? The obvious—to meet and hide with others of their kind. The stop-off in Pretoria was simply that, an opportunity for Gerhard Steuben and his escorts to connect with someone from the Iron Guard. Selepa made a mental note to check again on Gert van Koch and his subordinates, remain alert for any reported sightings, anywhere in the country.

Next question—what did Steuben and company want in South Africa? What was their objective, their intended goal?

Mitane Selepa didn't believe they had chosen his homeland simply as a place to hide. It was a long way from Kiev to Pretoria, along a route fraught with peril for bogus Israeli sportsmen. More to the point, South Africa under the current regime wasn't the safest or most logical place for a fugitive neo-Nazi to hide. Steuben would have been more at home in one of the Middle Eastern sheikhdoms, or perhaps one of the South American countries where Hitler's lieutenants had plowed so much stolen wealth into the blood-rich soil. For that matter, he could have found a more convenient, less imperiled sanctuary in Switzerland, perhaps even Australia or New Zealand.

So, once again, why South Africa?

The goal of every diehard white racist in the country was simply stated—namely, to topple the present coalition government and restore white-only rule under the guidelines of apartheid, the cruel system of segregation and oppression from cradle to grave. Under the old regime, blacks—and their occasional white allies—could be exiled or imprisoned for simply speaking out against apartheid, and for those jailed as enemies of the state, life was sometimes abruptly cut short. Of course, the same had been true for many of those outside prison, in a state that was itself—at least for the native population—one vast prison camp. In a land where civil disobedience was met with rifle fire, where torture was routine and where ministers of state conspired with law-enforcement officers to carry out wholesale assassination of their enemies, the only thing missing was the smoking chimneys of Auschwitz.

And those indeed might not be far away if diehard fascists ever succeeded in recapturing control of South Africa.

It was imperative, therefore, that Mitane Selepa do anything and everything within his power to find and detain—no, make that find and destroy—Gerhard Steuben and his little group of sportsmen. They had to be stopped, and forcefully, before they had a chance to implement whatever deadly scheme was brewing in their twisted minds.

Not easy, though, the small voice in Selepa's head reminded him. Not easy to break down the wall, slip past their guard.

There was, of course, a world of difference between "difficult" and "impossible." If necessary—and Selepa had begun to think it would be necessary—he could always grab a member of the Iron Guard and use his powers of persuasion to find out what pearls of wisdom the neo-Nazi was packing around in his mind. Should one refuse to talk, he could select another, and another, and…

The real enemy, the implacable and inescapable foe, was time.

In which case, Selepa thought, he should not waste more of it.

The hunter smiled, almost a grimace, as he went in search of his selected prey.

CHAPTER SEVEN

When in doubt, Bolan thought, always start at the top.

He lay prone on a flat, sunbaked rooftop, peering through the Nimrod telescopic sight that was standard issue with a Galil sniper rifle. He had acquired the "spot weld" of his face against the cheek rest on the folding stock, slowly scanning his target a hundred yards downrange.

The Iron Guard, while engaged in terrorist activity throughout South Africa, also maintained a legitimate public face in the guise of the National Renaissance Party. Its candidates were rarely elected to office, although the odd rural victory wasn't unheard of. More commonly, the NRP served its parent organization—and the Temple of the Nordic Covenant—as a public voice of protest against "black rule," and as a recipient of donations from angry or frightened whites.

Perversely, as a gesture of contempt for the biracial government in power, the National Renaissance Party had located its shoestring-budget headquarters in Vereeniging, a short drive south of Johannesburg, some eighty miles from the South African capital of Pretoria. A frontier outpost in the nineteenth century, Vereeniging had been a major center of resistance to British imperial rule during the Boer War, and it remained a hotbed of white intransigence after the fall of apartheid.

Bolan had found his way to the heart of enemy territory in South Africa, which wasn't to say that he had found his primary targets.

There was, predictably, no sign of Gary Stevens in Vereeniging, and no recent sightings of Iron Guard leader Gert van Koch. Still, even in their absence, Bolan reckoned he could send a message to the Nordic Temple, rattle his opponents just a bit, perhaps unnerve them before he got down to more serious business.

Still peering through the Nimrod telescope, the Galil's muzzle steady on its bipod, Bolan picked up the cell phone that lay beside him and keyed speed dial for the preset number. Downrange, through the plate-glass window of the office, he watched a ruddy-faced man with too many chins reach out for his own telephone, still speaking to a group arranged around a large wall-mounted map.

Plotting strategy? Some kind of action in the works?

A gruff voice answered, speaking Afrikaans. Bolan replied in English, suddenly uncertain whether anything he said would even be translated.

"I want Gerhard Steuben," he said, giving him the name Stevens had claimed for himself in his reincarnation fantasy.

"Eh?" It took the man of many chins a moment to shift gears. "Herr Steuben?"

"I want Gerhard Steuben *and* the warhead. Have you got that?"

"Ah, you wait now, for—"

"Wrong answer," Bolan said and set down the cell phone, bringing his left hand back to brace the rifle.

His first shot took out a fist-sized piece of glass and drilled a brass ashtray off Fat Boy's desk, resembling the base of a sawed-off artillery shell. Round two brought down the window in crashing ruins, punching through the left cheek of a tall, lean neo-Nazi as he turned from the wall map to gape at the wreckage behind him.

The others tried to scatter, but they had nowhere to go. Bolan's third 7.62 mm round caught a shorter, huskier target as he spun toward the door, lunging headlong for what he thought was safety in the outer corridor or waiting room. He never made it, slapped behind his left ear by a slug that tore through his skull, back to front, spraying the door with blood and gray matter before the dead man got there, stumbling on his own feet, surrendering to the relentless draw of gravity. His ruined face struck the doorjamb, leaving crimson skid marks as he slithered to the floor.

That left three still alive in the office, and Fat Boy had dropped the telephone, fumbling for something in the top right-hand drawer of his desk. Bolan left him to it, swinging back to find the others.

One of them was crouched behind a filing cabinet, trying to conceal himself, but one of his knees was visible and Bolan put a bullet through it, round four of twenty in the Galil's box magazine, impacting at a speed of some 2,600 feet per second. The effect was devastating, bone and cartilage exploding from a ragged wound, spilling his target in a wriggling, twitching heap of misery.

Instead of squeezing off a mercy round just then,

he swung around to catch the last man on his feet, midway through a desperate rush for the exit. The door was blocked by a fallen comrade, though, and the neo-Nazi was stooping to grab his good friend by the belt, haul him out of the way like a sack of dirty laundry, when Bolan shot him just above the swell of his left hip. The bullet tore through various internal organs—stomach, liver, lung—and pitched him forward. He sprawled across the dead man who had been his friend, shuddering the final seconds of his life away as their blood mingled and pooled on cheap linoleum.

Bolan brought the Nimrod's crosshairs back to Fat Boy, identified the item from his desk drawer as a semiautomatic pistol and shot it from the neo-Nazi's trembling hand, clipping off his trigger finger in the process. Fat Boy rocked backward in his swivel chair, his squeals audible to Bolan through the phone link still connecting them.

Remembering the knee-shot target, Bolan found him with the telescope and put round seven through his open, screaming mouth. The impact snapped his target's head back and brought blessed silence to the office as the echo of his final gun shot rolled across the street and vanished on the breeze.

Bolan retrieved his cell phone, speaking sharply into it, aware that he was nearly out of time. "Pick up the telephone," he said. And then, again, when there was no response from Fat Boy, "Pickup the goddamned telephone!"

The wounded neo-Nazi heard him that time, blinking at the handset lying on his desk, reaching out to snare it with his undamaged left hand. When it was nestled up against the neo-Nazi's sweat-slick face, Bolan spoke again.

"I want your führer and the warhead," he repeated, driving home the message. "Spread the word or die."

He stroked the sniper rifle's trigger one more time and blasted the telephone from Fat Boy's desktop, leaving the hit's sole survivor with the handset and dangling cord in one hand, a fistful of blood in the other.

It was a start, Bolan thought as he packed up his gear.

WAITING IN THE street outside the Iron Guard hideout in Johannesburg, Jacob Gellar felt the old rage returning, flowing warm through his body like the burn after a stiff shot of liquor. He knew where it came from, the message drilled into him from early childhood, as if it were predestined that he would be here this day, carrying a silencer-equipped MP-5 SD submachine gun in a plastic shopping bag.

Gellar would have preferred to wear the SMG on a shoulder sling, but concealment would have required a jacket—which would have made him stand out like a two-headed freak in the heat of a Jo'burg afternoon. Rather than blow the operation with a bit of inappropriate attire—which also, incidentally, may well have pushed him into sunstroke—Gellar made a show of window-shopping as he moved along the small stores facing the sidewalk, with apartments stacked two and three floors above. The Iron Guard flat was on the second floor, above a sandwich shop whose menu and aroma would have beckoned Gellar under other circumstances.

As it was, the best that he could do was focus on the job at hand.

At least four neo-Nazis were in the flat upstairs, and it would be his task to leave one of them breathing, if he could. It ran against his grain and lifelong training, but Gellar had questions to ask, and a message to impart, if answers were not forthcoming.

Time to go.

They had split up for the initial raids to cover more ground in a hurry, Mike Belasko well able to navigate on his own in a city where most inhabitants spoke fluent English in addition to the native Afrikaans. Mitane Selepa had provided a fair list of targets, and he was out seeking more even now, a kind of insurance against early failures.

God knew they'd had enough near misses, Gellar thought as he began to climb the narrow flight of stairs. At least, this time, he knew damned well that the primary targets weren't in the flat above. These men were merely foot soldiers in the cause of racial holy war, but they might, with any luck, direct him toward their leaders.

He reached the landing, found the door and drew his weapon from the shopping bag, tossing the bag to one side, where he could find it quickly as he left.

Assuming he was still alive.

As Gellar knocked, he knew the first man at the door would have to die. It was the only way, but he was troubled by the thought that he might thereby kill the only one among them who possessed the information he required. There seemed to be no way around it, though, and he resigned himself to stick with the original plan.

Footsteps approached the door, which seemed to

have no peephole. If the neo-Nazi asked his business without opening the door, Gellar would fire through the flimsy wooden panel, follow with a kick to clear the way and hope that no one else inside the flat could reach a gun before he had them lined up in his sights.

As luck would have it, the neo-Nazi was careless. He opened the door for Gellar without even engaging the slender security chain. A man that stupid had no right to live, much less rank himself as a member of the so-called master race.

"Vas is—?"

He never learned the answer to his question. Jacob Gellar fired a 3-round burst into the center of his chest at skin-touch range, striking at a muzzle velocity of 926 feet per second, hurling him back as if yanked by a lanyard, well into the room beyond. The guy was dead before he hit the threadbare carpet, shivering in his death throes, blood pumping from his mutilated heart.

Gellar followed him in and kicked the door shut behind him, tracking with the MP-5's thick muzzle to catch three more goons on the rise, bolting from their seats around a square card table. He had deliberately set the SMG's fire selector switch for 3-round bursts, thus offering better control, and the compact weapon served him to good effect now, as his targets scattered from their places, chasing weapons that were dangerously out of reach.

The gunner on his left was nearest to a shotgun leaning in a corner of the room, and Gellar didn't even try to spare him, shooting to kill as his adversary's fingers found the scattergun. Three Parabellum rounds slammed home between the neo-Nazi's shoulder blades and added their momentum to his lunge, propelling him headlong into the wall, his crumpling form taking the shotgun down and out of play.

That left two neo-Nazis alive, and one of them would have to be his pigeon if Gellar was to make the visit count for anything beyond spilt blood. They made it difficult for him, deliberately so, but he was faster, more experienced, with the advantage of surprise.

The middle player scrambled toward a breakfast counter where two pistols lay on a folded newspaper as if presented for inspection or field-stripping. Gellar shot him in the legs, an inch or two below his buttocks, and the man yelped out a curse as he went down.

Swinging around to face the fourth and final challenger, Gellar was staring down the muzzle of an automatic pistol when he squeezed off one more muffled burst. He let the muzzle of his MP-5 rise slightly as it spit out Parabellum rounds, blood spouting from his targets upper chest, his neck, his face as he collapsed. A dying reflex action led the neo-Nazi to trigger one shot from his pistol, high and wide. It missed, but sounded nearly loud enough to wake the dead. Gellar knew his time was running short before he turned back to the wounded Iron Guard trooper, closing on him from behind.

He had to give the neo-Nazi credit, still struggling to reach the pistols that were hopelessly beyond his grasp. Gellar kicked the man onto his back and crouched beside him, jamming the warm muzzle of his SMG beneath the neo-Nazi's chin.

"You speak English?" he asked his wounded enemy.

"Fuck you!"

"That's close enough," the Mossad agent said through a ferocious smile. "Tell me where Gerhard Steuben is, or Gert van Koch, and I may let you live."

"I tell you nothing, bastard!"

Gellar knelt on the wounded Nazi's groin, bearing in with his weight, cutting off the string of bitter curses with another squeal of pain.

"Once more," he said. "Where are they? Where's the warhead?"

Defiance shifted gears into confusion at his mention of the nuclear device, then came back bright and clear. "They have a bomb?" The neo-Nazi grinned at him through waves of agony. "I hope they blow the Jews and kaffirs straight to hell!"

"You'll be there first, the way you're bleeding," Gellar said.

The neo-Nazi hissed at him through clenched teeth, "It makes no difference. I am a soldier!"

Gellar rocked back on his haunches and rose to stand above the wounded man. "All right," he said, "enjoy your misery. But if you live, make sure to tell your führer that his days are numbered. He is running out of time."

"You think so, bastard? He will—"

Gellar made a point of stepping on the neo-Nazi's right hand as he turned to leave, grinding his heel until he heard the fingers snap and anything the Iron Guard trooper had to say was smothered by a sob. Gellar retrieved his shopping bag and tucked the submachine gun out of sight. He was already halfway down the stairs, bright sunshine in his face, before he heard one of the neighbors raising an alarm.

Too late for three young neo-Nazis in the flat, but Gellar hoped the fourth would hang on long enough to spread the word among his comrades. After that, it hardly mattered what became of him, whether he died or lived to walk again someday, perhaps with canes.

By that time, it would all be over, one way or another. Gellar and his people would have won or lost the game.

And if they lost, he thought, one limping neo-Nazi, more or less, would make no difference in the scheme of things.

KURT ROOYEN YAWNED and checked his watch again, the third time in the past half hour, wondering how time could pass so slowly without lurching to a halt. The midday heat had made him drowsy, even as it baked the perspiration from his pores. His khaki shirt was plastered flush against his back, soaked through, and that despite the shade where he was seated, on the warehouse loading dock.

Shade never seemed to make much difference on a day like this. Oh, it could buy you time, all right, if you were trekking in the desert, but it wouldn't really save your life. Without a handy source of water to replace the steady loss through sweat, a white man faced dehydration and death within a day or two, at most. The fact that kaffirs could survive the desert heat and function normally beneath the broiling sun was further proof, for Rooyen's money, that they were a separate, subhuman species after all.

Instead of simple water, he had bottled tea to keep him going, sitting frosty in the cooler to his left, within arm's reach. Off to his right, out in the open with no effort toward concealment, lay an R-5 assault rifle, South Africa's homegrown modification of the Israeli Galil.

There was nothing illegal about his possessing the weapon, per se. Indeed, the rapid escalation of violent crime over the past decade had made private security guards and paramilitary weapons almost as common in South Africa as they were in fortress Israel. The irony in that comparison didn't escape Rooyen, even though the heat had dulled his senses and he wouldn't have been taken for a genius on the best of days.

His task, quite simply, was to guard this warehouse on the outskirts of Pretoria, where the Iron Guard maintained a cache of arms, ammunition and other supplies. Approximately once every hour of his shift, Rooyen would leave his shaded post and make a walking circuit of the warehouse, checking doors and windows to make certain that no saboteurs or kaffir thieves had found a way to circumvent the antitheft alarms. The walking tour took perhaps ten minutes, and it always left him feeling like a baked potato by the time he got back to the meager shelter of the loading dock.

He could have used someone to talk to, but he didn't really feel like talking, and the boom-box radio that sat beside the cooler filled with bottled tea would keep him company. The news was coming on just now, behind a tune that Rooyen liked, with the announcer talking over final lyrics toward the end.

"Rude bloody bastard," Rooyen muttered to himself, and scowled.

The first item of news didn't improve his mood. According to the broadcast, sniper fire had raked the National Renaissance Party headquarters in Vereeniging sometime within the past two hours, and at least three members of the party's staff were dead on arrival at the local hospital. The gunmen hadn't been identified, but Rooyen could imagine who they were: black bastards from the African National Congress, not satisfied with kaffirs at the helm of government, determined to harass and murder white men any time they saw the opportunity.

Well, if it was bloody war they wanted...

No more than half an hour had passed since Rooyen's last walking tour of the warehouse, but he decided then and there to make another, scooping up the R-5 carbine as he rose from his folding patio chair. It couldn't hurt to double-check, what with so many savages about.

He made the circuit, walking briskly, carrying his rifle with the safety off this time. It was a bit of melodrama, but he didn't feel the least bit silly. Not with three of his comrades lying dead in Vereeniging.

Rounding the last corner, coming up toward his own patch of shade, Rooyen stopped short in his tracks, startled by the vision of a tall man standing on the dock, a few feet from his chair. The man was tall, dark haired, with shiny aviator's glasses covering his eyes, a loose safari vest worn over his short-sleeved shirt despite the heat.

A stranger, watching Rooyen with his head turned slightly, almost in profile.

Rooyen considered raising his weapon, but stopped short of following through. This was a white man, after all. A stranger, yes, but also possibly a comrade sent to bring him news or simply make sure he was on the job. It would look bad in the reports if he was jumpy, pointing guns for no good reason.

"Can I help you?" Rooyen asked.

The stranger turned to face him, bringing up a pistol with some kind of silencer attached, and it was too late for Rooyen to lift his rifle then, as the first bullet took out one of his knees, another ripping through the shoulder of his gun arm as he fell.

The pain was staggering—or would have been if he hadn't already fallen to the ground. A moment later the stranger stood above him, scooping up his R-5 carbine from the pavement.

Studying Rooyen's ashen face, the stranger spoke to him in English. "You don't know where I can find a certain Gert van Koch, by any chance?" he asked.

Against his will, Rooyen shook his head. There was no compromise in offering a negative response, he told himself, since it supplied the enemy with nothing in the way of useful information. Only afterward, aghast at his mistake, did it occur to him that he might have signed his own death warrant.

But the stranger didn't finish him. Instead, he spoke again, in measured tones. "If you should see him, tell him that I'm after Gary Stevens and the warhead. I want both. It's not an either-or. You follow me?"

This time, Rooyen found the strength to nod.

"Okay, sit tight. I'll be right back."

The stranger took Rooyen's R-5 with him, disappeared into the warehouse, which, Rooyen realized, was somehow magically unlocked. The man was gone for minutes, maybe hours. He couldn't have judged the time with any accuracy, and he couldn't raise his arm to check his watch. At last the dark-haired man returned and took him by the collar of his khaki shirt, ignoring Rooyen's cries of pain as he dragged him across twenty yards of parking lot to leave him in the pool of shade beside a garbage container.

They had barely reached that spot when the warehouse exploded, going up in flames. Inside, Rooyen could hear the cache of ammunition cooking off, understanding that the stranger had placed him behind the garbage bin to protect him from stray rounds.

An act of mercy from the enemy?

"Remember what I said," the tall man cautioned as he turned to leave. "Don't make me visit you again."

He wouldn't, Kurt Rooyen thought, uncertain whether he had voiced the words aloud. He really, really wouldn't.

MITANE SELEPA LIKED to think of himself as an easygoing man, and yet... It wasn't every day a black man in South Africa—even the "new" South Africa—had a chance to strike back at his white enemies.

Selepa was no racist. He understood that some black Africans hated white people as much as the Iron Guard hated "kaffirs," and while he understood the feeling well enough—his own grandfather had been executed by the white regime, for what they called sabotage and subversion, in June 1970—still Selepa couldn't bring himself to hate all whites for the harm some members of their race had done. It made no sense to him, and never would.

As for the Iron Guard and the other neo-Nazis, though...

Selepa smiled his broadest, brightest smile as he approached the small house in a suburb of Johannesburg. The neighborhood was open to all races now, though it had once been lily-white, and he had counted signs announcing homes For Sale in three yards on this block alone. The Boers were moving out as rapidly as possible, surrendering their turf to seek a more secure dwelling place.

It was ironic, then, that the Iron Guard would have a safehouse in this neighborhood, surrounded by the very "savages" who were the movement's enemies and targets. Perhaps it was a conscious effort at disguise, like taking off the swastika armbands and jackboots before the neo-Nazis went grocery shopping. It had, of course, fooled no one at all.

But Mitane Selepa was about to...or, at the very least, he was about to try. He reckoned that he had at least a fifty-fifty chance of coming through alive and in one piece.

On balance, those were better odds than most black men were used to in South Africa.

The paper bag he carried bore the logo of a Chinese takeout establishment, but there was no fried rice, chow mein or other tasty food inside. In fact, the bag was nearly empty—would have been entirely empty if Selepa hadn't sliced a hole on one side where he could insert his hand, clutching a Walther P-1 automatic pistol with a bulky suppressor attached.

The neo-Nazis hadn't ordered Chinese food, of course.

They were about to get a rude surprise.

Selepa rang the doorbell, waited, was about to ring again when the door was opened by a hulking skinhead, his bare chest and muscular arms festooned with tattoos.

"A bloody kaffir! What in hell do you want, boy?"

Selepa's smile was cheerful as he shot the neo-Nazi once, straight through the heart, at point-blank range. He would have made it two, but he was mindful of the eight rounds in his pistol's magazine, uncertain how many more targets remained in the house.

Shedding the paper sack, which had begun to smolder from the Walther's muzzle flare, Selepa stepped inside the house and closed the door to give himself some privacy. He followed gruff male voices toward a rear bedroom. The door was standing open, and he had a clear view from the threshold. Four more neo-Nazis stood around the bed in sundry stages of undress; a fifth, stark naked, was already stretched out on rumpled sheets, taut buttocks heaving between the splayed thighs of a terrified young woman.

She had been tied to the bed, wrists and ankles bound tightly with what looked like old strips of cloth. Her eyes found Selepa's, pleading with him through the glaze of shock.

The young woman was black.

He started shooting then, just as one of the neo-Nazis half turned toward the doorway. Any thought of leaving one alive to tell the story, any plan for questioning survivors, had been instantly forgotten as he glimpsed the savage tableau before him. He aimed for heads and torsos, saving three rounds for the bare-back rider as his final target recognized the sudden danger, scrambling clear of the girl and the mattress. Where he hoped to go was anybody's guess, but there was nowhere to run, nowhere to hide, as Selepa shot him first in the groin, then twice in the chest.

The girl watched in silence as he reloaded the Walther, released the open slide to chamber a cartridge and worked his way around the room once more, stooping low to shoot each skinhead once below the belt and once between the eyes, continuing the ritual until his second magazine was empty.

On the bed, the girl made no attempt to cringe from him as he removed a switchblade from his pocket, snapped it open and began to slash the bonds that held her down. That done, he turned away from her as she curled into a fetal ball, surrendering to a fresh wave of tears.

"You'll be all right," he told her softly, wondering if it was true. "This trash can't hurt you anymore. They can't hurt anyone again."

But there were more like these, Selepa knew. So many more.

"Let's find your clothes," he said. "I'll take you to the hospital, or anywhere you want to go, but we must hurry."

He had men to see, he thought, and questions to ask.

AFTER THE WAREHOUSE strike, Bolan changed clothes to shed the smell of gun smoke—or as much of it as he could lose without a long, hot shower, for which he had no time at all. The clean clothes he put on resembled those he had discarded: sport shirt, slacks, casual shoes. He might have been a Boer—at least until he spoke—and no one, black or white, gave him a second glance as he moved along the Johannesburg sidewalk, homing on a commercial address in the middle of the block. His blazer was too much for the weather, but it gave him the look of a laid-back businessman, while concealing the AT-2000 autoloader in its fast-draw armpit rig.

The print shop was ostensibly a normal business, open to all comers, though it found various ways to discourage black customers. The six-inch-square NRP decal in the shop's front window was a start, announcing the white management's allegiance to the anti-black, proapartheid National Renaissance Party. Any blacks who missed that not so subtle message were apt to find themselves patronized, insulted and grossly overcharged for mediocre service by the crypto-Nazis who owned and managed the establishment.

In practice, the shop was a subsidiary of the NRP and the Iron Guard, an organ of the Nordic Temple once removed, where fascist propaganda was cranked out by the case for distribution nationwide. The owner of record was a slope-shouldered troll named Gunter Gross—a name that seemed to fit both his appearance and his chosen lifestyle.

Bolan didn't know if Gross and company could put him on the track of Gary Stevens or the missing nuke, but he was bound to ask. Besides, he told himself, where better could he leave a message for the führer than on the editorial desk of the Iron Guard's very own propaganda mill?

To nail his cover—for the first few seconds, anyway—he carried a manila folder in his left hand, the file containing a single sheet of cheap white paper. The negligible burden left his right hand free for the pistol when things began to unravel.

A bell chimed somewhere overhead as Bolan entered the print shop, the sound attracting a squat, gray-haired figure from the noisy back room. A name tag on his bulging shirt read Gunter, and the print shop's owner—also a lieutenant in the Iron Guard—lived up to descriptions of his brutish mien, although he had aged several years since his last candid photo was taken.

"I can help you?" the fat neo-Nazi said, turning the statement into a question.

"I hope so," Bolan replied, placing the slim manila folder on the countertop between them. "I need a flyer printed up from this," he said, and tapped the folder with his index finger.

"Flyer?"

"Sorry. What you'd call a handbill."

"You're American, I think."

"That's right."

Gross opened the folder, blinking at the message printed in neat letters, angry color rising in his fat cheeks as he read it through a second time. It read: "I want Gerhard Steuben and the warhead. Give them up and you may live. If not…"

Gross raised his eyes to meet Bolan's gaze, sputtering in anger. "What means this—?"

He never had a chance to finish, as Bolan's pistol, muzzle-heavy with the black suppressor, smashed into the bridge of his nose. Gross's nose had been broken before and it showed, but he still barked in pain, recoiling from the strike, his well-padded buttocks colliding with stacked shelves of printing supplies as he staggered backward.

Bolan vaulted the counter, lashing out again before Gross could sound a warning to the employees in back. The clanking of an offset printing press combined with the groan of busy photocopiers, covered the sound as Gross collapsed to the floor.

Bolan entered the back room, checking out the three employees briefly. All of them were white, of course; that stood to reason. It wasn't enough to condemn them, but they had stripped down to skimpy T-shirts in the heat of the print shop, all three revealing arms and shoulders defaced with swastika and lightning-bolt tattoos.

It was enough.

He shot the first one from behind, dropped him beside a copier that kept on printing and collating copies as if nothing had happened. The other two were still oblivious as Bolan lined up his next shot, spattering one neo-Nazi's profile with the others blood and brains.

That baptism alerted number three, but it was too late for the man to save himself. He seemed to be unarmed, but you could never tell, so many shelves and cubbyholes, tables and drawers around the workspace.

Better safe than sorry.

Bolan put a Parabellum round between the neo-Nazi's eyes and watched him fold, then doubled back to check on Gross. The neo-Nazi was in dreamland, snuffling blood through flattened nostrils, but in no apparent danger of expiring. Bolan took his message from the countertop, careless of fingerprints that were no longer on file with any law-enforcement agency on earth, and folded it neatly, tucking it into Gross's breast pocket.

A little reminder, for when he woke up.

The message might reach Gary Stevens, or it might be intercepted, censored, somewhere on the way between the print-shop slaughterhouse and its intended destination. Either way, though, it would have an impact on the Iron Guard and the Temple of the Nordic Covenant.

It was the best that he could hope for, in the present circumstances.

Time to go.

The Executioner was doing well, but he still wasn't finished.

As a matter of fact, he was just getting started.

CHAPTER EIGHT

Gerhard Steuben washed down four pain pills with lukewarm coffee, then reconsidered the dosage and tipped two more tablets from the plastic bottle into his palm, sending them to join the rest. The last two left a bitter residue on his palate, threatening to gag him and bring back the greasy remains of his meager deep-fried lunch.

He should have seen the migraine coming, Steuben realized, but he had been distracted by the preparations for their big move in South Africa, the master stroke that would redeem his recent failures. Caught up in the vision of a victory that would erase all those embarrassing defeats and put the Temple of the Nordic Covenant back on track toward the Apocalypse, he'd been taken by surprise when a fresh disaster came calling.

The migraine had arrived, full blown, with the reports of new attacks upon his followers, this time within the very precincts of Johannesburg, Pretoria and Vereeniging. Their personnel losses were light so far—around a dozen men, none of them personally known to Steuben—but he understood the import of the new assaults.

His unknown enemies had followed him southward,

some six thousand miles from the scene of the last attacks in Ukraine, and they had arrived within a day or less of his own touchdown in Pretoria. They hadn't found him yet, but the Israeli-passport dodge hadn't deceived them, not if they had tracked him to South Africa, and the attacks upon his followers were clearly damaging morale. His chief lieutenant in the country, Gert van Koch, followed his restless pacing with a pensive look, as if expecting Steuben to produce a miracle from out of thin air.

At last, growing impatient with the pacing, Koch asked, "What would you have us do, führer?"

"What *can* you do," Steuben replied, "that you are not already doing? You are checking the hotels, yes?"

His lieutenant nodded. "It will take some time, but we are helping the police. We have friends there, as you may know."

"And you are checking all arrivals for the past two days, including private charter flights?"

"Yes, sir."

"Surviving witnesses have been debriefed?"

Another nod. "But as I've told you, sir, their various descriptions don't agree. We seem to have at least two different white men, based on height, complexion and the rest of it. The gunman in Johannesburg was black. Frankly, sir, I'm not convinced that shooting is related to the rest."

"Because your men were caught raping a black girl," Steuben said.

Koch produced a careless shrug that said boys would be boys.

"It was a stupid thing to do, bringing the bitch back to their house," the führer snapped at his subordinate.

"Doubly stupid at this time, when every man's full concentration should be focused on the task at hand."

"They've paid for their mistake, sir," Koch replied coolly.

"Ah, yes. And that removes the problem of publicity, does it? Their stupid deaths somehow turn off the spotlight that is tracking every move our people make today? I'm so relieved, Gert. For a moment, I was worried that their goddamned idiocy might have jeopardized the cause!"

"Führer, I didn't mean—"

"Damn what you meant to say! You think it's a coincidence this gunman turns up just in time to kill five of your stupid bully boys? Do you believe the Jew press won't connect these incidents and run with it because one of the shooters was a fucking kaffir?"

"Sir, I don't suggest—"

"That's right. You don't suggest. You follow orders, Gert, or I'll find someone else who can. You understand me?"

"Perfectly, sir." The flush of angry color in his face found no outlet through the Boer's mouth. He was playing it safe.

"We have a chance to salvage something from the series of disasters that has dogged us for the past few weeks. If we succeed with what we've planned for Saturday, this country will go up in flames, and when the smoke clears, order—racial order—will have been restored."

"Yes, sir."

"And if we fail..."

Steuben didn't complete the sentence, leaving it to Koch's imagination. One more failure, on that scale, and it would all come down to desperate, last-ditch tactics, with only a marginal hope of final victory. Blind faith aside, Steuben wasn't convinced that even a fulfillment of the last great prophecy could save the cause, if he was blocked at each preliminary step along the way.

As he had been, so far, by meddling bastards who were still faceless, nameless, visible only when they chose to be.

"How goes the preparation, then?" he asked after a silent moment stretched between them.

"It goes well, sir," Koch replied. "My men are ready for both phases, and the recent—um, unpleasantries—haven't affected those chosen for the assault teams. Barring any more serious complications, phase one shall be carried out tomorrow night, on schedule."

Steuben nodded. "Let us have no further complications, then."

"No, sir." Koch managed a mirthless smile. "Phase two is ready to proceed on Saturday, assuming that the target reacts as expected to phase one."

"Have you ever known it to fail?" Steuben asked. "The man's a goddamned glory hound. Give him half a chance, and he'd call a press conference to announce that his laundry was done."

"You're right, of course, sir," Koch said. "And with the nature of the provocation, so far from the capital, there'll be no reason for him to increase security."

"Be ready for an increase, just the same," Steuben commanded. "All this other business may put him on the alert, even it it's only white men dying."

"I'll see to it personally, Führer."

"As for discovering the men responsible for these

attacks, I want no effort spared. You understand me, Gert? It's top priority. They could surprise us yet and ruin everything. It wouldn't be the first time.''

''Right, sir. I'm prepared to move as soon as we have anything at all. A name, address, an auto license number...they're not ghosts, sir. Men leave tracks. You can't avoid it.''

''Don't overlook the kaffir from the shooting in Johannesburg. It's possible our enemies have found themselves a native ally. Someone from the ANC, perhaps, or some such revolutionary scum. No stone unturned, Gert! Make sure all your people understand. No stone unturned!''

''No, sir. No stone unturned.''

The pain inside his skull decreased a trifle as the painkillers started kicking in. Steuben wished that he had something stronger, but he would need his wits about him for the next two days, at least, while their final moves were under way. If they succeeded here, in this bastion of black power, it could be enough to light the doomsday fuse and start the final countdown to the great Apocalypse, the racial holy war that he believed would cleanse the planet of its various subhuman parasites.

Soon, now, he told himself. Let it be soon.

''AND YOU WOULD RECOGNIZE this man again if you should see his face?'' The question sounded casual, but no one watching Gert van Koch as he pronounced the words would have assumed the inquiry was anything but deadly serious.

''I would,'' Gunter Gross said. His flattened nose, the nostrils daubed with rusty bloodstains, made his voice even more annoying than usual. Instead of his normal raspy tone, his voice seemed to have picked up an octave somehow, becoming a rough nasal whine.

"So, describe him for me once again, this stranger."

Gross narrowed his blackened eyes to glinting slits, as if the squint would somehow help him see the past more clearly. When he spoke again, he made an effort to control his voice, but without much success.

"The man was tall," Gross said. "Six feet at least, perhaps a little more. Dark hair of average length, not short or long. His face was unremarkable, no scars that I recall. He wasn't pale or ruddy in the face, more of an olive complexion."

"But white?" Koch prodded. "You said before, he was a white man."

"Definitely white," Gunter agreed, nodding his battered head. "Certainly not colored or a kaffir."

"Possibly a Jew?"

Gross thought about it for a moment, frowning to himself. "Who knows these days?" he said at last. "They have black Jews and Chinese Jews. I'll say he didn't have the nose for it, no Star of David showing anywhere."

"All right. Proceed."

"Where was I?"

"You've described his face," Koch replied. "About the rest of him..."

"Ah, yes. I'd guess he weighed between 190 and 200 pounds. Athletic looking, you might say. He's strong, I give the bastard that." As Gross spoke, fat fingers rose to trace the outline of the tape that spanned his broken nose.

"What did he wear?"

"The clothes? Now, let me see. He wore a jacket. Shirt and pants, of course. No tie. He looked respectable enough. If I'm required to guess, I'll say the jacket was dark blue or black. I really didn't pay attention to his wardrobe."

"Never mind. Go on." The bastard could have changed his clothes a dozen times by now, in any case. He could have shaved his head or glued a false beard to his face.

"He handed me the folder and I opened it," Gross said. "You've read the message, yes?"

"I have," Koch replied.

"And then, I barely finished reading it before he knocked me down. He had a gun, you understand. I never saw—"

"Don't worry, Gunter. No one's blaming you."

There was a problem with the message, obviously. It wasn't intended solely for the eyes of Gunter Gross; indeed, he had been given no real chance to respond before he was clubbed unconscious, demonstrating that the note was meant for someone higher up the ladder of command.

"I want Gerhard Steuben and the warhead."

The first part was clear enough. The author of this note wanted someone in the Temple to betray his leader, give him up, as if that were an option. But the rest of it...

Gert van Koch had no idea what warhead the message referred to. Clearly, the term implied a nuclear device, but was personally unaware of any such weapon falling into the Temple's hands. It galled him to think that he, a national commander of the holy order, would be kept in the dark on a matter of such significance, and this note from one of their enemies would grant him the perfect excuse to ask Herr Steuben for details.

Not that there was any guarantee he would be told the truth, of course. Some actions were planned on a need-to-know basis, his own upcoming moves a perfect case in point. Would Temple officers in Germany or the United States be briefed on details of what was about to happen in Pretoria? He hoped not, trusting that security remained effective, even with the recent damage to the Temple's chain of command.

Still, if nuclear arms had been procured, if they were about to be deployed, Koch would hope to be informed, as the results and repercussions of a strike on that scale would be global, potentially catastrophic.

Yes, he would most certainly request more information from the führer when they met again.

As for the rest of the note, it set his teeth on edge.

"Give them up and you may live. If not..."

The threat struck him as personal, though it wasn't addressed to anyone by name or rank. Koch bore ultimate responsibility for anything the Temple and the Iron Guard were involved in, anywhere within the borders of South Africa, and Gerhard Steuben's safety was his personal responsibility, as long as the führer remained in the country. The choice of "giving up" his leader would rest with Koch, assuming such a thing was even thinkable. Of course, it hardly mattered, since the note demanded both Herr Steuben *and* the warhead, which Koch didn't possess.

The threat was clear enough to anyone with eyes.

There was no need to spell it out. The author of the note was threatening to kill those who resisted him, as other members of the cult, including several ranking officers, had recently been killed in the United

States and Europe, by persons unknown. Already there were casualties in South Africa—more than a dozen, in fact—and Koch had no reason to doubt that the mayhem would continue until such time as the interlopers were destroyed.

And how would he accomplish that, when all before him, including Sean Fletcher and the Ukrainian brute Onoprienko, had failed so miserably?

It was yet another question to be raised with his commander when they met again. But first he had to oversee the final preparations for the first move in what the Americans would call a double play.

It was a whole new game, and if the enemies who dogged his führer didn't interfere, Koch had every reason to expect that victory would soon be his.

If only he could stay alive to celebrate.

LARS KORSTIAAN WATCHED the thirty members of his team as they fell into ranks and snapped to attention, heels clicking together, their spines ramrod straight. Sharp eyes, approximately equal numbers blue and brown, were pointed straight ahead, most of the soldiers too keyed-up to blink.

The moment they had waited for, trained for, was rapidly approaching. They would soon be joined in battle with the enemy, upon a scale unwitnessed in South Africa since the collapse of the apartheid state. Most of them were too young to have participated in the final struggle of the old regime. For them, the young lions, this would be their first real taste of combat on the eve of the Apocalypse.

Korstiaan surveyed their ranks, moved among them while they stood at attention, no sound audible except for the click of his boot heels on concrete. His men were dressed in black from head to foot, their jackets stripped of any patches that would mark them as members of the Iron Guard. Each wore combat webbing, with suspenders supporting their pistol belts and surplus ammunition pouches, fighting knives and antipersonnel grenades. Approximately half of them were armed with R-5 assault rifles, the standard military issue, chambered in 5.56 mm. The remainder were armed with a mixed bag of Striker 12-gauge shotguns, each loading twelve buckshot rounds in its revolving cylinder, and Spanish Z-84 submachine guns, modeled on the Israeli Uzi design. The party's "artillery" section consisted of three troopers armed with RPG-7 grenade launchers.

Korstiaan moved among the men, stopping here and there to face a soldier squarely, daring them to meet his gaze. All passed the test, and he was smiling thinly to himself as he reversed direction, marching to the podium in front of them.

The troops had been assembled in a waterfront warehouse in Durban, well removed from the recent attacks on Iron Guard forces around Pretoria and Johannesburg. They had a long truck ride ahead of them tomorrow, but it would be as nothing compared to their weeks of intensive training, a trifle compared to their anticipation of the action scheduled for tomorrow night. Each man would do his part when called upon, and Korstiaan would lead them into battle, thus guaranteeing his own place in history.

"At ease, men!" he ordered, watching them relax in military style, with a perfectly coordinated movement and stamping of boots on concrete. They were perfect. They were his.

"Tomorrow night, at 2100 hours, you will meet the

enemy,'' Korstiaan told them, as if a reminder were needed. ''You will have the full advantage of your training, your superiority, and the advantage of surprise. Remember who your adversaries are, what they have done these past ten years to our beloved homeland, and show them the same mercy they've shown to our women and children. You are already heroes. Tomorrow night, you shall become living legends!''

That brought a cry from thirty voices, sounding off as one.

''Hoo-rah!''

Korstiaan waited for the echo to subside before he spoke again, his tone more solemn now. ''I know you're all aware,'' he said, ''of what's been happening around Pretoria, Johannesburg and Vereeniging. At least a dozen of our comrades have been slain, with several others gravely wounded. As of now, we still have not identified the men responsible, but they will be found out and punished for their crimes. Some of you may perhaps take part in teaching them their final lesson.''

''Hoo-rah!''

Again he paused, allowing them to simmer in the fury that was running through their veins. ''For now, though,'' Korstiaan told them, ''you must focus on your mission to the absolute exclusion of all else. Your wounded brothers won't be speeded on the way to their recovery by news of failure. Any outcome short of full and total victory will shame the memory of those already lost. Our enemies are gloating now. It is your task, when you meet them tomorrow night, to wipe the damned smiles off their faces and remind them who will always rule South Africa!''

The men were cheering now, their clenched fists

raised. Korstiaan wished that he had brought along a sacrificial kaffir, just to whet their appetite, but it was just as well that he hadn't. This way, there was no mess to tidy up, and they could brood in anger while they traveled north tomorrow, looking forward to the sweet taste of revenge.

When the tumult died down moments later, Korstiaan was ready to dismiss the troops. "You will be sleeping here tonight," he told them. "Cots and toilet facilities are available, also showers. You will be fed, and beer has been provided. Two bottles per man, and no more. I want no hangovers tomorrow. We leave after breakfast. Dismissed!"

They were the best, these men—or, anyway, the best the movement had to offer in South Africa. If pressed upon the matter, Lars Korstiaan would have compared them favorably to the Wehrmacht troops who invaded Poland in 1939 or Russia two years later. Most of them had done a turn of military service prior to joining the Iron Guard, while a handful had been— or were still—policemen. They knew their weapons and tactics, they were solidly committed to the cause and all of them were blooded, albeit without the ultimate test of fighting for their lives in a full-scale pitched battle.

Tomorrow night would be their true baptism of fire, the first step on a forced march to reclaim their homeland from the Jews and kaffirs who had taken over in the so-called peaceful revolution of 1991. Korstiaan had a list of race traitors who had been tried in absentia, sentenced to summary punishment upon capture, and he was looking forward to working his way down the list, beginning with the political trash in Pretoria.

But first things first.

Every explosion needs a spark to set it off, and that was Korstiaan's task, the job assigned to his commandos. In just over twenty-four hours, they would fire the first shots in a long-delayed counterrevolution, and there would be nothing peaceful about it.

South Africa was long overdue for a bloodbath.

And Korstiaan was about to turn the tap.

SOME MORNINGS, Hal Brognola would have sworn the telephone was his worst enemy on Earth. Forget about Augie Marinello, the Talifero brothers, any other mobsters, terrorists or wackos he had grappled with through the years. It all came back to Alexander Graham Bell. The telephone would wear him down and finish him one day, perhaps before too long.

That morning, it had been bad news for breakfast, with a side order of bad news via cell phone on the drive to work and a triple helping of bad news waiting for him at the office, red lights winking on three of his five normal lines. Able Team had hit a snag on its mission of the moment, in Costa Rica. Ditto Phoenix Force in Lebanon. A protected witness had vanished from a federal safehouse in Scranton, Pennsylvania, on the eve of a critical Mob trial, leaving behind his entire wardrobe and some ominous—albeit tiny—bloodstains on his pillow. The DEA was asking for Brognola's help in retrieving two of their top "extraditables"—homicidal twin brothers and cocaine millionaires—from a fortress compound near Yopal, Colombia. The State Department was concerned about snakeheads importing hundreds, maybe thousands, of illegal Chinese into the United States, and Justice feared that some of those were Triad soldiers, others possibly spies for Beijing.

It had the makings of a long, long day…which prompted Hal to groan and mutter choice profanity when the phone rang again and he saw that the incoming call was on his private, outside line.

Not good. In fact, if he was forced to bet…

He scooped up the handset instead. ''Your dime.''

''Make that a rand, and you'd be right,'' Mack Bolan said.

''I'm scrambling,'' Brognola stated.

''Standing by.''

He punched a button on the box attached to his special telephone and waited for the green light to come on. When it was glowing like a tiny traffic signal, he informed his oldest living friend, ''Okay, we're set.''

''I read you five-by-five,'' Bolan confirmed.

''You made it, then,'' the big Fed said, stating the obvious.

''We've got a few things going on,'' Bolan replied. ''The echoes may be reaching you a little later on today.''

''I'll listen for the heads-up. Anything at all about that parcel that was misaddressed?''

Even with the scrambler engaged, he had trouble naming the stolen nuclear warhead. The thought of such a weapon in die-hard neo-Nazi hands put a crimp in his gut and sent chills down his spine.

''Nothing so far,'' the word came back. ''Our pigeon's here somewhere, but nobody we've talked to seems to know a thing about the other deal.''

''You think he sent it somewhere else?'' It was the worst scenario, the nightmare realized.

"It's possible," the Executioner replied. "Too early to be sure of anything right now."

"So, what's the next move?"

"We've got the word out," Bolan told him. "It may take some time to get around. We're lying low today with some of Gellar's contacts, playing wait-and-see. I have some numbers I can check with by and by to see if anybody's biting."

"Just make sure you don't get bitten," Brognola replied.

"That's not the plan."

Of course not, Brognola thought. But how often did the plan work out as detailed on the drawing board? How many times had he and Bolan watched their best-laid schemes unravel like a cheap sweater.

Too damned many times.

"If you need anything..." he started to say, then cut it off. What help could he possibly offer to Bolan and Jacob Gellar in South Africa? It was more than mere distance, placing them halfway around the world from Bolan's support team at Stony Man Farm. There was a simple matter of mechanics, Brognola compelled to work through CIA, which would in turn want a piece of the action—or at least a plausible explanation—before field operatives were committed, and even then, what would he have? How did he know whom to trust in that troubled land, where the races had been locked in mortal combat for more than three centuries?

"I'll call you, sure," Bolan said, letting the big Fed off the hook.

He was good that way, always had been. It was one of his many talents, often overlooked when his ac-

quaintances took inventory. No big thing, perhaps…but no small talent, either.

"About this hideout," Brognola began, taking another tack, "where did you say it was again?"

"I didn't say," Bolan reminded him. "And I don't
know yet. It looks like we're going native for a little
while."

"Is that a good thing?"

"If it keeps us out of Stevens's people and the cops
are canvassing hotels, I'd say it is," Bolan replied.

"You mean the lady's going under, too?"

"She wanted to, but it's counterproductive in her
case. She checked into her hotel alone, with a fairly
decent cover, and anyone who might have recognized
her is long gone. She'd stand out like that sore thumb
everybody talks about, the angle we're pursuing."

"Whereas," Brognola put in, "you and the dude
from Tel Aviv will pass like you've been homeys all
your life. Is that the plan?"

Bolan chuckled at that. "You underestimate my
sense of rhythm."

"Well, excuse me all to hell," Brognola said. "I
didn't know you'd started watching *Soul Train*."

"Careful, chief. Someone'll have you up on
charges, you keep making jokes like that."

"My luck, they still won't fire me," Brognola
groused. "So, anyway, you keep in touch, all right?"

"Will do," Bolan replied, "as soon as I know
something."

"Even if you don't," Brognola said.

"Okay. You've got a deal."

The line went dead, the scrambler clicking off as
soon as he was disconnected, red light winking at him

until Brognola cradled the receiver, whereupon it switched off automatically.

"Going native," he muttered to himself, unaware that he was scowling. "Whose idea was that, I'd like to know."

Not that it mattered now. The decision had to be Bolan's and Bolan's alone. It might sound like madness to Brognola, sitting in his Washington office, a world away from the racially divided pressure cooker of South Africa, but he could have said the same— hell, he *had* said the same—about any number of Bolan's strategic choices through the years. Some of them were merely risky; others read like a blueprint for suicide the hard way, in the worst of all possible worlds.

But the damned guy was still alive, still out there on the firing line, in hot pursuit of yet another predatory scumbag. It had become almost impossible for him to picture Bolan any other way—like in a coffin, for example. Rotting in the ground.

Almost impossible...except in dreams.

"You'd better not get wasted over there," he told the brooding, silent room. "You'd damned well better not."

CHAPTER NINE

South Africa

South Africa's system of black townships dates from 1954, when the infamous Natives Resettlement Act evicted fifty-seven thousand Africans from Johannesburg ghettos, transporting them to the all-black reservations of Meadowlands and Diepkloof, ten miles southwest of the city proper. Overwhelmingly opposed to the move, Africans were herded aboard military trains at gunpoint, their ouster from Johannesburg deemed such a great success that the Sophiatown neighborhood, once cleared of blacks, was promptly renamed Triomf—or Triumph—by the white regime in power. Henceforth, no blacks would be allowed to remain in any urban area for more than seventy-two consecutive hours, without specific documents proving employment at the same location for a ten-year minimum. Violation of these laws, openly patterned on the anti-Jewish statutes of Hitler's Germany, meant imposition of a stiff prison term.

The downfall of apartheid in 1991 had swept such draconian laws from the books in South Africa, but many natives still remained in rural townships, for the same reason that many African Americans haven't purchased homes in Malibu, Beverly Hills or Miami Beach: they couldn't afford the asking price. Conversely, while no laws mandating racial segregation survived in the new South Africa, it was unheard of for whites, however destitute, to settle in the black townships. They weren't welcome there, both races openly acknowledging the fact.

There was a heavy-duty risk involved, therefore, when Mitane Selepa suggested that Bolan and Jacob Gellar should take refuge in the all-black township of Moseto, midway between Jo'burg and Pretoria, in the wake of their recent blitzkrieg. Selepa acknowledged the danger, including a threat of betrayal by residents of the township who supplemented their meager income, as in the old apartheid era, by serving as paid police informers.

"We take good care of spies," Selepa said once they were on the road, "but some always around. A man who sells his soul learns how to hide his true face from the people, sure."

"This may not be the best idea we've had today," Gellar remarked, a sour expression on his face.

"Tha's not a thing to worry 'bout," Selepa said, wearing his trademark grin. "We have a family waiting, very trusty. We be fine as long as no one see us going in."

That sounded dangerously iffy to Bolan, but he kept his concerns to himself for the moment. Selepa had not steered them wrong so far, and there was certainly no reason to suspect that he was setting them up for an ambush now. If worse came to worst, they still had their weapons, the ability to use them and at least a decent fighting chance.

The drive north from Johannesburg was uneventful.

Bolan rode in back, with Gellar in the shotgun seat, beside Selepa. Twice along the way, they passed police patrol cars, but the officers—two white and two black; with no mixture in the cars apparently—didn't give them a second glance. To any casual observer, they were simply two well-dressed white men with a black chauffeur, en route from Jo'burg to the capital, perhaps on some business of state.

Except, of course, that they wouldn't be going to Pretoria.

There were no patrol cars in sight when Mitane Selepa turned off the main highway, following a narrow gravel road that led across scrub desert spotted with thorny acacia trees, toward a smudge on the horizon that he took to be Moseto. Anyone of either race observing them would certainly have had his curiosity aroused by their change of direction, since white visits to Moseto almost invariably meant trouble with the law.

When they had traveled several miles along the gravel road, their destination assuming more positive form in the shape of clustered shanty houses showing faint lights in the dusk, with several larger buildings and three ancient-looking water tanks mounted on stilts, Selepa braked the Range Rover and turned to his companions as the trailing cloud of dust caught up with them.

"You both lie down now," he instructed them, "and try stay out of sight."

"Will there be guards?" Bolan inquired.

"Moseto is not guarded, but it is observed," their driver said. "Most of the people, I can trust. Some, I cannot. The problem is deciding which are who, you see? Two white men in Moseto cause much talk regardless, anyway. Tha's mostly why you hide. Stop gossip, just in case."

"You're saying there are people in Moseto who would help the Iron Guard?" Gellar asked.

Selepa shook his head. "Not purposely, I think. But some do talk to the police, for certain, and who knows where it may go from there?"

If nothing else, Bolan thought, two white strangers hiding in Moseto would be instant suspects for the series of attacks on neo-Nazis in the neighborhood. That bit of news alone would be enough to draw a flying squad of uniforms, complete with armored vehicles, machine guns, tear gas, snipers—many of them veterans from the old regime who still harbored fears of a not so peaceful revolution in the works.

He lay on the seat, nothing to cover him, but from the glimpse he had had of the settlement ahead, watchers spying from second- or third- story windows wouldn't be a problem. The houses were small, one-story structures, with three- or four-room models qualifying as substantial homes. Many were even smaller, one- or two-room shanties with free-standing privies nearby.

Gellar had noted the latter buildings at first glance, and now he asked, from his huddled place beneath the dashboard, "Is there running water in the town?"

"No running water," Selepa replied. "We have the water towers and communal wells."

"As for the, er, plumbing—" Gellar began.

"No worries," said their driver with a sparkling laugh. "You gentlemen won't have to go outside. We give you chamber pots!"

Johannesburg was looking better by the minute,

even with its legion of police and neo-Nazis hunting those responsible for the attacks on the Iron Guard, but he wouldn't insult Selepa by suggesting that they turn around and head back to the city, where flush toilets were taken for granted. They had agreed to cool off in Moseto, and he wasn't prepared to ditch the plan on grounds of personal comfort. He could live without a shower for a day or two, no problem. Anything he found here in Moseto, Bolan had seen worse, experienced more-primitive conditions in his time.

And still, he had to wonder: how and why did people live like this? Why did the revolution take three hundred years? And why on earth was it peaceful?

The answer to his final question was undoubtedly a testimony to Nelson Mandela and the human spirit. As for the rest...well, Bolan was a soldier, not an armchair philosopher. And he was here to fight, not write a history of human response to injustice.

Stay focused, he cautioned himself. Stay alive.

The car stopped several moments later, more dust settling as Selepa switched off the engine. A door banged, somewhere close at hand, and Bolan was cupping the butt of his Czech AT-2000 automatic when Selepa hissed, "Quickly now! Into the house, before someone comes!"

MARILYN CROUDER CHAFED at being left behind, but she couldn't complain. For one thing, it would do no earthly good. And for another, there was no one for her to complain *to* at the moment, since she didn't have a clue where Mike Belasko and his sidekick from Mossad had gone.

She hated hiding out in the hotel suite, like some effete celebrity dodging troublesome paparazzi, but it was still an improvement, Crouder realized, over running the streets in a strange city, hunted like an animal and fighting for her life.

How did Belasko do it, day after day, job after job? How many men had he killed? How many times had he felt the reaper's shadow fall across him, linger for a moment, then move on?

How many more times could he pull it off?

That train of thought was agitating her, so Crouder switched tracks, focusing once more on her irritation at being cut out of the loop. This whole damned fighting tour of the world had begun with her assignment to infiltrate the Temple of the Nordic Covenant and bust the cult, if possible, for federal crimes involving outlawed weapons and explosives. She had gleaned enough hearsay information to convince herself there was more at stake than simple gunrunning, but her cover had been blown before she could collect enough hard evidence to make a case in court.

Enter Mike Belasko.

He had saved her life more than once, and she had repaid the favor in Chicago—as if that kind of debt could ever truly be wiped off the slate. She wanted to do more, but it was clear to Marilyn that she was out of her element, had been since they left the States, little more than a squeaky fifth wheel on the soldier's private juggernaut.

So go home, then, she thought.

But she wouldn't. Crouder knew that, as surely as she knew her own name. She had booked through to the end of the line, even if it meant riding in the baggage car and catching only fragmentary glimpses of the passing countryside.

It's wasn't a pleasure trip, she told herself. It wasn't a honeymoon.

And where the hell did that come from?

Crouder knew enough of the world and the business of danger to mistrust her present feelings for Belasko, as muddled and confusing as they were. He was a handsome, virile man, most excellent in bed, but she had been through situations vaguely similar to this one in the past, as well. She knew that men and women thrown together in high-pressure situations often sought the quick-fix comfort of meaningless sex. *Casual* might not be the right word, since the circumstances were typically hectic, even perilous, but no long-term attachment was generally sought or expected.

It had nothing to do with love.

So, what was it she felt for the man who had twice saved her life?

There was gratitude, of course. A measure of embarrassment, perhaps, that she, a trained professional, had needed a stranger's help in the first place. There was certainly attraction and arousal, at some primitive level that almost reminded her of puberty. Raw lust, that would be, and Crouder knew enough not to trust it any further than she could throw the chest of drawers in her hotel room.

But there was something more, as well.

She admired Belasko, no bones about it—and that was something of a surprise to her, given his take-no-prisoners approach to solving problems. His tactics had more in common with guerrilla warfare than they did with law enforcement, and while the method had put her off at first, Crouder was amazed at how quickly she had fallen into step with his technique, discarding her training and by-the-book ethics as deftly as a reptile sheds its skin.

Long months of undercover work could do that to you.

So could torture, rape and being marked for death by neo-Nazi lunatics.

She had done enough, while they were still chasing Gary Stevens and Sean Fletcher in the States, to warrant prosecution for abuse of her lawful authority, perhaps reckless endangerment of civilians, maybe manslaughter or even murder two. She would plead self-defense, of course, against a charge of homicide, maybe throw in some kind of diminished-capacity defense, based on all she had suffered at the hands of Nordic Temple zealots. The abduction and rape alone would probably convince most female jurors to acquit, while certain men would probably admire her courage, maybe even enjoy a vicarious thrill from the idea of kicking neo-Nazi ass.

But it would never come to that, she thought.

The Feds weren't about to charge one of their own in a muddled, bloodstained case like this, if they could help it. Not with lingering memories of Ruby Ridge and Waco still fresh in so many minds across the country, from Capitol Hill to your average local jury box. Who needed more publicity like that, to start the new millennium?

Not ATF, that was for damned sure.

The prelims would drag on for months, the trial for months longer, with reporters dissecting every line of testimony, filing lawsuits under the Freedom of Information Act to fill in the back story. It would be a media nightmare for the men who had given her the assignment to start with, then cut her adrift when the whole thing got too hot to handle.

So, Crouder was covered in that respect, the legal angle pretty well nailed down. Now all she had to do was figure out what to do with the rest of her life, once the job was finally done.

Not so fast, she cautioned herself.

The first thing she would have to do was get back home alive.

And at the moment, that was far from being guaranteed.

MITANE SELEPA HAD considered the risks before he suggested that his white companions seek refuge in Moseto. There was no longer any law against their being there, no penalty for whites cohabiting with Africans, but their presence in the current circumstances would undoubtedly provoke suspicion, and that alone was enough for police to detain and question the strangers. That, in turn, would mean exposure to their enemies and almost certain death.

Still, Selepa had decided it was worth the risk, and both of his companions had agreed. If they were taken now, it would be his fault as much as anyone else's, at least in his mind, and he would share the burden of guilt.

If they were found by the Iron Guard, no doubt Selepa would share the punishment of death, as well.

But they would have to take him first. He wouldn't go without a fight.

As hosts for his companions and himself, Selepa had chosen the Ushante family, consisting of Moses and his wife Niala. They were older folk, fifty-something, with two grown children off in their own lives, and both had been political in their day. Moses had served three years in prison for distributing pamphlets from Nelson Mandela's African National Congress, and he had suffered inside, at the hands of white guards and black traitors alike. Somehow, the experience hadn't embittered him against all whites or humankind in general, but he remained steadfast in opposition to the paramilitary racists who campaigned for restoration of the old regime.

Moses Ushante had consulted his wife before agreeing to shelter Selepa and his Caucasian associates—it was, after all, her home as much as it was his—but Niala had raised no objection. Her children had begun to prosper under the new coalition government, without apartheid's weight to hold them down, and she knew only too well what a return to the bad old days would mean. Even if the Iron Guard and its allies failed in their ultimate objective, there was bound to be blood, and native Africans had always been the first to suffer in such outbreaks, the first to die.

Selepa parked his car beside the Ushante home, well back from the dusty street, and checked as best he could to make sure that no one was watching before he gave the signal for his passengers to make their move. They bolted from the car, duffel bags clanking, and slipped in through the back door of the house, where Moses welcomed them with handshakes, an embrace for Selepa.

"Welcome, my brother," he said.

Niala joined them in the kitchen, smiling tentatively, seeming a trifle surprised when the white men extended their hands to shake hers. It made her giggle, almost like a schoolgirl, shaking hands first with one, then the other.

"We appreciate your kindness," Jacob Gellar told them both. "However, if you're having second thoughts and feel there's too much risk—"

"No, no," Moses Ushante said. "You stay the night, at least. Let the Iron Guard run 'round in circles yet a while. They need the exercise."

"Fat bottoms, them," Selepa said, grinning as he slapped his buttocks with an open palm. "They sit too much and dream about how great the old days be."

The tall American was silent, smiled politely, something obviously on his mind. He glanced around the house, as if already planning his defense against assailants who—so far, at least—existed only in his mind.

The Ushantes were well-off by Moseto standards, both employed in Johannesburg, with the occasional contribution from their children to help out around the house. Their home had four rooms, one of which—a kind of den for Moses, now the boys were out and on their own—had been set aside for their guests, with sleeping bags rolled up in one corner. The rest of the layout included a master bedroom, the kitchen, and the parlor where a black-and-white TV set occupied a central place of pride. The house was spotless, well maintained, a monument to Niala's energy and thrift. There was much worse to be seen in Moseto, Selepa knew from personal experience, but it didn't intrude within these walls.

He hoped it never would.

The Ushantes understood the risk they were taking by sheltering strangers who, if not precisely fugitives just yet, would certainly be sought by the police, if they could only be identified. No reference to the particulars was necessary or expected. If they were caught harboring felons, there would be jail time involved for both of them—and that would be nothing next to the Iron Guard's inevitable retribution.

Taking in the strangers, then, was more than a simple act of kindness or political solidarity. It was an example of near heroic courage.

Selepa had impressed that on his two companions, to the point that they had both resisted coming to Moseto. Having done his job too well, Selepa then had been required to state the obvious: that native Africans had never felt truly safe in South Africa since the first Boers arrived, and little enough had changed since 1991 to make them feel any more secure. Apartheid's statutes and the hated passbooks were gone, but violence remained a harrowing fact of daily life, raising the specter of general bloodshed with each new incident.

It would only take the proper spark, Selepa knew, to set his homeland ablaze.

And the smoke from burning corpses would blot out the sun.

LARS KORSTIAAN DOZED as they drove north from Durban, enjoying dark and bloody dreams. They weren't nightmares, which imply unhappiness or dread. Rather, his dreams were littered with black corpses, lying underneath a pall of battle smoke. He strode across the killing field in triumph, laughing, spreading death and misery among his foes.

A blaring horn jarred Korstiaan from his dream. His eyes snapped open to behold an urban scene, with traffic heavy on the streets. Some of the cars were dusty, others old and battered.

"Where are we?" he asked the trooper seated next to him, a young man with a buzz cut and dark glasses.

"Just entering Bethlehem, sir," the young soldier replied.

"Jesus Christ," Korstiaan muttered, the young man at his side nodding and chuckling.

"That's a good one, sir," the trooper said appreciatively.

It took Korstiaan another long moment to appreciate his own wit. In fact, he had simply been cursing in frustration. They were less than halfway to their target, and he was already stiff from the road, feeling the achy tightness begin in his neck and the small of his back. He knew he should get up and walk around the bus, stretch his legs a bit, but he decided it could wait.

He had all day.

They would be stopping for fuel and food in Kroonstad, another two hours or so up the road. The next town of any size after that would be Vereeniging, scene of the National Renaissance Party's recent loss and humiliation at the hands of unknown enemies. Beyond that lay Johannesburg, and then their target.

It would be full dark before they reached their destination, just as planned.

The night would shelter them and give them the advantage of surprise.

The men were out of uniform today, their night garb and weapons safely hidden in the cargo bays of their respective buses, in case something went unaccountably wrong and they were stopped by the police for some vehicular infraction. It felt strange, traveling to battle in civilian clothes, unarmed, but there would be ample time to change and arm themselves when they reached their destination. Meanwhile, to anyone who asked, they were a group of football fans en route to watch their Durban favorites perform against a team of British wankers in Pretoria. It was a cover story that would stand, because there really *was* a game that night, with thousands of fans expected from Durban to watch.

The story would hold...unless someone got nosy and found their mobile arsenal.

In which case, Korstiaan knew, there would be hell to pay.

He respected the police—white officers, at least—as much as the next terrorist, but Korstiaan wasn't about to see this mission fail at the last moment, before he could lead his troops into battle. He wouldn't have that stigma of failure attached to his name. If it came down to the choice of a policeman's life or ultimate success, the choice would be an easy one to make.

The strike team leader checked his watch and thought it might be nice to sleep some more if he could recapture the dream that had been so rudely interrupted. Korstiaan often dreamed of killing blacks, though he had only done so twice in waking life. The first time was an accident, drunk driving on the way home from an Iron Guard meeting, though he talked it up and let his comrades think it was deliberate. Despite initial fears, there had been no investigation worthy of the term, which had surprised him, with the new regime in power, elevating blacks above their betters when and where it could.

The second time Korstiaan killed a black man, it had been deliberate, a shooting set up as a kind of graduation exercise, to test his worthiness for elevation in the ranks. The ''victim,'' as they called him in the Jew-owned kaffir-loving newspaper, had been a lawyer in the African community who sued policemen, bus drivers and any other whites whom he regarded as behaving disrespectfully toward blacks. Although he lost as many as three-quarters of his cases, he was still a menace and an enemy of every Aryan alive. Removing him had been a service to the master race...but it had still required a few stiff drinks beforehand, just to steady Korstiaan's aim.

This night would be his first time killing sober. He had vowed to bring no liquor on the road trip and to ban his troops from drinking, too. Dutch courage, as the booze was sometimes called, could breed mistakes. He would prefer his soldiers nervous but alert rather than cocky and oblivious to danger.

Sleep eluded him, and Korstiaan finally gave it up. He might feel more relaxed after the Kroonstad stop— or maybe not. It made no difference, either way, as far as Korstiaan was concerned. He knew that he would be alert tonight, when it mattered.

When he was on the firing line.

This night there would be no accidents or clandestine back-alley ambushes. This would be full-dress combat with an enemy force of superior size, albeit inferior training and arms. Korstiaan would prove himself. When the revolution's history was written, his name would be there in black and white, if only in a footnote.

Lars Korstiaan smiled and wondered if his parents would be proud.

THE NATIVE TOWNSHIP was a different sort of place after nightfall. Darkness helped conceal some landmarks of the settlement's near ubiquitous poverty, but it also drove many people indoors, seeking shelter in their homes, however meager those might be. Cooking smells mingled on the night breeze, and stray dogs prowled freely through the streets, but human wanderers were few and far between.

The vanishing act confused Jacob Gellar, and he decided to ask their hosts about it, when they sat down to deep bowls of delicious stew made with meat of indeterminate origin. As it happened, Bolan beat him to it.

"You roll up the sidewalks around here after dark," the American said with a smile.

"Sidewalks?" Niala Ushante seemed confused.

"Roll up?" her husband asked.

Gellar seized the opportunity to play interpreter. "He means that it is very quiet in the township after nightfall. I suppose we both expected more in terms of people being out and about on the streets."

The Ushantes shared a glance before Moses replied. "Tomorrow is another working day for many here," he said. "They need their sleep, you understand." He hesitated, as if deciding whether he should let it go at that. After a long moment, he added, "And there is the monster."

"Moses!" His wife looked aghast, raising a spotless napkin to her lips.

"Monster?" Bolan queried, frowning.

"The Monster of Moseto," Moses said. "Oh, not the kind you see in motion films from Hollywood. This monster is a man of flesh and blood, though he behaves as if a demon owns his soul."

"Some kind of criminal?" Gellar asked.

"A rapist and killer of women," Moses replied. "He has already nineteen victims in the past two years. He does fearful damage to the bodies. The authorities will not discuss it, but I have a friend who found—"

"Moses!" Niala's voice cut through his narrative, silencing her husband before he could describe whatever it was his friend had discovered.

"A serial killer," Bolan remarked.

"So the police have said," Moses replied. "Dr. Pistorius draws profiles of the monster in Pretoria. She talks to agents from the FBI. It makes no difference."

It was Selepa's turn to interrupt. "Some say," he interjected, "that the monster is a witch doctor, practicing *muti*." Blank looks from Gellar and Bolan prompted him to explain. "In *muti*, certain body parts are taken to make—"

"Mitane, that's enough!" Niala Ushante's voice was like a whiplash, taking control. "We do not speak about such evil business over food. You should know this!"

As if the people of Moseto didn't already have enough trouble, Gellar thought. He wanted to hear more about the case, but didn't wish to cause dissension or anger their hostess. This wasn't the first time police had been stymied by a psychopath, particularly in a poor community where some manhunters had little interest in—or sympathy for—the inhabitants. It was better to forget about the so-called monster and concentrate on their own immediate concerns.

Like the Iron Guard, for instance.

Like the Temple of the Nordic Covenant and a missing nuclear warhead.

He was about to ask another question, working his way back to politics in a general way, when a sudden, bloodcurdling scream tore through the night outside.

Gellar and Bolan instinctively reached for their concealed side arms, while Mitane Selepa bolted to his feet, clutching the knife he had been using to slice a loaf of homemade bread. Moses and Niala Ushante exchanged another glance, this one fearful, and breathed a single word in unison.

"Monster!"

The scream had come from somewhere close at hand, perhaps from the general direction of the nearby communal showers. Gellar was on his feet, one hand on his Czech autoloader, when Moses Ushante rose before him, stretching out a cautionary hand.

"You must not show yourselves," he said, reminding them. "There are no white men here."

"Sounds like someone's in trouble," Bolan said.

"It is our trouble," Moses told him. "Ours to live with, ours to solve."

So saying, he turned from the dining table and brushed past his wife, ignoring her whispered plea for him to wait, linger, stay. Moses Ushante took a long walking staff or cudgel from the corner where it stood beside their old refrigerator, and moved toward the back door of his house. Outside, there were new voices raised in the darkness, shouting questions, maybe curses from the sound of it, though Gellar could not understand a single word.

"What's happening?" he asked Selepa, as their guide and driver rose, apparently to follow Moses outside.

"They hunt the monster," Selepa replied. "He has struck again."

"One thing." Gellar detained Selepa with a strong hand on his arm. "This monster—what's his choice of weapons?"

"No one knows for certain," Selepa said, "because the ones who see him don't be talking after that. An ax, some say, or maybe panga—what you call machete."

"So," Bolan said, "Moses is going up against this psycho, with a stick against a blade?"

"I don't much like the odds, myself," Gellar replied, starting to smile.

"He has help, though," Bolan said.

"It hasn't done much good, so far."

"We really shouldn't," the American went on.

"I totally agree."

"So, are you coming with me or what?"

The gruff Israeli broke into a full-fledged smile.

"I thought you'd never ask," he said.

CHAPTER TEN

Lars Korstiaan stood aside and watched his soldiers finish suiting up, buckling on their combat webbing in the darkness, cocking weapons with the metallic click-clack sound of giant insects gnashing jaws and pincers in a science-fiction film. The buses sat with engines idling, bleeding diesel fumes, their lights switched off, shadows bulking in the night like darkened bunkers with indeterminate machinery grumbling away inside.

Korstiaan kept his voice down as he spoke to his assembled troops, no shouting to warn the enemy in their warren of shacks and shanties. The strike force had stopped a half mile short of its objective to proceed on foot, and thus insure the critical advantage of surprise that would be lost if they had gone ahead by motorcade.

They would be marching over unfamiliar ground, but only to a point. Each member of the team had studied aerial photographs and memorized his own position in the skirmish line that would advance upon Moseto under cover of darkness. There should be no great surprises, no gullies or fences unforeseen, no posted sentries in these days of ''peace'' and ''reconciliation.''

"Every man alert now!" Korstiaan whispered as he moved along the line, reviewing his troops for the last time before they engaged the enemy. "Remember that your only friends from this point on are those who wear this uniform," he said, slapping his chest. "The rest are targets. Big or small, young or old—all targets!"

There was no dissent from the ranks; he had expected none. These men were specially chosen, hand-picked for this mission that would finally open the flood gates and unleash the longed-for racial holy war. There would be no forgiveness, no reconciliation with the kaffirs after this night's work was done. And when the other hit team struck the following day, when they scored their coup, the ticking time bomb that had been South Africa these past ten years would finally explode.

And when the smoke cleared, days or weeks from now, the master race would once again be in control.

"All ready, then?"

No answer from the troops as they stood mute, their weapons poised.

"Advance!"

Lars Korstiaan led the way through no-man's-land. There was no lagging back for him, no hiding with the rear guard, much less waiting with the buses for his pointman to report contact. Whatever happened next, he would be there to see it, feel it, smell it, taste it.

What happened next—at least initially—turned out to be an uneventful march across the open plain that separated Korstiaan's troops from the light-speckled mass of Moseto township. Two or three of his soldiers stumbled on rocks or rat holes along the way, but they resisted the temptation to curse, recovered without breaking ranks. They made no sound beyond the crunch of boot heels on the desert hardpan underfoot, advancing steadily. They were prepared to open fire if challenged, but there was no challenge from the target as they closed the gap.

Korstiaan picked up on the smell of cooking from a quarter mile, a bit surprised to find that there was nothing strange or repugnant about it. Revulsion kicked in moments later, wrinkling his Aryan nose, as the reek of sewage wafted to his nostrils on the cool night breeze.

That was more like it, he thought. Filthy kaffirs!

Korstiaan didn't stop to consider what members of the master race might smell like, huddled together for decades on end in a primitive village, without plumbing or other sanitary facilities. It was beyond his capacity to draw such connections, to imagine such eventualities. His mind sought simple answers that confirmed and reinforced his prejudice; all else was "propaganda" spread about by Jews and Communists.

So far, so good, he thought as they crossed the quarter-mile mark, advancing steadily toward their target. On arrival in the township proper, his thirty-man squad would break up into four teams, three with eight men each and one with seven. They would fan out through the narrow streets, leaving fire and death in their wake, inflicting the maximum possible damage on their savage enemies before it was time to withdraw.

He had allotted half an hour for the strike, from start to finish. It was ample time, and while they had already dropped the telephone lines that served Moseto, there was still a possibility that someone in the township might possess a two-way radio, with which they could alert police to the assault in progress. By allowing thirty minutes on the ground to hunt at will, plus time for their retreat, Korstiaan had calculated that they should be on the road again and well away before patrol cars could arrive, either from Jo'burg or Pretoria.

That was, assuming any of the coppers cared enough to come at all.

And if they didn't come, so much the better. It only meant that more of the wounded would die.

They were a hundred yards from contact when a shrill, unearthly scream tore through the nearly silent darkness. Korstiaan froze in his tracks, holding on point like a trained hunting dog, his troops halting en masse behind him. Behind the scream came shouting voices, male and female, more lights coming on in houses that were previously dark.

Now, what the hell...?

Was this some kind of an alert? Or were the kaffirs merely partaking of some heathen ritual, perhaps including human sacrifice? Korstiaan had read of such things, but understood that proof in modern times remained elusive.

All the better then, if he and his soldiers could catch the kaffirs at it and reveal them for the brutes they truly were!

"Forward at the double!" he snapped to his soldiers. "After me, men!"

THE SCREAM, as it turned out, had issued from a narrow lane behind Moses Ushante's home. Its source, a young woman in her late teens or early twenties, streaked past Bolan and Gellar in a panting sprint, so frightened that she failed to note the two white men as she passed by.

"This way," Bolan said, retracing her steps. Gellar followed closely behind him, while the racket of what sounded like a lynch mob forming echoed from the next street over, keeping pace in the same general direction.

"This looks bad," Gellar suggested, as they hurried onward. "One good look at us, and that lot could decide that we're the monster."

"I don't plan on meeting them," the Executioner replied.

"I hope you're right," Gellar replied. "I'd rather that we didn't have to open fire on them ourselves."

Bolan was blotting out that ugly mental image when he came around a corner, found himself behind a long, low structure built from cinder blocks, with a roof of corrugated tin. A water tower loomed above it, at the north end, and he recognized the building as a public shower.

There, in the building's shadow that was darker than dark, screened from the meager light of the new moon, he made out two human figures. One lay crumpled on the ground; the other hulked above, stooped at first, recoiling and straightening to full height as the newcomers arrived. In one of the upright figure's hands, a long-bladed machete dripped crimson; in the other, a melon-shaped object did likewise, suspended by hair from the mute slayer's fist.

At the sight of them, the monster snarled—a low, almost inhuman sound—and pitched the severed head of his latest victim overhand. Bolan ducked, felt something wet and warm spatter his cheek in passing and couldn't suppress a fleeting thought about the prevalence of AIDS in sub-Saharan Africa. He had no time to brood upon the problem, though, because the panga-wielding hulk was charging at them now, blade raised high to deliver a death blow as soon as he came within range.

Bolan and Gellar fired together, five rounds, stopping the hulk in his tracks and dropping him onto his backside, a dazed expression written on his dying face. Both of their pistols were sound suppressed, which made the sudden echo of gunfire that much more startling.

It was automatic rifle fire, he recognized, and submachine guns.

A short block to the west, there were more shouts raised now, but the tone had radically altered. The would-be hunting party had been instantly diverted from its primary object, by the sound of things, and was lapsing rapidly from outrage into something more akin to panic.

"Can it be?" Jacob Gellar asked as they stood above the lifeless Monster of Moseto.

Bolan didn't have to ask what Gellar meant by "it." Short of an all-out civil war within the township proper, the echo of automatic weapons could only mean an attack from outside. And that, in turn, would most likely come from one source.

"The Iron Guard," Bolan said aloud, as if spoken words were required to make it real.

"We need more guns," Gellar remarked.

"You read my mind."

They left the Monster of Moseto and his victim there together, lying in the shadows, to be found by someone else when the smoke cleared. The scene would either speak for itself or it wouldn't; in either case, Bolan and Gellar had more-pressing matters with which to concern themselves than a dead psychopath and the victim of his rage who was beyond all earthly help.

There were other enemies abroad in Moseto, armed with worse tools than a panga.

They rushed back together through the darkness toward Moses Ushante's house, smelling cordite on the wind now, hearing cries that spoke of pain as much as fear or confusion. The battle was on, and first blood had already been spilled. Behind the voices shouting in Swahili, more were audible, barking orders and curses in Afrikaans.

No question now. It was the Iron Guard, come to call.

"How did they find us?" Gellar wondered aloud, as they entered the silent house of their hosts.

"I doubt they did," Bolan replied. "This sounds like something else."

"A random strike, then?"

"Or the start of something bigger," Bolan said. "Whatever, we can talk it over on the other side."

"Agreed."

They found their hardware, armed themselves and in another moment they were back out on the street, pausing to seek direction. It was difficult, because the firing seemed to come from everywhere at once now, all across the dark sweep of the town.

"They've split up," Gellar said.

"Sounds like."

"So, it's catch as catch can, then."

"Suits me," Bolan said.

"I'll see you afterward, God willing."

Bolan flashed a smile as he turned away, telling Gellar, "I'll take all the help I can get."

JACOB GELLAR HAD acquired his AKSU assault rifle days earlier, when he and Bolan were still hunting neo-Nazis in Eastern Europe, a long world away from South Africa. The little weapon had seen some hard use in those days, but it had served him well and was still in good condition, cocked and fully loaded as he moved along a dark and suddenly deserted street in the township of Moseto, following the transient sounds of combat.

No, he thought. Correct that.

The noises echoing across Moseto sounded less like battle, with the implication of a two-sided contest, than like the sounds of a massacre in progress. Automatic weapons prevailed, with the occasional random pop-pop of other small-arms fire, twice punctuated by the crash of explosions that Gellar was as yet unable to explain. He reckoned some of the Moseto residents were armed, legally or otherwise, but he had no reason to believe their homes were stocked with military hardware. Likewise, all the screams and cries of anguish he had heard so far were torn from native voices, indicating that the mayhem was still distinctly one-sided.

Gellar meant to balance those odds if he could, as soon as possible.

A burst of gunfire only one or two blocks to the north drew him in that direction, traveling through alleys where he could, ignoring the stench of uncollected garbage that mingled with the reek of dog and cat feces. Gellar didn't have a clue what he was stepping into, and he didn't care. He could replace a pair of shoes, but he might never have another chance like this to bleed his Iron Guard enemies.

He saw the first squad coming as he cleared the alley, ducking back at once to keep from being seen. He counted seven of them, all in black except their faces, which were neither painted nor masked. A certain arrogance there, he decided—the bastards didn't care if they were seen, because they either didn't plan on leaving anyone alive, or else didn't believe police would care enough about black deaths to call sketch artists in. All things considered, they were probably correct on the second count, and that knowledge made Gellar bare his teeth in a snarl as he edged back toward the sidewalk, clutching his rifle in white-knuckled hands.

Seven soldiers, five of them with automatic rifles, the other two packing submachine guns that resembled Uzis. He would need a bloody miracle to drop all seven of them with a single burst, the odds so long against it that he judged it practically impossible. That meant he had to pick and choose his targets, and he marked the nearest pair as the first to go, since their proximity made them more dangerous, and they were walking fairly close together, in defiance of normal military discipline. The others would be startled when he opened fire, presumably scattering in search of cover, but if he could drop these two with his first rounds...

Gellar waited, afraid to lean far out and track their approach, unwilling to expose himself before it was time to cut loose. He counted the seconds, listened to the sound of their approaching footsteps and offered up a prayer that they wouldn't be joined by any more neo-Nazis before he opened fire.

Another second, now...

One more...

He swung around the corner, leveling his weapon at the soldiers who were now no more than fifteen paces distant. As he squeezed the trigger, Gellar swung the AKSU's muzzle from left to right, sweeping across his moving targets with a spray of 5.45 mm slugs.

It took perhaps a second and a half, which meant that roughly half the contents of his AKSU's 30-round magazine had been expended, firing at a cyclic rate of some 800 rounds per minute. The reward, as he ducked back into the alley's darkness, was a cry of pain and the scuffle of boot soles on dirt, as the unwounded soldiers dodged and ran for cover.

They were calling back and forth to one another now, in Afrikaans, probably asking if anyone had glimpsed a muzzle-flash in the darkness. Gellar used that momentary confusion against them, leaning out to check his score.

Streetlights were as rare as rich men in Moseto, but there was enough errant moonlight to show him two forms lying crumpled in the street. One lay unmoving, facedown, while the other thrashed weakly, muttering in his pain and/or delirium, heels scrabbling at the dirt as if he hoped to rise to try the game again.

Game over.

The others had begun returning fire, albeit without a clear target, extrapolating range and direction from the posture of their fallen comrades. Gellar could have left them to it, gone in search of other prey, but he was bent on stopping these raiders here and now, while he still had the chance.

A distraction was required, and he had the perfect thing.

Detaching an antipersonnel grenade from his belt, Gellar hooked the pin loose with his thumb and side-armed the lethal green egg into the street downrange. He had no realistic hope of wounding any adversaries with the unaimed pitch, but that wasn't his goal. This time he would be satisfied with smoke and noise.

Five seconds from the toss, detonation brought him out from cover with shrapnel still singing through the air. There was moonlight enough for Gellar to see one of his enemies just struggling erect, from where he had fallen prone on the pavement. The neo-Nazi was retrieving his weapon when Gellar shot him in the face, a 3- or 4-round burst that punched him backward, nearly headless as he hit the deck.

That left four, and Gellar was regretting his failure to reload the Kalashnikov as two more emerged from the smoky darkness, firing as they came. They had a rough fix on his muzzle-flash, but their initial bursts were hasty, high and wide. Gellar dropped to a crouch as they tried to correct, nailing the shooter on his left with a rising burst that spun the man around like a dervish, dumping him in a heap.

The other had his fix now, but self-preservation made the neo-Nazi duck and weave, thereby spoiling his aim. The next rounds were closer, one of them plucking lightly at Gellar's sleeve, but the Mossad agent fought the urge to recoil, holding steady as he triggered another short burst. The neo-Nazi staggered, cried out as he fell, raising a puff of dust from the dry, unpaved street where he touched down.

Two left, and where the hell were they?

Gellar had to wait only a heartbeat for the answer to that question as the two surviving raiders broke from cover. They were several yards apart, converging on their target, firing as they came. He flinched involuntarily from bullets spitting dirt and gravel in his face, rolling and firing, then repeating the maneuver, praying for a hit.

That prayer was answered with the nearer of the two assailants, the last rounds from his AK magazine ripping through the Nazi's legs and dropping him in a headlong sprawl. Then Gellar's weapon was empty, incoming rounds still chewing the earth around him, giving him no time to reload.

He left the AKSU, rolling once more to his right, the movement allowing him to reach his pistol in the fast-draw shoulder rig. Its double-action mechanism was smooth on the first shot, barely shifting his aim as he sighted on the looming bulk of his would-be assassin.

Two rounds...three...four...the last of them fired at nearly point-blank range, before the running figure stumbled, slumped to his knees, then pitched forward onto his face.

The neo-Nazi didn't stir, but there was still unfinished business with his comrade who was only wounded in the legs, cursing and straining to reach the R-5 carbine he had dropped when he fell. Gellar beat him to it, closing the gap between them in four long strides and triggering a pistol shot into the neo-Nazi's skull, behind one ear.

All done.

He retrieved the AKSU, replaced its empty magazine with a fresh one and chambered a live round as he went in search of more fascists to kill.

KORSTIAAN HAD LOST radio contact with Team D, the seven-man squad, and it worried him. While it was difficult to be sure of anything at the moment, with the sounds of gunfire echoing throughout Moseto, Korstiaan was almost certain he had heard the trademark noise of a Kalashnikov rifle moments earlier, so distinctly different from the reports of any weapon carried by his troops. Moreover, there had also been what sounded like a burst of pistol shots—although, of course, he couldn't specify the caliber or type of weapon, and his men all carried side arms.

Still, he had to stop and wonder if the enemy was fighting back?

He couldn't rule it out. Some South African blacks had been armed for decades, dating back beyond the revolt of the African National Congress, and black possession of firearms per se was no longer a crime. The new rules and increasing self-reliance of blacks under the coalition regime made things difficult, risky for racial patriots like himself, but he still had no reason to believe the kaffirs in Moseto could resist his crack troops.

Except for the sudden, deathly silence of Team D.

Korstiaan tried the two-way radio again, raising his voice to be heard above the sounds of gunfire. "Team D, report at once!" When there was still no answer, he addressed the squad leader by name. "Gregor! Respond, damn you!"

Nothing.

Frustrated now—and frightened—he broadcast an

appeal to the missing squad at large. "Any member of Team D, report! I order it!"

Each member of the raiding party wore a headset with a single earpiece and a slim stalk microphone, allowing them all to keep in touch, receive his orders and call out for help if anything went wrong. There had been no such call from any member of the missing squad, which made their silence now all the more mysterious—and ominous.

Grinding his teeth in angry confusion, Korstiaan began again. "Team D—"

"Your bully boys can't talk right now," an unfamiliar voice came back to him, through his earpiece. "They've had a bit of trouble here."

"Who's this?" he demanded, feeling the short hairs prickle on his nape. "Identify yourself at once!"

The strange voice laughed at him and said, "I'd rather do that face-to-face, Adolf. Stay where you are. I'm on my way."

A hiss of static, and the link was lost. Korstiaan was uncertain for a moment as to how he should react. One of the enemy—a white man, by the sound of it, though Korstiaan couldn't be positive—had managed to locate their radio frequency. In all probability, that meant he had obtained one of the raiding party's headsets, which, in turn, virtually guaranteed that its original wearer was dead. Worse yet, the stranger's mocking words suggested that Team D had been annihilated. And if that were true...

The prospect staggered Korstiaan. Nearly a quarter of his strike force lost, within moments of engaging the enemy, and now his every order could presumably be overheard by that same foe. Casualties aside, his secure line of communication with his soldiers had been compromised and might be worse than useless to him now.

His brain hummed with questions, none of which Korstiaan could answer at the moment. He had no time to ponder the smirking enemy's identity or wonder what a white man was doing in Moseto, this night of all nights. He couldn't waste the time to mourn his soldiers, or even to wonder if all seven were truly dead. As long as others were alive and fighting, they were his priority.

And he had to keep himself alive, of course, to lead them safely home.

Without the two-way radio, Korstiaan had no method of communicating with Teams B and C. In order to recall them, form a flying wedge and blast their way out of what seemed to be a cunning trap, he would be forced to trust the airwaves, clinging to his faith that the savage enemy had to still be largely disorganized, despite intervention by one or more race traitors. If he recalled his soldiers now and warned them of the danger, if they kept their wits about them and fought their way through, he could still reunite his team for a forced march back to the waiting buses.

So be it.

"Teams B and C!" he barked into the headset's microphone. "Rejoin Team A immediately at coordinates J-12!"

It was impossible for any adversary in Moseto to know the simple map code Korstiaan had worked out with his troops in advance of the raid. They could, of course, be followed through the streets, but that should give them ample opportunity to shake—or even better, kill—the enemy who stalked them.

It could still work out, he told himself. It was unfortunate that they couldn't retrieve the bodies of his soldiers who had fallen thus far in the battle—all the more so since their presence here would point a finger of suspicion toward the Iron Guard, come morning—but mounting any sort of corpse-retrieval operation would simply amplify risk to the living.

And besides, this time tomorrow, it would make no difference what the Jew press or the coalition regime in Pretoria thought of the Iron Guard. They would all be scrambling to save their own asses, too busy to organize any kind of crusade.

How long before his squad was rejoined by Teams B and C? Korstiaan was about to check his wristwatch when a burst of fire from a Kalashnikov came out of nowhere, knocking down one of his pointmen, half a block away.

"Take cover!" he was bawling, well before the echo of the gunshots died away. "Defend yourselves!"

MITANE SELEPA WAS hunting. Armed only with a steak knife from Niala Ushante's kitchen when he ran into the night, seeking the Monster of Moseto, he had found and taken down his first Iron Guard adversary moments after the shooting began. The neo-Nazi's comrades hadn't missed him at first, and by the time they did, it was too late. By then Selepa had the dead man's R-5 automatic carbine and had donned his webbing, with the extra magazines, the side arm on his hip.

He almost felt a member of the team—except for his pigment, that was, and the abiding hatred that he nurtured for these men who came from nowhere, without reason, to disrupt and massacre a peaceful settlement.

Selepa wasted no time on preliminaries once he had the rifle in his hands. The other Iron Guard troops were moving, their apparent field commander barking orders to them, the six surviving members of his squad falling in behind their leader as they double-timed through the dusty streets, headed southwestward, in the general direction of the nearest communal showers.

Selepa followed them, jogging down the middle of the street, unnoticed for the first hundred yards or so, until the last man in line took the belated precaution of glancing back over his shoulder. At first glance, in the darkness, the trailing figure may have seemed almost normal, but there was something...

The Nazi did a double take, faltering in midstride, and wheeled about to face the man whom he now recognized as an enemy. Selepa shot him on the run, reached him before the dying man surrendered to gravity, whipping the butt of his captured rifle around to smash the neo-Nazi full on his jaw and put him down.

The six remaining gunmen, their leader included, were all aware of him now, swinging their eyes and weapons around toward the source of their unexpected peril. Selepa didn't know how many 5.56 mm cartridges remained in the R-5's 35-round magazine, but he cut loose on full auto just the same, raking the troops in front of him before they had a chance to aim and open fire. Two of them fell...three...four. The fifth was wounded when his magazine ran dry, the rifle's bolt locked open on an empty, smoking chamber.

Rushing at the wounded neo-Nazi with a shout of fury, Selepa butt-stroked him with the empty rifle, dropped it in the street and wrenched the compact Z-84 SMG from his hands as he fell. Praying that the safety was off, Selepa swung toward the rifle team's leader, caught him leveling his weapon from a range of less than fifteen feet and stitched him with a rising burst of 9 mm Parabellum slugs.

The dead man skittered through a jerky little dance, lurching and leaping with the rapid-fire impact of bullets, until Selepa released the SMG's trigger and let him collapse. Turning back toward the other fallen neo-Nazis he moved among them with the Z-84, firing short bursts here and there, where hints of life remained. When he was finished, satisfied that all of them were dead, he ditched the submachine gun and retrieved his liberated carbine, reloading the piece with a fresh magazine.

His work wasn't complete.

The hunt went on.

BOLAN SQUEEZED OFF another AK burst and took a second neo-Nazi raider down, almost before the first collapsed. He gave the black-clad figure four rounds, maybe five, and swung away in search of other marks as dead man number two was slumping over backward, toward a terminal collision with the earth.

Six men remaining in the rifle squad spread out before him, but the sound of voices calling out in Afrikaans told him that more were on the way to reinforce his enemies. Determined to inflict as much damage as possible before they reached the scene, he framed a third guerrilla in his sights and milked another short burst from the AKSU "bullet hose." His target staggered, stumbled and went down without a shot fired in return.

The same couldn't be said for those who still survived. They were unloading, fast and furious, in every direction at once. Some of the bullets came close enough to make Bolan wince, but others were fired into darkened homes and alleyways, some of them sprayed along the street in the opposite direction from where Bolan crouched, lining up his next kill.

This one appeared to be the leader, barking orders at the rest, fanning the air with his free hand while he brandished an assault rifle in the other, showing more restraint than his troops while he waited for a target to reveal itself.

Time to die, Bolan thought as he lined up his sights on the team leader's chest. The neo-Nazi was facing him, seemed to lock eyes with Bolan at the penultimate moment, but if there was recognition in that gaze, it came too late. A half-dozen 5.45 mm rounds tore through the neo-Nazi's chest and dumped him backward in the dust, his raspy voice forever stilled.

The team began to fall apart without him, soldiers sprinting off in all directions, Bolan tracking them, dropping one after another on the run. His magazine ran dry before he had a chance to finish number eight, and Bolan was reloading when the reinforcements arrived, their raised voices stunned into silence at the sight of their comrades sprawled in the dirt.

Bolan resumed firing, joined almost instantly by a second Kalashnikov, this one blazing from a side street to his right, away to the northeast. A third AK chimed in seconds later, triangulating fire, penning the Iron Guard raiders in a trap from which there was no escape this side of the grave.

But they fought back; he had to give them that. They went down firing, automatic weapons spitting toward the darkness rent by muzzle-flares, their RPG man launching one round to demolish a nearby house, struggling to reload his awkward weapon when a Kalashnikov burst took his face off, spilling him gracelessly to earth.

It was over in a matter of seconds, the ringing echo of gunfire lingering in Bolan's ears, the reek of cordite strong in his nostrils, mingling with the smell of dust and spilled blood. None of the black-clad raiders moved, except for one or two still shivering in the last of their death throes, no longer dangerous to anyone or anything in this world.

He waited for a further sound of gunfire, heard nothing but the cry of angry, frightened voices speaking Swahili, retreating from the scene of concentrating battle. When he raised his own voice, it was to the gunmen who had joined him in the final massacre.

"All clear?" he called.

"All clear," the voice of Jacob Gellar answered back.

"Tha's right!" Mitane Selepa chimed in, the trademark smile audible in his tone.

They emerged from the shadows in unison, moving toward the center of the killing ground. The dust of the unpaved street, blood moistened now in places, caked their soles. They spent a moment checking corpses, verifying what they knew already, then regrouped off to one side.

"That's all of them," Gellar said, stripping off a radio headset and tossing it into the street. "No more gab on the air."

"I'd say this blows our cover," Bolan said to no one in particular.

"Is true," Selepa said. "We should be going very soon, I think."

"How many friendlies down?" Bolan asked.

Gellar shrugged. "No way to tell, just now. I would not recommend that we remain to give first aid."

It galled the Executioner to leave this way, when so much damage had been done. He told himself the raid had almost certainly been planned ahead of time, without knowledge of their presence in Moseto, but the near certainty failed to pacify him.

It was a moan from the darkness, away to his left, that perked his spirits up.

"What's this?" Gellar muttered, moving toward the sound with his AKSU leveled and ready to fire.

"Not so fast," Bolan cautioned, coming up beside him as the Israeli reached a neo-Nazi, lying crumpled on his side, unarmed and bleeding from a shoulder wound.

"It won't take much to finish him," Gellar observed.

"Or make him talk," Bolan replied. "I have a hunch this raid had more in mind than finding us. It smells to me like something heavy in the works. And that means something else coming along behind. We need to find out what that is."

"You wish to question this one, then?" Selepa asked.

"Seems like the thing to do," Bolan said, "but not here. Not now."

"He isn't hurt too badly," Gellar reported, crouching beside the fallen neo-Nazi, probing at his wound with no great care. "I think he'll last some time yet if we stop the bleeding."

"Good. Let's take him with us, then."

"Come on, you bastard." Gellar wore a wolfish smile as he dragged the wounded neo-Nazi to his feet, swiftly stripping him of combat gear. "We're going for a ride."

CHAPTER ELEVEN

Gerhard Steuben stood, stone faced, his hands clasped behind his back, one gripping the other so tightly that he half expected to hear his own bones crack. He felt a shriek of fury building up inside him, struggling to break free, but he knew that once giving free rein to his anger there would be no turning back, and he couldn't afford the sort of chaos that would follow.

Not just now.

"And so," he said, surprised to hear his voice soft and calm, "another failure, then?"

Gert van Koch stood before Steuben, looking miserable, barely able to meet his führer's smoldering one-eyed gaze. "It would appear so, sir," he said, voice barely audible.

"It would appear so?" Steuben made no effort whatsoever to disguise the mockery in his tone. "Your elite strike force is annihilated, wiped out to the last man, and you say it would appear they failed?"

"Not to the last man, sir," Koch corrected him. "There are—"

"Ah, yes." The acid tone again, cutting off his subordinate's reply. "You managed to save the bus drivers."

"Yes, sir."

"And they saw...what, again? They've given you what vital piece of information, Gert?"

"Nothing," Koch replied, and this time he was slow to add the "sir."

"Nothing," the führer repeated.

In his fury, Steuben found that he was suddenly hyperaware of different sensations. His boots pinched his feet; his glass eye felt like an ice orb plugged into the empty socket.

"Still, you've left the enemy something, haven't you, Gert? Thirty-one Aryan corpses in full uniform, with thirty-one sets of battle gear. You've left a sign for them that reads The Iron Guard Was Here! You've given them a perfect reason to attack the Temple. That should count for something, yes?"

"It's not so bad as all that, sir," Koch replied.

"Oh, really? Pray, explain why not."

"We would have been suspected anyway," Koch suggested, "and it's not as if the coppers will have time for hunting anyone tomorrow, with the big event."

"You plan to go ahead, then?" Steuben was a bit surprised. He had expected some excuse, a stall. He had prepared himself to threaten and demand that Gert proceed according to their schedule, even in the face of the Moseto massacre. Now, all that righteous anger was preempted, wasted.

"But of course, sir." The man seemed honestly surprised that anyone would contemplate a deviation from the plan, despite phase one's abysmal failure. "I've already issued orders for the strike team to proceed. The only thing that will delay us now is if the target has a case of nerves and hides himself away."

"He won't do that," Steuben replied, speaking with

more assurance than he felt just then. "The press conference was scheduled—what, nearly a month ago? Last night's events may give him something else to talk about, but how would Mr. Courage and Integrity live with himself if he turned tail and ran for cover now?" His sudden smile surprised Steuben as much as his lieutenant. "If anything, he should be proud about Moseto, crowing over one more victory against the evil white man."

Steuben could almost see it now: the aging, worn, world-famous face behind a podium, doling out platitudes and tidbits of communism dressed up as "morality" and "social justice," the usual audience of sheep applauding and cheering the bastard's every word.

A blink of his good eye, and now he saw that lined face from a new perspective, through a telescopic rifle sight, the crosshairs meeting at a point between the eyes. If Steuben simply held his breath and curled his index finger, slowly, taking up the trigger slack, he could—

"Führer? Are you all right?"

"Of course!" he snapped, embarrassed, feeling color in his cheeks. Lying to cover his lapse, he added, "I was considering the problems that may lie before us, and should we proceed with the planned course of action. You have calculated all the risks, I take it?"

"Yes, sir...I believe so." Koch sounded hesitant, verging on confused. "But I assumed that you would want to go ahead, regardless of the danger, yes? It is our task to light the fuse, begin the final cleansing. Sacrifice must be expected, and—"

"Of course it must," Steuben said, interrupting his subordinate again. "And I most certainly intend to press ahead. But it is hardly worth the effort if we fail, now, is it? If we miss the target and sacrifice more of our best men for nothing? What have we achieved, in that case, Gert?''

"Um, nothing, sir?"

"Precisely nothing," Steuben answered, nodding. "You are perfectly correct. We must prepare ourselves, therefore, leaving nothing to chance. The strike must be perfectly timed and flawlessly executed. In short, it must be successful!''

"It will be, Führer," Koch replied. "We have a man inside the target's staff...well, close to it, at any rate. He tells us virtually everything the target does. If you would like," Koch said, smiling, "I could make a call and tell you what the kaffir bastard had for breakfast.''

"I'm not interested in his diet," Steuben countered, pinning his lieutenant with the glare of his one good eye. "This time tomorrow, I don't expect him to be eating anything at all, ever again.''

"No, sir. As I explained, our very best men are assigned to handle it.''

"That's what you told me yesterday, about the action in Moseto," Steuben caustically reminded him. "Your 'best' weren't nearly good enough, as it turns out.''

"The men assigned to this task are a different sort," Koch explained. "A different breed, you might say. They've been trained as soldiers, granted, but their true skill lies in simply killing. They're assassins, plain and simple...but devoted to our cause, of course.''

"Of course." There was no sarcasm apparent in the

führer's tone this time. "And how have they prepared themselves for the event, if I may ask?"

"They've visited the stadium, of course, and we have many photographs. We built a kind of mock-up in the desert, on some property one of our brothers owns. They have rehearsed the action time and time again. They're flawless, Führer."

"Meaning, I assume, that they were able to assassinate a melon of a mannequin, while suffering no interference from police or members of a huge, imaginary audience?"

"Well, sir, they couldn't very well—"

"Of course not." Steuben made a conscious effort to relax, finding it difficult. "I understand the problems that you face, believe me, Gert. Your efforts are appreciated and will not be overlooked, I promise, when the history of these last days is written. At the same time, you must understand—and make your soldiers understand—that *nothing* must prevent them from accomplishing their goal. If they must sacrifice themselves, so be it. It is not a case of 'victory or death,' my friend. We simply must not fail."

"I understand, Führer."

"In that case, I'm sure that everything will be all right."

But he wasn't.

He had a sickening sensation that the worst was yet to come.

HENRICK GODEWYN WOKE up in hell, then realized that he was being far too optimistic. It became apparent to him, in short order, that he wasn't dead at all, which meant, of course, that he hadn't yet reached the limit of his earthly suffering.

In fact, he feared that it had only just begun.

His ruined left shoulder was the worst of it so far, a wet morass of pain that throbbed and ached, sending off white-hot flares of agony when he tried to move. Godewyn remembered being shot—that was to say, he recalled the stunning impact of the bullet, though he'd never seen the shooter, hadn't even heard the shot per se. One moment he was firing into darkness, some foul alley in the kaffir village, and the next he was falling, his shoulder on fire, the earth seeming to open up and swallow him alive.

There had been more pain after that, some sensation of movement, but full consciousness had only returned to Godewyn in the past few moments, and it found him mightily confused. Beyond the fierce, erratic pain lay something else: the beginning of fear.

It took a moment for Godewyn, waking, to realize that he was sitting in a chair, more or less upright, with his arms secured somehow behind him. The pressure on his wounded shoulder made it burn insufferably, bringing hated tears of pain to Godewyn's eyes. He couldn't strain against the bonds that held his wrists—they felt like loops of narrow wire, but he couldn't be sure—because the effort brought more pain and made him want to sob, scream, weep.

Above all else, he had to appear before his captors as a man.

Godewyn's discomfort was amplified by the fact that his ankles were also bound—with what, he couldn't tell—to the widely spaced front legs of his straight-backed wooden chair. With effort that would cost him blood and tears, Godewyn supposed that he could tip the chair to one side or the other, given several tries, but what would that achieve? To fall upon his wounded shoulder, and perhaps crack his skull on the cold concrete floor of what appeared to be a vacant warehouse, didn't strike Godewyn as much of a tactical victory.

So he waited, as patiently as he could, for a look at his captors. He could already hear them, two men by the sound of it, and while their low-pitched voices weren't loud enough to make out any more than random words, he recognized that they were speaking English. Eavesdropping availed him nothing, since he couldn't pick up anything resembling a coherent sentence, but he drew some minor solace from the tenor of the voices. Both men sounded white to Godewyn, and he drew a marginal relief from that.

At least he wasn't being held by kaffir savages.

But, on the other hand, they could be Jews.

Make the best of it, a small voice in his brain advised, and he began to look for silver linings on the dark clouds that roiled in his personal sky. First and foremost, he was still alive, when they could easily have finished him off in the street—but survival had a downside, too, since it implied they wanted something from him and were simply keeping him alive to use him somehow.

Fair enough, Godewyn thought. Two could play that game.

Fairly soon, he reckoned, they would start to question him. He would resist, of course, but Godewyn cherished no illusions of invincibility, particularly in his present weakened, wounded state. The good news was that he could tell them only what he knew about the Iron Guard's leadership, deployment and operations. And thanks to internal-security precautions, his knowledge of such matters was distinctly limited.

There was consolation, of a sort, in knowing that he could only do limited harm to the cause.

The voices behind him fell silent, and Godewyn heard footsteps approaching. He considered feigning unconsciousness, then decided it would be a waste of time. They would have no trouble "waking" him with a jab to his wounded shoulder, and he preferred to spare himself any additional pain for as long as he could.

There were two of them, as Godewyn had surmised from listening to their muted conversation. One came around each side of his chair, the man on his left somewhat taller than his companion on the right, both stern faced but regarding him dispassionately, as if he were a specimen on the dissection table in some laboratory. It made Godewyn's skin crawl, having them examine him that way, while he sat helpless, at their mercy.

"You speak English?" the shorter of the two asked.

Godewyn debated playing ignorant, pretending that he only spoke Afrikaans, but he finally dismissed the notion as a useless exercise. Better to play along for now, perhaps buy himself some time with worthless, fabricated information, before they got down to the rough business of no-holds-barred interrogation.

"I speak English," he confirmed, surprised to hear his own voice crack, his mouth gone desert dry.

"You are a member of the Iron Guard," the shorter man said. He didn't phrase it as a question, and Godewyn saw no reason to reply.

"You and your friends committed murder in Moseto tonight," the taller man said. "Mass murder, in fact."

Godewyn considered that, supposing that it had to

be true. His team alone had certainly killed several kaffirs, before they were so rudely interrupted. Still, these men didn't appear to be police, and this place clearly wasn't an official detention facility. If he had been arrested, Godewyn thought, he would have seen the doctors first, for treatment of his wound. He wouldn't be tied to a chair, still bleeding, in a dusty old warehouse.

All of which combined to make him answer, "So did you, I think. You had no business in the kaffir town. No business shooting people."

"Some would call it self-defense," the shorter of the nameless strangers said.

Godewyn assayed a shrug, but the movement sent bolts of stunning pain rippling through his torso. It was all that he could do to bite his tongue, to keep from crying aloud. When he recovered somewhat, feeling clammy sweat on his pale face, he rasped out, "You should certainly report all this to the police then, eh? In fact, I must insist on it. Call them at once!"

The strangers laughed at that. Their mockery would normally have made him furious, but in the circumstances, Godewyn felt a sudden fear.

"He must insist," the shorter man said, almost cheerfully, when he was able to control his laughter. Leaning closer, with a broad smile on his suntanned face, he told Godewyn, "You're not in a position to insist on anything, my Nazi friend."

Godewyn would have liked to spit in the smug bastard's face, but he seemed to have no available saliva at the moment. He settled for a sneer and croaked out, "Fuck you both, then. I have nothing more to say."

"I told you," the shorter man said to his companion. "This one is a stubborn Nazi bastard. I believe that I will have to operate."

"You'd better get the tools, then," his companion suggested.

"I think you're right," the first man said, and passed beyond his captive's line of sight, heels clicking on the concrete floor.

JACOB GELLAR RETURNED moments later, carrying a rolled oilcloth packet tightly clenched in his left hand. He circled the chair where their captive was bound, moving back into the neo-Nazi's line of sight.

"We need to get that bullet out," he told Bolan in a bland, conversational tone. "This boy is losing blood. Infection could be setting in at any time. It's for his own good, really."

"You're the doctor," Bolan replied.

"Not quite," Gellar said, smiling at the neo-Nazi, "but I fancy I can handle this. It's relatively minor surgery, after all. In and out, with any luck."

He dropped to one knee, placed the oilcloth bundle on the floor in front of him and released its Velcro fastener with a harsh ripping sound. That noise was replaced by a metallic clatter as he spread the bundle wide, revealing an array of shiny surgical instruments inside, each tool slotted into its own narrow pocket. There were scalpels, forceps, probes, hypodermics, curved needles and surgical thread, a wicked-looking pair of bone shears.

"Damn!" The Mossad agent feigned surprise as he surveyed his implements. "No anesthetic here. That's inconvenient, I must say. Oh, well—" he shrugged "—we'll have to go ahead without it, then. No time to waste, a wound like this."

Their prisoner was looking worried now, eyes flitting back and forth between the instruments of stainless steel and Gellar's placid face. "You're no doctor!" he challenged, fairly wheezing out the words.

"That's true," Gellar admitted to his prisoner, "but I'm the best you'll get tonight. You may prefer bleeding to death, but I'm afraid I can't allow it. You already have too many martyrs for your cause."

"You can't do this!" the neo-Nazi said. "I have my rights!"

"You would, of course...if we were the police. We have no link to the authorities, no sanction to interrogate suspected criminals. No rules at all, in fact. I find it rather liberating, if the truth be told. No rules, no regulations. I'm restricted only by my own imagination."

"I've already told you that I don't know anything," the neo-Nazi said.

"I do recall that, yes," Gellar replied. "Which doesn't change the fact that we must get that bullet out of you as soon as possible."

He pulled on latex gloves, snapping the rubber at his wrists, then chose a scalpel from his tool set, with a wicked-looking pair of forceps some ten inches long. The neo-Nazi followed every move that Gellar made, his bloodshot eyes unblinking now.

Gellar stood, moved closer, the surgical tools in his hands reflecting glints of light from the fixtures overhead. "I'll need to get this shirt out of the way," he told Bolan, reaching out to slit the blood-soaked garment here and there, along its seams—no matter if the blade was dulled a bit—until he could separate fabric from flesh with a sound reminiscent of the Velcro on his oilcloth bundle.

The neo-Nazi clenched his teeth, biting off a whimper as his wounded shoulder was exposed. The blood had begun to clot, but it was dribbling again now. Not enough to kill the man, perhaps, unless it was encouraged to flow more freely. Still, he was obviously weakened, frightened.

Gellar leaned in closer to examine the wound, tracing its scabbed outline with the tip of his forceps, while the neo-Nazi cringed and grimaced. He could smell the man's breath, stale and rancid, flavored by something that had once been edible. Prepared to leap back if the neo-Nazi snapped or spit at him, he watched blood pulsing from the shoulder wound.

"I'll need to cauterize this when I'm finished," he informed Bolan. "Could you fetch the propane torch? I left it in the office cubicle."

"Okay."

"I must apologize," he told the neo-Nazi when they were alone, "for any small deficiencies in my technique. I've done this several times in battlefield conditions, and the patients all survived. Of course, they were my friends."

"I know a kike when I see one," the Nazi grated.

"Your eyesight's unaffected by the injury, at least," Gellar replied. "You should be pleased, in that case, since it's well known that my people make the finest doctors in the world. Please don't regard my lack of formal training as a handicap. Consider it, let us say...an adventure!"

"My comrades will kill you for this!"

"Your comrades from Moseto?" Gellar smiled at that. "I doubt that very much, my fascist friend. Unless, of course, they find a witch doctor to raise them from the dead. I've never seen a neo-Nazi zombie. It should be…unique.''

"You always think you're so damned smart,'' the neo-Nazi said. "You scheming Jews. We'll see who has the last laugh.''

"I guess we'll have to wait and see,'' Gellar replied.

He heard Belasko coming back and watched him set the small propane torch beside the oilcloth bundle of surgical tools. It was a squat, unlovely instrument, resembling something that a scuba diver or an emphysema patient might employ. Gellar waited for another moment, watched the neo-Nazi staring at the torch before he spoke again.

"Right, then,'' he said. "We're wasting precious time.''

"I DON'T CARE what became of the Moseto expedition,'' Gert van Koch informed the seven men who stood before his massive wooden desk. "It's history, an object lesson to be studied at some later date, when we have more time for reflection. Those who gave their lives were friends and valued comrades, but they haven't sacrificed themselves in vain. By simply managing to infiltrate Moseto and raise havoc with the kaffirs, they've achieved the greater part of their original objective.''

There was no response from any of the seven soldiers who regarded him with cold, unflinching stares. Koch couldn't have said with any certainty if they were sad or angry at the news emerging from Moseto—where Lars Korstiaan's expedition had gone horribly, spectacularly sour—but in any case, their concentration didn't seem to be affected.

That, of course, was what made them professionals. The best of the best.

He had handpicked these soldiers, winnowing a list of fifty candidates until he satisfied himself that he had picked the best, most efficient and cold-blooded killers that the Iron Guard had on its membership rolls. Each man who stood before him was a certified life-taker, all of them with victims numbering into the double digits. They had proved themselves in combat and on individual assignments where race traitors were the targets and liquidation the prescribed remedy. They wouldn't flinch from spilling blood, even if some of it turned out to be their own.

"Your preparations are complete?" he asked the strike team, well aware in advance of the answer.

"We are, sir," said the chosen leader of the team. His name was Groot Vanderpool. At six foot two, he was the tallest member of the team, though not the heaviest. His close-cropped hair was dirty blond, with pink scalp showing through on top. Not quite a skinhead, Koch thought, but close enough. To Koch's personal knowledge, Vanderpool had personally killed at least a dozen Africans and four white traitors to their race within the past four years. His comrades in the Iron Guard sometimes called him "Tick-Tock," for his skill in building time bombs, but he had proved himself equally adept with long-range weapons and at killing hand-to-hand.

"Excellent," Koch replied. "I have informed the führer of your preparations and assured him that you will succeed. At any cost. You understand me, gentlemen?"

This time, all seven of them answered him as one, a crisp "Yes, sir!"

How could they fail with men like this? the Iron Guard leader asked himself—and thought at once of the disaster in Moseto, only hours earlier. Thirty men dead and one missing in action—also undoubtedly dead—in an operation that had been planned to perfection, described by those in charge of final preparations as a sure-fire victory.

Still, there was some truth in what he had told the men who stood before him. The Moseto raid, while costly, had served its primary purpose. The local kaffirs were terrified, their spokesmen making outraged noises in Pretoria and in the media. The target for this afternoon's event had already announced his intention to proceed with the scheduled press conference, refusing to be intimidated by what he called "a handful of fringe-dwelling fascists." Now more than ever, the walking dead man told his disciples, a show of courage and determination in the face of hatred was required.

It was perfect.

Successful execution of phase two, now ready to proceed, should guarantee resumption of the full-scale mayhem that had marked the last years of apartheid in South Africa. Black rioting and terrorism would demand a white response, and once a few atrocities had been recorded, who on earth could find fault with the Boers for striking back in self-defense? More to the point, who would remain to make condemnatory statements once the smoke cleared and the deed was done?

No one.

At least, no one who dared to speak.

"I shall report your confidence," Koch told his

commandos. "I expect the führer will be pleased...as long as you succeed, that is."

"We will, sir," Vanderpool assured him.

"I expect no less. The cause demands no less. Dismissed!"

The seven troopers snapped to attention as one, their right arms shooting out in the trademark salute as they shouted, *"Sieg heil!"*

Gert van Koch returned the salute without rising from his high-backed swivel chair, then watched them turn on a dime and march from his office in single file, the last man out closing the door behind him with a snap of grim finality.

Good men, he thought...and hoped that they were good enough. Their preparation would be useless, wasted, if anyone or anything prevented them from taking down their target on schedule. A near miss in this case would be worse than useless, only adding to their target's reputation for an almost supernatural ability to duck and dodge his racist enemies.

This time, the hunters absolutely had to succeed.

But it was out of Koch's hands from that moment forward. He could only trust in fate and in his men, perhaps offer a prayer up to Wotan, for whatever good that might do. The years of skirmishing and sabotage came down to this at last: one chance to strike a mortal blow against their enemy and watch him crumple to the dust.

If they didn't succeed, Koch was able to predict without the benefit of any psychic powers, it would surely mean the end of the Iron Guard. His soldiers would be hunted down, and those who weren't killed on sight would be shipped off to prison, there to end their days. The movement would be broken in South

Africa, his opportunity for greatness flushed away like so much offal down the toilet.

It galled Koch to be helpless now, at the penultimate moment, when he so wished to join in the action, to assist his chosen warriors in any way he could. Instead, he knew, his place was with the führer, to watch and wait, encourage and console.

And if the mission failed, his task would be to offer up his life. For nothing less would satisfy the führer's rage.

Taking a loaded pistol from the top drawer of his desk, Koch went off to wait and watch, counting what might turn out to be the final hours of his life on earth.

CHAPTER TWELVE

Despite his stern resolve, the neo-Nazi cracked. Of course. They always cracked, regardless of determination, strength or courage. The only unbreakable men in the face of determined interrogation with no holds barred, were those who died somehow, before the inquisitors found their personal weakness through a system of trial and error.

Every living, breathing human being had a breaking point.

Years earlier, Bolan had briefly perused a manual—a series of manuals, in fact—that detailed techniques of physical interrogation. The methods ranged from passive to atrocious, including everything from sleep deprivation to gang rape and dismemberment, but one point was stressed repeatedly: different strokes for different folks.

It accomplished nothing to threaten a masochist with torture, for example. Putting a gun to the head of a terminal cancer patient might evoke a heartfelt thank-you. Certain kinds of sexual assault might leave a particular kinky subject panting for more instead of spilling his guts. Threatening a captive's family was no threat at all if he despised his relatives anyway.

Different strokes.

The neo-Nazi, as it turned out, was relatively soft, all things considered. The initial bluster had been mostly for show. Jacob Gellar had barely touched the shoulder wound with his scalpel when the goon broke down, sobbing and wailing, promising to tell them anything if Gellar would just for Wotan's sake leave him alone!

Some superman.

Bolan dismissed the master-race delusion with a passing scowl and thought about their captive as a frightened human being, spilling everything he knew and certain things he had undoubtedly surmised or put together on his own from bits and pieces overheard along the way. Most of it struck the Executioner as trivial, and some of it would be impossible to check without a man inside, at the führer's right hand, but one thing made him sit up and take notice.

Because he had heard it before.

A variation on the theme, at least—and very recently, when they were in Croatia, on their last whirlwind stop before "Israeli sportsman" Gary Stevens escaped to Pretoria. A plan to rock the ruling government, if not dismantle it, by taking out the head of state.

The refinement, in South Africa, was a cunning one-two punch. Croatia had offered no highly visible minority—or repressed majority, in this case—that was likely to erupt if their national leader was suddenly, violently removed from office. South Africa, by contrast, was a historical pressure cooker, centuries of native fury and frustration dissipated only by degrees over the past decade, since the abolition of apartheid and the popular election of the country's first black president. Even then, white bigotry and violence remained an obstacle to anything approaching full equality, and an assassination of the sitting leader now, following hard on the heels of the bloody Moseto incident, could well be the spark that set the whole damned place on fire.

Welcome to racial holy war.

The sheer audacity of it was almost stunning. South Africa's whites—good, bad or indifferent—were outnumbered more than six to one by blacks, and the days were long gone when white troops held all the military hardware, with blacks compelled to arm themselves with sticks and stones. Short of calling air strikes on the various black townships and rural native villages, there was no reason to believe whites would prevail in—or survive—any full-scale outbreak of ethnic cleansing in South Africa.

Then again, with a black hand forcibly stripped from the helm, and white officers still prominent in both the military and police, why should mass retaliation in force be deemed implausible or even unlikely?

By the time United Nations referees arrived, he thought—assuming that they ever came at all—it could already be too late. A decade's worth of progress could have been reversed, burned out and washed away with blood.

"All done," Jacob Gellar said as he came back to the waiting car and slid behind the steering wheel. He had volunteered to dispose of their captive and clean up the mess.

"What's the deal?" Bolan asked as the rental's engine growled to life and Gellar took them out of there.

"Propane torch," Gellar told him, "with the flame

directed toward a fifty-gallon drum of fuel. It shouldn't be much long—''

The blast, two blocks behind them, sounded like a muffled thunderclap, mostly contained within the warehouse proper. It got louder and brighter in a hurry, though, as secondary blasts ripped through the other drums of gasoline that had been cached inside the warehouse. Half-turning in his seat, Bolan could see flames leaping through the broken skylights in the long, flat roof.

''That ought to keep them guessing,'' Gellar said. ''By the time they identify our Nazi—if they ever do—we should be done and gone.''

One way or another, Bolan thought, and kept the observation to himself. He didn't know the neo-Nazi's name and didn't care to know it. The dead man probably had some kind of a family whose members might or might not miss him, might or might not grieve when his charred remains were interred. None of that mattered, now, because the Executioner had far more pressing business on his mind.

Like trying to avert an all-out civil war.

The problem being that he didn't know if such a thing was even possible.

''Somebody needs to warn the president,'' Bolan said, ''and we'll never get within a hundred yards of him. We need to make some calls.''

''My embassy, perhaps, can be of some assistance to that end,'' Gellar replied. ''There is no guarantee, of course, that anything I pass along will be regarded seriously.''

''Maybe if we both try,'' Bolan said. ''I'll call my people, too. Two warnings may jar someone loose who wouldn't blink at one.''

The problem, as he saw it, was that South Africa's black president, surrounded by enemies in Pretoria and the nation at large, had to receive death threats from white racists—and undoubtedly from certain disaffected blacks—on a near daily basis. Given the political climate of the country and the prevalence of arms, at least some of those threats must be regarded as credible and serious.

The first immediate problem was that they knew where and when the hit was supposed to take place, but the target had already promised his constituents, in the wake of the Moseto bloodbath, that he wouldn't be deterred by violent enemies. The speech-cum-press conference was on, come hell or high water.

Which brought Bolan to his second immediate problem. While he knew the where and when of the attack, he didn't know the who. Iron Guard assassins would presumably be white, but that description was so vague that it amounted to no real description at all. And if a president committed to courageous progress would not hide himself from hostile guns, neither would he segregate his audience by barring white spectators, journalists or security personnel.

Any one or more of whom could be the shooters, right.

"Beside the calls," Gellar remarked, sounding unhappy, "we should also be there, I suppose."

"I can't see any way around it," Bolan said.

The Mossad agent scowled. "I was afraid of that."

"THE PRESIDENT? Again?" Marilyn Crouder was surprised to feel outrage, after all that she had seen, experienced and felt in the past eighteen months. "What is this, déjà vu?"

"It's close enough," Bolan's voice came back at her through the telephone earpiece. "We're taking care of it the best we can."

"Okay," she said. "Why don't I—?"

"No!" he cut her off, not waiting to hear what she might have in mind. "You stay put where you are. We agreed."

He agreed, she felt like telling him, but kept the angry words penned up behind her teeth. "Right. You're right. We had a deal."

"This shouldn't take much longer," Bolan told her. "One way or another, we'll have it wrapped up in a few more hours."

One way or another. She knew what that meant.

"Please be careful," she told him, knowing it was wasted breath. No matter what she said, he was about to put himself at mortal risk. Again. That was the built-in problem with a hero, dammit. Always looking out for someone else, regardless of the peril. She might just as well have told him to watch out for gravity, sunshine or oxygen.

"I will," he said to quiet her. "I'll call you when we're done."

"Okay. I'll be here. Just take care."

He broke the link, no great one for goodbyes. She cradled the receiver and began to pace her lonely hotel room.

"I'll be here," she had told him, but she wasn't sure that she could sit the action out this time.

They had a deal, of course. She had promised to stay on the distant sidelines, avoiding any repetition of her risky actions in Chicago and Los Angeles. If Crouder broke that promise now, it made her...what?

A liar? She could live with that, she told herself.

Or maybe someone Mike could never trust again?

It wouldn't make any difference if he was dead.

She had to laugh at that, the notion that her interference in whatever plan he had cooked up with Jacob Gellar would somehow make the difference between success and failure, death and survival. As if *she* could charge in from left field, play the hero for a change, like some modern Joan of Arc, and rescue the two soldiers from their own folly.

Imagine!

And yet...

She knew where the hit was supposed to take place. Bolan hadn't spilled it, but simply naming the target was enough. You couldn't turn a television on today without blundering into another announcement of the president's upcoming speech. Everyone was welcome to the open-air event, broadcasters said. Never mind the previous night's violence in Moseto township. Come one, come all!

If it was going down today, it would be happening there, with the target exposed, a sitting duck despite best efforts to impose security. That much was crystal-clear.

The problems was that she didn't know how many shooters would be working, who they were or what they looked like, what they would be carrying or whether any members of the president's security detachment might be hooked up with the other side. That made it tough in terms of heading off the enemy.

Damned near impossible, in fact.

Or not.

Bolan and Gellar were laboring under the same handicaps, two pairs of eyes, four hands, against what might turn out to be a firing squad of trained professionals. They had no more to go on than Crouder did at the moment, but that wouldn't stop them from putting their lives on the line.

And why should she do any less?

Because it wasn't her fight, the whining little voice inside her head shot back. It wasn't even her country, for God's sake!

"Shut up!" she told the little voice, and went to change her clothes. Jeans for this deal, she decided—the black ones. Pick a short-sleeved blouse to match, as a concession to the weather, since she had to wear a windbreaker.

To hide the pistol.

That was something else. She wasn't technically unarmed, but going up against a hit team with a pistol and a single extra magazine—what kind of crazy plan was that?

Answer—the only one available.

She would have much preferred an M-16, even an Uzi, but larger weapons meant more difficulty with concealment, lugging a gym bag or sweating through a longer, heavier coat, instead of the lightweight windbreaker. Either choice would make her stand out in the crowd, perhaps attract unwanted attention from the president's own security team.

The pistol it was, then.

Crouder finished dressing, wedged the Czech AT-2000 automatic into her waistband, at the small of her back, and slipped on the jacket to hide it. The windbreaker had an inside pocket, above her left breast, and she slotted the spare magazine into its place, within easy reach.

Still early, she discovered as she checked her watch,

and that was fine. She wanted time to look around the killing ground before the party started.

Crouder was nervous, but felt strangely upbeat—almost euphoric—at the same time, as she made her way downstairs to hail a cab.

STEUBEN WAS WAITING when Gert van Koch returned to the safehouse. It was a ranch of sorts, outside Johannesburg, patrolled by a dozen armed guards. The single road that served the property was long, straight, unpaved and totally exposed to watchers from the house. Any vehicle approaching trailed a plume of chalky dust behind it for the best part of two miles before it reached the gate, where riflemen would greet all comers, invited or otherwise. The alternate approaches were by air—in which case they were ready with the RPGs—or on foot, across the sunbaked desert that surrounded the ranch on all sides.

Steuben was up and pacing when Koch entered the "library," a room devoid of books, but well-stocked with videotapes and nudist magazines. The führer's rapid back-and-forth scurry didn't suggest a caged panther so much as it did a cornered rat.

Koch paused a moment, waiting for the automatic guilt to kick in on the heels of that silent observation. When it didn't come through, he shrugged, plastered a fake smile on his face and went to join his not so fearless leader.

"All is ready, sir," he said, keeping the smile in place. "The speech will go ahead as planned."

Steuben frowned, as if perplexed. "He's speaking to the legislature?"

"No, sir. The legislature sits in Cape Town."

Now, the führer clearly *was* perplexed. "I thought Pretoria was the capital," he said.

"Yes, sir. It's the administrative capital. We are unique, I think, in having three capital cities—the extreme version of your own separated powers in America. Cape Town is the legislative capital, while Bloemfontein is the judicial capital."

"Bizarre!" Steuben said with a brisk shake of his head that left his false eye slightly out of line with its mate. "How does the president control his legislature and the courts from such a distance?"

"That's the point, of course, sir. He isn't expected or supposed to run the other branches of the government."

"The people tolerate this?" Steuben asked.

"Quite well, in fact," Koch replied. "There are local courts, of course, but in the event of major trials— black terrorism, for example—removing the subjects to Bloemfontein from their respective townships also helped disperse the enemy."

"Still, it's confusing, Gert. We'll have to see about correcting all this...afterward."

"Yes, sir." Shifting gears, he said, "The strike team is prepared. Its members send their fond regards and solemn promise to succeed."

"They are good men?" the führer asked unnecessarily.

"The best we have," Koch assured him.

"We live in strange times, Gert."

"Yes, sir."

"Strange and perilous times for an Aryan warrior."

Steuben had ceased his scurrying, rooted now at a point near the seldom-used fireplace, which had once been painted black to hide soot stains but was flaking now, showing sporadic glimpses of the red brick underneath. Koch stood facing him, his hands clasped behind his back, and waited for his leader to complete the thought.

"There have been moments, recently," Steuben said, "when I was moved to doubt my calling, Gert."

"No, sir!" Koch could feign dismay when necessary. Truth be told, he had begun to doubt the führer's calling, too—and to have major second thoughts about his leadership abilities.

"It's true," Steuben replied, wearing a rueful smile. "I realize it was ridiculous, of course, but there were several times within the past two weeks or so when I have stood and watched our best-laid plans go up in smoke, our fine young soldiers die, and there was absolutely nothing I could do to stop it."

"Sir—"

The führer raised a cautionary hand to silence him. "I know what you're about to say," Steuben pressed on. "Of course, I know the gods aren't capable of making a mistake. I have been chosen for a purpose, to complete the grand design and save our planet from the demon Jews."

Koch hung on to his smile with a supreme effort of will. He hadn't been about to offer any comment of the sort. His own train of thought had run more toward, *Perhaps you need a rest, sir. You might consider stepping down, retiring as it were, and giving someone else a chance. Someone like me.*

Such words were dangerous, though, at the best of times. Just now, with Steuben's shooters parked in the television room, no more than twenty feet away, they could be tantamount to suicide.

Strange and perilous times for an Aryan warrior.

Instead of correcting the führer's erroneous presumption, Koch merely smiled and nodded, playing along. This was no time to be considering a palace coup. He hadn't even sounded out his own aides on the subject of a change in leadership, much less secured their support for an armed revolt. More to the point, his troops were recently depleted, not to say decimated, and the best shooters he had were embarked on a mission that would—with any luck at all—tumble the nation into chaos.

That, Koch suspected, was the time to make his move. Steuben could be dead when the smoke cleared, preferably the victim of a black assassin, while his loyal lieutenant—

"You agree with my position, Gert?"

The voice cut through his reverie, jerking Koch rudely back to the present. He blinked, clueless as to what Steuben was saying—and what did it matter? The words "my position" said it all.

He took a chance and said, "Yes, sir. Of course I do."

"Good, good. You'll see to the arrangements, then, as soon as possible? Tomorrow, perhaps?"

"I will, sir." Thinking, what arrangements?

Never mind.

Steuben wanted "arrangements" made, and Koch wouldn't disappoint him. He already had a plan in mind, filling the details in.

Tomorrow, perhaps?

His smile was more sincere, now, as he thought, perhaps tonight.

Washington, D.C.

THE TELEPHONE AGAIN, his private line. Brognola wished for one of the cigars that he had given up on doctor's orders, months ago, and lifted the receiver to his ear.

"Hello."

"It's me," the deep, familiar voice informed him.

"Right. Hang on a second."

The big Fed went through the scrambling ritual and waited for the green light to come on. It took perhaps two seconds, feeling more like twenty minutes as he sat there, sweat welding the phone to his palm.

"Okay, we're green," he said. "What's happening?"

"I don't know if the news where you are has picked up on last night's deal," Bolan replied.

"We're getting bits and pieces, coming through on CNN," Brognola said. "I can't say it looks good."

"It looked worse on the ground," Bolan said.

"You were there?" Brognola asked, knowing the answer in advance.

"Coincidentally. I told you we were looking for some downtime."

"This is not what most of us would call low-profile, guy."

"Agreed. Thing is, the shooters didn't come in looking for us," Bolan said. "It was a raid, all right, but targeting native civilians."

"And the reason is…?"

"They're turning up the heat," Bolan replied, "before the main event."

"I'm listening."

"Have you got someone you can talk to, maybe from the State Department, in Pretoria? You need to do it quickly."

"What's the rush?" Brognola asked.

And then, he listened as his oldest living friend explained the problem, laying out the meager details he possessed. A hit against the black elected president, by neo-Nazis, following the slaughter in Moseto by a few short hours. The big Fed didn't need a working knowledge of Afrikaans to know that that combination spelled "deadly trouble" in any language.

"I can find somebody," he told Bolan. "I'm not sure exactly who. What kind of deadline are we looking at?"

"About four hours," Bolan said. "The crowd's already gathering, of course. I'm on my way, as soon as I get off the line."

"I don't know how much good a call will do, at this point," Brognola said gloomily.

"It couldn't hurt," Bolan replied. "Mossad is reaching out at the same time. I'm not expecting any miracles, but if they hear it twice..."

"I'll see what I can do."

"Fair enough. I'm out of here."

The line went dead, and Brognola dropped the receiver back into its cradle, green light on the scanner winking out. Fishing inside one of his trouser pockets, he withdrew a key ring and unlocked the upper left-hand drawer of his large, blocky desk. Inside it, tucked beneath a short stack of manila folders, questing fingers found a small leather-bound address book.

Here were Brognola's "special" contacts, those he hadn't committed to his larger card index or to his secretary's computerized files. The men and women named within his little book were secret contacts, covert allies whose careers—whose very lives—would be at risk if their association with Brognola was revealed. The short list included diplomats and dealers, politicians and police, with others whose careers defied simple description. Roughly one name in eight had been crossed out over time, the simple red-ink X serving as an obituary.

Brognola found the name and number he was looking for, dialed out on his private line to avoid the Justice switchboard downstairs and waited while a distant telephone rang once, twice, thrice.

"Hello?"

"You recognize my voice?" Brognola asked.

"I do. It's been a while."

"I'm scrambling."

"Go."

The green light glowed again. When they were set, the big Fed said, "I have a problem in South Africa. I need to contact someone in Pretoria, our embassy. This person needs to be reliable, discreet and well connected on the other side, able to reach the president."

"May I ask why?"

"There's been a threat against his life."

Soft laughter on the other end. "That isn't news, my friend. He gets at least a dozen every day, before he breaks for lunch."

"This one is credible," Brognola said. "It's in the works. It's going down in just about four hours' time."

There was a momentary silence on the other end, and then, "You're sure about this?"

"As can be."

"Because this guy I have in mind values his contacts and his reputation."

"He'll have one less contact if the hit goes down," Brognola said.

"And I'll have one less if this thing turns out to be a false alarm."

"Three hours and fifty-eight," Brognola said.

"All right, hold on." A brief delay. "You have a pen?"

"Right here."

Brognola wrote the name and number in his secret address book, then said his hasty thanks and broke the link. The address book stayed open as he calculated time zones, lifted the receiver one more time and dialed eleven digits for Pretoria.

His final conversation of the day was short, if not so sweet. On the receiving end, a diplomat and sometime freelance asset for the CIA listened to Brognola's report with skepticism, once suggesting that he would have known about a full-scale plot against the president, if one were in the works. Of course, the Iron Guard was a problem—there had been another bloody incident the previous night, in fact, with dead on both sides—but security was tight, and... No, he couldn't swear that every member of the president's security detail was loyal, but... All right, dammit! He would pass the word along, for what it might be worth, without his personal endorsement.

"You're a credit to your race," Brognola said, and hung up on the pompous ass.

Now, all that he could do was wait and hope that it was good enough. And he would know if it was not.

Another name would be crossed out in his address book if the game went sour.

South Africa

WAITING WAS THE WORST of it, in Bolan's view. Anticipating action, standing idly by and watching players take their places—or not watching in this case, because he didn't know whom he was looking for. Once someone started shooting, there was only time to act, to hit your mark and keep on moving, covering the ground and covering your ass until the skirmish ended, whereupon you knew if you were still alive or not.

The waiting sucked.

Still, it was part of what he did—had always done—and Bolan was a pro. The waiting was a part of him, as it was part of every sniper, every soldier, every hunter. Training and experience had taught him to endure, hang in there, waiting for the perfect shot or settling for next best if the perfect shot never came along.

But while he could perform his task with tactical precision, that didn't mean he enjoyed it, any more than a skilled physician enjoyed diagnosing terminal cancer.

And despite his professionalism, of course, there was always a chance that he might fail.

There was no way to check if either Brognola's or Gellar's warnings to the president through their respective embassies had carried any weight. The speech was going on as scheduled, and he had no frame of reference for judging whether the security force on hand was larger or smaller than usual.

Ground zero was a soccer stadium, where the president of South Africa planned to address his constituents, black and white alike, in just under one hour. The crowd had been gathering by slow degrees since early morning, at least three quarters of the faces black, although the target had his share of white supporters, too. He was, in fact, the people's president as none had been before him in South Africa. It could be argued that white support for the sitting president was pragmatic or opportunistic, rather than ideological, but such distinctions meant nothing to Bolan at the moment.

He simply hoped to keep the man alive for one more day.

Bolan wasted no time scanning the crowd for Gerhard Steuben. The would-be führer might be crazy, but no one had ever mistaken him for an idiot. He would be safely tucked away somewhere behind the lines, perhaps in Jo'burg or even farther afield, waiting for the news of the assassination to be broadcast.

Bolan had suffered a few grim moments at first, considering the possibility that Stevens might use his newly acquired warhead here, to take out the crowd and most of Pretoria along with his personal target, but their neo-Nazi captive had put his mind at ease on that score, at least for the moment. The action was conceived as a conventional hit, albeit with a strike team of unknown size and firepower. Whatever happened here this afternoon, the end result would not turn out to be a mushroom cloud.

So where had Stevens stashed the nuke? After spending so much blood and money to obtain it, what was his ultimate target? Where and when did he plan to strike the final spark for Armageddon?

Security precautions at the stadium so far struck Bolan as mediocre. There were armed guards in evidence, both black and white, a few of them walking leashed dogs, but they employed no metal detectors, stopped and frisked no one for weapons, as far as Bolan could see. Half the people in the crowd might be packing concealed weapons—side arms, hand grenades, maybe something larger—and no one would know it unless a clumsy shooter dropped his piece in front of a uniformed officer.

Bolan, meanwhile, was dressed in a denim jumpsuit with Vogel embroidered over his heart. Mitane Selepa had liberated three outfits from a maintenance locker, tucked away beneath the bleachers, and while the fit was imperfect—oversize, thankfully, helping to conceal his hidden pistol—it provided Bolan with a convenient disguise as he moved through the crowd, carrying a heavy metal toolbox.

No one paid attention to maintenance men in Pretoria, it seemed, any more than in New York or L.A.

Inside the toolbox—underneath a tray of screwdrivers, wrenches and pliers—Bolan had concealed a mini-Uzi submachine gun and spare magazines. He carried no grenades, because of the civilian noncombatants all around him. Automatic weapons would be risky enough, as it was, and he would have to watch his line of fire at all times to avoid inflicting needless injury.

Gellar and Selepa were similarly armed, working different sectors of the stadium, three men doing their best to cover an area with seating for some thirty thousand, plus public toilets, concession stands and service tunnels.

It was needle-in-a-haystack time, all right...except that these needles were deadly on contact and could strike without warning, from any direction.

The upside was that Bolan doubted the hit team would make any move before the president arrived and took his place on the dais down below, at the north end of the soccer field. Even if the shooters were already present, therefore—and Bolan strongly suspected that they were—he still had time to spot them before their target stepped into range.

Time...and what else?

No descriptions, beyond the fact that they would obviously be white men. No numbers for the team, which could turn out to be a single man or a much larger firing squad. No clear idea of how the shooters would be armed, whether with rifles, submachine guns, even RPGs.

So, watch and wait.

The Executioner kept moving, searching for the faceless strangers he must find and kill.

CHAPTER THIRTEEN

Looking at the buses lined up in the parking lot outside the soccer stadium, Marilyn Crouder feared that she had set herself a hopeless task. Two more buses were unloading as she crossed the broad expanse of sunbaked asphalt, feeling its heat through the soles of her shoes. The disembarking passengers were black, many of them dressed for the occasion in traditional African garb as they fell into line, two abreast, and made their way toward the stadium's main entrance.

Too damned many people, she thought, shaking her head in disgust.

She would be lucky enough just to spot a familiar face in this crowd, Belasko or Gellar. Finding a total stranger, black or white, before he had a chance to fire upon the president, seemed nearly impossible; the odds against her being close enough to intervene were astronomical.

Go back to the hotel, then, quitter, if you feel that way.

But she wouldn't go back. Having come this far, she would see the job through, however ill conceived. If she wound up as nothing more than one of several thousand witnesses to a grim tragedy, at least she would have tried her best.

Fat lot of good that would do.

"Shut up!" she muttered to herself, and pressed on to the gate, joining a line that seemed to stretch halfway across the parking lot.

She was initially relieved to see no evidence of metal detectors in use at the gate, then realized that her unknown adversaries would likewise have no problem entering the stadium with weapons. Crouder assumed they were already here, finding their places well ahead of time, to avoid the last-minute rush. If there were snipers, they would seek the high ground, whatever that was. Close-range weapons, on the other hand—shotguns or SMGs—would mean gunners working closer to the target, near the dais at the north end of the playing field.

She had a clear view of the stage and podium once she had worked her way inside the stadium, ignored by most of those around her, though she caught a number of the men trailing her with their eyes. Crouder was used to that, though she had never considered herself a great beauty. In any case, none of these watchers appeared to be armed or positioned for a clear shot at the field.

Forget about them. Concentrate!

She didn't try to find a seat. Her chances as a stationary watcher would be even more pathetic than if she kept moving. As it was, at least she had some small possibility of being in the right place at the right time, if only by chance.

Where to start?

She assumed that gunmen wouldn't rise from the bleachers to open fire on the stage, unless they planned on making this a suicide mission. Even then, surrounded by thousands of blacks who supported their target, the shooters might well be disarmed before they could get off a shot.

No good.

Altitude for snipers. Close range for SMGs.

Close range, for all practical purposes, meant thirty feet or less from the stage. Beyond that distance body armor became increasingly effective against small-arms rounds, while clean hits were more difficult to score. Thirty feet from the stage meant joining the TV cameras and reporters down below, on the playing field itself, where presidential security officers were double-checking press credentials and poking into camera bags.

Scratch that.

Crouder found herself running out of options, increasingly nervous that she would bump into Belasko or Gellar by accident and cause some kind of scene that would fatally distract all concerned. She kept moving, thinking two steps ahead, charting the geography of the stadium in her mind.

There should be service tunnels underneath the bleachers, she recalled from her collegiate days at USC and football games on Friday nights, but how did that help her? It was one thing to move around the stadium unseen, but assassins still needed a shot at their target, and they wouldn't get it through tons of concrete.

Unless…

Stupid! she cursed herself. Of course!

There was more tucked away beneath the bleachers in most modern sports stadiums than plumbing and broom closets. The opposing teams had locker rooms and showers down there, the administration had offices and there was storage space for all manner of supplies.

And there was access to the playing field.

You didn't want your teams trapped underground when it was time to play, and Crouder recalled the cheering now, each time the football squad appeared at the beginning of a half, emerging from the cavelike entrance to the locker room.

Downstairs.

Before committing to the move, she turned back to the nearest aisle between two banks of bleachers, made her way to a point from which she could see the access tunnel nearest to the stage. A single uniform was posted there, his back turned to the darkness within as he scanned the audience for signs of trouble. Crouder didn't need to see the other tunnel, the long shot, to know that it would be the same.

One guard, with access to the target from his blind side. He could be down and out in a heartbeat, shooters moving into range before security personnel on the stage could react. Full-auto fire from the closer tunnel, a volley of rifle fire from the farther—or why not some of each to really nail it down?

She had a choice to make: which way to go? Near or far?

She felt a stirring in the crowd, shoes scraping concrete as the thousands came to their feet, cheering and clapping hands in a storm of approval. If there was a hostile voice in that throng, it went unnoticed for the moment.

Downrange, the president mounted the stage and raised both arms in welcome to his people. He made quite the target, standing there.

Move, dammit!

Painfully conscious of passing time, the seconds spilling through her fingers, Crouder chose the closer of the locker rooms, whose access tunnel would provide a better shot at the dais for short-range, rapid-fire weapons.

Now all she had to do was find the damned place without getting lost.

GROOT VANDERPOOL'S first choice for a sniper's nest had been the stadium scoreboard, something he had seen once in an old American movie, broadcast on late-night television, with a deranged gunman shooting up fans at a big football game. Was it the Rose Bowl? Super Bowl?

What bloody difference did it make?

He had scrapped that plan after a dry-run visit to the stadium, which had included an examination of the scoreboard. He could get inside, all right; the padlock on the access door in back wouldn't have stopped him, but once he saw his chosen vantage point close up, it had occurred to Vanderpool that once the shooting started there would probably be no escape.

The guards might not pinpoint him right away, but even if he made the kill with his first shot, the stadium would still be thronged with uniforms and guns. To get away, once he had done the job, meant climbing down a ladder in full view of everyone, then crossing thirty yards or so of open grass to reach the nearest exit from the field. An exit that, he realized, would probably be blocked by presidential bodyguards as soon as the first shots were fired.

Vanderpool was proud to be a warrior for the master race, but he didn't intend to be a martyr. Not if there was any way for him to do the job he had been assigned and make it out alive.

He had divided his seven-man team on arrival at the stadium, sending four soldiers off to the locker room nearer the target, while Vanderpool and two others proceeded to the opposite end of the structure. All seven wore standard-issue police uniforms, purchased from a costume shop in Durban. Each man carried a standard-issue Browning Hi-Power pistol on his belt, with a Heckler & Koch MP-5 submachine gun slung over his shoulder. It would require a second, closer glance to note that several of the MP-5s were silencer-equipped, and no human eye could penetrate the heavy duffel bag Vanderpool carried in his left hand, brushing against his leg with every step he took.

Inside the duffel bag, two PSG-1 sniper rifles lay blanket-wrapped, to protect their zoom telescopes and prevent them from clanking together. Also inside the bag, secured in special pouches, were half a dozen 20-round box magazines for the semiautomatic weapons.

Vanderpool wasn't inclined to think that they would need all sixty rounds, but who could ever tell? In the confusion, once the president was dead, he hoped to slip away, lose himself in the milling crowd, but something could always go wrong at the last moment. His pointmen in the close-range strike team might not generate sufficient chaos to cover Vanderpool's retreat.

In any event, experience had taught him that too much firepower was always preferable to too little. It was a law of nature, seemingly immutable.

They had rehearsed their movements with a blueprint of the stadium and knew precisely where to go, which doors to open with the pass keys provided by a patriotic janitor. It was cool in the locker room, not steamy at all with the showers off, a relief from the simmering heat of the day outside. Making sure that they had the place to themselves, Vanderpool locked the door from inside and proceeded to break out the rifles.

He kept one for himself and passed the other to Hans Kroger, the second-best shot on the team. Between them, Vanderpool was confident that they could drop a man-size target at twice the hundred-meter range confronting them. The third man in his unit, Bleecker Carstens, would support and cover them, providing added firepower for their retreat, if necessary.

Vanderpool loaded his rifle and tucked the spare magazines into his pants pockets, stretching the gabardine fabric. Leaving the chamber empty for the moment, he slung the PSG-1 over his left shoulder, muzzle pointed toward the floor, and retrieved his submachine gun from a wooden bench worn shiny by the naked bums of countless athletes.

They left the locker room, their footsteps echoing, and moved along the access route toward the playing field. Sunlight streamed through the opening ahead of them, the proverbial light at the end of the tunnel. Framed there, his back turned toward them as he scanned the field, was a single uniformed figure, armed as they were, except for the rifles and the silencer mounted on Groot Vanderpool's SMG.

Vanderpool didn't know the constable's name, but he prepared to address him by rank, hoping various members of the security detail might be strangers to one another, the momentary lapse no great cause for alarm. In any case, he would only need a moment. One clear shot...

As it happened, Vanderpool wasn't required to test himself. The officer heard them coming, turned to face them, moving deeper into the tunnel as he met them halfway. His eyes were still adjusting from bright daylight to the deeper gloom as Vanderpool and his companions closed the gap between them.

Smiling foolishly, the constable—his name was Wevers, etched into the tag above his heart—asked them, "Am I relieved so soon?"

"You should be," Vanderpool replied.

Before that could sink in, Wevers made out the rifles Vanderpool and Kroger carried, frowning at the sight of them.

"What's this?" he asked.

"The end," Vanderpool replied, and shot him in the chest, three rounds from six or seven feet away. Wevers collapsed as if someone had pulled his plug, blood seeping through his shirt where he had failed to wear his Kevlar vest this day.

Carstens bent down to grip the dead man's feet and drag him farther down the tunnel, Vanderpool and Kroger moving up to take position just inside the shaded mouth of the tunnel. As they reached their position, the stadium erupted with cheering and applause.

"We're just in time," Vanderpool said, smiling.

THE EXPLOSION of audience sound told Bolan he was running out of time. He had already scanned the west side of the stadium as best he could, briefly spotting Gellar at the far end, moving slowly through the crowd, before a fresh glance at the field put him right—or so he hoped, at any rate.

In truth, it was a fluke. One moment, he was looking toward the south end of the soccer field, where a uniformed constable stood in the mouth of a tunnel. Bolan glanced away, checking the stage, and then looked back again.

The constable was gone.

So what?

So nothing, maybe. But perhaps...

Bolan did the math, checked the distance with a sniper's practiced eye. It was a hundred meters, give or take, over level, unobstructed ground. No wind that mattered, in the basin of the stadium.

A perfect shot.

If he was wrong, of course, the trip to check it out would be more wasted effort, but he had accomplished nothing, as it was.

The gray Employees Only access door was locked. No one was around to see, as Bolan took a long screwdriver from his toolbox, used it on the locking mechanism, bearing down. It was a contest for a moment, touch and go, but then he was rewarded with a loud metallic snap, before the doorknob turned and he was through.

A long cool tunnel, leading to a door marked Locke Room, the *r* scratched off. It could have been prophetic, for this door was also locked. Instead of reaching for the screwdriver again, he drew his pistol with its sound suppressor attached and blew the lock away.

So much for stealth, but if his first hunch was correct, his targets weren't waiting in the shower area. They would be well beyond, along the access tunnel to the field, where they could sight down on the dais at the far end of the stadium.

He kept the pistol in his hand and took the toolbox with him, through the locker room, until he reached the second tunnel. There, he set the box down, opened it and took out the mini-Uzi, shifting its spare magazines to the cargo pockets of his jumpsuit. With the pistol holstered once again, he cocked the Uzi, left its safety off and moved along the tunnel cautiously, lifting his feet and placing them precisely, avoiding unnecessary noise.

He saw the dead man first, a crumpled silhouette that could have been someone's discarded laundry on the ground, until Bolan got close enough to smell the cordite and fresh blood. There was a slick trail on the concrete where the body had been dragged from somewhere closer to the field, as if a wounded giant snail had passed that way.

The dead man was a cop; he saw that now. Multiple gunshots to the chest had finished him, a tight pattern, but not close enough for powder burns beneath the seeping crimson. Whoever shot the constable had left his weapons with the body, a holstered automatic and an MP-5 bearing a double magazine.

Bolan helped himself to the latter, easing it off the dead man's arm, slinging the backup piece across his own shoulder. You never knew when sixty extra rounds would come in handy in a firefight, and he barely felt the extra seven pounds.

He moved on cautiously toward daylight, following the blood trail, noting where a footprint marked it, here and there. Careless, but there had obviously been no reason for the killer to believe he would have company down here.

Another moment, and he saw them: three men huddled near the tunnel's exit, bright daylight beyond to obscure their features. He could tell they were in uniform and armed, a sudden chill enveloping Bolan as he thought they might be police themselves, somehow allied with the Iron Guard. Police membership in right-wing extremist groups wasn't unusual, in South Africa or elsewhere, and this wouldn't be the first time that an honest cop had paid with his life for opposing corrupt, brutal colleagues.

And the Executioner, for all the violence in his life, nad vowed that he would never drop the hammer on a lawman, regardless of the provocation—even if it meant his life.

Were his hands tied against these shooters?

There was something wrong with that scenario, and in another heartbeat, Bolan knew what it was.

He had no doubt that there were white cops in Pretoria—across South Africa, in fact—who would be pleased to see the present government dismantled, with apartheid reinstated. Some of them were probably affiliated with illegal paramilitary groups, and some of those were doubtless guilty of assorted felonies. The scene before him, though, struck Bolan as a transparent setup. A sham.

How difficult would it have been, with neo-Nazis on the presidential guard detail, for them to draw the tunnel watch without killing one of their own? And how tough could it be to obtain police uniforms, simulated or genuine, on the eve of an all-or-nothing terrorist strike?

Child's play, on both counts.

How certain was he? Call it ninety-five percent, and that would have to do.

Downrange, two of the figures shouldered rifles bearing telescopic sights. Their target had to be the dais at the far end of the field.

Distract them, dammit!

"Hey!" the Executioner called out. "Is this a private party, or can anybody play?"

The third man spun to face him, muzzle-flashes winking from some kind of automatic weapon, bullets swarming through the air as Bolan hit the deck and pressed his face into the concrete floor.

THE FIRST STACCATO sound of gunshots startled Jacob Gellar, even though he was expecting it. A moaning started somewhere in the dark heart of the audience and spread in waves, the sound of mortal danger recognized, as Gellar tried in vain to trace the source of the reports.

Below him, on the dais erected in the soccer field's penalty area, uniformed guards were leaping to shield their charge from danger without recognizing its source. Weapons raised, they formed a human screen around the president, prepared to sweep him off the stage and off the field.

A second burst of fire erupted, and Gellar still couldn't place it. The sound was muffled, as if coming from a distance, or perhaps—

Underground?

Gellar was trying to fix a direction in his mind, work out an angle of attack, when another burst of automatic fire ripped through the sound of wailing voices. This time, it was definitely closer—almost close enough, he thought, to reach out and touch.

Spinning back toward the dais, where the president was huddled in the midst of something like a dozen bodyguards, Gellar saw muzzle-flashes winking in the shadows of a nearby access tunnel built beneath the bleachers. An instant later, he saw the first gunman, at least three others rushing from the darkness behind, coming into the light.

These shooters clearly weren't the source of the original gunfire, but Gellar had no time to think about that at the moment. He was too busy setting down his toolbox, ripping it open and discarding the top tray of tools, removing an MP-5 K machine pistol from the hidden compartment beneath. Scooping up spare magazines with his free hand, he was halfway to the railing that separated bleachers from the playing field, when a cry went up behind him.

"There's one!" someone shouted.

"White man has a gun!"

"Stop him! Somebody stop—"

Gellar was jolted by a hurtling body, strong arms wrapped around him as he slammed into the metal rail. Fists pummeled him, one of them finding his kidney in a white-hot flare of pain. Gellar smelled garlic breath and sweat, struck backward with his elbow toward the source of panting curses, and connected with a skull. The man held on with one arm, striking more body blows with the other, while Gellar tried to swivel in his grasp.

Not easy, but he managed it—enough, at least, to swing his fistful of MP-5 K magazines against the side of his assailant's head. That rocked the man, loosening his grip on Gellar's torso, and the Mossad agent slashed a knee into his adversary's groin to make the point. No sooner had the first man fallen back, however, than half a dozen more surged forward to attack, clawed fingers groping for Gellar in defiance of his visible weapon.

Repulsed by the thought of shooting them down, Gellar chose the only other course of action open to him, hooking one elbow over the rail at his back and somersaulting backward toward the track and field below. It was an awkward, ill-timed move, rough contact with the rail igniting another flare of pain from his bruised kidney, and Gellar landed badly, twisting his left ankle on touchdown. It hurt like a bitch, and he dropped his spare SMG magazines as he threw an arm out to keep himself from sprawling, tasting red dust that rose from the track as he landed.

There was no time to think about the pain, however, no time to worry about the audience members who were already clambering over the rail to pursue him. In front of Gellar, less than fifty feet distant, a pitched battle was raging in the soccer field's penalty area, and the attackers seemed to be winning. Several of the presidential guards were down and out of action, either dead or badly wounded, while the survivors, still returning fire from their assailants, tried to force their charge into a crouch behind the dais, maximizing their minimal cover.

The attackers, for their part—dressed in identical police uniforms, Gellar noted—had thrown themselves prone on the grass and were raking the stage with measured bursts from their machine pistols, apparently coordinating their bursts by some kind of prior agreement, so that no two were forced to reload at the same time. It was an effective technique, and it was taking its toll on the defenders, whittling their ranks with a vengeance.

Gellar scooped up a couple of his scattered

MP-5 K magazines, firing the machine pistol one-handed as he double-timed toward the gunners disguised as policemen. One of them was hit, his body jackknifing from the impact, before another unarmed adversary slammed into Gellar from behind, thrusting him forward and spoiling his aim. A second blocker hit him almost simultaneously, the combined weight of the two bodies dragging him down to his knees.

Cursing, struggling in the grip of his misguided opponents, Gellar tried to bring a second target under fire, but one of them had seized his gun arm, hoisting it skyward, away from the shooters. Even as a fist slammed into Gellar's head, setting bright-colored pinwheels in chaotic motion behind his eyes, he saw one of the gunmen turning, sneering down the barrel of his submachine gun.

It was a truism of battle that a person never heard the shot that killed him or her. Jacob Gellar heard these shots, although he felt the bullets first, drumming his torso with the impact of a jackhammer. Some of the Parabellum rounds were also striking his two adversaries from the audience, evoking cries of shock and pain.

The three of them collapsed together on the grass, with Gellar on the bottom of the heap. The last thing he remembered was the crushing weight of someone crawling over him, then slumping into immobility across his head and shoulders, pressing his face into the turf.

He couldn't breathe, but Gellar didn't panic.

It was all irrelevant, he thought, as darkness swallowed him and vanquished conscious thought.

THE SHOOTING STARTED as Marilyn Crouder entered the large locker room, showers and toilets away to her left, another exit to her right with the legend Field painted in green above it.

Never trust a jock to know which way he was going, she thought, if he couldn't see the goalposts.

The gunfire was coming from that direction, somewhere beyond the access tunnel's yawning mouth, and Crouder picked up her pace, fairly sprinting now, the Czech pistol clenched in a white-knuckled death grip. She had her finger on the double-action trigger, ready to fire at the first sight of a living target, praying that she wasn't already too late.

There was a storm of gunfire now, as she drew closer to the source. It sounded like a dozen automatic weapons, maybe more, but with the tunnel serving as a kind of echo chamber, she was not prepared to stake her life on any long-shot estimates.

Forget the numbers. Any one of them could blow her away.

And that was true for members of the presidential guard, as well, she realized. The cops wouldn't know her from Eve, another strange civilian with a piece, and they would just as likely fire on her as on the Iron Guard assassins. There would be no opportunity for her to plead her case or reason with the white hats, now that they were under fire.

Back off! the small voice urged, but she ignored it, pressing on. Another moment, and she saw daylight ahead of her, green grass, a slice of sky, with bleachers in between the two. No sign of gunmen yet, but from the sounds of combat roaring in her ears, she knew that they couldn't be far away.

She hesitated for an instant, just inside the tunnel's shady mouth, then risked a look around the corner, to the dais where the president had been about to speak short moments earlier. At first she was surprised to see policemen firing at one another, some of them already sprawled in blood, but then she understood what she was seeing, recognized the four men lying on the grass and firing toward the dais as assassins in disguise.

Go for it!

She lined up a target, her index finger taking up the trigger slack. The pistol's hammer was creeping backward toward full-cock when her target suddenly convulsed, blood spouting from vents in his shirt. He shuddered, died, and Crouder swung around in the direction the gunfire had come from in time to see Jacob Gellar leveling his machine pistol for another burst.

She also saw the two black men rushing from behind him like pro football tackles, saw them strike him, one after the other, bearing him to earth beneath their weight. She missed the second neo-Nazi pivoting to bring that awkward trio under fire, but Crouder saw his bullets chopping into them, shredding flesh and fabric, all three human targets crashing down into a bloody, writhing heap.

She swung back toward the fight and marked the shooter, squeezing off too hastily, and only winged him, crimson mist airborne from a superficial gash across his biceps. Still, it got the killer's attention, and he wriggled through a forty-five-degree turn to spray the tunnel's mouth with 9 mm Parabellum rounds.

Crouder lurched backward, jagged shards of something—copper or concrete—stinging her face. Her eyes were spared, but she could feel the warm blood on her cheek, and dribbling from a cut on the bridge of her nose.

Too damned close for comfort.

Even as a part of her demanded that she sit and wait the firestorm out, Crouder knew she had no time to spare. Each second that she hesitated left the president in danger, not to mention thousands of civilians in the audience.

She forced herself back to the mouth of the tunnel, arriving just in time to see the various combatants scatter. Three surviving members of the hit team were retreating toward the tunnel where she stood, while the remnant of the president's guard detail—still surrounding a slumped, jogging figure—were beating a hasty retreat toward a gate on the far side of the stadium, apparently designed to admit vehicles. Both groups were still exchanging gunfire, and she saw another of the presidential guards collapse, clutching his throat, blood pumping from between his fingers.

Crouder took her shot, lining up on the gunner who had tried to kill her, squeezing off a double tap from forty feet as he turned to face the tunnel, gaining speed. Both bullets struck him in the chest, although a bit off center, halting his run as his legs turned to pasta and dropped him facedown on the turf.

Crouder was sweeping toward another target when the other two goons opened fire, spraying the tunnel with their SMGs, driving her back under cover. A bullet plucked at her sleeve, another tracing fire along the outside of one thigh as she squeezed off three aimless shots in futile counterpoint.

They might have killed her then, but as the moments passed, she realized that she had bluffed them, faked them out. Another cautious sweep of the field, and she saw the two neo-Nazis sprinting away from the tunnel, toward a flight of concrete steps that served the bleachers. A metal gate barred the steps, pad-locked now, but they vaulted it with ease, taking the stairs two and three at a time.

She left the tunnel, running after them, afraid to try a shot on the run as her targets plunged into the mill-ing audience. The combination of confusion, plus their uniforms and weapons, seemed to hold the crowd at bay. If any of the noncombatants in the bleachers had observed these two "policemen" firing on the presi-dent, they were apparently prepared to let it slide.

Would Crouder receive the same courtesy?

She'd know in a minute.

She cleared the low metal gate like a gold-medal hurdler, then almost ate it when she lost her footing on the steps, skinning a palm as she caught herself and saved her face from a collision with concrete. Above and to her left, the two faux constables were making fairly decent time, occasionally glancing back to check for any tails.

"Stop them!" she cried to no one in particular. "They're not police! They tried to kill the president just now! You must have seen them!"

No one was listening, and then a tall, dark figure lunged into her path, hands groping for her weapon. Crouder ducked underneath the reaching arms and whipped the muzzle of her pistol hard into his crotch. As he was doubling over with a gasp, she raised a knee to meet him, felt the snap of nasal cartilage.

"Back off, goddammit! Back the fuck off now!"

Between the pistol and her tone, she held the rest of them at bay, charging along behind the disappear-ing gunmen, as they turned hard right along a corridor between the ranks of bleachers, searching for an exit from the stadium.

GROOT VANDERPOOL WAS startled when the guns went off behind him, swiveling to meet the threat, still staring through the sniper rifle's telescope. It was a dizzying experience, and he was forced to lower the weapon, blinking rapidly to regain his equilibrium.

He had a brief impression of a man-shape diving to the floor, as Carstens sprayed the tunnel with his MP-5 SMG. The bullets made sharp cracking noises as they struck concrete and ricocheted into the darkness, toward the silent locker room and shower area.

Before he could focus on the prostrate form of their opponent, Vanderpool was distracted by a storm of automatic fire from the north end of the field. The other members of his team were right on time, either oblivious to his own failure or tired of waiting for a rifle shot to drop their target. Snapping the PSG-1 rifle back to his shoulder, Vanderpool clenched his teeth against the rush of vertigo and swept the dais, seeking the familiar face.

Nothing.

A phalanx of guards had already closed around the president, reacting on instinct to the first sounds of gunfire. Enraged, Vanderpool shot one of the big man's civilian hangers-on, a weasel-faced race traitor he recognized from television news reports, and watched the man pitch over backward with a blank expression on his blood-drenched face.

He could have fired blindly into the crush of bodies on the dais, but they were already surging away from him, dropping down behind the platform, and his hollowpoint rounds lacked the penetrating power needed to cut through human shields in search of a secondary target.

Vanderpool felt the scream building up inside him

as he turned his back on the field and the sunlight, squeezing off three rapid-fire rounds toward the shadowy form of his unknown enemy. Ears ringing from the rifle's loud reports, he missed the impact sounds this time, but he could see the muzzle-flashes of an automatic weapon winking back at him, the adversary still well able to defend himself.

Bullets swarmed past his face in the semidarkness, buzzing like blood-hungry flies. A moist sound of impact from somewhere behind him, and Vanderpool heard Kroger grunt as if someone had punched him in the gut.

Firing again toward his shadow-enemy, retreating toward unfriendly daylight, Vanderpool risked a backward glance at Hans. He was in time to see Kroger slumped against the far wall of the tunnel, spilling scarlet from multiple chest wounds as his legs folded, his head and shoulder scraping down the curved concrete wall until he landed in a kneeling posture, like some odd religious supplicant.

Too late for Kroger, but Carstens was still laying down a stream of cover fire from his MP-5, fighting the rearguard action. Vanderpool took advantage of the moment, clearing the tunnel in a rush, ducking instantly to one side for cover. Blinking in the sunlight, he turned, looked upward toward the bleachers and found a cluster of black faces staring at him, bending over the rail.

"Clear off, you lot!" he barked at them, brandishing his rifle. "Police business here!"

They drew back a few inches, moving almost as one, but they didn't seem overly impressed with Vanderpool's command. He wondered whether he would have to fight his way out through the whole damned crowd, and whether that was even possible.

"We've got some of the shooters cornered here," he told the dark, suspicious faces ranged above him. "If you want to help your president and keep yourselves from harm, you'll clear out. *Now!*"

Mounting a nearby flight of steps to reach the bleachers, Vanderpool took a chance, advancing briskly on the huddle of suspicious bystanders.

"Off with you, now!" he snapped. "Or face arrest for interfering with an officer's performance of his duty!"

That appeared to do the trick, his dark-skinned audience retreating, leaving Vanderpool to find his own way up and out. It was a start at least.

Now all he had to do was slip away before that bastard from the tunnel started after him or someone with a real badge saw through his disguise.

No worries, he told himself with more confidence than he felt. He was halfway there.

THE CROWD WAS going crazy. It wasn't a riot yet, but fistfights had already broken out between black and white members of the audience, the former lashing out in a moment of panic at strangers who shared common pigment with their historical oppressors. There was nothing new or surprising in that, and Marilyn Crouder frankly didn't give a damn, as long as she was left alone to pursue the fleeing assassins.

The pistol in her hand helped out in that regard, though it wasn't a shield. Somebody in the bleachers lobbed a bottle at her head and missed, while others screamed and cursed at her in passing. They presumably mistook her for a member of the hit team, having somehow missed the fact that all the shooters had worn uniforms and *she* was chasing *them*. It made no difference at the moment, though, since rationality had vanished from the stadium the moment the first shots rang out.

Whatever happened in the next few minutes, it occurred to Crouder that Gary Stevens had achieved at least some measure of his goal. The president was still alive, but the attempt upon his life had already sparked racial violence and more was sure to follow. Unless she missed her guess, there would be rioting tonight, as word of the attack was broadcast nationwide. Black violence would guarantee an armed response from the police, while any outbreak increased white fears and drove more potential recruits into the arms of "defensive" groups like the Iron Guard.

Too late to stop that now, she thought, and focused on the task at hand.

She had almost reached the corner where her uniformed quarry had vanished when a large black man lurched into her path, crouching like a wrestler. Something glinted in his hand, a wicked-looking pocketknife, and there was no time to consider options as he moved to intercept her, wild-eyed, flushed with rage.

Crouder shot him in the knee from six paces, the crack of her pistol sending ripples of shock through the crowd. Around her, some of the combatants separated, diving for cover in fear of a new fusillade. Women screamed and men shouted. Those among them who had thought of tackling the woman with the gun instead got out of the way.

Crouder sprinted for the nearest aisle between bleachers while the mob was unsettled, before anyone dredged up the nerve for another rush. Her quarry had a growing lead, which made her less than cautious as she dashed around the corner, running full tilt.

Two things happened almost simultaneously. First she glimpsed the two retreating figures she was after, shouting out a futile call for them to halt—and then she stepped in something with her right foot, wet and slippery it was, legs crossed and scooting out from under her before she even had a chance to fan her arms. She hit the floor as if she had been dropped from a much higher altitude, grunting with pain.

And the fall saved her life.

Downrange, the uniforms *had* heard her call and they turned to face her, submachine guns stuttering from sixty feet or more. The first rounds might have missed her even if she hadn't fallen, but the extra margin gave her time to thrust the pistol out, lips curling back around a snarl of pain, and squeeze off two quick shots.

One of them missed; the other slapped into the right thigh of the shooter on her left and cut the leg from under him, dropping him flat on his rear end. He kept firing, though, and his comrade stood fast, still hosing the aisle with his SMG.

Crouder had nine rounds left in the pistol, and she used two more now as she scrambled upright, blasting at the gunner who was still on his feet. Was that a hit? He seemed to stagger, but it could have been a near-miss flinch, no blood in evidence.

She fired twice more and saw him rock this time, no doubt about it. There was scarlet splashed across his shirt—no Kevlar, then—but he was tough enough to stand his ground and return fire, his bullets slapping concrete on either side of her, chips from the damaged floor stinging her ankles.

She fired again, two-handed, and she hit him in the chest a second time. The prick was going down now, slumping to his knees, but even as he toppled over on his face the trigger finger clenched enough to empty out his weapon's magazine.

The impact spun and stunned her, dropped her on her back. If questioned at that moment, Crouder couldn't have said that she felt pain, so much as shock. There was an ache, of course, but overall a certain numbness and a sense of spilling deep inside herself.

With a supreme effort of will, Crouder rolled over onto her side, surprised to find the fingers of her right hand still securely wrapped around an automatic pistol. Hers, it seemed to be, although it weighed nearly too much for her to lift.

Lift it she had to, though, since the second gunner was approaching her, hobbling on his wounded leg like Chester from *Gunsmoke,* in the prehistoric days of black-and-white TV. He could have tried to get away, but he was coming back to finish it. So much the better, since she couldn't have pursued him any farther in her present state.

Hold on, she told herself, her brain spinning, her vision fading in and out as if someone were passing an old sheet of Plexiglas back and forth before her face. He had to get closer.

The phony cop was firing now, and she could feel the bullets chopping at her, solid hits, as she unloaded with the pistol, cursing him with everything she had until her lungs ran out of breath. The slide locked open on her gun, and the last thing Crouder saw through the lazy smoke curling from its chamber was the scuffed sole of a dead man's shoe.

BOLAN'S LAST Uzi burst caught the rearguard shooter as he paused to reload, no help for it, down on one knee and half-turned in profile to minimize the target he offered. It was hopeless with the sun behind him as it was, and Bolan knocked him over like a fat tin rabbit in a shooting gallery.

Up and running as he switched magazines in the Uzi, Bolan didn't hesitate as he reached the tunnel's exit. He had lost too much time already, ducking bullets in darkness while the last of the shooters made tracks. Away behind him, toward the north end of the soccer field, there were no more sounds of gunfire and the stage was clear. Bolan couldn't interpret that—it might be good or very bad—but it was something, telling him the rest of it was settled, one way or another.

All except his own pursuit of number three.

Or was this number one?

It made no difference to him at the moment, whether he was chasing the hit team's leader or a simple grunt whose nerve had broken. Either way, he meant to finish it. Clean sweep.

There was no sign of the shooter as he exited the tunnel, checking both directions on the field and glancing up into the stands, where most of the crowd had evacuated. They were heading for the north end of the stadium en masse, following the smell of cordite and the sight of bodies being laid out on the grass.

Was one of them the president's?

He couldn't tell and dared not stop to ask.

A gate stood halfway open at the near end of the field, some kind of access for vehicles onto the field and its surrounding track. He ran in that direction, his feet raising puffs of ocher dust from the athletic track.

The gate was made of chain-link fencing, with the parking lot beyond. So many cars and other vehicles, how could he ever hope to find—

He felt the bullet ripple past his face, sucking the sound along behind it like a tiny fighter plane. As Bolan lunged for cover in the shadow of the nearest car, another round punched through the driver's window, exiting the near side in a shower of glass.

The shooter was somewhere in front of him and firing on a level plane, which meant that Bolan had a chance to flank him now, if he stayed low and took advantage of the intervening cover. On the downside, his enemy could also keep moving, while renewed gunfire was sure to draw officers from the stadium in a matter of moments.

Hurry up, then! Get it done!

Which way to go? The choice was either left or right, northwest or southeast, and either pick meant he would have to wind his way through untold ranks of vehicles while searching for his prey. He couldn't get a fix on distance, though he knew the shooter had to be fairly close. The echoes made it difficult to judge precise direction, but he had at least a vague idea of where to go, assuming that the shooter wasn't moving, too.

Bolan cleared the gap between one vehicle and the next in a scuttling crouch, staying low. No shots were fired, and none again as he worked his way around the tailgate of a dusty Range Rover, edging closer to the point from which his assailant had earlier fired. He tried to listen for scuffling shoes on asphalt, but it was hopeless. There was too much traffic on the nearby streets, still too much noise from the stadium behind him.

He heard an engine come to life somewhere nearby, and while it startled him at first, he had to wonder why more people weren't evacuating, fleeing from the scene of so much carnage. Was it morbid curiosity? Concern for the president? Or had police already sealed the stadium?

The vehicle was moving now somewhere not far to Bolan's left. The next shot startled him, more so because it wasn't coming his way and it had been fired at least a little farther off than the first two.

The gunshot was immediately followed by a squeal of brakes. He knew in a flash what it meant, what it *had* to mean, and he was on his feet a heartbeat later, throwing caution to the wind. If it had been a trick, the shooter could have nailed him then, no sweat.

But it wasn't a trick.

His target stood erect and plainly visible, some twenty yards away. The shooter had stepped out in front of a gray compact car, his warning shot designed to stop the vehicle. He had achieved that purpose, moving swiftly toward the driver's side and leveling his weapon at the slender Asian man behind the steering wheel.

The shooter didn't hesitate. Another round punched through the driver's window, blew his human target over to his left and out of sight. The faux policeman reached out for the door handle, gave it a yank and found it locked. He drew his rifle back, prepared to smash out the remainder of the window glass, and he was on the down stroke when a burst from Bolan's Uzi ripped across his back.

No warning preceded the impact that slammed him hard against the driver's door. The corpse behind the compact's wheel chose that moment to slump further, shifting position, dead foot slipping off the brake pedal. The compact started rolling, pulled the dead or dying shooter with it, blood-smeared paint marking his passage as he slithered to the pavement. The compact's right rear tire passed over the shooter's outflung arm and crunched his face as the car veered off course, colliding almost gently with a stationary vehicle.

Bolan considered going back to look for Gellar and Selepa, but it was a passing thought, a fantasy. They had a rendezvous arranged, taking for granted that they would be separated in the chaos of the moment if a move was made against the president.

And so they were.

He ditched the Uzi and the MP-5 beneath a rusty Morris Minor, knowing he couldn't hope to conceal them on the walk back to the rendezvous point. His pistol would have to do, in terms of personal defense.

Ignoring the voices behind him, keeping it casual, Bolan struck off across the parking lot, his heels clicking on the asphalt as he walked beneath a broiling sun.

CHAPTER FOURTEEN

Mitane Selepa was embarrassed. When the shooting had begun, he was on the wrong side of the stadium and high above the field, overlooking the center flag. His plan had been to spot the shooters from on high, perhaps spot a sniper lining up his shot, but it backfired on him, catching him out of range from the action that broke on the field. Instant confusion in the stadium, with bodies filling up the aisles, kept him from the action until it was too late, the police mopping up.

But that wasn't the worst of it.

Selepa had seen Jacob Gellar die.

His mind was racing as he headed for the rendezvous that had been prearranged, in case the three of them were separated. Only two would make the meeting now, at best, and he couldn't be sure about the tall American.

Which would be worse—to learn that Mike Belasko had been killed, as well, or telling him of Gellar's fate?

No contest there, at least. He hoped the tall American was still alive.

Selepa didn't want to think about the options, in that case. No one expected him to carry on alone, of course. He wasn't troubled by that. The thought of failure nagged at him, shamed him. Those men were his responsibility. He was—had been—their contact, guide, interpreter. At some level, however seemingly irrational, Gellar's death—and Belasko's, too, if he was lost—translated into failure and shame for Mitane Selepa.

Ridiculous, he told himself. Absurd!

And still, he couldn't shake off the feeling.

Because he hadn't fired a shot at the stadium, Selepa still carried his toolbox with the Ingram MAC-10 machine pistol and spare magazines hidden inside. It sat unopened on the seat beside him, where any workman might carry his tools on the way home from work. Police at the stadium had ignored him completely, their black-white train of thought working to his advantage for once, since the shooters in this case were white and their target was black. The men inside the uniforms couldn't conceive of paramilitary whites enlisting some black traitor to assist them, even after generations of police corruption in the native African community.

This one time, Selepa told himself, it was just as well.

He had considered discarding his weapon when the shooting broke out and it became apparent that he couldn't join the battle. Just as quickly, though, he had determined to bluff it out as far as possible, taking his leave as would any other frightened black laborer in the same circumstances. He hadn't been detained or molested, slipping out before officers had the presence of mind to seal off the stadium to contain their witnesses. By the time they started blocking exits, Mitane Selepa was already gone.

And he had witnessed something odd along the way. Something he hoped the tall American might be able to explain, assuming he was even still alive.

The rendezvous point was a small apartment occupied by a friend of Selepa, presently visiting with relatives in Soweto at Selepa's request. He had left keys behind, one each for Selepa and the two white men. Police would have one of them now, from Jacob Gellar's corpse, but it would be impossible to trace unless they tested it on every locked door in Pretoria. The fact that Selepa's friend was black compounded the problem, since the dead key holder at the morgue was white, and most police would never think he had connections to a black or mixed-race neighborhood. If he was ever finally identified, the trail would veer even more radically away from Selepa and his friend.

All to the good.

At the moment, though, Mitane Selepa was more concerned about the American. Was he still alive? If so, had he been captured at the stadium? And if he was arrested, would he talk?

The latter possibility seemed so remote that Selepa put it out of mind. Belasko—or whatever his name was—didn't strike him as a man who would crack easily, even if police forgot themselves and used the techniques they had once reserved for black suspects. More likely, in the heat of the moment, they would simply kill him at the scene if they were able and declare another job well done.

Selepa hoped he would survive and keep their rendezvous, however. He had questions to ask, as well as information to transmit.

Climbing old wooden stairs to his friend's second-floor apartment, Selepa heard them groan beneath his weight. It was a simple but effective warning system, audible inside the flat if you weren't asleep, and sometimes even if you were.

Outside the door, he kept the toolbox in his left hand, fished the key out of a pocket with his right. The room was dark inside, with all the curtains drawn against daylight. He stepped inside and fumbled for the light switch. He knew it was somewhere on his right but—

"Are you alone?"

Selepa recognized the voice, and even startled as he was, couldn't suppress the makings of a smile. Relief washed over him, despite the knowledge that a gun was no doubt pointed at his chest.

"I am."

"All right, then."

When he found the switch a moment later, Belasko stood before him, legs and lower body screened behind a large, square couch. There was no weapon in his hand, but he had taken off his denim coveralls, the pistol in his shoulder holster readily accessible. Selepa knew that he couldn't have reached his own gun, drawn and fired before Belasko cut him down.

"I have bad news," Selepa said, wishing to have it done and over with.

"I'm listening."

"Your friend is dead."

"You saw him?" the American inquired.

"I did. A group of gunmen rushed the dais, four or five, I think, and he ran out to meet them. He was shot. Some people from the audience, as well. It was confusing there."

"The shooters?" Bolan prodded.

"One of them he killed, before the rest shot him."

Selepa felt a sharp twinge in his chest, below his heart, and recognized the pang of guilt. "I could not reach him. I was...there was nothing I could do. I tried...."

"He knew the risks," Bolan said. "He chose the game."

"There is another thing," Selepa said. "Perhaps you find it strange."

"What's that?"

"After the gunmen killed him, one of them was shot. At first, from where I stood, it seemed police had shot him. Then I saw a woman firing from the tunnel where the gunmen must have come from. She killed one of them and chased the others up into the stands."

Bolan's face had paled as he was speaking, but Selepa forged ahead. "I thought it strange to see this," he continued. "Female police, of course, we recognize, but this one had no uniform. She almost seemed to fear the other officers, the way she ducked and ran."

"What did she look like?"

"White, with yellow hair, I think. Blond hair. The rest, I cannot say. I was a fair way off."

"What happened to her? Did you see?"

Selepa shook his head. "She was across the stadium, far side. I lost her in the crowd." He blinked at the American's stony face and asked, "Is something wrong?"

RUNNING AGAIN.

The prospect didn't sicken Gerhard Steuben as it had the first time, or the second, and that very fact—that he was getting used to fleeing from his enemies—left him disgusted with himself. What good was he to anyone, much less a revolutionary cadre, when his every plan went up in flames and he was always on the run?

It could be worse, he told himself, watching the images that shifted, flickered on his muted television set. The president had managed to escape unharmed, but there had been some kind of miniriot at the soccer stadium and now police were on patrol throughout Pretoria, expecting further trouble from the outraged blacks. Before he shut the sound off, there had been predictions that unrest would spread into Johannesburg by nightfall, perhaps even farther afield. All police and military leaves of absence had been canceled in anticipation of more violence.

Steuben assumed his men were dead. The televised reports had mentioned several uniformed policemen being killed. They weren't named, no photographs were shown, but Steuben didn't know the shooters his subordinate had chosen for the job in any case. If even one of them had managed to escape, he should have been in touch by now, reporting his view of the hit and why it had gone wrong.

Wotan, let them be dead, he thought, and not in custody.

The last thing he needed at the moment was a worried soldier locked away, spilling his guts.

There would, of course, be raids against the Iron Guard and other patriotic groups, once everything was sorted out, but that didn't concern him. He would be long gone by then, safe from the heat.

In fact, he would be very, very cool.

As cold as ice, he thought, and smiled.

His men were almost finished packing, rounding up the bags, making a final check around the hotel suite for anything they might have overlooked. They were a thorough team, this group, and wouldn't let him down.

The helicopter would be waiting for them, ready to go when they reached the airport. The first leg of their journey was a relatively short one, three hundred miles from Johannesburg to Kimberley, refueling there and on to Cape Town. There, a transatlantic charter flight was waiting that would carry them to Buenos Aires. And from there…

The irony of fleeing to Argentina wasn't lost on Steuben. How many soldiers of the Third Reich had made that journey in the dark days after World War II? Were any of them still alive, after so many years? He knew that some had settled there, also Bolivia and Paraguay, where Dr. Mengele had put down roots. It had been almost sixty years, by now. If any of the fugitives remained, they would be doddering old mummies now, most likely senile, prone to babbling incoherently about their glory days in Germany or on the Eastern Front. Some of them had established families and prospered; this was known to be a fact. Their children would be getting on in years, grandchildren off to college now or raising families of their own.

How many cherished the ideals their forefathers had fought so grimly to preserve in France, in Italy, in Russia, in North Africa? How many even recognized their heritage, the proud blood coursing through their veins?

Loyal fascists still remained in South America. He knew that for a fact, since some of them had joined the Temple of the Nordic Covenant and pledged their lives to help remake the world. The Temple didn't have large numbers there, but they would be enough. Steuben and his companions didn't need much help from this point on. A simple place to stay, until their final transit was arranged. Protection from their enemies for two, perhaps three days.

So little, really...but it could make all the difference in the world.

Steuben didn't regard his flight today as cowardice, whatever might be said by fools behind his back. He wasn't running from a fight, but rather racing toward his rendezvous with destiny, a moment that would change the world and—if his calculations were correct—produce a great new age for man on earth.

Some men, at least.

The Jews and muds would rue the day when Gerhard Steuben came into his own and brought the full force of his personality to bear upon the problem of a decadent, corrupted race. A few more days, and he would show them all exactly how deluded they had been to shun his message and disparage him. As in the days of Noah, so another prophet would be vindicated and avenged.

Except, of course, that Noah hadn't been an Aryan.

"All ready, sir." The leader of his bodyguards spoke softly, as if worried he might spook the führer otherwise.

Steuben switched off the television set, dropped the remote control onto the bed. "We should be going, then," he said.

"Yes, sir."

His men kept weapons handy as they left the hotel through a service entrance at the rear. Two soldiers from the Iron Guard were on watch there, waiting with the van that would convey them to the airport. Steuben checked both ways along the alley, seeing no one else, no trace of any enemies.

But they were out there somewhere, Steuben knew. There was no doubting that. Even if the fiasco at the soccer stadium didn't involve the faceless strangers who hounded him halfway around the world, he knew that they were tracking him, that they were somewhere in South Africa—perhaps within a short drive of the very spot on which he stood.

You're too late, Steuben thought. You've missed again.

"Beg pardon, sir?"

Confused, the führer turned to face his acting chief of security. "What?" he demanded.

"You said something, sir. I missed it, I'm afraid."

"Missed it?" Embarrassed by the thought that he was talking to himself and didn't even know it, Steuben snapped, "You're hearing things!"

"Yes, sir," his bodyguard replied, frowning.

Watch that, he told himself. You're no good to the movement if you come off acting like a goddamned lunatic.

And this time, Steuben bit his tongue to make sure that he didn't speak the words aloud. Another moment saw him in the van and they were rolling through the alleyway, left turn, a merge with traffic, headed for the airport.

Headed for a date with epic destiny.

BOLAN STOPPED en route to Crouder's hotel and telephoned her room. No answer, and the desk clerk told him that the lady had to be out. Was there perhaps some message?

There wasn't.

He tried to think of reasons why she might not answer the phone. Maybe she was in the shower when he called, or she had gotten tired of room service and went downstairs to try the hotel restaurant. Why not?

Because she wouldn't, Bolan thought. She promised not to leave the room.

Same promise, more or less, that she had broken in Chicago. And in L.A. she had promised not to leave the car. Both times, she had decided on a whim to put her life at risk. She had survived those lapses.

This time, though...

A sense of dread had taken root in Bolan's chest. It was a dull, dead feeling. He remembered it too well from situations in the past, although it hadn't troubled him of late. It was the feeling he had grown accustomed to during his lonely one-man war against the Mafia, when innocents attached themselves to his cause for one reason or another and wound up suffering as a result.

It wasn't the same, he told himself as he continued navigating through the after-work rush-hour traffic. There were more police cars on the street than he remembered seeing previously, and they all seemed to be going somewhere in a hurry with their flashing lights, a siren whooping now and then when traffic failed to yield. The radio, tuned to an all-news channel, spoke of scattered vandalism and incendiary fires, a few reports of bricks and bottles being thrown at cars driven by whites.

Things fell apart, some poet said.

And when they did, the predators came out on top. Focus!

He told himself that Crouder had learned her lesson, that she wouldn't break her word again, but he wasn't convinced. Bolan had seen her, listened to her, sensed the buildup of frustration that was a predictable result of being sidelined, watching others hunt the prey that was supposed to be her own. Her life had been disrupted, effectively turned upside down, her career with ATF pulled up by the roots. She had faced death and suffered grave indignities, finally reduced to trailing a virtual stranger around the globe and watching while he mopped up her original targets.

Would it be enough to push her over the edge, drive her out on a desperate mission in unfamiliar territory?

It might.

Bolan hated that answer, but there was no way around it. He drove on, switching off the radio after another block or two. No news, in this case, was good news.

At the hotel, he parked himself in lieu of using the valet and breezed through the lobby to the bank of elevators, keeping an eye out for lurkers along the way. No one appeared to follow him upstairs, and he had the fifth-floor hallway to himself when he stepped from the elevator car.

Palming the spare key to Crouder's room, Bolan kept his right hand empty, ready to receive his pistol, as he neared her door. Pausing, he knocked, waited and knocked again before he used the key.

Dead silence in the room as Bolan entered, pausing on the threshold to call out her name, then closed and double locked the door behind him. It was useless calling out her name again, but Bolan did it anyway.

No answer.

There was nothing out of place about the room, no evidence of ransacking or any signs of struggle. That would fit with what Selepa had reported from the stadium, assuming that the woman he had seen *was*

Crouder, and not some member of the president's security detachment.

"A woman firing from the tunnel where the gunmen must have come from," he had said. "She almost seemed to fear the other officers, the way she ducked and ran."

According to Selepa, the blond Jane Doe had killed one of the shooters and chased two others out of sight, lost in the crowd on the far side of the stadium. Assuming it *was* Crouder, that didn't mean she had been harmed. She could have managed to escape the same way he had, slipping out before the stadium was sealed.

Where was she, then? the voice in Bolan's head demanded.

"I don't know," he told the empty room.

He made another quick search of the suite, as if he might have missed her lying in the bathtub, maybe crouching in a corner of the bedroom closet. Bolan felt absurd and knew that he was wasting time.

He switched on the television and flipped around the dial until he found a channel running footage from the stadium. There had been several minicams throughout the audience, it seemed, besides the regular contingent of media gear. The action had been covered from at least six different angles, and he stood there watching Jacob Gellar die in instant replay, half a dozen times, like something from a bloody action film. The camera work was unrelenting, as if calculated to inflame.

When they were finished killing Gellar and the others who had fallen with him, an announcer started reading off the names of dead and wounded constables, together with a short list of civilian casualties.

The punch line was a series of still photos, showing lifeless faces, that depicted those described as unnamed terrorists involved in the attempt to kill the president.

Nine faces, eight of them male. One of them belonged to Jacob Gellar. The ninth, a blond-haired woman who had carried no ID and was reported trading shots before she died with two of those disguised in bogus uniforms. The talking heads suggested that there may have been some falling out between assassins, cause unknown, since the police denied a hand in killing any of the nine.

Bolan switched off the television set and locked the silent suite as he left.

GERT VAN KOCH didn't know whether he was angry or depressed. The move against the president had cost him seven more of his best men, and all he had to show for it so far was scattered rioting in several of the native townships, nothing serious enough as yet to warrant calling out the troops. He feared that it would all blow over in another day or two, leaving the president to launch a hunt for those who schemed against him. And that hunt could only lead investigators back to the Iron Guard.

The TV news reports had spoken of nine terrorists, including a woman, but Koch had long since given up on hearing truth from the Jew media. Assuming that a white woman had died at all, Koch assumed she was some crazy from the audience, one of the kaffir-loving race traitors who always flocked to hear the president, applauding every word he spoke as if he were some kind of deity himself. Her death didn't concern the

Iron Guard's leader. She wasn't a member of his team, and who else really mattered?

It was typical, he thought, that the new "enlightened" media would paint the lone white female victim of the shooting as a part of the assassination team. Koch recalled a time, not very long ago, when kaffirs would have been the instant suspects in her death and the police wouldn't have rested till at least one of them had confessed. Now blacks were presumed innocent unless a videotape of the crime in progress was produced, at which time leftist lawyers would contend that it was staged, complete with stand-ins and special effects, to frame a poor innocent victim.

Worst of all, worse even than the failure of his effort at the stadium, was the fact that the führer had slipped through his fingers. Koch had worked out a plan in his mind to shift the burden of responsibility for the attempted murder. Steuben was responsible. He would confess it in a note, which the police would find beside his lifeless body. Suicide was good enough for Hitler, Goebbels, Himmler—why not Steuben? Who would think it out of character or question Gert van Koch's capacity, his right, to take the führer's place?

Indeed, who else was left?

But Steuben had eluded him, his last chance vanishing like smoke. Koch wished he had told the führer's escorts to detain him, but he had been fearful one of them would let it slip, say something inadvertently to one of the American bodyguards. He had played it safe, and thereby lost his golden opportunity.

Now it was time for *him* to run away.

He saw no other choice, all things considered. Once the shooters were identified—a matter of hours at most, given the police records two or three had boasted—raiders would be scouring the landscape for Iron Guard members, plastering his face and those of his surviving officers across every TV screen and front page in the country.

South Africa's Most Wanted, he thought, and nearly choked on bitter laughter.

Koch wasn't the world's best packer, but he trusted no one else to fill his bags before a trip. Especially not this time, when he knew it was entirely possible that he wouldn't be coming back. What did it matter if the things he packed were wrinkled, creased or badly folded? When he reached his final destination, Koch was confident that he would find a maid or laundry service standing by.

And if he didn't, if he wound up on some tiny tropical island like a castaway, what did it matter if his clothes weren't immaculate?

The more he thought about it, tossing things into his sturdy leather bags, the more Koch thought hiding out in some remote, unsullied paradise might be a grand idea. He didn't want to be alone, of course. He would be taking soldiers with him, and he could afford to staff a modest home with servants if their needs were modest. Someplace virginal, he thought, smiling, like nineteenth-century Tahiti, when the sailors of the *Bounty* first arrived.

A place like that, Koch could be the führer of his own small empire, and it wouldn't matter what Steuben did with the rest of the world, whether he lived or died. A place remote enough to be forgotten, overlooked, ignored.

Locking his bags, he called out to his soldiers in the other room, "I'm ready. Let's get out of here."

No answer.

"Come and get the bags, will you?"

Dead silence from the living room.

Scowling, prepared to blister someone's hide, he moved to the connecting door, which stood ajar, and threw it open. "Are you all asleep in here? I said—"

Koch couldn't continue, as his voice dried up, a kind of raspy whistle emanating from his suddenly constricted throat.

His men were dead. All five of them, sprawled on the carpet or the furniture, blood soaking into pile and fabric from assorted ghastly wounds. Directly opposite, blocking the only exit from the room, a black man with a pistol in his hand stood facing Gert van Koch. Despite his shock, the neo-Nazi was alert enough to note the pistol's sound suppressor.

He turned to run and found the second man behind him, leveling a silenced automatic at his face. This man was white, well built, with grim death in his eyes.

"We need a moment of your time," the stranger said.

HAL BROGNOLA SMILED at recognition of his old friend's voice. "You did it, guy," he said. "It's on the tube. The president came through without a scratch. Congrats to all concerned."

"I'll need a Ouija board to pass it on," Bolan replied.

"Say what?"

The warrior answered with a question of his own. "You hear about nine shooters on the news?"

"That's right." Hal felt a worm of dread begin to wriggle underneath the pink skin of his scalp.

"The Iron Guard only sent in seven," Bolan said. "The other two were ours."

"You mean...?"

"Gellar was hit down on the field. He stopped them getting to the president, apparently, but couldn't save himself. The cops here have him down as some part of the hit team, working on a theory that the shooters started capping one another. God knows why. I don't know if Mossad will want to claim him, in the circumstances, but someone should let them know what happened, at the very least."

"It's done," Brognola promised. Even dreading it, he had to say, "That's only eight."

"The ninth was female," Bolan said.

"I heard that on the—" Brognola imagined that his heart had skipped a beat. "Aw, shit. Oh, no."

"She was supposed to stay at the hotel," Bolan explained, an unfamiliar stiffness in his voice. "We had a deal. She kept her word the last two rounds. We'll never know what set her off this time."

"She knew where it was going down?" The words had barely left his lips before Brognola recognized his critical mistake.

"I kept her up to speed," Bolan replied. "She seemed to take it better that way, being sidelined. How's that for your basic gallows irony?"

"It's not your fault."

"You're absolutely right. She broke her word. Sometimes, you lie, you die."

And leave the hurt to someone else, Brognola thought, but kept it to himself. Instead, he asked, "Where's Gary Stevens in all this?"

"Long gone," the Executioner replied. "He

skipped while we were reinventing contact sports. Lost him again.''

Brognola closed his eyes. "You have some kind of line on him?"

"Better than that. I know exactly where he's going.''

"Oh?"

"I had a little one-on-one with his lieutenant here in Jo'burg. Guy thought he could buy himself a pass with information.''

"Yeah?"

"It didn't work."

"You trust his intel?"

Bolan thought about it for a moment, then said, "Yes, I do. It's too damned crazy to be plucked out of thin air.''

"How's that?"

And Bolan told him. Brognola could feel his jaw drop, snapped it shut again to keep from looking like some inbred idiot. The plan was crazy, sure—but it was also dangerous as hell.

"Antarctica?"

"You heard it right." Bolan's voice was ice-cold, a perfect complement to Brognola's mental image of the frozen continent that capped the bottom of the globe.

"But, what the hell…?"

"You spelled it out the day you briefed me on this job, remember? Hitler and his pals believed the Earth was hollow and the old-line Aryans were tucked away inside, descendants of the early Norsemen or whatever. If memory serves, the SS sent an expedition up to the North Pole—a zeppelin, I think it was—to try and find the entrance to the hidden world.''

"Yeah, I remember that," the big Fed said. "But what—?"

"Stevens has worked out in his head somehow that Adolf and the others got it wrong. Instead of going *up,* they should have sent their people *down.* That's why they missed it, see? Who knows where he comes up with this demented crap. You ask him, I imagine he could talk your leg off quoting chapter and verse from some ancient scroll or tablet. Personally, I don't care what's on his mind, as long as I know where he's going."

"Antarctica," Brognola repeated.

"Antarctica."

"And you don't think this guy you grilled was maybe snowing you? No pun intended, here. You don't think maybe he was sending you off on the ultimate wild-goose chase?"

"The guy thought he was buying life," Bolan replied. "He anteed up the only thing he had to trade."

"But even so—"

"I know the signs," Bolan said, "and this guy believed what he was saying. There's a chance that Stevens lied to him, of course, but I can only check that out by going down to have a look around myself."

"You plan to search Antarctica." Brognola's voice flat-lined to a monotone, weighed down by disbelief. "You're Admiral Peary now?"

"Peary went north, just like the Germans," Bolan said. "You're thinking Amundsen, from Norway."

"Whatever. Can we get real here, for a second? Antarctica has to be—what, three million square miles of ice and snow? Maybe four?"

"More like five and a half," Bolan said.

"Well, hey! You should be done with that around

the halfway point of the millennium, if you don't stop for lunch.''

"I have a fix on where he's going, Hal.''

"You do.'' Somehow the news was not encouraging. ''Terrific.''

"Stevens has the portal marked,'' Bolan explained.

"You mean, he's found the elevator that will take him down to inner Earth?''

"Not quite. That was the second error Hitler's people made, the way he's worked it out. First, going north. And second, thinking that the entrance would be standing open, visible to anyone who happened by.''

"Hey, anyone can see that's crap,'' Brognola said. "Who leaves the front door open when it's ninety-eight below outside?''

Bolan ignored him, pressing on. "That's why the Nordic Temple's team needed a key to help them open up the way.''

"A key?'' It hit him then. "Oh, shit. You're telling me...''

"That's right.''

The nuke.

"He's setting off the bomb so he can meet the supermen downstairs?''

"And call them forth,'' Bolan explained, ''as reinforcements for his ethnic cleansing plan.''

"I missed my guess,'' Brognola said. "This prick's as crazy as they come.''

"You need to find somebody who can calculate the impact of a tactical device exploded at or near the pole,'' Bolan went on. "I'm hoping it will just irradiate the ice and snow, but if it's something worse than that, we need to be prepared.''

"I'm on it," Brognola replied, grabbing a pen and paper, scribbling notes. "And you'll be where, again?"

"I thought I'd crash the party," Bolan said, confirming Brognola's worst fear. "Chill out a while, you know? See if Stevens needs some help with that ignition fuse."

"The smart thing is to call an air strike in and vaporize his Nazi ass."

"Not knowing if the warhead's armed? I don't think so."

"I hate it that you're always right."

"I'm leaving the coordinates with Gellar's contact in Pretoria," Bolan explained. "He's got your number, there. If there's no word from me by Saturday, he'll call and tell you where to go."

"Oh, great. I get that all day long around here as it is, and now some guy I never met is jumping on the bandwagon."

"You'll know him if and when he calls. He'll ask for Striker."

Bolan's code name.

"But you won't be here," Brognola said.

"That's right. You get that call, I won't be anywhere."

"Goddammit!" Brognola relaxed the fist that he had clenched in anger and frustration. He was on the verge of telling Bolan to stay frosty, but he caught himself. "You watch yourself down there, all right? It's not some frigging ski resort."

"I'll be in touch," Bolan replied, and broke the link.

"You'd better." The big Fed was talking to the dial tone, but he still repeated it for emphasis. "You'd better just."

You'd better bring a coat in case our flight down is delayed, but be well expected in the snowplace. "You'll love this."

CHAPTER FIFTEEN

Antarctica is not particularly large, as continents go. In fact, of the earth's seven continents, only Europe and Australia are smaller. In terms of population, the planet's southernmost ice cap loses hands down: it is officially unpopulated, although research teams from several nations are perpetually in residence. Published estimates of its total area range from 5.1 to 5.4 million square miles, all of it sheathed in ice and snow year-round. The coldest temperature ever logged on Earth—a mind-numbing -129° Fahrenheit—was recorded at Vostok in July 1983.

Although Antarctica is inhospitable in the extreme, it hasn't been ignored by humankind. The date when some unhappy sailor first laid eyes upon the frozen wasteland is unknown, but British navigator James Cook is named as the first to cross the Antarctic Circle, in 1773. American and Russian expeditions made the first tentative explorations of Antarctica, in 1820–1821, while Norwegian Roald Amundsen won the international race to the South Pole in 1911.

Politically, Antarctica is open territory, much like Las Vegas and Miami on a Mafia map of the United States. The Antarctic Treaty of 1959 barred any military presence on the frozen continent, and new agreements signed in 1988 permit several competing nations to exploit the region's natural resources, including fish and krill, natural gas, iron ore and offshore oil. Scattered scientific research stations are the only year-round settlements. The only natives of Antarctica are penguins and assorted dwellers of the ice-cold seas.

Bolan had borrowed Jack Grimaldi for his hop from Argentina to the bottom of the world. The two men had been friends since Bolan plucked Grimaldi at gunpoint from his erstwhile occupation as a private pilot for the Mafia and managed to persuade him that there was a better way to spend his time. Both men were veterans of combat in their nation's service and of war against domestic predators who lived outside the law. If asked, Grimaldi might have said that he had seen and done it all.

At least, until the day he dropped his old friend on a barren plain of ice the maps called Queen Maud Land.

"There's no way I can talk you out of this?" he asked once more as Bolan finished packing gear onto his military-issue ATV.

"No way," the Executioner replied.

"We could go back and get some napalm," Grimaldi suggested. "Maybe use a fuel-air bomb instead. Damned Nazis wouldn't know what hit them, and it shouldn't blow the nuke."

"Can't take the chance," Bolan had told him. "Anyway, I still need confirmation that the warhead's really there."

"Try talking sense to some people," Grimaldi muttered.

"It's a bitch, I know." Bolan was smiling as he said, "I'll call you when I'm ready for the pickup."

"I'll be standing by." The pilot didn't sound convinced that he would ever get that call.

"Stiff upper lip," Bolan said.

"Cold like this, you'd better know it," Grimaldi replied.

Now, sixty miles and counting from his drop-off point, Bolan was skimming ice that made the all-terrain vehicle shudder beneath him, rattling his skeleton from head to heels. His four-wheeler was large and sturdy, built to haul a payload that included extra fuel and motor oil, arms and explosives, food and water, plus cold-weather camping gear that might save Bolan's life if he were somehow stranded for any length of time.

Exactly how long it would save his life was anybody's guess, but an extended outing on the ice would definitely be the death of him. That much was crystal clear.

The ATV was open to the elements, a kind of hulking dune buggy, and even though its speed topped out in the vicinity of forty miles per hour over ice and snow, the wind chill it produced was fearsome, shaving eighty-four degrees off the balmy ambient temperature of -20° Fahrenheit. Bolan felt the bone-deep cold gnawing at him despite his head-to-toe layered ensemble that included thermal underwear and socks, insulated pants and cleated snow boots, the thickest sweater he had ever seen, a hooded parka, a ski mask and tinted goggles, knitted gloves under a pair of fur-lined mittens that felt like boxing gloves.

Beneath the heavy parka, Bolan wore a new Beretta 93-R in a fast-draw shoulder rig, for all the good that it would do. Unzipping, fumbling off the mittens, he would give an adversary all the time required to take him down, unless he managed to secure the critical advantage of surprise.

To that end, Bolan had insisted that Grimaldi drop him off a hundred miles from his intended target, to defeat—or at the very least *confuse*—whatever radar might be mounted at the neo-Nazi base camp. Flights across Antarctica weren't uncommon, and while most touchdowns occurred in the vicinity of well-known research stations, random landings on the ice cap weren't so unusual as to excite undue suspicion when the plane came down a hundred miles away.

Who in his right mind would be coming overland from such a distance to intrude upon the führer's privacy?

Grim death, perhaps.

The warrior's other armament included an M-16 assault rifle and M-203 40 mm grenade launcher, with bandoleers of ammunition for both. The 40 mm loads included high explosive, thermite and fléchettes. He also carried C-4 charges with a variety of timers and remote-control detonators, plus frag and smoke grenades. If all else failed, he had a sturdy Ka-bar fighting knife and braided wire garrote, together with his knuckles, boots and teeth.

A crash course on disarming Russian warheads had been offered by a nondescript expert, talking over photos and schematic diagrams in Bolan's Rio Gallegos hotel room the night before he jumped off with Grimaldi for the big freeze. Details of the procedure were hazy in his mind just now as he jolted across the frozen landscape, but they would come back to him when they were needed.

What would happen to this vast deep freeze if Stevens and his neo-Nazi thugs set off their nuclear device? Would the explosion be a futile gesture, briefly melting ice for several miles around ground zero, with no long-term effect?

Or would it make for a disaster that would dwarf the fright films of the 1950s by comparison?

Did anybody even have a clue?

Bolan could only hope it wouldn't matter in the end, that he could reach his target, neutralize all personnel and render the device inoperative before the pointmen for the so-called master race did something even more insane than usual.

It was the best that he could hope for.

And if necessary, he would die in the attempt.

THE ENDLESS SNOW and ice reminded Gerhard Steuben of home. It was no home that he had ever seen, but more of a psychic flashback, what some anthropologists and shrinks referred to as race memory—that is to say, an image branded on the gray matter and on the genes of prehistoric man, so powerful that even after several hundred thousand years of evolution it could still evoke a primal gut response from certain Homo sapiens.

The frozen wasteland spoke to Steuben of Norsemen who had sailed around the world nine hundred years before Columbus conned Spain's king and queen into providing three small ships and a disreputable jailbird crew. The Vikings had been pioneers and warriors, pure of blood and purpose. They had sacked the settlements of those less hardy than themselves and taken what they wanted—*whom* they wanted—when they wanted it.

If only there had been an opportunity for them to meet the Jews, he thought, the rotten world might be a very different place today.

Steuben enjoyed a stroll around the base camp, though he had to dress up like an astronaut prepared to walk in space, and even then couldn't remain outside for more than twenty minutes, maximum. He liked to face the cold, relentless wind, lean into it and feel its power, test himself against the boundless might of nature. An environment very much like this—albeit with some mountains, caves and trees—had spawned the race of which he was a part and launched the members of that race on a divine crusade to rule the world.

It felt like *Roots*, without the slave ships, cotton patch or Chicken George.

He laughed at that, but no one could have heard him twenty feet away. Between the moaning wind and Steuben's thickly insulated mask, the woolen scarf wrapped several times around his head beneath the parka's hood, he could have screamed his lungs out and nobody would hear him, much less any of his soldiers, safe and warm inside the Quonset huts.

He had a two-way radio, of course, bulking the right-hand pocket of his parka, but to use it, Steuben knew that he would have to doff at least one glove, together with his scarf and mask. Skin froze within minutes, in that kind of cold, the damage frequently disfiguring and irreversible.

Besides, he thought, if there was an emergency out here, he'd probably be dead before he had a chance to use the radio.

That thought struck him as curious, even disturbing. He didn't require a psychoanalyst to help him understand what troubled him. He had been hounded for so long and so relentlessly by unseen enemies that Steuben half expected them to turn up here, rise from the ice itself like elemental demons and renew their assault.

As if in response to that image, he felt a fluttering against the left side of his rib cage, like a sparrow trapped inside his clothing, battering itself against the heavy parka to be free. It was the pager, set to vibrate since an aural tone would probably have been inaudible, reminding him that it was time to end his morning constitutional. Steuben possessed no wristwatch that would fit around the parka's sleeve—or that would not freeze up at wind-chill temperatures of -65°—and so one of his soldiers had agreed to page him twenty minutes after he had suited up and gone outside.

He started to ignore the signal, certain he could stand another ten or fifteen minutes, but he understood what that would mean: a panic in the ranks, troops scrambling into thermal gear and snatching weapons from the arsenal, rushing to seek him out and drag him back to safety. As arrogant as Steuben was—and he admitted that; the master race had reason to be arrogant—he wouldn't put his soldiers through that kind of trauma on a whim.

Perhaps tomorrow, he thought, smiling, as a training exercise.

There was an air lock on the east side of the Quonset hut. No coded keypad on the outer wall, since the mechanism would freeze solid in minutes and no hand inside a heavy mitten could manipulate the buttons anyway. The outer door was locked from the inside, forming an airtight seal, except when someone from the live-in team had work to do outside. As soon as they returned, the door was bolted tight behind them, warm air filled the air lock, and gloves could be removed to operate the key pad on the second, inner door. By that time, though, the person trying to get in was already on camera and power to the key pad's locking mechanism could be cut with the flip of a switch by the sentry on duty.

Intruders were unknown in this part of the world, but it would only take one breach to ruin everything, doom everyone on-site. The air lock system, in addition to providing crucial insulation for the living quarters, also let them trap an uninvited visitor, ask questions via intercom and open special hidden vents to freeze his ass if any of the answers were unsatisfactory.

Steuben believed the system was unbeatable, but he experienced a moment of anxiety each time he came back to the Quonset complex from another of his walks. Suppose the others schemed against him when his back was turned but lacked the guts to face him, kill him outright. They could simply lock him out and let the frozen desert do their dirty work. They could—

The outer door resisted Steuben for a heartbeat, then swung open to admit him. That was half the danger gone, right there. He waited for the air lock to warm up a bit, then stripped the mitten and the knitted glove from his right hand, tapping out the five-digit code. Another moment, and the inner door popped open with a sigh that could be welcoming or mournful, all depending on your mood.

Today, he thought it sounded breathless with desire.

The whole place knew what's coming. It could hardly wait.

"So, YOU DON'T KNOW what happens if an A-bomb detonates at the South Pole?"

Brognola's incredulity had to have been registered as anger by the NASA physicist who had consumed the past eleven minutes of his day. "Well, um…" The man seemed desperate not to give offense. "That is essentially correct. I mean, there's never been a nuclear device exploded on Antarctica before. They aren't allowed to be there, if you follow me."

Brognola followed him, all right. The trouble with this young man and his multiple degrees from Yale or Princeton, was that he had spent his postgrad life imagining how things should work in outer space. He obviously didn't have a clue as to how real-world problems came about or were resolved.

"We're talking hypotheticals, all right? Let's just assume there's a nuke on the ice and it happens to blow. Can you give me a working scenario or not?"

Brognola didn't want to spook this character, much less leak any information that was strictly need-to-know. He was already skating on thin ice by consulting "experts" he had never heard of in his life before today. This one, Steven Kaplan, Ph.D., was number four, and the big Fed was beginning to see what the jokester had meant about piling it higher and deeper.

"That depends on the type and size of device," Kaplan replied. "Low yield? High yield? Fission or thermonuclear? Airburst, surface or subterranean? There are devices that kill strictly via radiation, with no appreciable shock wave. Others flatten everything within a radius of several miles. In other words—"

"It all depends," Brognola finished for him, making no attempt to cover his disgust.

"Well, um, exactly. Yes, that's right."

The hell of it was that Brognola couldn't fill in any of the blanks in the equation. They had no description of the nuclear device, except that it apparently could fit inside a large suitcase and be transported by a single man, at least for a limited distance.

"Let's pretend it's small," Brognola offered. "Call it suitcase size. That any help at all?"

"Not terribly," the physicist replied. "I still don't have a clue as to the nature of the bomb or the material employed to build it. Is the suitcase small, large, medium? Is it packed full of fissionable material or—?"

"Go for broke. Assume the worst."

"Well, from the vague dimensions," Kaplan said, "we can rule out the worst, I think. We know it's not a planet killer. Beyond that, however—"

"Not a what?"

"Sorry?"

"You said, 'We know it's not a'…what, again?"

"Oh, right. A planet killer."

"Spell that out for me in simple language, will you, Doc?"

"Of course. A planet killer—theoretically, at least—is a device so large that it would have a global impact, catastrophic and irreparable, resulting in eradication of humankind, perhaps all life as we know it."

"A single bomb can do all that? Such things exist?"

"On paper, certainly. As for reality…you'd have to ask the Kremlin and the Pentagon, assuming anybody in the know would give you more than terse 'no comments' or a lot of double talk."

"Blow up the world, huh?"

"Not exactly," Kaplan said. "You don't need to

destroy the planet to eliminate most forms of life. An axis shift or deviation in Earth's standard orbit. You'd be surprised at the impact a relatively minor deviation in our distance from the sun could have. Throw in earthquakes, tsunamis and volcanoes, wrap it all up in some nice dirty fallout, and you've got the recipe for a new Dark Ages, assuming anyone's around to see it."

"But you said a suitcase bomb can't do all that," Brognola reminded him.

"It's hard to picture one that could."

"Hard to picture, or impossible to build?" Brognola asked.

"Nothing's impossible," Kaplan replied. "The size of the device described suggests that if it detonated on its own, without some kind of chain-reaction link to other nukes, it wouldn't generate sufficient force to cause a global shift."

"Not even if it's detonated at the pole?" Brognola pressed.

"It shouldn't matter. As to impact on the ice cap, though—in terms of melting or displacement, things like that—I'd just be guessing. Someone at the Pentagon or at the AEC may have computer models, but I wouldn't bet the farm on it. Getting a peek at them, assuming that they do exist, would open up a whole new world of problems in itself. Nobody stalls like apathetic or vindictive bureaucrats."

"I heard that," Brognola replied. "Thanks for your time, Doc."

He hung up on whatever the physicist said next, dismissing Dr. Kaplan and the others from his mind. "We know it's not a planet killer." But they really didn't know a goddamned thing. It was a game of odds and probabilities, in which Brognola didn't even have the necessary stats to ante up, much less to bet his hand.

Okay, the good news: Gary Stevens didn't *want* to wipe out life on Earth—unless you counted Jews, blacks, Asians, gays, Hispanics, liberals and any other living soul who disagreed with him about the holy mission of the master race. He didn't want to crack the globe or send it shooting off toward Pluto like a table-tennis ball knocked out of bounds.

All he wanted to do was open the doorway to another world, right, and let all the happy Aryan Vikings come bouncing out to join ranks with the Temple of the Nordic Covenant for Armageddon.

"Jesus H.!" Brognola muttered to himself. "Where do they find these freaks?"

But that, he knew up front, wasn't the question that counted. It didn't matter where Gary Stevens came from, only where he was going and what he would do when he got there.

Correction, he thought. He was already there, already counting down.

Would Bolan be in time to stop him?

Glancing down, the big Fed was surprised to find he had his fingers crossed.

"WE'RE FIVE-BY-FIVE, sir," Eric Glass announced in answer to the question from his führer. "Radar's clear, no bogeys. I believe you lost them this time."

Steuben frowned at that, Glass wondering if he had gone too far, implied that his leader was some kind of coward perhaps, but in the absence of a verbal reprimand he let it go. There was enough to think about now, at ground zero, without dreaming problems up out of thin air.

A time and place for everything, he thought, including paranoia.

They were on the verge of something here. Glass felt the tingle of anticipation like a mild electric shock, coursing along his nerves, lifting the short hairs on his nape and arms. He wasn't sure exactly what would happen when they triggered the device, if it would truly open up a whole new world or simply leave them a giant mess of melted ice and snow, but faith had carried him this far. Faith and determination that the master race would rise again to rule the world within his lifetime, rather than some future generation yet unborn.

He would be part of it, Glass thought. His finger on the trigger when the precious moment came.

"If they were coming, they would have to fly in, yes?"

The question hauled Glass back from his reverie of mushroom clouds and chimneys spewing Jew smoke. "Yes, sir, that's correct," he said with perfect confidence. "The journey overland's a ball breaker. If they could even put a team ashore—I mean, there *is* no shore, per se, but if they could—that team would have almost six hundred miles to travel from the nearest point along the coast. That's over mountains, glaciers, skirting any crevices a man can't step across—and some of them can swallow tanks, no problem."

"It's impossible to take us by surprise, in other words?"

"Well, when you say 'impossible'..."

"I mean exactly that. Can it be done, or not?" Steuben demanded.

"I suppose, if they could drop someone beyond our radar range and let them go from there, it's long-shot possible," Glass grudgingly admitted. "Even so, sir, they'd still have to choose a route, know the terrain—"

"I want patrols out on the ice," Steuben announced. "Around the clock, beginning now. I should have ordered it first thing."

"Sir, you'll recall that we have fifty men on-site...well, fifty-two, including you and me. There are significant logistics problems for the kind of operation you're suggesting."

"Solve them!" Steuben snapped. "And I am not suggesting anything. I'm issuing an order."

"Yes, sir. Right away, sir."

Glass snapped a salute at his führer and marched off to obey, moving with strides that verged on being angry goose steps, through one corridor and then another.

It wasn't his place to argue.

They had a staff of fifty men; that was the good and bad news, all rolled up together. He couldn't send sentries out alone into the wasteland, and while two might be enough for simply hiking over ice and snow, a larger group would be required if they seriously meant to stop encroaching enemies.

What enemies?

Glass understood that Steuben had been shaken, maybe even traumatized, by the events of recent weeks. He had been hunted like an animal from the United States to Europe, on from there to Africa, and now Antarctica. His first chief of security, Sean Fletcher, was among the scores of Temple soldiers who had died along the way; so were his ranking officers in Germany, Croatia, the Ukraine—and now, perhaps, South Africa. There had been no word from Koch since Steuben left Johannesburg, and Glass wouldn't have bet a dollar that the man was still alive and at liberty.

So, maybe there were enemies approaching, even though they left no trace on radar and should have no way of knowing Steuben's destination once he left South Africa. It was a strange world; weird things happened every day, and some of them could be the end of you unless you kept your guard up all day, every day.

Patrols.

To be effective, they should range at least a mile out from the base camp; two was even better. They had brought along a dozen two-man snowmobiles, which meant that he could send four men toward each point of the compass, have them execute a sweep and then return. Call it two hours, out and back. Upon returning, they would find another sixteen men on standby to refuel the snowmobiles and take them out again, a third shift ready in rotation after that. With detonation scheduled in eleven hours and forty-seven minutes—calculated by the führer, God knew how— each team would therefore make two runs: four hours total in the cold, eight hours warm and dry inside.

The Quonset complex was laid out in a kind of ladder formation, as if three giant capital *H*s had been set down on the ice, connected end to end. Living quarters were located at the north end of the complex, with administration and control facilities on the south, storage space in between. Glass still marveled at the fact that the base camp had been constructed without interference, proof positive that the vaunted "superpowers" were sometimes fatally myopic.

Too late now, he thought, and smiled. The lazy bastards could have stopped it once upon a time, but they had missed their chance.

His men would grouse and mutter when he asked for volunteers to take the first shift on patrol, but they would ultimately do as they were told. They were the very best available, and each man recognized his duty to the cause. They would lay down their lives if necessary, and they wouldn't jump at shadows while they scouted fields of empty snow and ice.

ANOTHER SEVENTEEN or eighteen miles to go, by Bolan's calculation; call it half an hour if he held his present speed and didn't launch the ATV into a crevice that had opened since the final round of satellite surveillance photos had been snapped and forwarded ten hours earlier. All bets were off if something happened to the vehicle before his scheduled drop, a mile out from the target, in the shadow of a long snow-covered ridge.

He would be hiking in from there, white clad and hopefully invisible to any watchers at the compound. Would they bother posting sentries, Bolan wondered, or would they trust Mother Nature to protect them from their enemies this time? Approaching the base camp on foot, he would have minimal mobility and virtually nothing in the way of cover if they spotted him and opened fire. Even retreat would be untenable, a long run to nowhere while the gunners framed him in their sights.

One problem at a time, Bolan chided himself. Right now, the wind chill was his enemy, despite the layers of thermal clothing specially designed to trap and hold his body heat. A man could freeze to death in cold like this no matter what he wore, without an independent source of warmth. He had considered ordering one of the sci-fi suits with built-in heating elements, but finally rebelled at the idea of strapping on a battery pack and oxygen tanks, in addition to the mandatory battle gear.

He would make do with what he had and somehow manage to survive.

At least, until he met his enemies.

The ATV was making decent time, its fat tires slipping now and then, but mostly hanging on. There had been no way to completely neutralize the engine noise, but heavy-duty mufflers did the best they could in that regard. The wind helped, too, staying in Bolan's face and helping carry any noise he made away behind him, toward the distant South Atlantic.

Would the Nordic Temple's outpost be equipped with seismic gear to herald a vehicle's approach? He doubted it, but there was no way to be sure. For all he knew, there could be mines planted somewhere up ahead: HE to flip him like a turtle on his back, or Claymores to obliterate him in a giant shotgun blast.

Keep moving.

If a soldier fixated on everything that could go wrong about a mission, he would never leave the barracks. Problems should be recognized, identified and filed away. Obsessing over them was a pathetic, self-defeating waste of time. It played into his adversary's hands and made the enemy more powerful than he had any right to be.

The snowy ridge where Bolan planned to leave the ATV was larger, viewed from level ground, than it had seemed in the surveillance photographs. He took this as a hopeful sign, parked on the ridge's leeward side and pocketed the keys. Bolan already wore white combat webbing; all he had to do now was strap on snowshoes, unpack the M-16/M-203 and load both weapons, chambering a 5.56 mm round.

Whatever happened in the next half hour, even if he blew it somehow, he wouldn't go down without a fight.

The ridge stretched for a mile or so in each direction, roughly north-south, and since there could be no circumnavigating it, he went over the top. A scramble to the summit, then a long slide down the windward side, snow tumbling down behind him in a miniavalanche. Once he had shaken off the worst of it and cleared his weapon, Bolan faced due west and started walking.

Equipped with a compass but no walking odometer, Bolan could only guesstimate his progress as he slogged across the frozen waste. The snowshoes mostly helped, but there were times he would have gladly traded them for cleats to bite the underlying ice. He didn't fall, but it was close, a time or three, Bolan imagining what it would be like if a roving pack of hunters found him here, exposed, nowhere to hide.

At first, he thought the distant whine of motors had been conjured by his brain, to grant the nightmare some verisimilitude. Another moment passed before he recognized the sound as real and understood that he was hearing two engines, at least, approaching rapidly from somewhere to the south-southwest.

Dammit!

Resignedly, he kicked off his snowshoes and lay down in the deepest nearby drift that he could find, to watch and wait.

CHAPTER SIXTEEN

Eight hours and counting.

All of human history came down to this: the final grueling wait before a hero struck a blow for destiny. Given a choice, Steuben would have preferred to arm the nuclear device and start the final countdown now, without delay, but he wouldn't play fast and loose with prophecy.

The hardest part, when all was said and done, was simply trusting in himself.

Prophecies were tricky items at the best of times, and it was no reflection on his officers that some of them should doubt his calculations, even his interpretation of the sacred texts. He had them on that point, of course, because he was the only member of the Temple who could actually read some of the languages—Enochian among them—in which the most critical texts had been written. If no one else could translate what was written down, their argument against Steuben's interpretation of the text lost most of its thrust at the outset.

And still, the waiting was a problem for his men.

Some of them had been cooped up in the Quonset complex for over a month. Rotation and relief had been eliminated when the trouble broke Stateside, after Chicago and Sean Fletcher's death. From that point on, the core group stationed at what they were pleased to call Fatherland South had been cut off from all but sporadic emergency communication, surviving on their ample stores, uncertain as to if or when they would be liberated from their frozen exile.

Soon.

A few more hours now, barely a normal workday's stretch between the time they punched a time card coming in and going out again. A soldier who could not wait eight more hours to win the world was obviously not cut out to rule it in the first place.

Steuben's prophecy was vague on what exactly should occur after the warhead detonated. Tons of ice would naturally melt, and he expected shock waves, even though the bomb was sunk in ice three quarters of a mile due west of the complex. It should be nothing catastrophic, but they were prepared for minor damage, double rigged and battened down.

Choosing the perfect place to sink a shaft and plant the warhead was another challenge, every bit as critical as the selection of the date and time for detonation. He presumed that there were many hidden entrances that granted access to the world within, but if a certain portal has been specified in prophecy, no other may be used without dire consequences, a disastrous boomerang effect. Steuben preferred to follow all the rules as they had been revealed to him—and pray that he hadn't fucked up.

What a pathetic epitaph might still be his: Here Lies A Man Who Could Have Ruled The World...If He Had Only Paid Attention During Ninth-Grade Algebra.

Feeling a hyper moment just around the corner, Steuben told himself that he'd made no errors. None.

Who was there to dispute his painstaking translation of the ancient texts? Who dared to make a claim of having put in longer hours, studied more obscure material, before determining the date and place where a strategic blow would open up the path to inner Earth? Reichsführer Himmler himself had wasted untold money and man-hours trying to find that portal at the North Pole, rather than the South. Was it a clumsy error of interpretation, or was Himmler meant to fail, the honor held in trust for someone who would come along behind him, generations later?

Someone like Gerhard Steuben?

If a person had no faith in himself, why should anyone else?

It was a fact of life, he understood, that small-minded fools often mistook true genius for insanity. Why not, when their own thought process was so stunted that they could not grasp the obvious? How could they appreciate a man of boundless vision, when they themselves were blind?

How could—?

The shock of the explosion sent a shudder through the Quonset complex, rippling through the walls and floor beneath him. Steuben's first reaction was to check his wristwatch, even though he knew it would be more than seven hours yet before he joined Glass in the camp command post to set off the nuclear device. A flash of panic told him something had gone wrong: some fool had keyed the button prematurely or the weather had done something to the firing mechanism, causing it to trigger on its own. The years of work and planning all were wasted, ruined, just because—

A blaring fire alarm told Steuben he was wrong, his fear misplaced. The blast a moment earlier hadn't been nuclear; it had occurred within the base camp proper and some portion of the structure was on fire.

A different kind of panic gripped him now. He couldn't guess the source or cause of the explosion—they had gasoline and diesel fuel aplenty, propane for the stoves, conventional explosives, arms and ammunition—but he knew that any major compromise of their manmade environment could be lethal. If they lost their heat and shelter, Steuben and his soldiers faced the prospect of an icy death.

And there was something even worse, in Steuben's view.

If they lost power, if the generators went, they also lost the ability to detonate the warhead on command.

What could have—?

Steuben hesitated, halfway to the exit from his private quarters. What if the explosion hadn't been an accident? he asked himself, feeling a clammy sweat break out beneath his clothes, although the temperature inside the Quonset complex was—so far, at least—a constant seventy degrees.

What if his nameless enemies had found him once again?

Preposterous! Unthinkable!

But Steuben thought about it anyway and doubled back to find the pistol that he kept beneath his pillow on the narrow wall-mounted bunk. Its solid weight provided a measure of comfort as he tucked it into the right-hand pocket of his jumpsuit. Leaving nothing to chance, he removed two spare magazines from the top drawer of his small dresser and slipped them into his left-hand pocket.

Better safe than sorry, as the old cliché proclaimed.

He had been sorry quite enough in recent weeks, and was no longer sure exactly what "safe" felt like anymore. One thing seemed certain, though: if his relentless enemies had tracked him here, to the very root of the world, it was bound to be the last act of the drama, one way or another. He didn't expect the helicopter pickup for another seven hours and fifty minutes, well after the warhead had been detonated and its impact judged. There would be no escape, except perhaps across the ice.

And how far could he travel on a snowmobile, before the hunters ran him down?

Determined not to waver this time, Steuben left his quarters and went looking for his second in command.

THE HUNTERS HAD been easy.

Lying in the snowbank, watching them approach, Bolan knew that he could take them down. Two snowmobiles, four passengers. All four of them were armed, but they were carrying their weapons slung, drivers grappling with the handlebars of their vehicles, passengers hanging on with both hands.

At first he thought they might have been dispatched specifically to hunt him down, the hardsite's radar more effective than he'd hoped, perhaps some more sophisticated gear in place that he had missed. On second thought, however, it was clear the snowmobiles were only traveling in Bolan's general direction. If they held their present course, the nearer of the two would pass some twenty-five or thirty yards to his left and keep on heading eastward to the ridge where he had left the ATV.

Was that their fix? Had they picked up on the machine somehow, but missed it when he moved ahead on foot?

Unlikely, Bolan thought. In fact, their almost casual approach made him doubt their consciousness of any lurking threat. More likely, he decided, this was a routine patrol sent out to scan the ice and reassure the brass that they were all alone in no-man's-land. He took for granted that they would be carrying at least one two-way radio and knew that anything he did would have to be decisive, brisk and bold.

He edged around to track the lead snowmobile with his M-16, the rifle set for semiautomatic fire. He chose a point well ahead of the snorting vehicle, calculating its velocity, allowing for windage on gusts that now and then drew veils of drifting snow across his line of fire.

The hard part, Bolan calculated, wouldn't be the first kill; it would be the double play.

The M-16, like most modern assault rifles, is built specifically to minimize recoil. Unlike the classic hunting rifle with its angled stock, which actually encourages the muzzle to buck with each shot, the M-16's "straight-through" design with high-set sights vastly improves accuracy, without appreciable recoil from its high-velocity 5.56 mm ammunition. At the delivery end, those rounds compensate for their .22-caliber size by tumbling on impact with flesh and bone, producing gross internal damage even from a relatively minor hit.

His first shot struck the driver in the left side, at a point midway between his armpit and his hip. He had already fired a second round by then, knowing the pillion passenger would occupy the driver's space a heartbeat later, just in time to feel the 5.56 mm tumbler rip into his shoulder socket and explode into his upper chest.

Bolan ignored the dead men riding, shifting slightly for his first shot at the second snowmobile. It took only a second, but the passenger on number two had noticed something out of place about their teammates, angling one hand past the driver's face in their direction as he shouted something through his insulated mask.

Too late.

The Executioner's third round punched through the driver's parka, jolting him. A gloved hand rose from the accelerator, swooping toward the wound, but only made it halfway there before a fourth shot echoed on the frozen flats.

That one, reserved for the excited passenger, slammed into him at 3,250 feet per second and lifted him out of the saddle, as if an invisible cable had yanked him from behind. The snowmobile went on without him for another thirty yards or so, then slewed around in answer to a dead hand at the helm, kicked up a fan of snow, and died.

The other snowmobile was still in motion, chugging on despite the loss of both its passengers. It ran on, arrow straight, until it found the snowy ridge and tried to climb it, failed at that, and settled back to run in place, its tracks displacing snow until they found the ice beneath and spun in vain.

Bolan was on his feet by then, moving among the dead. One of the point riders had landed on his side, a crumpled form that showed no sign of life besides the crimson bloom soaked through his parka at the back. His passenger was also dead but didn't know it yet. He used one arm to drag himself across the ice, leaving a bloody trail and going nowhere fast. He didn't seem to have a radio—or if he did, wasn't inclined to use it. Bolan let him crawl in lieu of squeezing off another shot that might alert some other team of hunters that he couldn't see.

Both riders from the second snowmobile were down and out. He spent enough time with them to be sure that they weren't about to rise again, then turned and walked back to their vehicle. The snowmobile had stalled out, but he got it started on the second try, familiarized himself with the controls in nothing flat and pointed it in the direction of his target.

It would save some time, now that the enemy had been engaged, and Bolan couldn't say for sure if any ears still living had picked up the sound of distant rifle shots. He gunned the snowmobile westward and held it steady, feeling the vibration in his guts and groin, riding until he saw the hardsite as a smudge on the horizon, maybe half a mile ahead. He killed the engine then and started walking in.

He met no other riders, heard no challenge as he neared the Quonset huts, circling toward the north end. He had already seen the hardsite's layout from the air, in photographs, but didn't know how many troops were present in the complex, how they were distributed or where the nuclear device was stashed. Would Stevens keep it here, or was it hidden somewhere else? In either case, would it be armed by now, some kind of timer counting down to the apocalypse?

Refusing to be cowed by doubt, Bolan proceeded with the plan he had worked out before he went aboard the cargo aircraft with Grimaldi. He removed a brick of C-4 plastique from his pack, attached and armed a detonator, jogging briskly onward to the west.

He needed cover now, such as it was. A place where he could wait and see what happened when the C-4 blew.

And forty-seven seconds later, he found out.

"THE STRUCTURE HAS been compromised by an exterior explosion at the north end of the complex, source and cause unknown." As Eric Glass pronounced the words that could spell death for every member of his team, he felt a preview of the chill that would be permeating corridors and rooms within the next half hour, tops.

"Can you explain that to me, Eric?" The expression on his führer's face would have been comical, in other circumstances. Steuben's features twitched, as if he didn't know whether to laugh or scream.

"No, sir," Glass said. "At least not yet. I have some people checking out the damage. They can tell the blast occurred outside, because the wall and insulation were punched inward. Otherwise—"

"North end, you said. That's living quarters. What is there at that end of the complex to explode?"

"Nothing that I can think of, sir. I—"

Glass was grateful for the sharp hiss of the two-way radio, one of his people at the blast site checking back. "Go on," he said.

"Smells like C-4 down here," the soldier told him.

"Are you sure?"

"It's fuckin' hard to miss, sir." And, belatedly, "Um, sorry, sir."

"What can we do about the breach?" Glass asked, ignoring the lapse in military courtesy.

"If we can cut away the ragged edges, throw one of the prefab sections up and get a spot-weld going, we can close it, sir. I couldn't tell you how long it'll take. No expertise on that end, sir."

"I'll get some people on it ASAP," Glass replied. "You men stay put and keep an eye out for intruders. You see someone, take them out—but make sure that it's not one of our own patrols returning from the sweep."

"Affirmative," the eager voice came back at him. "We won't cap anybody on a snowmobile, sir."

"Well," he turned to Steuben, wishing he could keep the scowl from dragging down the corners of his mouth, "it was apparently a bomb, sir. C-4 plastique, planted on the outside of the northern wall."

"A bomb? How can there be a bomb outside the northern wall, Eric? We're in the middle of Antarctica. You look up *nowhere* in the dictionary and you'll find a map with arrows pointing here. There's miles and miles of flat-assed nothing all around us. How could anyone get close enough to plant a goddamned bomb?"

"I don't know, sir." His mind was racing, coming up with more questions than answers. "You remember we decided not to go all-out on the exterior-security devices when the site was built. Motion detectors, mines, closed-circuit cameras. The thought was that our radar would pick up on any hostile presence in the neighborhood and give us time to set a trap or bail."

Glass didn't mention that the thought was Steuben's, issuing commands from somewhere in the warm-and-sunny U.S.A. while miserable, frost-bitten workers were putting the base camp together. In all fairness, the skimping on security had seemed entirely reasonable at the time. How did you sneak up on an armed camp in the middle of a snow-white frozen wasteland, where cover was restricted to windblown snowdrifts and the occasional upthrust ridge of ice?

"This can't be happening," Steuben declared. "We have patrols—"

"That's it!" Glass fairly shouted out the words as revelation dawned.

"That's what?"

"They picked off one of the patrols somehow and rode the scooters back. It has to be."

"One team?" There was a sudden glint of hope in Steuben's eyes. "Two snowmobiles can only seat four men," he said.

"If they took out all four patrols, it means we're totally surrounded," Glass replied. "I can't believe they put those kind of numbers on the ice without a radar blip."

"Four men," Steuben repeated, close to smiling now. "That means we have them outnumbered by more than ten to one."

Glass didn't care to spoil his führer's mood by stating the obvious: that a larger team could have ambushed the patrol, with infantry trailing the snowmobiles back to their base. Why borrow trouble? And besides, if there were dozens of commandos on the ice, all poised to strike, what were they waiting for?

And one more thing...

"I think they're still outside," Glass said. And then, before Steuben could ask, "There would be shooting, otherwise."

"Of course!" The führer positively beamed. "If we can keep them out and keep the complex in one piece—"

"We win," Glass finished for him. "I'll get on it, sir."

Glass moved to the command console and keyed the intercom, began dictating orders to his troops. It made no difference if the commands were audible to adversaries crouched in freezing cold outside. In fact, he wanted them to know that they were standing in the path of a relentless juggernaut. Breaking an enemy's resolve was half the battle, and Glass wanted all the edge that he could get.

Something told him that he would need it, very soon.

THE WAIT WAS relatively brief, and Bolan huddled in a relatively wind-free pocket where two Quonset huts were joined to make an elbow or perhaps a T. He lay in the snow, which was remarkably dry at -30° Fahrenheit, like artificial flakes on a Hollywood soundstage. It was the best that he could do in terms of cover, while he waited for his enemies to show themselves.

Another way to go would have been planting more C-4 and blowing down their house, but Bolan balked at further random demolition of the site, at least until he had some hint of where the stolen nuke was stashed. A C-4 charge might not unleash the warhead's blinding light, if it was still unarmed, but it could breach the shields and unleash radiation in a lethal dose.

And a protracted, agonizing death by radiation poisoning wasn't on Bolan's daily list of things to do.

He heard the shooters coming, even though they tried to run a stealthy sweep. Given the circumstances—their confusion and excitement, geographic isolation and a barren landscape, deathly silence in the wake of the C-4 explosion—Bolan doubted whether any unit could have pulled it off.

Again, there were four men; all dressed in white, all armed. They spilled out through a doorway to his left, some fifty yards away. The door eased shut behind them, no slam to betray their exit, but it is impossible to walk silently on ice and frozen snow. Each step the gunners took produced sounds that reminded him of creaking Styrofoam.

Four shooters he could see, but Bolan didn't take for granted that these were the only four dispatched to scout around the site's perimeter. He would assume that there were other teams, emerging even now from different exits, but the four in front of him had Bolan's full attention at the moment.

Lying in the powdered snow, he watched them drawing nearer, moving cautiously across the ice. Three of the hunters carried M-16s, their pointman having opted for a Remington 870 shotgun. Both weapons were lethal at Bolan's distance from the gunners, but the pointman was marginally more dangerous, since buckshot or fléchette loads would eliminate the need to pause and aim.

The shotgunner was thirty paces out, give or take, when Bolan lined up on his chest and put a 5.56 mm tumbler through his parka and the sternum underneath. The guy was dead before he knew it, but he had his finger on the shotgun's trigger, squeezing off a blast that fanned the air away to Bolan's right with whistling death.

There was no time to watch the pointman fall, as Bolan shifted toward his secondary target, scoping on the next soldier in line. All three of the survivors were reacting as if they had trained for such a moment, crouching, falling out of their formation, numbers two and three breaking to right and left, respectively, while number four fell back in the direction of their exit from the complex.

None of them were firing yet, still scanning for a likely mark, and Bolan took advantage of their hesitation, drilling number two with a head shot. Staggering, the neo-Nazi tried to bring a hand up to his face, but all his mental circuits were misfiring, shutting down at once, and he wound up simply fanning the air as if he were waving goodbye.

Number three had glimpsed Bolan's muzzle-flash, or thought he had, firing from the hip with his M-16. The bullets kicked up spouts of snow and chipped ice in a ragged line, perhaps a yard to Bolan's right. He didn't know if nervousness had spoiled the gunner's aim or if he had misjudged the range, but either way, it was an opportunity that he couldn't afford to miss. His rifle cracked out twice, the human target lurching, going down on one knee like a drunkard, holding there for several beats before he toppled over on his face. He raised a little cloud of snow on impact, as if he had fallen into talc or dust.

The last surviving member of the team was running for his life, mission forgotten as he sprinted for the nearest door that would admit him to the Quonset complex. Bolan tracked him, milked another tumbler from his M-16, and saw the quilted fabric of the runner's parka ripple as the round went home. It punched the neo-Nazi forward, giving him additional momentum, but he couldn't handle it and made the last three paces on his toes, like an ungainly skater heading for a fall.

Instead of simply sprawling on the ice, though, he collided with a corner of the Quonset hut before him and rebounded with a muffled thunk! The dead man landed on his back with arms outflung, as if someone had staked him to the ice, a frosty crucifixion. For a moment it appeared that he might try to rise again, his back arched, boot heels scraping at the ice, but then he slumped back into flaccid death, a final puff of steam escaping from behind the fabric of his mask.

Bolan got up, moved past the dead men, homing on the door through which they had appeared brief moments earlier. There was a foot-square window in the door, a dimly lighted corridor beyond, but when he risked a look in through the heavy Plexiglas, he could see no one waiting on the other side. There were shapes moving farther back, beyond a second windowed door, but none of them appeared to be concerned about the fate of the patrol he had wiped out.

He tried the door handle, but it refused to budge. Self-locking, with the likelihood of accidents and loss of crucial heat in mind should someone fail to latch the door securely on his own.

No matter.

Bolan had no lock picks with him, and it would have been a foolish error to discard his gloves in any case, as he would surely have to do if he was planning a clandestine entry. As it was, he thought a more direct approach might be appropriate.

Retreating from the doorway several yards, he braced the M-16 against his hip, left index finger curled around the trigger of the M-203 launcher mounted underneath the rifle's barrel. One HE round coming up.

Assuming that you had to crash a party, Bolan thought, it was the only way to go.

THE SECOND BLAST wasn't as loud as the original explosion—or perhaps it came from farther off, more insulated walls and airtight doors between ground zero and the place where Gerhard Steuben stood, in the command post. Even so, the echo made him jump, and that in turn made Steuben furious. He spun to see if any of the others in the CP were regarding him with scorn, amusement or contempt, but only caught them sharing worried glances, double-checking weapons, monitoring life-support controls.

The Quonset complex was constructed like a submarine or space station. Its occupants wouldn't explode or drown upon exposure to the frozen world outside, but they were certainly at risk of major injury or death from any long exposure to the elements. Without the complex as a base camp—its sustaining shelter, warmth, food, water and communications with the outside world—they would be stranded in an Ice Age wasteland where no unprotected person was able to survive.

A brilliant plan, Steuben thought. All except the part where enemies came sneaking up and blew in the walls with plastique, and no one did a thing to head them off.

It wasn't true, the would-be führer thought, that in the final moments of your life, when death was near, the images of bygone days appeared to soothe or haunt. Steuben had reason to believe that he might die within the next few minutes, based upon the luck his troops had had in dealing with these nameless, face-less enemies before. And yet no images from Steuben's past were coming up—not even when he closed his eyes.

Instead, he glimpsed the future as it might have been, if he had been allowed to carry out his plan, fulfill his destiny. He saw a planet purged of Jews and mud people, with clear-eyed Aryans in charge and harmony the order of the day. A moment later, and he watched that beatific vision crumble as if rotting from within, consumed by cancer, all the worse in Steuben's mind for knowing that the cure had been within his grasp.

If only...

What?

If only he hadn't been stopped before he set the warhead off at the predicted time and place.

But he hadn't been stopped! Not yet!

A glance at Steuben's watch confirmed what he already knew: he still had hours to wait before the blast could manage to achieve its purpose. If he waited where he was or tried to hide somewhere inside the Quonset complex, Steuben sensed that he would be long dead before that crucial time arrived.

If he stayed where he was...or if he tried to hide inside the complex?

But there was, of course, a third alternative.

He couldn't flee and hope to live, but he could get away. There was a difference between the two. And in the process, Steuben thought he might be able to confuse his enemies, at least enough to keep them hunting through the ruins of the complex, finishing his men, perhaps assuming that the warhead they could not locate was somehow neutralized with the destruction of the camp's command post.

Let them dream.

Steuben could beat them yet, the bastards whom he still hadn't identified. It didn't even matter if he lived to see the end result or not, as long as he was faithful to his mission and the prophecy that guided him. Perhaps his sacrifice had always been the hidden element, obscured from Steuben's eyes in case a sudden glimpse of death might frighten him off course.

It was doable! he thought, and there was even a slim chance—well, slim to none—that he might manage to survive. In any case, if this turned out to be his final living act, at least Steuben would know that he had died in a good cause.

But first he had to make his way outside. And that meant suiting up, arming himself, finding an unattended and undamaged snowmobile. He would need certain basic tools, a compass, weapons and a source of electricity. That part, at least, was easy: he could always use the scooter's battery.

But getting out could be a problem.

If he didn't watch his step, it just might get him killed.

And that, the führer thought, would be an awful waste.

CHAPTER SEVENTEEN

The high-explosive charge took down one door, and its concussion, ripping through the air lock, bowed the other in its frame, springing the lock. Bolan reloaded with another HE round and entered through a swirl of acrid smoke, feeling the tendrils wrap around him and insinuate themselves into the fabric of his thermal garb. It was like going to a bar where everybody smoked but you, and coming home with the tobacco reek all in your hair and clothes.

Except that this time, no one in the place was having any fun.

The tinted snow goggles were a hindrance now, and Bolan pushed them well back on his forehead, up under the hood of his parka. Heavy mittens dangling by their cords like swollen, not quite severed hands, he cleared the second door with three swift kicks that left his right leg sore and jittering from impact.

The corridor was empty as he entered, but it didn't stay that way for long. It was as if his HE blast had cleared the hallway, forcibly expelling any nearby enemies, but at the same time caused a vacuum that would shortly suck them back in even greater numbers than before.

They came with guns, no time to stop and count

them as they opened fire on Bolan from the far end of the corridor and from the open doorway of at least two rooms ahead. He answered with his M-16 set for full-auto fire, saw one of his assailants drop, another reeling back along the wall and clutching at a dangling arm. The first door Bolan tried was open and he ducked inside, a storm of bullets rattling the ceiling, walls and floor where he had stood a moment earlier.

Bolan unclipped a frag grenade from his web gear, primed it and pitched it out into the firestorm, angling for a ricochet off the opposite wall. He couldn't hear the impact with so many weapons firing together, and if anyone on the home team saw trouble coming, his warning shout was lost in the general chaos.

Bolan heard the blast, though, and he was ready for it, bursting from cover with shrapnel still airborne, picking targets from the haze of battle smoke and dropping them with short precision bursts. This time he counted, made it seven by the time he flushed a gunner from the last room on his right and nailed him with a rising burst of 5.56 mm tumblers. With the snowmobile patrol and scouts outside, that made it fifteen down.

How many more to go?

The only targets Bolan really cared about were Gary Stevens and the stolen warhead, but he understood that he would have to face the tinhorn führer's troops before achieving either one of those objectives. Even now, looking around the place, he had to wonder if the nuke was even there. Glancing around as he moved on, Bolan saw nothing to suggest it was the storehouse for a nuclear device.

A bullet zipped past Bolan's face, the gunshot audible a split second later, and suddenly there was another firestorm brewing. Scattered pop-pop-pops at first, increasing like the tempo of exploding fireworks, building swiftly toward the main event, Fourth of July in Hell.

He had to find cover or die, but the first door he tried, on his right, wouldn't budge. A bullet creased the left sleeve of his parka, spewing eiderdown, and another stroked his thigh with liquid agony. No penetrating wound—not yet—but he was definitely out of time and borrowing against his next life as he ducked and weaved across the killing floor.

He rushed the door directly opposite and threw his weight against it, rebounding from the first solid impact. Another bullet slapped his parka, missing flesh by some minute percentage of an inch. Firing the M-16 one-handed, Bolan tried the knob, turned it and spilled headfirst across the threshold, small arms snapping at his heels.

The room was occupied, its tenant juggling pants and pistol, teetering on one leg with a rumpled bunk behind him. Bolan shot him in the chest without a second thought, the reek of loose bowels wafting to compete with those of cordite and fresh blood.

Outside, the firing squad was edging closer, yard by yard. Bolan knew what he had to do, ejecting the high-explosive round from his M-203 launcher and replacing it with a buckshot cartridge. That done, he hauled the slim, dead neo-Nazi upright, trousers hobbling his ankles and dragged him to the open doorway.

"You won't feel a thing," he told the flaccid mannequin, propelling it into the corridor beyond. It would have slumped immediately to the floor if anxious trigger fingers hadn't taken over, hosing it with automatic fire. They held Bolan's fresh kill upright for what seemed an endless moment, waltzing him across the floor while bloody bits and pieces of himself were blown away and plastered to the walls.

It clicked with someone on the hit team finally, and Bolan heard a ragged voice call out, "Cease fire! That's one of ours! Goddammit, stop!"

It took another moment for the order to sink in, but then the firing faltered, stopped, and Bolan's meat puppet collapsed in ruin, half the man he used to be. Bolan was ready, made his move immediately, while his enemies were still recovering from shock. He lunged into the corridor, unleashed the 40 mm buckshot round and raked the hallway with full-auto fire. Five startled neo-Nazis tried to save themselves, but it was already too late. The blast of leaden pellets from his M-203 launcher cut three from the pack, leaving Bolan to pick up a split with shooters to his left and right.

The left-hand target was a little closer, Bolan's high-velocity projectiles ripping through him, speckling crimson on the curved, beige-painted wall. His comrade had an MP-5, short muzzle sweeping toward Bolan, taking up the trigger slack. Unfortunately for the master race, the piece was empty, its last rounds expended on a dancing corpse. The soldier's face went slack with disbelief a beat before another burst from Bolan's automatic rifle took him down.

He took a moment to reload the launcher and switch magazines on the M-16. The old one wasn't altogether empty yet, but it was getting there. This way, he was prepared for anything and wouldn't be caught short.

Hunting, the Executioner moved on in search of other prey.

THE MOVIE IMAGERY came out of nowhere, startling Eric Glass. Kenneth Tobey in *The Thing,* with James Arness in monster makeup as the veggie vampire from beyond the stars, terrorizing scientists and soldiers at an Arctic research station. One by one the humans were picked off.

Screw that!

The soldiers won in the original 1951 production, which for Glass's money was vastly superior to the remake, filmed thirty years later. To hell with the new age of special effects.

The soldiers—his soldiers—would win this fight, too.

Granted, he didn't know whom they were fighting yet, but they were obviously dealing with a relatively small shock force, no aircraft, armor or artillery. A large force would have overwhelmed them by now or simply pounded the complex flat with heavy fire. Glass couldn't say how many troops were on the strike team, but he guessed that his men had the enemy outnumbered five or six to one, at least.

Depending on how many of them had been killed, that was.

He had reports of losses, but they were disjointed and included no specific body counts. Glass guessed that he'd lost at least half a dozen men so far, and maybe twice that number. The uncertainty infuriated him, but there was little he could do about it at the moment. Running up and down the smoky corridors himself would not accomplish anything except to make the situation even more chaotic—and of course jeopardize the base commander's life.

And speaking of commanders, where had Steuben gone? One moment he was standing right at Glass's elbow, kibitzing, but then, when Glass had turned around to ask the führer something, he had disappeared.

No sweat, Glass thought. He couldn't go far.

But that wasn't what troubled him. He wasn't even terribly concerned about his führer's safety at the moment, when he had the base camp and a team of fifty soldiers to defend. It would be an embarrassment if Steuben died on his watch, but it was a sure-fire way to win promotion, too.

What troubled Eric Glass right now was an oppressive sense that Steuben hadn't run off in a panic, to hide in his quarters, but rather that he had some kind of wild hare up his ass, some crazy scheme to save the day.

Instinctively, Glass turned to check the firing console they had set up for the nuclear device, feeling a surge of almost sexual relief when he discovered that the firing key was still in place. So much for *that* fear, anyway. It was irrational, of course: what could Steuben have done with the key if he took it? There was no alternate trigger mechanism in the complex. To set the nuke off without using the console, a guy would have to cross the open ice, three quarters of a mile, and jury-rig some kind of trigger at ground zero. It could work, if the mechanic knew what he was doing, but there was no timer attached to the warhead. It would be a flat-out kamikaze mission with no hope at all of survival.

"Fuck a goddamned screaming duck!" Glass blurted out.

Two soldiers blinked at him from their combat stations, one with nerve enough to ask, "Say what, sir?"

"Nothing!" Glass snapped. "I want reports from

all positions, and I want them now. Get on the PA system. Have them use the intercoms, walkies, whatever. How the fuck can I direct troops if I don't know who's alive or where they are?''

''Yes, sir!'' one of the soldiers answered.

''Right away, sir!'' his companion echoed.

''I'll be back,'' Glass said. Another movie line, but what the hell.

It wasn't victory, in Eric Glass's mind, unless he came out of the fight alive and relatively whole. The dueling voices in his head enjoyed a brief but spirited exchange on whether he should even try to locate Gerhard Steuben. Would Steuben scrap all his long-winded talk about the prophecy to blow the nuke ahead of schedule? More importantly, if that was his decision, why should Glass attempt to stop him?

Let him go.

But something—call it duty—made Glass go in search of the man he had once idolized, whom he still admired despite certain lapses of reason that seemed to come with the territory of genius. Glass was a soldier first, and that meant pursuing a standard of loyalty that sometimes flew in the face of self-preservation.

If Steuben was already gone, that was one thing. Glass wasn't about to follow him across the ice, abandoning his post and men in pursuit of a suicidal prophet. On the other hand, if Steuben hadn't left the complex yet, there was a chance Glass could restrain him, reason with him—knock him out cold, if necessary.

Think how very different the modern world could be if someone in the führer bunker had prevented Hitler from committing suicide in 1945. He could have slipped out through the sewers of Berlin if need be, rallied loyalists in the mountains of Bavaria or fled to South America with Bormann and the rest. Who could predict what would have happened with the great man himself in charge of preparations for the Fourth Reich's challenge to effete democracy?

Passing the arsenal, its door unlocked and standing open, Glass ducked in and helped himself to an Uzi, loaded and cocked it, shoving spare magazines into his pockets. Glass had no clear use in mind for all that firepower, but he knew it was madness to move through the smoky halls of a compound under siege without some means of self-protection.

"I'm coming," he muttered to no one. "Just hang on."

FOOTSTEPS APPROACHED in a rush.

Rather than seek a place to hide, Bolan dropped to one knee and fixed his rifle sights on the T-intersection before him. His ears were ringing from incessant gunfire and explosions, but he judged his adversaries were approaching from his left, along the north-south corridor.

A moment later they were visible, one of them squawking at the sight of Bolan with his weapon leveled, losing traction in a skid that dropped him on his butt. The acrobat's companion was a little more coordinated, lurching to a halt and seeking target acquisition with a silencer-equipped Ingram subgun.

The little "room broom" could shred any man alive at thirty feet, but Bolan's adversary never had a chance to use it, as a 3-round burst of 5.56 mm slugs ripped through his chest and hurled him back against the nearest wall.

The dead man's friend had dropped his rifle when he fell, a fatal error in the present circumstances. He was rolling over, groping for it, when a second burst from Bolan's M-16 sheared off the left side of his face, pitching the tattered rag doll over on its back.

Based on the aerial surveillance photos and his early walking circuit of the hardsite, Bolan estimated he had covered roughly one-third of the complex, killing everyone he met along the way, and there was still no trace of Gary Stevens or a recognizable command post. Every moment spent without primary target acquisition felt to Bolan painfully like wasted time, the doomsday numbers thundering inside his skull. It was a short half second's work to fire the nuke, assuming it was armed for detonation, and he was aware of moving down the smoke-filled hallway with his muscles clenched in grim anticipation of the white-hot supernova that would end his life.

Not yet.

If it were just that simple, Stevens could have blown the warhead at the first sign of a hostile presence at the hardsite. Why had he delayed? Was there some glitch in the technology, or did he have another reason Bolan hadn't fathomed yet?

Beyond a vague, generic understanding of the racial and religious hatred that propelled him, it was difficult to grasp the mind-set of a man who thought some ancient Nordic deity had handpicked him to rule the world. He was delusional, at least in some respects, but that didn't prevent him from devising battle plans, dictating strategy. Each move he made was leading toward the same apocalyptic goal, and even though he stood no chance at all of conquering the earth, that built-in limitation didn't make him harmless to the human race or the environment. Brognola's efforts to determine what a nuclear explosion at the pole might mean had been a waste of time, as far as a consensus was concerned, but Bolan didn't need a degree in nuclear physics to know that permitting the blast was a lousy idea.

But where was the nuke?

So far, no clue.

Bolan was setting charges as he went, each hundred feet or so, digital timers counting down as he proceeded on his way. Whatever lay ahead of him, the portions of the complex he had checked were clear, and they would soon be uninhabitable. He was shutting down the neo-Nazi base at the South Pole, whatever happened with the missing warhead.

In the process, he had whittled down the home team, mopping up resistance where he found it, leaving C-4 packages behind and moving on. The neo-Nazis seemed to lack determination now, almost as if their will was broken and they simply wanted to get out of there by any route available. At one point, he had found an emergency exit propped open, its alarm disabled, tracks of several warriors leading off across the snow outside.

He wished them luck and went back to the hunt.

As focused as he was, he nearly walked into a trap. The shooters would have nailed him, staking out a major intersection where four tunnels met, but one of them was nervous, fidgeting, as Bolan came around the corner into range. The movement wasn't much to speak of, just a flicker at the corner of his eye, but it did not belong there and he hit the deck a fraction of a beat before all hell broke loose.

At least three automatic weapons were unloading

on him, Bolan trying to return fire with his M-16 before they pinned him down. It wasn't having the effect he needed, so he tried the 40 mm piece, launching a high-explosive round downrange as he retreated with a kind of wriggle in reverse.

The blast brought down some ceiling tiles and silenced one of the shooters, his companions laying down erratic cover fire as they tried to withdraw. Before they could accomplish that, however, Bolan heard somebody raging at them, rattling off a submachine-gun burst for emphasis.

"You will not run!" the new arrival shouted, furious, his voice cracking. "You will hold the line or die a fucking coward's death!"

A glance was all he needed to identify the owner of that voice. Bolan had seen the face ages ago, it seemed, among the mug shots Hal Brognola had displayed for him at Stony Man. The soldier's name was Eric Glass, heir to the role of security chief for the Nordic Temple after Sean Fletcher was killed in Chicago. This was the first time Bolan had seen him in the flesh, and it occurred to him that they should have a chat about the stolen nuclear device.

He fired his second high-explosive round deliberately high. It detonated overhead, ripped through more ceiling panels, insulation and the hut's outer roof. Concussion and debris flattened his human targets, Bolan taking full advantage of the moment as he rushed to cover them.

A bitter pang of disappointment stung him as he saw the piece of blackened, twisted steel protruding from Eric Glass's throat. The neo-Nazi's talking days were over; any information he possessed was going with him to an icy grave.

Checking the other two, he found one breathing and began to slap his face until the young man came around, eyes swimming into focus on a soot-and bloodstained mask.

"You have one chance to live," Bolan informed him. "Nod if you would like to walk away from this."

The neo-Nazi hesitated, finally bobbed his head.

"One question— Where's the warhead?"

"N-not here," the hostage gasped, as if it hurt to speak.

"Outside the complex?" Bolan pressed him.

Nodding. "West, three quarters of a mile. Fire in the hole."

Bolan went through the soldier's pockets in a rush, somewhat surprised to find a billfold with a California driver's license in the plastic window. Alan Grant from Bakersfield, age twenty-three.

"If I find out you've lied to me, there won't be anyplace on earth for you to hide. You understand me, Alan?"

"Yes, sir." Nodding rapidly.

Bolan stood, dragged the young neo-Nazi to his feet and shoved him back in the direction he had come from. "Time for you to split," he said. "A few more minutes and this place is going up in smoke."

Fire in the hole.

He backtracked to the open emergency exit and ducked outside. Fifty yards to his left, or west, four parka-clad soldiers were dismounting from snowmobiles, another patrol coming home, scoping out the drifting clouds of smoke in bewilderment.

They never had a chance to work it out, as Bolan came up on their blind side, firing from the hip. Four up, four down. One of the drivers still had keys clutched in his fist. The snowmobile came back to life and Bolan nosed it toward the open wasteland, revving it across the ice.

Three quarters of a mile. Not far, although he had no clear idea of what to do once he got there. The crash course in disarming nuclear devices had been adequately thorough, but it would not help him if a signal from the complex set the nuke off in his face.

Forget about the complex.

He had covered some three hundred yards when the explosions started, tearing up the ice in rapid fire. Behind him, roughly half the neo-Nazi base camp was disintegrated, while the other half went dark, the generators blown.

"Stay frosty, guys," he muttered through his mask, then focused on the great white void ahead.

STEUBEN COULDN'T believe it when the snowmobile ran out of gas, halfway between the complex and the firing pit. At first, he thought the fuel gauge had to be wrong, but when the engine wouldn't fire again, he felt the manic rage explode inside him, swirling in his head until it was a challenge to remain upright.

The spell broke when he realized that he was shouting curses at a cloud bank looming to the west, its shadow racing toward him like a breaker over sand. Steuben sucked in a deep breath through his woolen mask, welcoming the sharp bite of frigid air in his lungs, the spreading chill that damped his fury down.

He was tempted to sit right there on the ice and simply wait for death, but that would mean defeat— or worse, abandonment of his prophetic mission. Dying in the line of duty was one thing; surrender, even in the face of overwhelming odds, was something else entirely. It was shameful, a disgrace that would most certainly exclude him from Valhalla.

Shrugging off the morbid mood, he walked back to the silent snowmobile and fetched the canvas satchel that contained his tools, electric wire and a spare battery. He wasn't sure exactly what he would require to do the job—had no real skill with things electric or mechanical, in fact—but it was all that he could think of as the world came crashing down around him, threatening to crush his dreams.

He couldn't see the scaffold yet, but knew approximately where it was. The compass Steuben now extracted from his pocket seemed to function properly; at any rate, if there was something wrong with it, he would know soon enough, when he got lost and froze to death.

He checked the compass again, turned his back to the dead snowmobile and began his trek across the ice. He had been walking for perhaps ten minutes when a string of rapid-fire explosions echoed hollowly across the ice. He turned in time to see a fireball wafting skyward from a swirling cloud of smoke and wondered whether any of his men were still alive back there.

No matter.

Facing west again, the compass held in front of him as if it were a talisman, the would-be ruler of the world began to run.

WITH NOTHING to obstruct his view but the sporadic gusts of wind that dragged long veils of drifting snow across his track, Bolan saw the abandoned snowmobile from close to 150 yards out. He slowed his own vehicle and unslung the M-16, bracing it across the handlebars for forward firing as he continued on his way, chugging along at reduced speed.

At eighty yards he knew Gary Stevens was either lying flat behind the snowmobile or he had gone ahead on foot. Approaching cautiously, he verified that Stevens was gone, noting that the snowmobile's ignition key was still in the on position, the needle on its fuel gauge resting solidly on Empty.

"Best-laid plans," he muttered to himself, and urged his scooter forward, letting the compass and his own sense of direction guide him. There were no tracks to follow, the ice field wind-scoured, its snow shifting like fine desert sand. He wondered briefly whether Stevens had the wherewithal to navigate the wasteland on his own, or if he would collapse and simply freeze to death. In that event, if he was wearing white, Bolan might pass his body on the ice and never even know it.

Not important, Bolan told himself. What counted was the warhead—more specifically, disarming and defusing it in such a manner that it couldn't be set off. Eliminating Stevens would be frosting on the cake, but it could wait.

The scaffold was a dark speck on the skyline from three hundred yards away. At two hundred, it took on shape and definition, recognizable as something in the shape of a pyramid. One hundred yards, and Bolan could see through it, as if he were looking at the skeleton of an abandoned teepee, nothing but the lashed-together poles remaining once the occupants had fled and taken all their hides along.

And he saw something else: beside the scaffold, kneeling on the ice, was a huddled figure dressed in white. The lurker gave himself away when he moved sideways, blocking out a portion of the scaffold with his body, one leg winking in and out of view.

Stevens.

Bolan didn't ease off the throttle. On the contrary, in fact, he revved up the scooter and let the engine wail, announcing his approach. It would give Stevens time to draw and aim a weapon, but if Bolan had a choice, he would prefer to face a bullet rather than a nuclear explosion.

He had closed the gap to eighty yards or so before the neo-Nazi heard him coming. Probably distracted, layers of insulated fabric covering his ears, Stevens was slow to recognize the danger closing on his flank. When he woke up to Bolan's presence, though, he demonstrated a remarkable agility, unfolding with a hop that brought him to his feet and left him facing Bolan with a compact submachine gun in his hands.

There was a ripping sound as Stevens opened fire, and Bolan heard the bullets snapping past him. He ducked and gave himself a three-count before leaping clear, hoping the snowmobile would hold its course.

It did, and Stevens concentrated on the scooter, hosing it down with his SMG as it charged him. One of his bullets struck the handlebars at some point, and the snorting vehicle was forty yards from contact when it veered suddenly off course, to the northwest.

Stevens saw the empty saddle, recognized his mistake and was swinging around to bring Bolan under fire when the M-16 cracked twice and sat him down. He dropped the submachine gun as he fell and it spun out of reach, across the ice. Rising, Bolan advanced to meet the enemy he had pursued halfway around the world and back again, holding his rifle steady, knowing that the neo-Nazi still might have a hideout gun.

No blood was visible around the small holes in his adversary's parka, but that came as no surprise. Layered clothing made for an effective sponge, and chest wounds often did their most dramatic bleeding on the inside of the body cavity. From the location of the bullet holes and the bright scarlet soaking through the would-be führer's white ski mask, Bolan made it at least one lung shot, maybe two.

Out here, that was a death sentence, and Stevens had to know it. Still, he raised his head, examining his enemy through tinted goggles.

"Who are you?" Stevens asked, the blood-wet fabric of his ski mask fluttering.

"What difference does it make?" Bolan replied.

The neo-Nazi tried to shrug, but only one shoulder would cooperate, making the effort look more like a nervous tic or seizure.

"Do you call yourself a white man?"

"Not your kind."

"My kind is all there is," Stevens informed him, adamant despite a certain grogginess. "The rest are traitors, half-breeds, Jewish scum."

"You need a rest," Bolan said. "Take this with you, guy—you blew it. You go out with nothing."

"That's what you think. Someone else will come along behind me to complete the work."

"And I'll be waiting for him when he gets here," Bolan told him.

Stevens tried raising his right arm in the traditional salute, but had to settle for the left. *"Sieg—"*

Bolan's bullet cut the parting comment short, drilling the left lens of the neo-Nazi's goggles and dumping him backward on the ice.

His rifle slung, Bolan advanced to stand before the

scaffold, where Stevens had winched the warhead up from a circular pit in the ice. It sat in a canvas cradle supported by chains, swaying ever so slightly with the stronger gusts of wind.

There was a small box mounted on the top, dead center, with a keypad and a digital display. The timer had been set and it was running, counting down with sixteen minutes and change left to go before detonation.

Bolan pressed the button labeled Dis, for Disarm, and frowned behind his ski mask as the timer kept on running. Stevens had bypassed the primary control.

So, use the code.

He had the numbers memorized, a bit of information channeled from a member of the former KGB to someone in the CIA and on from there to Stony Man. He didn't know how much the code had cost; perhaps it was enough for someone with the vestige of a conscience to prevent a grave atrocity from being carried out with Russian surplus hardware. Then again...

Eight digits. Bolan tapped them out and waited, while the doomsday countdown rushed ahead. A separate LED display beside the keypad suddenly winked red at him, its message simple and succinct: Access Denied.

Strike two.

It took three minutes, with his clumsy gloves, to unscrew and detach the faceplate of the warhead's detonator. Once inside, he felt a moment's panic as he noted three red wires instead of one.

What was it Hal had said when he relayed instructions for the worst-case scenario? "You pop the top and clip the red wire to your left." For some reason, Bolan had taken that to mean there would be one and only one red wire. Confronted with a trio now, he had no logical choice but to follow his directions.

Jesus, if this was wrong—

The wind made too much noise for him to hear the cut, but Bolan felt it, waiting for the ground to open up beneath him in a blinding flash. When nothing of the sort occurred, he checked the timer's LED display and found that it had frozen at 11:13:33.

He had a few more things to do, detaching certain other wires and flinging them away, extracting a computer chip that went into his pocket. Short of bringing up a whole new detonator mechanism now, no one could blow the warhead even if he wanted to.

Game over.

Veering wide around the corpse of Gary Stevens, Bolan walked to where his borrowed snowmobile had stalled. A brief inspection showed the headlight had been blown away, the paint job bullet scarred, but there was no apparent damage to the fuel tank or the engine. It was flooded, but he got it running on the third attempt and nosed the scooter eastward, back in the direction he had come from.

He could navigate by following the black smoke from the neo-Nazi base camp and rely upon his compass for the last leg of his journey to the waiting ATV.

If he ran into any neo-Nazi stragglers on the way, it would be their bad luck. The wise ones would avoid his path and take their chances on the ice.

It was a long way home, and it would take some time before he fell out of his killing mood.

EPILOGUE

"They're mopping up the rest of Stevens's people as we speak," Brognola said. "Besides the FBI and ATF, you've got GSG-9 in Germany, militia in Croatia and Ukraine and the South African Security Police. It's getting done."

They occupied a corner booth in a small mom-and-pop bar and grill. It was Brognola's choice, the outskirts of Bethesda, Maryland, with Bolan one day back, still feeling the effects of freezer burn around the edges.

He was warming up, but it would take a while.

"Survivors?" Bolan asked.

"More than you might expect. Without Stevens at the helm, it seems like most of those remaining on the team would just as soon pack up and split. Fact is, they're rolling over left and right for plea bargains. So many of them singing that the deputy director of the Bureau's started calling them the Nordic Tabernacle Choir."

"I didn't know he had a sense of humor," Bolan said.

"That's it for the millennium, I wouldn't be surprised."

"So," Bolan asked after a moment's hesitation, "was it worth it?"

"I leave calls like that to someone else," Brognola said. "I know you shut the Temple down, prevented several massacres, assassinations, plus the detonation of a warhead on the polar ice cap—which, if nothing else, would have the Green team screaming for the next five years, at least. I'd say it was a good day's work."

"Considering it took the best part of a month," Bolan reminded him. "And cost some decent lives."

"Soldiers," Brognola said. "From what I hear, Mossad's coining some kind of medal with Gellar's name on it for special service above and beyond the call. Of course, the guys who win it won't be allowed to wear it in public or admit it exists. It ought to look nice in the closet, though."

"And ATF? Are they cutting a medal, too?"

"Those guys," Brognola said, and fanned the air in front of him with one large hand. "Between the GAO and OMB, congressional oversight and internal reviews, the NRA and the *Washington Post,* it's a wonder they're not all schizophrenic. Or maybe they are. They definitely want to eat their cake and have it, too, but they'll be sweeping this one underneath the nearest rug."

"Too bad." There was a bitterness in Bolan's tone that he made no attempt to hide.

"The lady did her part," Brognola said, "but what the hell. She made some bad calls, too. That last bit, in Pretoria…" Brognola shook his head and took a sip of beer. "Dissect that in the media, the chances are she'd come off looking like a loose cannon, maybe a flat-out Section Eight."

"From where I sit, it looks more like she saved the president."

"You'll get no argument from me," Brognola said, "but I'm not well respected in the fourth estate."

"No family. It's like she's gone without a trace or never lived at all."

"You think?" Brognola frowned. "I would have said the ones she helped—the ones whose lives she saved—were family enough. They don't know where to send the thank-you notes, but there's no doubt they feel a debt and they'll remember it. That makes a legacy in my book, any way you break it down."

"You ever want to quit your day job," Bolan said, "you could consider writing eulogies."

"And give up show business?"

"You know the Temple has collaborators on the government payroll," Bolan remarked. "Berlin, for sure. They talked about connections in Pretoria, as well."

"I wouldn't hold my breath for racists and reactionaries to be weeded out of law enforcement in this lifetime, over there or here at home," Brognola said. "The jobs a draw for natural conservatives and some who cross the line big time. Others sign on with good intentions and get sick of paddling around the cesspool every day, hoping a simple answer really works."

"I'm talking criminal conspirators, not rotten attitudes," the Executioner replied.

"I know that. But the past is very much alive for certain people. Take a look at Austria, if you're in need of a reminder, with that joker going on about the 'decency' of the SS. The Germans have been living Hitler down for over fifty years, and lots of them are tired of it. You get the same thing here in Dixie, if you bring the slavery issue up—'Just let it go, for heaven's sake.' South Africa, same thing—except their bad old days are fresh enough that many of the players haven't had a chance to fade away. You want the bitter truth? Some of them never change, and they'll be bragging of their great 'achievements,' trying to convert another generation, till the last of them lies down and dies.''

"I'm glad we had this little talk. You've really cheered me up.''

"You want somebody to blow sunshine up your skirt,'' Brognola said, "call up a psychic friend. She'll tell you everything looks great and you're about to meet a tall, dark stranger. What you won't hear is that he'll be coming up behind you with a cleaver.''

"Bearing that in mind,'' Bolan said, "do you ever wonder if we even make a difference?''

"Never once,'' Brognola replied, without a moment's hesitation. "Hey, I know we'll never change the world, much less the nature of the human race. Nobody will. The only guy I ever heard of who was perfect wound up getting crucified, and there are some who'll tell you he was just a myth, to start with. What I *do* believe is that we hold the line. We clean up where we can and try to keep the mess from getting any worse. You think about it, in the scheme of things, that's not so bad.''

"I guess.''

"It gets old,'' the big Fed admitted, "but we're doing what we can with what we've got.''

"It's not enough,'' Bolan replied.

"It's all there is.''

Bolan considered that, then said, "I hate it when you're right."

"Me, too." Brognola finished off his beer and said, "You need to take some down time. Grab some R and R."

"Sounds like a plan."

"Take all the time you want. I shouldn't need you for another two, three days at least."

"You're all heart, guy."

"I know, but hey, don't let it get around, all right? Get soft with one, first thing you know, the whole damned crew is asking for an eighty-hour week."

"I'll take it to the grave," Bolan replied.

But not this day.

Right now, this minute, he was standing down. He might be called upon to face another enemy tomorrow or the next day after that, and that was fine.

In fact, the Executioner wouldn't have had it any other way.

James Axler

OUTLANDERS®

TOMB OF TIME

Now a relic of a lost civilization, the ruins of Chicago hold a cryptic mystery for Kane. In the subterranean annexes of the hidden predark military installations deep beneath the city, a cult of faceless shadow figures wields terror in submission to an unseen, maniacal god. He has lured his old enemies into a battle once again for the final and deadliest confrontation.

In the Outlands,
the shocking truth is humanity's last hope.